BLACK AND WHITE AND READ ALL OVER

BLACK AND WHITE AND READ ALL OVER

a novel

William Kinsolving

PRAGMATIC PRESS

BLACK AND WHITE AND READ ALL OVER

Copyright © 2026 by William Kinsolving

This work is a novel. While inspired by historical events and real persons, the characters, dialogue, and narrative are works of fiction. Any resemblance to actual persons, living or dead, is coincidental or used fictitiously.

This work was written without the use of artificial intelligence in the creation of the manuscript.

Paperback ISBN: 979-8-9952201-0-7
Hardback ISBN: 979-8-9952201-1-4
Ebook ISBN: 979-8-9952201-2-1
Audiobook ISBN: 979-8-9952201-3-8

First published in 2026 by Pragmatic Press
United States of America

To Susan, again and ever,

with thanks for finding the footnote,

and for everything else.

AUTHOR'S NOTE

Most of the story you're about to read is a pure romance, its struggles, its perseverance against impossible odds, and its joyful triumph—though brief.

This is a work of historical fiction based on actual events. While the narrative and certain details have been imagined, the social attitudes and legal practices depicted reflect the period in which the story unfolded. It includes language and descriptions that may be considered offensive by today's standards a century later, particularly in its portrayal of gender, race, and class, as well as in the invasive scrutiny of a woman's private life. These factors are presented as part of the historical record and are essential to understanding the forces at work in the trial that concludes the book.

The novel does not endorse the prejudices it portrays. It seeks to examine one extreme example of the human cost of a society that so adroitly could turn private lives into public spectacle.

This story has been told in magazine articles, scholarly books, novels, and endlessly in the newspapers a century ago, mostly for the sensation of it. Well, it was sensational, and scandalous, shocking in its legal conclusion, revelatory of the nation's insidious flaw—racism—despite the decades-old Constitutional Amendments intended to purge it.

After following up on the footnote from Nella Larsen's novel *Passing*, that referenced the Rhinelander trial in 1925, I found that the research revealed extraordinary and unique personal disclosures, struggles, and finally family revelations that previously had not been fully considered.

The temptation was strong to write the story as non-fictional history. I overcame it. The fiction—the story—begins here.

PROLOGUE

It was called "The Rhinelander Affair," probably the kindest headline the newspapers could give this story. They fed on it for a year before the trial, for nearly a year after, until the scandal dissolved in other public distractions. Most journalists ignored truth for sensation—easily done in the racist, sexual, and financial context of the Twenties. But not one of them got the story right. Of course, their readers didn't care much about truth, being so addicted to front page shocks that they craved ever-more vivid, salacious smears.

To conjure a couple so unsuited to such notoriety as were Alice Jones, my younger sister, and Leonard Rhinelander, an imperfect scion, would be impossible. Because of the times in which they fell in love, they became framed in tight focus by the insidious and violent white fear of miscegenation that only America's unique intolerance can nurture. Their story began in 1921, during the fracturing years that followed a war—The Great War in Europe, 1914 to 1918—when the certainties of pre-war life were never again going to be the same. What we'd thought were the solid traditions of our civilization, including the evil ones, began to crack and shift with the power and violence of earthquake moves. Even in the middle of that wild, buckling decade, theirs might have been the most glittering Cinderella romance of all. It's surely a love story, but not one either could have anticipated, or, in the end, have wanted.

When the trial was happening, I swore that I'd never say a word to anyone about it. Afterward, I'd hoped that time would do my work of forgetting, letting the fury in me cool to a simmer and then go cold. I'm not much of a talker anyway, and thinking clearly about what had happened to my sister remained difficult. Over the years since, it seems that ignoring memory worked for everyone but Alice and me. She told me once she'll never let it go, holds it all in with her fierce determination that the Rhinelanders will never beat her down, will never defeat her as they've so adroitly destroyed others.

I don't have her personal motivation. I'm just stubborn. A pressure of rage kept building up in me for all the damage the trial did, for how they tried to break my family, and didn't care about doing it, even if they divided the nation. Years passed, but I still feared that something in my head was bound to blow. It was a frightening edge to live on.

One night, I came close to going down. I met someone at a party, a fundraiser, as I remember, for dear Alain Locke's impossible project to build a Harlem Museum of African Art. My husband and I still try to support the effort, despite this Great Depression engulfing us all. I'd had a few drinks, which might have helped the conversation along. This is what was said, probably shouted, as the room was crowded and noisy. "Aren't you Alice Jones Rhinelander's sister?"

No stranger had made that connection for more than ten years, and back then, it was usually said mean. "What about it?" He was a white man in a good suit. I expected a snide remark, and I was ready to fight.

"I remember you at the trial. I covered it for *The New York Times*." I adjusted. He seemed okay. "Long time ago."

"You haven't changed."

"More than you could know."

"It came to mind a while back."

"Never left mine."

"I can understand that."

I believed he did. I said, "You and I are two of the few who even give it a thought." We exchanged a quick smile, old collaborators.

"I remember that in the courtroom, you sat behind your sister and never spoke. But you sure watched. I'd bet you never missed a thing."

"I was listening to the Rhinelander lawyers trying to destroy her."

"Didn't quite work."

"Did some deep damage, though... I remember *The Times* published a courtroom summation every day on the front page."

"Oh yes. I wrote them. After all, it was 'The Trial of the Century'."

"You treated Alice and my family kindly... although you didn't get it right, either!" Abruptly, the old fury came down. "We were only... trying to be human! ... Nice to talk to you." I was going to explode—bellow, scream or cry. He didn't deserve it, and I had to get out of there.

I managed two steps, and he said to my back, "Have you ever thought writing about it?"

Something happened, air leaking out of the near-bursting balloon. I turned back. "No. I read. Books. Never written anything."

"How many books have you read?"

"Well, I don't count them... About one every week or two for the last twenty years, except when my daughter was little... and during the trial."

He reached into his pocket for a black-enameled case of calling cards and handed me one "I'm in publishing now. I'd say you might be ready to write about it. Call me when you agree."

I took it and then said something that gave a bare hint that, out of the blue, I was intrigued. "I wouldn't know where to begin."

"Bet you can figure that out." He smiled, knowing what I'd admitted before I did.

"It's a long story. Racism goes way back around here."

He thought for a moment. "That's not the story I remember. When I covered the trial, racism was certainly the atmosphere. But power and family—both the Rhinelanders, and sure as hell yours—were the essence." He smiled again and drifted away into the noise.

"The essence"..."Power and family." He was right. Trouble was, the Rhinelanders had all the power. But by God, we had the family!

A NOTE ON SOURCES

The reader should know I'm not a scholar nor a historian. I asked for that to be put right up front. To be clear on how I worked, I used four main sources:

1. The New York and Westchester County daily newspapers of the period. A journalist at the time, Barbara Reynolds, now owner and publisher of Tri-State Media Papers, was instrumental.

2. The transcript of the trial. It is massive and is carefully housed by the constantly helpful people at the Library of the New York State Bar Association in Manhattan. When I requested the transcript, I was told that the Rhinelander lawyers had sequestered it with some spurious legal curlicue. I am indebted to my attorney (and husband), Robert Brooks, New York State Assemblyman from Harlem, for negotiating my access.

3. Alice Jones Rhinelander's diaries. On her seventh birthday, my sister was given a small leatherette-bound diary with a chrome lock and key. A single-minded, at times obsessed habit commenced, one that has continued to this day. The shape of the volumes varies, but her entries became consistent. Each one has a large date, a hurried list of subject matter she didn't want to forget, and then the details of the day. In this book, I quote two entries verbatim. The rest of the time, the diaries were my most vital reference and corroboration, along with my own memory.
    When I told Alice of this project, I didn't even have to ask: She volunteered any of the pertinent years of her diary that I wanted. Her single condition was that she be excluded from anything to do with the book's publication and be given notice in time for her to be away when it was released.
    Alice did not request, nor has she made any editorial contribution. She has not seen the manuscript and begged me not to be offended if she didn't read the book.

4. Jason Macleod Steiner. He is the journalist at the trial who went into publishing. I told him I could never write high-literary glitter; even so, he took a very big chance on this book and this writer. Not only was he a creative, line-editing, teaching scourge throughout my struggles, but—having been at the trial—was an invaluable source as fact-checker and editorial guide to my often formless storytelling effort.

CHAPTER ONE

Here's the racist "atmosphere" that Jason Steiner, *The New York Times* man, now my editor, was talking about:

In September 1921, President Warren G. Harding addressed a large but carefully segregated, though biracial audience in the Capitol's Rotunda. They'd been assembled for his much-touted statement on race in America. He said, "Since last year's two constitutional amendments were ratified, which established Prohibition and gave women the vote, our country has changed noticeably. But another continuing change is as significant as those two. It commenced before the Great War in Europe began. America has experienced a steady migration of several million of our Negro citizens from the farms of the South to the great industries of the North, and to other employment opportunities throughout the rest of the country. The social conflicts, vicious violence, and race riots that have resulted have stained our history. Perhaps they were inevitable with such a massive societal shift. But democracy in America is a lie until the Negro is granted economic and political equality wherever in the nation he may choose to go."

Loud cheers rose from the black section of the hall.

The president continued. "But a black person cannot be a white person. There must be a natural segregation because any kind of racial amalgamation cannot be!"

Extended and taunting cheers erupted from the white section of the hall that were then countered by fury from the black section, causing the Capitol police to drive both groups out.

So that's something of the "atmosphere" of where America was, although Harding's view was pretty naïve, pretty simplistic. It's doubtful that he learned anything from the meeting. As to "the essence" of my sister's trial—the Rhinelanders' power coming up against our family—that is complicated. It's the main subject of this book, and my challenge.

I met Leonard Rhinelander the same day Alice did, September 21, 1921, but later than she by about four hours. The date is easy for both of us to remember, for her because of him, I because that morning I learned for sure I was pregnant. That was no surprise, but it was a vital event toward healing what had become a deep family wound.

Explaining it involves explaining some convoluted Jones family history. Our father, George Jones, was born in Walkington, an East Yorkshire village in England, to a young widow who owned the local pub. A West Indian sailor had harbored there, captured her heart for a week, but then sailed on. The result was young

George, who learned hard work from the beginning of consciousness. He grew strong and tall during the effort, and as an added benefit, was as classically handsome as a British movie star. Even so, these qualities were only noted, if at all, after the fact that his dark skin was absorbed. Apparently, it was the only feature inherited from his long-gone father, a rather homely, cheerless man, as his mother had begrudgingly remembered, she having been desperately lonely at the time.

With no time or money to indulge in idle romance, George managed to become a young man before he met and immediately courted Elizabeth Bowton, a kitchen maid at the local grand estate of an owner of distant factories. The English-rose-like product of generations of Yorkshire serving-people, she too was at first put off by George's "African complexion" as she had referred to it. Even so, he was very handsome once one became used to his "shade"; he was also kind, smart and even charming. Each evening during haying season, he worked on the estate and slept with other laborers in the barn. He'd leave a bunch of field flowers on the windowsill of a scullery where Elizabeth worked with a note of sweet nothings and plans to take her to America. When she found out he had nothing to do with Africa, but was "descended from the West Indies," somehow her resistance was vanquished, and they married.

The new Mr. and Mrs. Jones saved every penny they could until they had enough to survive for a time in a new country. They finally arrived on Ellis Island on March 18, 1891. (Our family used to celebrate the date every year with high tea, singing "God Save the Queen" for Victoria, who was the monarch back then.) My parents lived in a New York City slum, both working at any job available. After the first winter, George was hired to dig trenches for sewer lines in New Rochelle, New York, a half-hour north of the city by train. Always looking for more income, he returned to the train station after work and, for several hours, offered to carry bags and parcels for the passengers returning from New York. Any number of his patrons remembered him and got to like him. Even after his work in the sewer trenches led him into the construction trade, he continued to work at the station.

After two years of thankless labor, the Joneses finally moved to New Rochelle. It took another two years for George to buy a second-hand rig and a slightly spavined horse to deliver commuters from the station to their homes. (His series of used automobiles for taxis came later.) He had gained a genuine acceptance, even admiration in the community for his humor, courtesy and reliability. It was a decidedly white community, and many of his regular fares enthusiastically offered their idea of a fine compliment: "Well, George, if we're going to have a Negro (or colored man, or darky, etc.) in New Rochelle, a British West Indian with a Cockney accent is the best we could hope for!" It wasn't Cockney but a Yorkshireman's lilt.

All too soon, we daughters came along, me first named Emily or "Em," then Alice, and finally Grace. Beneath the general happiness of adding to the family, each birth came with a gnawing bitterness for our mother. She had suffered and fought against the vicious jeers that came her way back in the slum. They'd called him a word that she would never say, and never allowed us to say. (And I won't use even now in writing this book.) New Rochelle had offered Elizabeth Jones solace, as its citizens accepted the family with little racial regard beyond their unconscious patronizing tolerance. Having been a staunch churchgoer in England, she made a point of joining the local Episcopal Church and found a gratifying welcome for the entire family. She made friends at all the shops and had new acquaintances over for tea.

But as each of us was born, a bureaucratic blemish spoiled the joy of it for her. Each birth certificate had a required space to be filled in to describe the infant's "race." Judgment about that status was made by busy nurses or doctors and filled in by one registrar or another. My document said "black." Alice's certificate said "mulatto." And Grace's said, "octoroon," the latter being the result of someone asking my parents enough questions to figure out that the child surely wasn't white but was maybe barely black. Actually, according to the racist definitions, "quadroon" is what we sisters are, our sailor-grandfather presumably being the only full-blooded black man in the line, but to what degree of West Indian "shade," who could tell?

In the Caribbean, one could be of infinite racial mix descended from a Spanish hidalgo and/or a Senegalese slave. In these United States, however, our father was officially considered half black, and we sisters were a fourth. The basis for prejudice in America, however, is the infamous and ridiculous "one-drop rule": If you have one drop of black blood in you, you're one hundred percent black.

We sisters talked about it, but—and this may be hard to believe—it was never any great concern. For whatever genetic reasons, we all grew up looking white enough for the country club—not that we ever went there. Each of us had small areas of skin "mis-colorings," small blemishes that were hardly noticeable and were covered by our clothes—at the base of my spine, for instance, or the dark hues of Alice's breasts and on her thighs. Grace had a kind of birthmark high up on her left thigh, among others. We compared them once in a while but didn't worry about them. In New Rochelle, we were treated as white girls, at school, at jobs, at church, and thought of ourselves as such. Nobody paid any attention to our birth certificates, and Mum never showed them to us.

Even so, for Mum, those gradations of race on an official document were like a brand on our foreheads that she could see as plain as day. "I will not be the mother of black children," she blurted out once in an unguarded moment of rage. She never admitted that possibility to herself or anyone else. We never discussed the subject with her, although over the years we heard tears in the kitchen, or at night in their room when she was with Daa (what we called our father).

This was why—on September 21, 1921—my pregnancy was so important. A year before, I'd married Bob Brooks, the first and only love of my life. I'd met him on the train to New York. He was smart from the moment he sat down across from me, bold in that, although the trains weren't segregated, it was unusual, to say the least, for a black man to sit anywhere near a white woman. Yes, a black man. He was funny by Larchmont, and by the time we arrived at Grand Central, I knew his ambitions, all of which seemed impossible in white America.

Be assured, I've read most of what Freud has written that I can find. My decision to marry a black man had nothing to do with my father, although giving in to it was probably easier because of my parents' example. It was simply Bob himself. Both of us knew what was going to happen, and he asked me to marry him two weeks later. I was ready, but I knew what it would do to Mum (we used the English term for mother). When I told her I had a Negro boyfriend, she went stiff and silent, saying nothing. He came to call at our house in New Rochelle, and I introduced them. She was rigidly gracious, then excused herself due to a migraine headache. She'd never had a migraine in her life.

Bob returned several times, but always after her iron greeting, Mum found an excuse to escape. The rest of the family was immediately taken with him, and Daa particularly enjoyed talking business, admiring his plans for the future. Grace flirted with him as she did with anyone in pants, and Alice laughed at his stories and asked questions about his life. He'd graduated from high school at the top of his class, gone to a school for fancy butlers, and, at present, ran the Weingold mansion. They were a rich Jewish couple who lived across town in the fancy part of New Rochelle.

Alice and I had always told each other everything, so after Bob left each time, we'd go up into my room and lie around. She had a thousand questions about how "falling in love" had happened, what had happened, and why it had happened. I was as honest as possible, but it seemed to be beyond her understanding. She was excited by it, so very happy for me, but baffled, as if love were a geometry problem that she would never understand.

"Did his being a black man ever mean anything to you?" Alice asked one night.

"I had my automatic defenses like any other woman, but they didn't last long, particularly when he started making me laugh. His being black stopped meaning anything at all. He was just this handsome guy, comfortable in a suit who knew where he was going, and it took me about half an hour to know I wanted to go along."

Alice pondered that, and then a familiar look of total certainty came on her face. "Em, it so completely depends on the luck of meeting the one person on earth that makes it work for you. And you did it, against those impossible odds!"

"Not at all. More than one person on earth can fit the bill, Alice. For me, Bob happens to be one of them and just happened to be on that train."

"I don't believe it. You're 24 years old, and you've met hundreds of men—in suits!—that you never even looked at. No. You were incredibly lucky. What if he'd taken the next train?"

"I'd've become a nun."

I thought that was kind of funny, but Alice didn't laugh. "Em, you went to secretarial school, have a steady job, always neat, always well-dressed. I'm 21, I work as a waitress, a laundress, a maid, whatever I can find. I always look barely put together. The boyfriends I have don't last, or they're slimy... Okay, it's because I'm a prude about sex. And if they can't dance, I have no interest in them at all. My odds are ten times, a hundred times worse than yours. I'll never find him."

"I'd say you're talking yourself into a hole, Alice. There's not just one guy in the world for you. You're a smart, good-looking girl, and you'll find someone. And what's this 'prude about sex' stuff? You look pretty flirty on the dance floor."

"Look, the dance floor is where I rescue what's left of my life. What I do there is like, well, the cocaine the other girls at the laundry used for the same reasons. Yes, I'm a prude. It's the only way to think about sex that makes sense with men being the way they are, mashers just taking what they can get without any idea of something that lasts. You started telling me about sex when I was nine..."

"Only because Mum the Victorian wouldn't talk about it, and Daa had such a hell of a time explaining it to me."

We laughed at the memory. "God knows he tried," Alice said.

"It was when I asked about The Curse that stopped him cold."

"Oh my God! What a dear man he is... So listen, yeah, I've made my choices about sex. I know what fucking is, and I know what some of it feels like. Oh, yes, I do! And these guys that come around are always willing to show me the rest. My God, if they could find a knothole, they'd fuck a tree!" We both laughed at that. Then she went quiet and serious. "But it seems to me it's too wonderful, too personal to just do it with anyone, to Joe Nobody hanging around who's ready. And they're all ready. I want to share sex with... him. You know, Mr. Billion-to-one Shot."

"You're a romantic, Alice. I've always thought so."

"What's wrong with that? Are you and Bob...? You told me you'd never done it."

"I've never had the choices you do. I wear glasses. My nose is always in a book. I don't talk much, and I'm as flat-chested as two raisins on an ironing board."

Alice howled with laughter. "That's terrible, Em, and not true."

"Let's just say we have different attractions, and no, Bob and I are holding out, thinking it'll motivate us to get married quicker."

And it did, which caused the crisis. The night Bob and I told the family we planned to go to the town hall to get married, we asked them all to be with us as our witnesses. Before anyone else could say anything, Mum shouted—literally— "If you marry him, you'll no longer be allowed in my house!"

All of us stood in shocked silence until Daa said, "Elizabeth, you promised not..."

"I lied! That promise is no more!" She turned to Bob, then me. "You are not welcome here, and if you marry him, neither are you!"

"Mrs. Jones," Bob said calmly, "I love your daughter and will make her happy."

"This is my home, too," Daa said, "and we'll have no forbidding. We can work this out."

"NO WE CAN'T," Mum bellowed.

I said, "We don't want to be where we're not wanted. Goodbye, Mum. I'll miss you terribly," which sounded phony like I'd taken it from a Jane Austen novel. Then I hugged Daa, Alice and Grace, who was crying. I took Bob's hand, and we left. I didn't notice until we reached Bob's used Model T at the curb that Alice had followed us out.

"This is so right!" she said. "Do anything to win against those odds." She hugged us again, promised to pack my things and bring them to Bob's place. Even with my own worries and sadness, I was concerned about her as she ran up the steps to the front door and disappeared. She'd convinced herself of a certain crazy ideal about love, and she was stubborn enough to hold to it. She'd write these things down in her diary, and once written down, they had to be true. I knew stubborn, and her waiting for the one man in the world for her to show up might lead to a lonely life.

Bob and I made plans to be married in a week. We both went to tell the Weingolds, hoping the arrangement wouldn't affect his employment. As an elderly couple who had lost a child to diabetes years before, they were surprisingly delighted, and Mr. Weingold insisted on opening a bottle of champagne. Before it was finished, they heard of our need for witnesses at the town hall and volunteered on the spot. At the ceremony, Mrs. Weingold wept. Then, Mr. Weingold sang "Od Yishama," a Jewish wedding song. So we all wept. The event was quick but memorable.

Bob and I hadn't been back home since Mum's outburst. After we were married, most of the family came over to visit our apartment above the garages at the

Weingolds' estate, Alice more often than the others. But never Mum. As time went on, Bob and I thought of a thousand strategies to find a way back. When we tried them out on Daa, though, he held out little hope that they'd work. "Elizabeth has a soft heart but a steel will." The night he said that, Alice had come over with him. It was late in 1920. We were drinking what was left of Daa's last bottle of good whiskey. "Em, you'll never change Mum's will," Alice said. "But I think she hates this separation as much as we do, maybe even hates herself for what she feels. But she's hard stubborn, which is where we get it."

She looked around to see if any of us would disagree. No one did. Then she looked at me. "Go for her heart, Em. And here's the key: When are you two planning on having a baby?"

She knew we were planning already, because I'd told her how hard we were trying.

"I'm not sure that's the answer," Bob said. "Would she be happy waiting through pregnancy to see if she had a mulatto grandchild?"

That hung in the air until Alice said, "I'm not smart enough to explain why, but yes! She'll be happy. On some level of love, it won't matter to her. I know she wants this over, and I know she'd love to have a grandchild."

I so hoped she was right, although at the same time, in my big sister way, I wondered if Alice believed too deeply, too idealistically in the so-called powers of love. From what I knew, she'd had little if any experience of it with her revolving swarm of "slimy" dancing hulks. This lack of exposure to real life allowed an emotional vacuum that her too rosy, and therefore distorted theory of affection could fill. Being so inexperienced myself, I didn't know how to warn her about where such a vulnerability could lead, which, after all, I only knew about from books.

It didn't take us long, and the night my doctor told me I was pregnant, Bob and I drove over to New Rochelle with no warning. We thought if Mum knew we were coming, she'd have left the house. Daa opened the door, was startled, and for a second, we weren't sure he'd let us in. But suddenly, he was alert, suspecting why we were there. "Luv, we have visitors."

They'd finished dinner, and Mum was sitting at the dining room table, peeling apples for a pie. I remember the knife falling on the floor. She stared at us open-mouthed, debating rage or relief. I didn't give her a chance to decide. "Mum, you're going to be a grandmother."

Alice had been right. Tears gushed forth even before she stood up, saying, "Oh! Oh! Oh!" She came around the table and hugged me, trying to talk and failing. I saw Daa shake Bob's hand, shouting congratulations. Then Grace trundled down the stairs in a tight blouse that showed off the breasts she was so proud of, her eyes wide, calling out, "What's going on down here?"

Mum turned around and said, "The third generation of the American Jones family is on the way!" As Grace screamed and came to hug me, Mum stepped over to Bob. "Welcome, Bob." It was hard for her but genuine.

"Mrs. Jones, it's a joy to be here."

"Where's Alice?" I asked.

"She went out," Grace said, full of insinuation, "for 'a w-a-a-lk,' dressed up as if she were going to a speakeasy."

"What's that?" Mum asked. "She missed her dinner."

"It's what they call the illegal bars and nightclubs that serve illegal liquor," Daa said. "Our little Grace is always up on the latest terms."

"Well, that's what she looked like," Grace said, and flounced toward the kitchen. "She was wearing her new gold dress and her church cloche hat with the feather and..."

"Today's her day off," Daa said. "After a week in her maid's uniform, she just wanted to look nice." He turned to Bob. "I have to go out for a tiny bit, so Bob, protect yourself from these women."

Mum kissed him. "The pie'll be ready in an hour, Grand-Dad!"

Daa owned some rental property in New Rochelle that he had to visit every two weeks. We heard his ancient taxi drive out of the garage and down the street as we all went into the kitchen to keep Mum company as she baked her pie. I suddenly had many questions to ask Mum about having a baby. Grace had as many and wasn't shy at all about asking them in front of Bob. He stayed silent with the coffee Mum made him, listening intently as our questions went into details about a woman's world he knew little about, having had no sisters.

Deep in conversation, we heard a car drive up and stop in front of the house. After a while, Grace wandered into the living room to look out the front window. She whooped and came running back. "You should see the car Alice is in!"

We all hurried into the living room, but before we reached the window, the front door flew open, and there was Alice. I noticed that the feather in her cloche hat was missing.

"What are you doing here?" she said to me, hoping she knew the answer. I noticed right away that something was different. She was glowing. Behind her, a very tall, too-thin boy in glasses and an elegant dark green tweed suit came in and stood against the door frame. Alice saw that Mum's eyes were still glistening with tears. Grace was looking devilish, Bob seemed amused, so I said as casually as I could, "Oh, hello, Alice. I'm pregnant."

Alice bellowed and grabbed me in a bear hug. I whispered in her ear, "It worked on Mum."

She whispered in mine, "I found him!"

"Who?"

Everyone started talking except Mum. Her gray hair in her careful curls on her proud head, wearing a flowing blouse, sweater and full-length skirt, she impatiently wiped away whatever tears she'd allowed, as each over the other described how I'd come in and said what I said, how each of them felt and reacted.

Alice looked around the room. "Where's Daa?"

"He'll be back," Mum said. "He had to…" Abruptly, she and the rest of us noticed the tall person standing by the front door.

"Oh my gosh!" Alice went over to him. "I'm so sorry. Mum, everybody, I've brought a friend to meet you. This is Len Rhinelander."

We all chorused wry comments about "friend." As he was introduced to each of us, good-humored greetings were made, allowing him to say nothing. He looked to me like Ichabod Crane with glasses. I figured this was "him." He made a little bow to Mum, and finally said to me, "C-C-Congratulations." I was mildly amused, but I caught a stutter. Then he reached out his hand to Bob and said, "Hello, B-B-Bob, isn't it?" That time, everyone noticed it.

Bob replied with mock-martyrdom, "Yes, Len, like everyone else, you overlooked the father-to-be who's made all of this possible." They shook hands as we hooted derision, except Alice, who was watching Len. He seemed bemused and certainly curious about Bob.

Mum assumed her usual primacy in the house. "My husband, hearing he'd soon be a grandfather, has gone off to drive the tenants of his building mad, so his place at the table is yours, Mr. Ringlander, if you'd care for some dessert."

"Rhinelander, Mum. He's from New York."

"Len Ringlander!" he said, looking at Mum in wonder. "W-w-wouldn't it be w-w-wonderful to be someone else!" The stuttering was very strange.

As everyone went back to the table, Grace asked suggestively, "Alice, did you go all the way into New York to meet him?"

"No, I'm sure not," Mum said, enjoying Len's holding her chair out for her. "Tell us, Mr. Rhinelander, all about your good self, and how you happen to be here."

Len took his place at the table, seeming to concentrate on what he was going to say. "Alice's amazing honesty w-w-w-with m-me this afternoon is my guide tonight. First of all, you'll n-notice that I stut-t-t…" He shrugged, then stopped to concentrate. "I'm at a clinic called The Orchards up near Stamford that's sup-pposedly curing me of that and a nervous stomach. You see, I'm k-k-kind of a mess." He laughed as we objected. "It's not c-c-completely..." he paused to focus, "successful so far, but it's getting better."

"You're doing pretty well, Len," I said. "Goes well with this crazy family."

"Thanks, Emily. That's n-n-not the usual reaction. People get really n-n-nervous or embarrassed and actually f-f-flee!"

"I know just what you mean, Len," Bob said. "Try being black and walking into a white church sometime."

"Yes," Len agreed. "It must be something like that. Not that I'd know."

"I'll get you some blackface, and you can give it a try."

Len gazed at him with delight. "How I'd love to w-w-walk into St. Thomas w-with my father as his colored stuttering son!"

"That'd get you some attention," Bob laughed. "You live in New York, Len?"

"It's w-where my family is, but I'm not there much, sent away to camps, boarding school. I turned eighteen in May, and I w-w-was...supposed to go to Harvard this fall, but my father thought the clinic for my stuttering and stomach w-w-would be time better spent. I suppose he could have made w-w-worse choices. Um, 'w' is my hardest letter." He looked at Alice. "My family regards m-m-members who disappoint their standards as failures. My being a stutterer, w-w-with explosive digestion, I'm definitely a failure to them." Thinking he'd said too much, he smiled at everyone. "I w-w-was terribly disappointed about Harvard... until today."

He looked back at Alice. She looked startled. The rest of us gaped back and forth between the two, until Alice did a mock look-down-in-shyness, and we all joined in laughter. Mum and Grace served the pie. The conversation turned back to focus on the future blessed event, the date of arrival, the names for either a boy or a girl, and which sex was preferred. Bob opined, "I'm pretty sure we're going to keep whatever kind of thing comes."

"What do you mean, 'kind of thing'?" I demanded. "I'm not going to produce a 'kind of thing!'"

As the banter and affection went on, Len seemed enveloped in it. Everyone had opinions about my firm decision that the baby be named for Bob, whether a boy or a girl, Robert or Roberta. Bob suggested "Atlas," but was laughed down. "Here's another piece of pie." Mum served it onto Len's plate. "You're too thin for a young man of your height."

"That's as g-good an excuse as any for more, and the pie is as good as any I've ever had."

"Oh, thank you, Len."

"And I have to s-s-say, I'm honored to be here on such a h-h-happy occasion, with the family back together."

Mum turned to him sharply. I was pretty surprised myself. Alice seemed to have shared a whole lot with him. Having intended his comment, Len met Mum's look.

"I see you've made swift progress with my daughter, Mr. Rhinelander, learning more of our family than might be appropriate."

"It's a great p-privilege to me, Mrs. Jones. I've heard you h-have a great family, and b-b-because mine is something q-q-quite different, I envy you very much."

Mum watched him. "Thank you, Len. I agree. My problem with this great family is my trying to prevent trouble from coming to it. So often, it doesn't cooperate." She smiled pointedly at us. "Oh, the stories I could tell."

As conversations continued, Grace strolled over to the Victrola in the living room and wound it up. She put a record on the turntable and switched it on, swinging the needle arm over to the record. The moment the music started, Alice stood up and looked around at the Victrola but then didn't move. It was her favorite song, one we'd heard her listen to, over and over.

> *Love will find a way,*
> *though skies now are gray,*
> *Love like ours can never be ruled,*
> *Cupid's not schooled that way.*

Len obviously didn't know the song, but the whole family grew quiet. One by one, each of us took to glancing at him with strange smiles. Then Alice turned slowly toward him with a look of longing I doubted he'd ever seen. I certainly never had.

> *…Dry each tear-dimmed eye,*
> *Clouds will soon roll by.*
> *Fate may try to lead us astray, But,*
> *Dearie, mark what I say,*
> *Love will find a way.*

When the song was over, and the needle was going around on the remainder track, no one said anything. All eyes were on Len, and he didn't know why. "I think that's about the loveliest song I've ever heard."

"And you didn't stutter!" Grace blurted as she turned off the Victrola.

"No, I didn't, did I? Grace, it must have been the song!"

"Perhaps the pie," Mum suggested.

All of us started talking except Alice, who only smiled at Len, and sat down again, as did Grace, filled with her musical triumph. Bob and I made more coffee, and conversation flowed, changing tone with every new story or old memory, until Len saw for the first time a Big Ben wind-up alarm clock on top of the upright piano in the living room.

"Good glory!" He stood up. "I'm very late. I'm s-s-so sorry, but I have to go."

Expressing regret, we all rose and went with him to the front door. Alice took his hand again.

"I can't thank you enough, Mrs. Jones. It's been the most w-w-wonderful evening."

"That's because of us," Grace said.

"Yes," I said. "Alice had nothing to do with it."

"Now, Len," Mum hastened to add, "I wish to presume you'll come back to see us."

"Did you actually make that pie?"

"Of course I did."

"I'll come back."

Surprisingly, the front door opened, and on entering, Daa saw Len. "Good gracious, who have we here? A door-to-door casket salesman, I'll be sworn, selling his goods out of that very new Oldsmobile convertible out there."

"No, Daa," Alice laughed. "This is my friend, Len Rhinelander. My father, George Jones." Daa's startled reaction and swift glance at Leonard's shoes were visible to everyone, and certainly to Len.

"Good evening, Mr. Jones." Len put out his hand, taking in Daa's dark coloring, his white hair and clipped mustache, the lilt of his Yorkshire accent. "I'm so pleased to meet you."

"Good evening, sir." Daa was unusually awkward. "Hope they've looked after you. Would you be needing a car to the city, sir?"

"No, thank you, Mr. Jones. That's my car outside. I've had a wonderful time with your family. You're such a lucky man." He looked at us. "You're all so lucky. I'm sorry, I have to leave, sir, just w-w-when you came in, but I'm very late. Goodnight, everyone, goodnight, Alice."

"I'll walk you out."

As they left, the family called out their goodbyes. The moment Bob closed the front door behind them and Grace ran over to the window, Daa said with considerable aggravation: "Good Christ! Do any of you realize who the bloody hell the Rhinelanders are?"

CHAPTER TWO

My husband knew about the Rhinelanders. Bob hadn't said anything when he heard the name, which is his way. He saw that Len was struggling to talk. He told me later why he knew Len was one of the famous family: because of his green tweed suit. From his own job, Bob knew luxury British tailoring and cloth; the quality of Len's suit defined the wearer. Besides that, Bob worked on a committee of the NAACP's New York chapter involved with confronting slum landlords who mistreated their tenants. The first time I'd met him on the train, he was on his way to the committee's weekly meeting on his day off.

He told me that by the 1920s, Rhinelander Real Estate owned or controlled one-third of the property in New York City. Their holdings included most of the prime buildings and construction sites in Manhattan, but also areas of slums that they bought up, milked for income, waiting for the right moment to develop them into even more prime real estate. Much of the time, the Rhinelanders' methods in the slums took intimidation to physical levels of damage and hurt, particularly against their Negro occupants. The NAACP's Housing Committee investigated, gathered evidence, and turned it over to the organization's legal arm.

"They're kissing each other!" Grace announced from the window, as the rest of us were trying to understand what Daa had just said.

"Stop peeping, Grace," Mum commanded. "But they only met today!"

"And God did greater wonders in the time," Daa said. "Come away from the window, Grace."

"Who are the Rhinelanders, Daa?" I asked, not yet knowing what Bob knew.

"I'll wait for her to come in. What in the world was he doing here?"

"We'll wait for her to come in," Mum said, "and then we'll ask her, won't we?"

So, we waited without moving from where we were standing, all with our eyes on the front door. We finally heard the car drive away. When the door opened, and Alice came in, she saw us at attention like expectant penguins.

"What's the matter?" She seemed already prepared for a family reaction.

"Did you happen to notice his shoes?" Daa had taught us that you could judge both a man's soul and bank account by his shoes.

Alice closed her eyes. "I just had a talk with myself out there after he left. I said, 'Don't dream a minute about his world, whatever it is, or getting out of mine. It'll be up to him, and it may have been nothing more to him than a nice day, a nice drive, a couple of kisses.'" She suddenly burst out laughing, but with tears at the same time, continuing. "'So, Alice, don't dare feel what you're feeling, that you must have fallen so in love with him that you're crazy with it. Think about..." she was gulping for air, "'about getting your uniform washed and ironed, about Em's baby, about anything but him kissing me, us talking about all the things in the world that matter, and wondering about all the other things he obviously wanted to say to me." Then she put her hands up to cover her face.

Mum and I went over and held her. I saw Daa and Bob exchange a helpless look of male uselessness. No one said anything until Grace said, "You kissed each other TWICE?"

We all groaned and then laughed, as did Alice, who admitted it. "We did. We sure did. I saw your reaction when you heard his name, Daa. Who is he? An axe-murderer? I mean, a rich axe-murderer?"

Daa knew more about the Rhinelander family than just their real estate, mainly because people left the New York newspapers in his taxi. While he waited for fares, he read them— including the financial and society pages.

"My darling daughter, the Rhinelanders are one of the most powerful families in New York City. They started buying up Manhattan before the Revolutionary War. One of them gave the money to build the Metropolitan Opera House, others to build every hospital in the city, and art to the museums. They were part of the original 'Four Hundred,' and they belong to all the private clubs. Give huge parties. They live like royalty."

"He told me about some of that."

"What's 'Four Hundred?'" Grace asked.

Daa shrugged. "I'm not sure, four hundred very exclusive people. Do you know, Emily?"

Strangely enough, I did. "Some of it. Before the turn of the century, a very rich lady wanted to be in charge of whom she thought was worthy to be in New York society." My knowledge came from my reading about the Gilded Age in Edith Wharton's books. "Her name was Astor, and she had a ballroom in her mansion that could fit in only four hundred people. So she gave a big party, and sent the guest list to the papers, calling them 'The Four Hundred.' They, and their descendants, remain part of it right up 'til today."

"Rather tacky to send a guest list to the papers," Mum sniffed and headed to the kitchen. "I'll make you some tea, Alice."

"Thanks, Mum. I have to get out of this dress. Em, come up with me?"

Before Grace could ask to come too, Daa said, "Bob, I think it's time we teach Grace the evils of gin rummy."

"Hey, would you?" she said.

I looked at Bob, he nodded, and it was fine. I hurried up the stairs to join

Alice. She'd had my old room ever since I left, letting Grace have the room across the hall as her own. When I got there, Alice was already in a chemise and quickly closed the door.

"I've gotta tell you!"

"Everything, I suppose."

"Yes, my dear pregnant sister, or I'll melt!" We hugged each other, both feeling triumphant. Then she told me of her day in a stitching of detail that it would be hard for me to forget.

***

Even so, her diary tells it better, and something of who she is as well. It's the longest diary entry that I found. This is who Alice is, in her own words:

> *September 21, 1921*
> 5. *Day off, black hole*
> 6. *Car crash (bump)*
> 7. *Him*
> 8. *Taking the air*
> 9. *Beach*
> 10. *His history, mine*
> 11. *Stuttering, stomach*
> 12. *Telling the truth, crazy?*
> 13. *His family, deaths*
> 14. *Other world*
> 15. *Kissing!!*
> 16. *Him and the family!*

***

Thursday. Another day off, like every other live-in maid in America. Daa picked me up at the Sondersons and brought me home. Mum had made scones as usual. The rest of the day has been magazines and records, then a nap. But even after a long bath, I still feel blue. Nowhere to go tonight. I have no idea what I'm going to do with myself. I thought of taking the train into Manhattan again, to kill time. Doesn't work. The last time there, I walked up the Avenue to Saks to look at the furs I'd never be able to afford. The saleswoman had treated me like dirt. How did that woman know I couldn't buy anything?

The idea of staying home is really depressing. The bath helped, except for

Grace coming in and out of the bathroom, needing Vaseline or floss as an excuse to barge in and talk about one more boy that she was carrying on with. After that, I came back to my room and stared at my maid's uniform that still lay on the floor. That slow, dull ache of hopelessness spread again, starting below the center of my ribcage, the dreariness going into my arms, down my legs. I picked up my uniform and dropped it on the bed. I couldn't wash and iron it right then. Later tonight, since I don't have anything else to do.

What I want to do is go out dancing, meet up with Kitty Thurston, and have some fun. The speakeasies are everywhere. They have the best jazz in the world. Kitty bobbed her hair and wants me to do it, too. It costs too much. Anyway, Kitty's doing something else tonight.

I love to dance. I'm really good at it if I do say so myself. I can pick up new steps almost as soon as I see them. Yes, I'm tired, as I am every Thursday night, but I could dance the Baltimore buzz, the shag, and wear out any partner that dares to take me on the dance floor! Gives me a real charge; most boys are convinced that they can out-dance anyone. I put them to shame! Yeah, I stop in the middle of the floor with the dancers and the smoke and the music churning around, thinking it's nothing more than a distraction from the slow dying my life's becoming. But then the music gets me again, and I dance!

Downstairs, just now someone— probably Grace— started my record on the Victrola again. What was that nice boy's name? I met him at Chatsworth's. He invited me to see *Shuffle Along* in New York. When I heard the song performed that night, it went right through me. It was the words:

> *Love will find a way,*
> *Though skies now are gray…*

I'm listening to the record, and got up, looked in the dresser mirror. In the reflection? Me and my life: the apron, headpiece, short-sleeved puffy dress—the uniform— on the bed, then beyond, my chest of drawers, the years and years of my diaries—my best friend except Em—locked up in the bottom drawer. Just like my life! Ha! The closet was closed to hide the mess inside it, my dressing table, the surface cluttered with two bottles of my cologne, a box of powder, make-up containers, an eyebrow pencil, an eyelash curler, and lipsticks. I love and hate this room: love it because I have it all to myself and made it my own; hate it because it's small and crowded like every room in the house, and I have to come back to it whenever I have free time. I don't want to believe that this room is all there is for me. Still, I'd rather be here than that tiny maid's room at the Sondersons.

I just went over to the half-mirror on the closet door and stood there naked, looking at myself. What's wrong with me? Why am I still alone? How can I be twenty-one already? So what if I can vote? How many women who are twenty-one are still single, or worse, like me, without even a connection to some possibility?

The mirror tilts downward. The autumn light comes in the windows at a slant, so the beams light those bits of dust that float around. The mirror reflected the bottom half of me. I just painted my toenails after my bath. I shaved my legs, too, even though I don't need to. There isn't much more than fuzz to shave. I put the two blocks of wood under each lower corner of the mirror and stood back in the new angle. The other half of me, belly first, flat, hipbones showing, ribs a little bit, too. Good. A lot of girls my age have already started going to fat. I'd hate it if that happened to me. But what does it matter? Every one of those girls has a fellow!

My breasts are kind of pretty. I can't compare them to anyone else's except my sisters'. I just wonder if mine are desirable, if they're done growing, if the nipples are going to get any darker, if I should show off in clothes and moves as Grace does or keep them to myself, as Em does. But does it make any difference?

My face. My head. Well, there it is. Shoulder-length straight brown hair that Mum taught me how to curl with finger waves, all pretty much washed out now from the bath. My lips really are too thin, not "luscious" like Grace brags that hers are. My nose is long and straight, handsome like Daa's, my skin is still "lustrous and radiant, lustrous and radiant" as Mum always tells me, and the brown eyes supposedly "flash" when I smile—as those boys at a speakeasy said.

I tested the smile in the mirror but couldn't be sure of the flash. They'd said I was "so pretty" too, then suggested I get in the backseat of their car with them. I never trust boys, but that must have been what they thought of me, pretty or not, that I was the kind that'd get in the backseat with them. I stared at myself, trying to see who I might be, asking myself if I was going to be someone other than who I thought I was, and why I was so alone and feeling so empty.

I went over to my dressing table and sat down, elbows on the top, and let my head fall into my hands. And that damn wonderful song was still playing.

Let's keep our love fires burning bright.
Your love for me is a heavenly beacon
Guiding me through love's darkest night.

No, no, dammit, no, I'm damned if I'm going to sit here listening to that love song, in this room, in this house. I'll fix up and get out of here, even if I just go walking around.

(Hours later! Oh my God! I can't believe it! I ought to go to sleep or do my uniform. I can't! I just told Em. I have to write it down! I don't want to forget a thing!)

Back earlier in my room: I put on full make-up, with my favorite lipstick, "Torch." Picking out panties, I chose the lacy black ones, what the hell! The matching brassiere, no. I threw it back into the drawer and put on a chemise. I don't like those new-fangled wired things. Then I took my new dress out of the closet, the shimmering gold flapper one that I'd saved up for all summer working at the resort, and never had a chance to wear! Since I was going walking, I didn't put on the high-heels I wear to go dancing, but some pumps. My coat isn't new, but that squirrel neckpiece I'd attached made it feel newer. It was chilly enough outside to wear it. Then, for no reason, I put on my yellow cloche with a pheasant feather sticking up that I usually wear to church.

When done, I stood in front of the mirror again. "Where the hell's my 'heavenly beacon'?" I said that out loud and laughed at myself. I looked good, I felt sly, in other words, a whole lot better just to be getting out of the house.

Downstairs, I went straight to the Victrola in the living room. I picked up the needle arm and said, "You'll wear it out, playing it over and over. It's my favorite record."

Grace and Mum were shelling peas at the dining room table. What a homey scene, I thought, Grace "thin with pleasing round accents," as one department store salesman had flattered her once, and at eighteen, like a filly in heat kicking to get out of the barn! And Mum? A force of electric nature she can barely hold onto in her plump body of creamy skin, topped by that lovely face and tight curls of gray hair.

How am I supposed to fit in here for the rest of my life? "Well, aren't you all dressed up," Grace said. "What for?"

"Just going for a walk."

"Ha! In that dress? She's sneaking out to meet up with that Eddy Lee."

"Eddy Lee drives a delivery truck, starting every morning at five. He doesn't go out much during the week."

"Please be back in time for dinner, luv," Mum said. "You know your father'll start groaning for his food."

The front door opened; Daa heard the last sentence. "Me, groaning? Nonsense." Holding his stomach, he moans. "And where might my princess Alice be going, all in her best?"

"I've been in that uniform for a week. I just wanted to get out of it and take a walk, just feel the sun." I kissed him. "I'll be back soon."

"I just might have found you a job, right here in New Rochelle."

"Oh, Daa, that'd be wonderful!"

"Won't say more until I'm sure. You go on, now."

The sun hit me at that sharp angle as I went out the front door and walked down the steps. When I got down to Pelham Road, I took a deep breath, happy to be out, glad the gloom had lifted even though I still had no place to go. I saw one of New Rochelle's police cars parked down the street, probably Daa's friend, Sergeant Kelly. I've always liked him and walked over, hoping to say hello.

Pelham Road usually has traffic that time of day. It wasn't surprising to hear a car approaching behind me. I love automobiles, so I turned to watch it come. It was a beautiful convertible, bright red, an Oldsmobile, I thought. Top down, it was coming fast, driven by a young man in glasses and a dark green suit, his hair blown back in the wind. As he got closer, his smile was so, I don't know, confident that I had to smile, too. In that moment, he was a picture of what? Pure freedom, able to do anything, go anywhere, live anyway he wanted. When he saw me, he stared too long before looking ahead again. Jamming on the brakes, he wasn't in time to prevent the Oldsmobile from skidding forward and just bumping Sergeant Kelly's car.

I just watched. The driver didn't move, sat bolt upright, gripping the steering wheel. Sergeant Kelly got out and went to the point of contact on his car, stared at it, then looked at the Olds. It was beautiful! I wandered over in time to hear, "Well, young fella, you've a nice new car, and naturally you had to drive it a wee bit fast." The sergeant went up to the driver to look him over. "It _is_ new, isn't it?"

The driver nodded rapidly.

"And next to this fine car, mine's a heap, wouldn't you say?"

"Y-Y-Y-Y... I mean, n-n-n..." He was struggling to talk.

"How fast were you going in this thing?" Sergeant Kelly demanded.

The driver tried to answer, but the first word caught. No sound came.

"Oh, not fast at all, Sergeant Kelly," I said without thinking about it. "I saw the whole thing."

Kelly looked at me doubtfully. "Hello, Alice. You know this young man?"

"No, not at all. I only saw him go by... kind of slow."

I saw that the driver was watching me. He started to get out of his car, then thought better of it.

"Might you be in possession of a license?"

The young man then got out of the car to reach for his wallet. I was surprised by how tall he was. Sergeant Kelly read the license and raised an eyebrow. "'Rhinelander.' That's an old name around here."

The driver was nervous. Then he laughed. "Yes! You see, my forebears f-f-founded New Rochelle in the s-s-seventeenth century, and..." He went silent, then desperately said, "I w-w-was just 't-t-taking the air.' Oh God, I d-d-don't even know w-w-what that means."

I'd never seen anyone work so hard just to talk, and I felt sorry for him. He looked anxious, his hair blown back, and he was so thin and tall. "From New York?" the sergeant said.

The young man nodded again.

"Well, Mr. Leonard Rhinelander, I have to say you're a very lucky man that no damage was done, and to be having an eye-witness for your defense saying you were going 'kind of slow.' Alice, please inform this young fellow that in New Rochelle, we don't look kindly on those who plow into our police cars, particularly when the policeman sitting inside is just finishing his corned-beef sandwich."

"I sure will, Sergeant Kelly."

He winked at me, then returned to his car, starting it up and driving away. The driver and I looked at each other from opposite sides of the Oldsmobile.

He tried to speak. Breath caught in his throat. Other cars passed by behind him.

So I smiled. "Hello." I don't know why, but I could feel my heart beating hard and fast. Yes, I know it was more than the automobile accident! I thought of his smile just before he saw me, just before he bumped the police car. That smile had been such a pure thing.

He was dressed in a dark green tweedy suit. His glasses kept reflecting the sun as he turned away from me to look at anything else, then turned back to try to say something, which he didn't seem able to do. "Hello," he managed. "My name is Leonard. And th-th-th-th-..." He paused and then almost shouted, "*Thank you!*"

I pulled back at the force of his thanks, then I smiled again. "You're welcome." I wondered if I was making him nervous. Dressed like that, driving a brand-new Oldsmobile convertible, what did he have to be anxious about?

"I mean," he took a deep breath, "I'm g-grateful for your help."

"I didn't do a thing." I realized that it was more than him being nervous.

Maybe he had that stuttering thing. "Just happened to be here."

"I'm very glad you w-w-were." He looked around and jammed his hands in his jacket pockets. "Do you live here in New R-R-Rochelle?"

"All my life." I thought he'd probably been everywhere. "All my whole life long, just waiting for a big red Oldsmobile to drive by and crash into a police car." I laughed to make sure he knew I was joking, but he just kept smiling at me with his eyebrows raised above his glasses, as if he was surprised by everything I said or did. He seemed nice enough, just awkward with talking.

"And h-h-here we are," he shrugged, looking down as he leaned forward to grip the door and prop himself against the car.

I nodded. "Uh-huh, we sure are."

"May I give you a lift somew-w-where?"

I liked the car a lot, but "Naw, I don't think so."

"I see." He looked crushed. He started to get back into the car but stopped. "W-W-Why not?"

"Well, look here, a girl doesn't just jump into a stranger's car."

"Of course not. I'm so s-s-sorry."

I waited. He seemed to be thinking about something, and then he forced out the words.

"You s-s-saved me getting a traffic ticket. I c-could drive you home."

Not wanting to admit that home was about a twenty-foot drive, I considered. I didn't think getting into his car was accepting the idea of fooling around, as it did with Eddy Holland or Bobby Al Rose. "I don't need to go home right now, thanks."

"I s-s-see." His disappointment again was really obvious. "I'd better be going."

Well, why not go with him, I thought. He's interesting, in fact, kind of nice. There was something about him that I saw in that second before he hit the police car that I wanted to find out about. It was Thursday night. What else did I have to do? "Listen, you said something to Sergeant Kelly, something about 'taking the air.' That sounded... pleasant." The word is one that Mrs. Sonderson uses <u>a lot</u>.

"We could d-d-definitely do that."

"What's it mean?"

"Just driving around, t-t-taking deep breaths." He smiled.

"Where'll we go?"

"Anywhere you'd like... this side of hell."

I was startled, as much as he was for saying it. So, I laughed. "Well, if we go there, you might find a couple of New Rochelle fire engines, so just don't crash into them."

He smiled and went around to open the door for me. I sure took that in. He was actually opening the door for me. Eddy Holland never did that. Neither did Bobby Al, not even when I had to get out of his fish truck on my own, him driving up to the curb and saying goodnight, sitting there like a frog in mud until I opened my own door and got out.

I stepped into the Oldsmobile and slid across the passenger seat. My coat parted and showed how short my gold dress was—above my knees! I saw him look, allowed it, then covered my legs again with my coat as he shut the door. "You b-b-better hold onto your hat!" He came around to the driver's seat. After a lurching start— "Have to g-get used to the clutch"—he turned the car and made his way out of New Rochelle. I held on to my cloche, sat back in the seat, comparing it to any seat I'd ever ridden in before. They were all lousy. This one had a sweet, pungent tang.

"Why does your car smell like this?"

"New leather, best smell in the w-w-world."

"Listen, I'm awful bad with names," I said. "Is it Laurence?"

"No. Leonard."

"Hi Leonard. I'm Alice Jones. Glad to meet you in all this air we're taking."

"Umm, you seem to be d-dressed up to go somew-w-where. I'll be glad to drive you."

I considered making up something but then didn't. Why? Because I'd probably never see him again, so why would it matter? "Well, to tell the truth, Leonard, when I got dressed up this afternoon? I had no idea where I was going. I just felt like dressing up. So maybe, without knowing any better, I was getting dressed up 'to take the air.' "

"Really? Then how very f-f-fortunate I came along and crashed into that police car."

We laughed. "Where are we going?"

"W-Would you like to take a w-w-walk on the beach? W-we're perfectly dressed for it, you in a gold dress, me in a tweed suit. And the air there is very good for the taking."

He said "perfectly" as if there was no "r" in it, but not "poificly" like the Brooklyn boys in the kitchen did at the resort last summer. "That'd be perfect," I said, not daring to imitate him.

"It's amazing to admit," Leonard said, "in s-such an easy way, that you'd gotten all dressed up w-w-without having anywhere to go."

"Well, it's the truth. I didn't. What's so amazing about that?"

"It's so... honest. I have a sister who'd never admit to such a thing. She dresses up to brush her teeth. If she doesn't have a reason, she'll make one up, something like, 'I have to dress for the shopkeepers. They expect it of me.' "

A sister, Alice thought, dresses up for the shopkeepers. A different world.

"You live in New York?" Alice said.

"Yes, w-w-we've lived there a long time."

"Yeah, after you all established New Rochelle in the 1700s."

"It w-w-was the 1600s. 1688 to be exact."

"I thought you said seventeenth century."

"Yes, but that's the 1600s."

"What? The seventeenth century is the sixteen hundreds? Well, that's confusing."

He glanced over. "It really is, isn't it?"

I changed from one hand to the other to hold my hat. We were tearing along. "Leonard, I gotta tell you, there's a whole lot of stuff I don't know."

He glanced over at me again, then drove for a moment before saying, "You're the only person I've ever known who was straightforward enough to admit it."

I liked that very much. He obviously had more education than I ever had, or ever would, and it felt good just to go ahead and admit it. To get a compliment back for being honest about it, yes, I liked that a lot. Then I realized: He hadn't stuttered.

Leonard interrupted the thought. "Um, how d-d-do you know the p-police so well?"

So it comes and goes. Strange. To the question, I thought of making up a better answer about knowing our policemen, but why? He'd just complimented me for telling the truth. I didn't think it would matter anyway. I thought of last summer, when I told the milkman who delivered to the resort that I was the illegitimate daughter of a Ukrainian princess. He'd believed me, and I don't even know where Ukrainia is. But this guy, this "Leonard," seemed to like the straight story. And if I never see him again, what does it matter?

"My father started a taxi service in New Rochelle. Still drives, but he owns some rental property, too. So he knows all the policemen pretty well. Went through a blizzard to get one of their wives to a hospital once, pulled another one out of his police car who'd turned over in a ditch. Sergeant Kelly's an old friend, comes in for coffee on winter nights."

"He started a taxi service," Leonard said with a kind of wonder. "That's wonderful, to start something on your own, something new. Everyone in my family has done the same boring thing for generations. Where does your family come from?"

"From England. My parents came here, oh, thirty years ago."

"So you're English."

"Well, they are. I was born here, so I'm American. My father started his taxi-driving when he saw all the men needing rides at the New Rochelle station coming out from New York." Should I tell him that Daa was a porter at the station and digging sewer trenches when he got the idea?

"Filling a need," Leonard said before I had the chance. "My family has never even imagined doing anything like that." He laughed again.

"Why's that funny?"

He stopped laughing. "W-W-What I meant was, w-what my family does, doesn't do anything for anybody, except make more and more money for the family."

"My golly, that's not so bad, is it? What do they do?" He hesitated. "They trade in property... real estate."

"You're right."

"About?"

"It's b*ooooooriiing.*"

He took a quick glance to see me looking at him, smiling. He threw back his head to laugh, swerved on the road and steadied the car as I braced myself and yelled, "Hey, you aren't Barney Oldfield, you know."

"Sorry. It was your fault."

"Mine?"

"You distracted me with humor." And he laughed again but held the car steady.

"Okay, I'll go all glooooomy while I'm out here taking this air. You scared it all out of me back there anyways." It was really fun. He's really nice. "Do you come up from New York a lot?"

"Ah, I'm not l-l-living in... I'm staying n-n-near Stamford now."

"Oh. That's... even closer."

"Yes, it is, isn't it?"

We drove for another quarter of an hour, me thinking about how close Stamford was, wondering if this Leonard person might actually want to meet again, planning how to find that out, and if he did, inventing some way to make it happen. When he pulled the car onto the shoulder of the road and stopped, I was thinking hard about the next step.

"W-W-We're here."

"Oh. It's beautiful."

"Shall w-we w-w-walk?"

"What'll we do with our shoes?"

"The backseat."

"What if someone steals them?"

"I can drive barefoot, and w-w-we'll go buy new ones."

What a simple solution. Another world. He hurried around to help me out, and we both sat on the running board to take our shoes off. I was so glad I had bright red nail polish on my toes! I noticed that his socks were striped up and down, blue and green, the green close to the same color as his suit. Was that by chance?

He threw the socks with his shoes into the backseat and rolled up the legs of his pants. When he stood up, he looked off as if he didn't know what to do next, maybe whether to offer a hand or an arm. So, I got up on my own and took off my coat, throwing it as casually as possible into the backseat with my pumps. The breeze off the Sound was chilly, but I wanted him to see me in that dress! I put my hand in his and said, "Let's go," as if it was the most natural thing to do, which it was, but he looked at me as if I'd just performed a miracle.

We trudged through the soft sand until it grew hard, approaching the low tide. Neither of us reacted to the cold water, but stood in it ankle-deep, gazing at the clouds that the sunset was turning into fire.

"'Red s-s-sky at night, sailors' delight.'"

"What's that mean?"

"Oh. Um, I used to sail. It's an old saying, 'Red sky in the morning, sailors take warning. Red sky at night, sailors' delight.' If it looks like this in the evening, it'll be a pleasant night. But in the morning, a red sky means hard weather."

He said all that without a stutter. Should I ask? No!

"So you're a sailor?"

"No, no, a number of my relatives have boats, and..." He stopped abruptly, as if it was something he didn't want to talk about.

"What kind of boats? Floating-in-a-bathtub boats, or those big ones with sails all over 'em? Come on, let's walk."

"W-W-With some sails."

"You mean, yachts?"

"Ummm..."

"You ever sail over to the New York Athletic Club at Travers Island?"

This surprised him. "Yes, any number of times. Why?"

Should I tell him this? If I did, would he think I was white trash, drive off after leaving me out at the curb? No, he liked the truth. And he might as well know this. I'd probably never see him again anyway. "I worked there."

"You did?"

"A couple of summers. In the laundry." I didn't turn to see his response but kept walking. I'd know how he felt soon enough. "I saw a lot of yachts. From a distance, of course."

But he stopped, and still gripping my hand, turned to gaze at me. I watched him, figuring that was that. But he kept hold of my hand and didn't even try to say anything, just looked at me until a high wave came in, probably the first of the changing tide. It hit above our knees, and both of us leaped back to the dry sand.

"Be careful, Leonard. You'll get your pants wet."

"It doesn't matter. Alice, you..."

"What do you mean it doesn't matter? Do you know what salt water does to wool?"

"It's all right, someone at home'll take care of it. I meant..."

"Oh, you mean you expect your momma to..."

"No, my mother is dead. I meant that we have someone at home who..."

"Oh, no. I'm so sorry, Leonard. I didn't mean...That's so, so sad."

"You couldn't have known. And yes, it was very sad."

"What happened?"

He didn't answer. I thought: *dumb*! For asking about something so personal. But he said, "Alice, something's happening. I don't think it's ever happened to me before."

"What?"

"I don't know." He took my hand again, and we started walking. "Just being with someone, and talking, not just blabbing, not just trying to say things to fill some empty silence." He stopped walking. "And I'm not stuttering."

"I noticed that. How come, you think?"

"I don't know. They tell me at the clinic it happens when I'm thinking about what I'm saying instead of worrying how I'm sounding, or who I'm saying it to." Walking again, he said, "So I must be doing that."

"You say things just fine. Better'n me. What are you thinking so hard about?"

"Here and now? You've just told me about your father driving a taxi, about where you worked, which was so... honest."

"Sure. Why not? There's no big secret. Just saves time getting to know somebody, families and all."

"Yes. It does." He walked on, changing his grip on my hand, holding it tighter. "So, this is what happened. My mother used a very bright alcohol spirit lamp on her dressing table when she fixed her hair to go out. One night, it exploded in her face. She died two days later from the burns."

"That's... horrible."

"Yes. It was. I still miss her."

"Course you do. How old were you?"

"Twelve."

"Oh, dear God. I can't imagine that. What'd you do?"

"I became very silent, because earlier I'd started to stutter. It got worse and I didn't know what else to do."

"Did your father look after you all right?"

"Not in the slightest. He got rid of me as quickly as he could."

"What? How'd he do that?"

"He sent me away to school."

"You mean, you lived there?"

"Yes. Boarding school."

"What was that like?"

"Well, if you don't talk, and when you do, you stutter, and then when your brother is killed, if you add another problem of having a very nervous stomach that leads to any number of embarrassments in public, boarding school is hell."

"Your brother was killed?"

"In the war. I missed one weekend at school to go home for his memorial service. Then right back to hell."

"That's about the cruelest thing I've ever heard. My father'd never do that."

"Know how lucky you are."

"I do. Did you have any other brothers and sisters?"

"Originally, two older brothers, at the time one already at another boarding school, the other at Harvard, before he joined up. My older sister, well, she was becoming a debutante."

"What's that?"

"Ah, well, it's when a young woman is introduced to society."

"What society?"

"It's a ritual, a lot of big dances that make up a season in the fall. Girls who are around eighteen from certain families dress up in white dresses to start the process of finding a husband."

"Are you kidding me?"

"No. It happens every year."

"What about your brothers? Were they debutantes?"

"No. Just girls are. My brothers attended a lot of the debutante balls, though. I did, too."

"Oh, I get it: You guys were maybe going to be the husbands. Did your brothers ever marry one of them?"

"P.K. did. Nice girl, good family, the usual thing. She raises their two children and goes to the Colony Club."

"Oh, she likes jazz?"

"Um, no, different kind of club. P.K. works with Father in the family business. The oldest brother, Oakley... w-w-well, he was the one that was killed."

"I'm asking all the wrong things. I'm so sorry."

"You said nothing wrong. It's all about *my* family. Oakley was the only relative I had that I think liked me. P.K. thinks I'm a jerk, Adelaide something worse, and my father just wants to get rid of me." He looked over at me, deciding something. "You see, Alice, I have these imperfections: the stuttering, the crazy stomach, glasses, and being awkwardly tall. The family doesn't consider me a real Rhinelander."

"That's so sad, Leonard. Doesn't anyone in your family realize how, well, swell you are? That's a compliment."

"I got it. Thanks. Well, I have an aunt, Aunt Lucy, a kind of fairy godmother who seems to like me."

We walked toward the sunset, forcing seagulls to run or fly in the opposite direction. I said, "Our family's never had any tragedies like that. It's the best, strongest thing in my life. My father, we call him 'Daa', he's just a fine man."

(Without thinking, I went ahead and said it! I can't believe I did that!) "He's half West Indian, Spanish, maybe slave or something, the other half British, talks like a real English gent. His Yorkshire accent bamboozles people, him being so dark-skinned, but everyone loves him." I never talked about this! Why did I say anything? BECAUSE OF HIM!

"That's amazing. Do you, I mean, well, you don't seem to have inherited any of... that."

"You mean his color? No. Just his gorgeous looks, long nose, thin lips." I made a joke of it but watched him carefully and struck a pose. "Judge for yourself."

"I already have. He must be a very good-looking man." He smiled. "That's a compliment."

"I got it. Thank you."

"Tell me about the rest of your family?"

"My Mum is as English as can be, rules our little kingdom like a queen. I have two sisters, Grace and Emily—I'm in the middle. Both are a whole lot different from me. Grace is a show-off and just wild. And Emily, who's the smartest, married a Negro, a butler." I kept walking but knew the chance I was taking telling him that! "He's a wonderful guy, graduated high school and all. But it nearly killed Mum, and they still can't come to the house."

I waited for him to respond. He'd trusted me with all his family stuff and seemed to accept what I'd told him about Daa. But the world draws lines about marriage between races, particularly fancy people like this "Leonard" certainly seemed to be.

"We had a family marriage crisis like that," he finally said, "not about race, but it was..." Then he stopped.

I sure wasn't going to ask anything more! "Every family does, probably."

"No, not like this." We walked a short distance. "Alice, I want to tell you everything. Maybe I will one day. My family had a predicament once that caused great cruelty and destruction." He gazed at me. No! I'd asked too much already. "Of course, this situation with your sister is completely different. It's sad that she's forbidden to come home. I don't know any colored people, but if her husband is as fine as you say…"

"Wait a minute. You don't know any colored people?"

"No. Not one, not even a servant. All ours are either English or Irish. I've seen Negroes play jazz in clubs, is all. I certainly understand how intermarriage is, well, difficult. But people can find reasons to be prejudiced about anything. My family's filled with it to degrees of disgust and hate you can't imagine. Not that they allow it to show. But if your sister's husband is a good man, your mother should accept him, for all of your sakes. If she doesn't, it'll only cause greater pain as time passes, it seems to me."

I looked at him in wonder. It was a long speech, and he didn't stutter once.

"You think so? I wish you could tell Mum that. She won't listen to us about it anymore."

"Maybe I will."

The idea that he'd do that implied things to both of us. This time, I stopped and turned to him. "'Maybe' is a nice idea."

There was his smile again, the one I'd seen while he was driving, of such huge happiness, of being free enough to do anything. Well, I'd not felt so happy in a long time either, and hoped it didn't show too much. Walking and talking on a beach with him seemed so—what's the word? So vital! Yes! Whoever he was, what kind he was, I sensed he'd done something to me without him even knowing it. I didn't know what it was, but I wondered if I'd done something like that to him. I was so damn glad I'd worn that dress! "You know, Leonard, I'm getting kind of cold."

"We lost the sun, and a beach in late September…"

"I didn't even notice. Oh, gosh, then I'm late for supper."

"Now may I drive you home?" He took off his green suit jacket and held it for me to put on. I was dwarfed in it, the sleeves coming down to my knees. Turning and starting back toward the car, we saw a flock of seagulls standing together down the beach. I began running toward them, making bird sounds, flapping the sleeves of Leonard's jacket up and down. I figured he might as well know I'm crazy right now!

Back at the car, I returned his jacket, picking up my own coat that he held for me. Daa does that for Mum, but nobody else I know does it. We put our shoes on, and Leonard managed to put the Oldsmobile's top up — amazed, he said, by how easy it was. The drive back to New Rochelle seemed to take no time at all. We spoke about places we'd been, Leonard describing as best he could exactly what a Venetian gondola was, and me telling the various Catskill delivery methods for illegal alcohol I learned about last summer. We discovered we both loved going to clubs and listening to jazz, something that neither of us had the chance to do very often. But it let us think about those teasing little hopes for the future. Neither of us expressed more than a casual possibility, but I sure grabbed hold of the idea hard.

We turned onto Pelham Road, and without thinking about it, I dared to say, "Leonard, why don't you come in, meet my parents, have something to eat. We probably missed dinner, but…"

"It's awfully late to come in unannounced."

"'Unannounced'? Hey, we don't do that fancy introducing to society around here. People come in all the time." Then I saw the Model T. "Oh my gosh! That's Bob's car, my sister's husband, I told you about, who is forbidden to be here? What are they doing here?"

Leonard parked the Oldsmobile just behind the old Ford. "Is this your house? Up there is where I hit the police car."

"Oh. Yeah, just up there a little bit."

"So that's why you didn't want me to drive you home. You really wanted to come with me."

"Well, I guess so. The air, you know."

"Alice, I'm so glad…" and he lurched over and tried to kiss me. For whatever reason, I drew back, and he lurched right back to his own side of the car. "I'm so s-s-sorry…"

"Len, Len, we…"

He sat up straight. "Say that again."

"What? 'Len?'"

"Alice, call me that! Will you? No one's ever called me that." Smiling in wonder, he collapsed back against his car door. "Alice, I haven't talked to anyone as we've talked in my whole life."

I believed him. And I knew damn well that the afternoon's relief from my own life had allowed my part of the talking. I leaned over and kissed him on the cheek. He turned and enfolded me, gazing at me a moment before kissing me on the lips, which, without a thought, I parted. Amazed, he copied me, and when our tongues touched, I thought my bones melted. He seemed unable to breathe. The kiss went on, and on. I finally pulled back and said, "Len, we have to go in."

"Yes," he said, breathing hard. "I liked that."

"I liked it, too. A whole lot."

We looked at each other, not wanting to move. "We better…" I said.

"Yes, we sure better."

I got out of the car without waiting for him to help, breathing hard. He joined me on the front walk. I tried to think of something else. Anything! "If Bob and Em are here, it might mean..." I hurried to the top of the steps. Then I stopped and turned back. "Oh gosh, Len, I forgot your last name."

"May I make something up?"

"No, you may not!"

"It's Rhinelander. Yours is Jones, isn't it?"

"Rhine what?"

"Rhinelander."

"That's a mouthful. Okay." I opened the front door...

CHAPTER THREE

Before the supervisors could see the reason to fire me, I quit my secretarial job at the insurance company where I'd worked for the previous four years. The day I left, I happily told everyone why. When I said goodbye to the men in my section, they looked at me with pity, as if my life were over. The women were thrilled for me, most offering happy advice, some quietly admitting their envy. That same night, Bob chose to tell me that he was starting classes whenever he could get to NYU, with the idea of going on to law school. He figured it would take him ten years, so our future seemed to be set for a while. I was very pleased. I'd known about his idea of becoming a lawyer since our first train ride together, and now he was going to make it real.

Daa found a maid's job for Alice in New Rochelle so she could live at home. This meant she could be there any night that Len could drive down from The Orchards. He came often, picked her up, and took her away to do whatever they wanted to do: drive and talk, a moving picture, sometimes on the night before her day off, a jazz club. I'd hear all about it, how he barely stuttered at all with her. He often dropped her off at the Weingolds' garage on his way back to The Orchards. Usually, Bob was up at the main house until late, as the Weingolds entertained a lot. I'd let her talk as long as she wanted, and when she finally gave out, I'd drive her home. That's when I usually heard what was really going on.

For instance, sometime in October, about a month after they'd met, she told me about a conversation they'd had that night. "We're different kinds of people, Len. I'm ordinary, and you're... what? So... grand. I know that and so do you. I work as a maid in people like yours' houses.

"Len watched me for a second, then let my hand go and started the car. The cold windshield was fogged by the heat inside, so he turned on the wipers. We drove away in silence from the beach. Then all of a sudden, he started talking, kind of angry. 'Let me tell you what's ordinary to me. During my sister's season, I was brought home from school as the darling little brother wearing white tie and tails who wouldn't speak. I had to go to a whole mess of debutante balls. I watched those girls, in masks of make-up wearing massive white dresses and high heels, they didn't know how to walk in, trying so hard to look, I don't know, regal. It was like some pagan ritual. Their fathers lead them wobbling down a set of stairs to the sacrifice, and the girls do an awkward curtsy to the God of sexual attraction, hoping it'll all end up in a grand society marriage.' He shook his head. He seemed so sad to me, as if he felt sorry for them. But then he got angry again.

"But then after the formal performance, they rush to change into 'rags,' they call them, and head up to Harlem in their fathers' limousines to jazz clubs, to drink and smoke, to dance and grope and tell dirty jokes, without any curiosity about anything other than about the comforts they were born to enjoy—expensive travels, expensive clothing designers, expensive parties, and the wealthy men to pay for all of it. They don't even listen to the jazz! Alice, in my pathetic moneyed world, that's what's ordinary to me. Next to any one of those girls, you're a goddess.' We drove a long time, neither one of us looking at the other.

"I don't know about any of that stuff," I told him. "It's all on a different rich planet—and it can stay there for all I care. I'm just glad you found your way to mine." I leaned my head on his shoulder. "I hate every night when you can't come down, or when you're at your family's house in New York. I love the letters you send, but they're no substitute for having you here. Because, for better or worse, I've fallen in love with you, Len, and I don't have any idea what to do about it."

"He said as he drove, 'I hope you already know I love you so very much. I love your planet much more than mine, I love your family, I love your home, and I don't know what to do about it either. We just have to—like your song says—find a way...'"

Alice told me this without her usual excitement, calmly, as if it were a column of figures that added up the first time she totaled it. "Don't tell anyone," she said. "Even with you, I'm scared that talking about it'll break the spell."

"Doesn't sound like a spell to me, just your basic falling in love."

She looked at me to confirm what I'd said, wanting to believe it. I suppose I wanted her to believe it, because I did. Not that I knew Len well enough to judge yet, but from what I'd seen and heard from Alice, I liked him, even as damaged as I thought he must be. And I don't mean just the stuttering.

"Thanks, Em. It helps so much to talk with you. What are you doing tomorrow? Maybe I could come over again..."

That was fine with me. Suddenly, I had a lot of free time as I was supposed to be preparing for the life-changing arrival. Of course, Bob and I bought the usual things and fit out a small storage room in our garage apartment for a nursery. It had a window to the north for good light. He bought two carved wooden signs for the door, one "Robert," the other "Roberta," and leaned them on the floor nearby. But even with all the preparation, I had time to myself and, at first, was guilty about it, having worked most of my life. But then I came across *The Age of Innocence*—Edith Wharton had won the Pulitzer Prize for it that year, the first woman to win it—and I started reading a whole lot of books in time-clouds of long and wonderful hours. I caught up with what I wanted to read about Bob's involvement at the NAACP, then took on learning about Mrs. Weingold's cause of Margaret Sanger and what had just been retitled the Planned Parenthood Federation of America. The world was changing, and I had to stay ahead of it for the child I was carrying.

The worst thing—and I read up on this too—was the resurgence of the Ku Klux Klan, more in the North than in the South, started right after the motion picture The Birth of a Nation came out in 1915. Its racist fiction glorified the Klan for rescuing civilization from the intrusion of the Negro, the uppity kind as well as the savage, both scornfully portrayed in the film. According to the newspapers, the KKK was growing in every Northern state where blacks fleeing Jim Crow in the South had come looking for jobs. Race riots and lynchings had become routine news, along with the illegal-liquor gangs murdering each other and all the government corruption that Prohibition was enabling. It scared me for the life my child would have to live. That's when I started thinking about whatever truth there was in my being black, and what "shade" my baby would be.

One night in November, when Bob and I were going over our budgets, we heard Len's car drive up, the motor turning off, and the doors slamming shut. Surprised, I opened our front door as Alice and Len came up the stairs outside, laughing, he was carrying a bottle. We greeted them, all of us talking over the others, and he was asking for a corkscrew, Alice saying, "You have to hear what he told me. His family is so crazy complicated." I found four glasses of varying sizes for whatever was being opened, as Len said, "I stole it out of our cellar. It's Chateau d'Yquem, liquid ambrosia!"

When we had our glasses, Len directed a toast toward my stomach. "In the presence of what's to come, here's to the future!"

We sipped the sweet, astonishing wine. "Is this a special occasion?" Bob asked. "Because it should be with this."

"I admit that when I smuggled it out of Father's cellar, I hoped we four would be the ones to drink it. Did we come over too late?"

The letter "w" no longer seemed his enemy.

"I'm not called to the main house until ten in the morning," Bob said.

"And tomorrow is Thursday, so I'm off."

"And I have nothing to do but lie around eating bonbons and thinking about diapers, so it's only you that'll suffer, Len."

"The Orchards thinks I'm home in New York. New York thinks I'm at The Orchards. And frankly, neither of them cares. What else shall we drink to?"

"Howzzabout Bacchus," Bob said, "for allowing us this beautiful stuff?"

"How about 'Gally Curtsy?'" Alice struck a hoity-toity attitude. "She's having her debut at the Metropolitan Opera next week, la-de-daa."

Len laughed as Bob and I looked at each other. "What's that supposed to mean?" I asked.

"Len, you have to tell them about your Opera Ball night."

Smiling, he nevertheless seemed hesitant, but the mood seemed to carry him along.

"This'll give you an idea of the life I'm trying to get away from. Last week, I went home to face a family obligation. I wouldn't dare drive the Olds in to be inspected and criticized, so my father sent his new Packard out to get me. I've always dreaded going home, but this time seemed so different. You see, I knew that no matter how thoroughly I might be ignored or ridiculed, I had Alice."

"Not that part," Alice said, embarrassed but pleased.

"I anticipated the usual repressive meals, the terse conversations with my father, the snide remarks from P.K., my older brother, and the usual nasty comments my sister, Adelaide, so enjoys making in front of me as if I weren't there." He smiled. "None of it mattered. You see, I had Alice." She rolled her eyes, more pleased than before.

"All right, all right. The purpose of the visit, as I thought, was to discuss my part in Adelaide's upcoming wedding to Larry Shackno. The whole family disapproves of the match, admitting no good reason why, but all knowing that because his family was unknown in the Rhinelander social realm, he wasn't good enough to marry one. The wedding means nothing to me, so I wasn't prepared for what was coming. I was wearing a tennis sweater and white flannel pants. I don't play tennis, but Alice had mailed me a clipping of a movie star wearing the outfit, saying it'd be exactly right for me. I bought it and liked it a lot."

"He looked spiffy!" Alice toasted the image.

"Chidester, our chauffeur, let me out and gave me his latest stock tip: a Peruvian gold mine. I said, 'That's a pretty crazy investment, Chidester.'"

"'I keep my ears open,' he said. 'As they say, gold is money, just needs digging up.' He usually isn't supposed to speak, but we've become friendly and have some common interests. I told him, 'Get me information on it, will you? And listen, I heard there's a new jazz joint down on East Fourteenth.' He told me about it, and I walked up the steps to the front door that Maxwell, our butler, held open, as usual, looking severe. God, Bob, I wish you could give him lessons on being human!"

"I give those lessons, but he couldn't afford me."

"He greeted me with, 'Master Leonard. I'm afraid you're late,' and immediately led me toward the drawing room.

"'What am I late for? 'The Opera Ball, sir.' 'That's tonight?' He slid open the drawing room's doors, and I went in. Considerable surprise! Adelaide was the first to welcome me: 'Oh my God, look at him!'"

"'Hello, dear boy,' my Aunt Lucy managed to get in. She isn't really my aunt, more a distant Rhinelander cousin who often is on Father's arm for social occasions. She was wearing a long blue dress with some kind of elaborate Aztec embroidery on it. The blue brought out her eyes and even more, the sapphire earrings she was wearing. You'll see in a minute why the colors matter.

"'Tennis anyone?' P.K., my older brother, added, already dressed in his white tie. 'No, Leonard's probably dressed for ping-pong.' He was a star squash player at Harvard, very good-looking, and could have been a model for one of Charles Dana Gibson's adoring swains, except that he adores no one more than himself. This includes his ever-absent wife and two daughters, whom he happily tolerates, but largely ignores."

I shot a glance at Bob, suddenly a little uncomfortable with all we were hearing, wondering if the wine was having its way with Len. Bob gave a small shrug as Len went on.

"My father, also in white tie, commanded, 'Leonard, we're due at the Opera Ball. Go up and change at once. You have ten minutes.' As usual, Father stood in front of the fire, posed for power. You don't know what he looks like, do you? He pays very careful attention to his walrus mustache—in imitation of old J.P. Morgan, one of the few people he ever admired. What's left of his graying hair is brushed and cut carefully. His face?" Len smiled as he searched for the description. "His entire face... is raised as if by pulleys attached to his forehead. He's therefore unlined by care, creating an imperious look he presents to the world as his own acceptance of his cunning superiority."

Happy with his description, he continued. "I then purposely stuttered, 'I feel so w-w-w-w-welcome coming home.'"

Bob guffawed. I looked at Alice. She was proudly smiling at Len's storytelling.

He was enjoying himself. "Adelaide, using her piercing shriek, said, 'Do you see what I mean?' She barged past me in her chic but dull black dress. 'He can't talk, and I won't have him in the wedding!' and left the room.

"'Great,' I thought, 'that's settled.'

"'Go along, Leonard,' Aunt Lucy said. 'We mustn't keep Galli-Curci waiting.'

"'Who?'

"'She'll sing an aria at dinner. It's her debut when the Met opens. Go quickly, my dear.' She smiled affectionately, and I loved her for it. So I hurried out and was met by Maxwell, who followed me upstairs to my room. Clive, my father's valet, was already there and said urgently, 'I took the liberty of loading your shirt and waistcoat with links, buttons and studs. The back collar button is in, but we'll have to do the front one when you're in the shirt.'

"'Thank you, Clive. Maxwell, who's Gally Curtsy?'

"'I believe a soprano from Europe,' he sniffed, the biggest snob in the world, and hurried back downstairs. With Clive's help, I was out of the tennis outfit and into the white tie and tails. As always, gathering the four buttonholes of both the stiff-shirt and the damned starched bat-wing collar onto the front collar button was maddening, but Clive was an expert and finger-wrestled them into place. I stood stiffly as he quickly knotted the white bow tie... All these ridiculous details are part of the story, I promise."

That self-awareness surprised me, and I listened more carefully.

"I thanked God that Aunt Lucy was there, obviously the only one who was glad to see me. She's one of the great conversationalists, has that skill to keep talk going in order to prevent any awkward silence. As Clive worked, I remembered the etiquette class that I'd been sent to in the sixth grade. Did I tell you this, Alice?"

"Yes, but tell them."

"The pompous instructor said that fifteen seconds was the limit allowed from the end of one conversation to the beginning of the next, whether with your dinner partner, at tea, at a ball, dancing or not. Some poor soul in the class dared to ask him what one was supposed to talk about. The instructor swelled up, shot a vicious glance at the questioner and said, 'Anything! And if nothing intelligent slips into your vapid little mind, discuss a cheese!'

"Aunt Lucy never fell back on anything like that. She's a beautiful woman who had a rotten marriage and seems to understand what despair is. I assure you, it's a response that no other Rhinelander has ever revealed. Aunt Lucy had rid herself of —as the family had dubbed him—a 'bounder' in an all-too-public divorce proceeding. She then reclaimed the family name and did her best to erase any memory of her marriage that she or the family might have retained." He finished what was left in his glass and poured himself some more.

"I want to tell you about something else. Alice, I left it out before. When my tails were on, I turned to the dressing table where, as always on opera night, a white carnation had been left there in a bud vase for me. I put it through the buttonhole in my lapel, staring at myself in the mirror. The tailor always puts a small loop of strong thread attached to the buttonhole behind the lapel to hold the stem of a boutonniere in place.

"This is when it happened." Len was staring at nothing, abruptly back in his room, all buoyancy gone. "As I attached the stem in that thread, it seemed, just for a moment, as if the Earth stopped turning; that time no longer passed. I know I didn't breathe. I saw all the intricate requirements that made up this grotesque costume, one designed by weird rules for the gigantic ritual of going to the opera. It wasn't the performance. That's creative art on six hundred different levels. I'm talking about what just attendance is, socially.

"In that moment, everything that I'd had to wear all through my life—the studs, the cufflinks, the coats, the ties, the handmade shoes, the right cuffs on the trousers, the right lining in a suit coat, and on and on—seemed ridiculous, meaningless. Details, thousands of details! An unseen loop of thread to hold a stem in place, for Christ's sake! The camelhair coat, the Chesterfield coat, the astrakhan coat and for that night, the opera coat that the valet was holding for me, another goddamn white carnation already in its lapel, held in place by another goddamn loop of thread! I felt that if I couldn't think of Alice, I'd get sucked down under all that junk in my life."

I was strangely alarmed. His intensity was frightening. Bob watched him steadily. Alice was wide-eyed, not having heard this part of the opera story.

"Alice, all that stuff is like... the cement in the wall between us. I stared at that white carnation and wondered what you were doing. It was Thursday night. You were at home, probably, listening to records, in pajamas—oh God, to be there with you in pajamas!" He glanced around at us to see if he'd gone too far. He had, but by that point, it didn't matter. "Maybe you were writing a letter to me, but you were so free of all this stuff, these idiotic details."

He was watching Alice, hoping for understanding, but by then, that didn't matter either. I couldn't tell if she was embarrassed by his strange moment or not. Quietly, she said, "Tell them the rest."

"Oh, well, Clive said, 'Master Leonard, I believe they're going to the car.' The moment passed, and the Earth moved again. I went down the hall to the stairs. Adelaide met me there and, as usual, chose to ignore me. I noticed her change of dress to one that was a clash of orange and yellow. Knowing better than to offer a compliment, knowing even better that she'd changed into a lot of garish color so as not to be overshadowed by Aunt Lucy's magnificent blue, I followed downstairs as the others were being helped on with their coats—in P.K.'s case, an opera cape lined in scarlet silk that he managed to swirl as he put it on.

"Then my brother and sister had one of their usual snake-hiss contests, which tells you what it's like around there. As she was putting on her fur, she asked, 'P.K., why is your ever-perfect wife Helen not joining us yet again?' Adelaide squirts malice wherever she can.

"'Because she's being the perfect mother at home with our loving children,'

P.K. said as they went out the door, 'behavior one day I'm sure you'll emulate, once married and breeding your forthcoming tribe of Jewish Shacknos.'

"She rose above the slur. 'Well, I'll never name a daughter "Living."' "'An ancient and honored name in her fine old family, as you know.'

"'Yes, but I've always wondered why she didn't name the other one "Dead."'"

Alice, beaming, looked at us, expecting laughter. Bob and I tried to, but we were considering more than Len's sister's grotesquely funny line.

Len finished his story. "I followed my loving siblings toward the Packard, asking myself what the hell I was doing there. Aunt Lucy turned on the top step and took my arm. I wanted to ask her how I could get out of it all, but didn't. She'd chosen to stay in the family maze. I'd just have to get out of it on my own if it were possible. All I knew for certain was that I had Alice in my life." He put his glass down and reached over to take her hand. "My dear, darling Alice, can you possibly imagine putting up with me and all that crap?"

As Alice answered by kissing the hand that held hers, I felt intense trepidation and ambivalence that I couldn't yet describe. We talked some more and enjoyed the wine. Only after the conversation turned to how late it was and they left did I even try to express my concern.

"Well?" Bob asked me, knowing I'd have plenty to say.

It took me a moment to start. "I fear for him. What he describes as his family, they seem to me to be a monstrous juggernaut locked into the intricate traditions that work for them like a Swiss watch. Rhinelander influence seems so massive that it faces no real resistance. Aside from making money, it can destroy—without taking much notice of doing it—anything or anyone that fools with how it works."

"Even one of their own?"

"My question exactly. I don't know how, but look at what they've done to Len already. I fear for him."

Bob nodded. "I like him."

"I do, too. But I'm not clear as to why."

"I think he's honest... in a distorted life that's slanted quick and easy by money toward self-deceit."

"He's so naïve!"

"He's eighteen, Emily. But to survive, the kid's been forced to a maturity beyond his years by that very strange, destructive family. I thought that moment he described tonight was a huge step toward realizing who he doesn't want to be."

"You mean, when the Earth stopped?" I said it sarcastically as I hadn't really gone along with that magic moment.

"Whatever it was, for Len it was shucking off a snakeskin. I almost laughed at him getting into his white tie. I do all that for Mr. Weingold, and that front collar button is a torture! But all those details—the limousine, the servants, the jewels, the dresses, the white tie, the opera—usually people drop that stuff to impress. But Len was honestly describing his usual life, without any conceit about it. And then his moment of truth—that it was all ridiculous, even dangerous, and that he wanted to get out of it? Seemed authentic to me."

"All because of Alice..."

He nodded. "When you think you're going under, you grab on to any lifeline that comes along."

I didn't disagree but was less than reassured. "I fear for her, too."

CHAPTER FOUR

I began to show and started to feel heavy. The morning sickness came and went, after which I didn't feel I could ever recover my usual level of energy. Therefore, I did little that required more than sitting. I'm not assuming my maternal progress is of any interest. It's only meant to explain the time I had on my hands to do research. I did want to know more about the Rhinelanders.

Until it became too cold, I drove over to the New Rochelle library to spend hours with old newspapers and social histories. Because the Rhinelander progenitors had established the town and moved on to great fame and fortune, the library proudly had a lot of what I wanted to know. It did little to counter my apprehension about Alice's and Len's future.

The original Rhinelanders landed—literally—in New Rochelle in 1688, the place being little more than a collection of farms. The family lasted there for less than two generations and was drawn to New York City. The true family history began in 1794. In that propitious year when George Washington was in his second term as president, the City of New York magnanimously gave Trinity Church a "water grant" covering all the Manhattan coastland from Washington Street to the North River, presuming that the donation would help finance charitable good works from the church to the city's citizens long into the future. Such a grant gave the Church not only the land on the river, but the right to extend ownership out into the Hudson River, should anything useful ever develop for the use of property that was underwater.

In a very short but discreet time, however, Trinity Church, for unknown reasons, conveyed that grant to the Rhinelander family progenitor, William, an upstanding and powerful member of the congregation. At the time, he also happened to be the Assessor for the Fifth Ward as well as an enforcer in the original Tammany Hall political organization. Subsequently, the Rhinelander family proved adroit in using the corrupted powers of city government to get land grant after land grant for virtually nothing. Over generations, those water rights allowed them, for little expense, to fill in the submerged areas of that original grant to double or triple their original landholdings. This practice, as well as massive financial leverage, led ineluctably to their ownership of a large part of Lower Manhattan Island, as well as to their heritage, to their power, and to their family's grand reputation.

Currently, Philip Rhinelander, Len's father, headed the family firm, Rhinelander Real Estate, from four floors of offices high in a skyscraper overlooking New York Harbor with a view of the Statue of Liberty. Any number of

Rhinelanders had distinguished lives and careers in other pursuits. The basis of the family's power and financial position, however, came from RRE. Among their more public projects was the accumulation of six square slum blocks on the West Side in what was called "Hell's Kitchen" in order to develop a self-contained, carefully priced and racially controlled "village." They also gained control of the area between 48th and 51st Streets and 5th and 6th Avenues, a project in which the Rockefellers already had expressed interest. And they were squeezing the Vanderbilts, who had to sell their majestic apartment building on Park Avenue to pay their taxes. "The Vanderbilts have come to the Rhinelanders when they needed money ever since they were farmers on Staten Island," was a contemptuous quote from Philip Rhinelander that had escaped into the papers—"escaped" because the family and firm retained any number of people to keep their name away from public consideration.

All of this information I managed to collect from the library in several weeks. Then, when Adelaide Rhinelander was married in "The Wedding of the Century," I stayed home and read all the New York papers for a few days. Len had been in the ceremony as a groomsman, but as several papers noted, without a bridesmaid to process with, walking alone at the back of the procession. Also, I couldn't find a single picture of him in any of the papers, even those of the bride and her family. He told Alice that his sister had instructed that he be cropped out of all photographs.

It was surely interesting to see what the other Rhinelanders looked like, and to get some idea of what a big society wedding involved, in this case, St. Thomas Episcopal Church (Mum was pleased) on Fifth Avenue, and five hundred guests seated in the Grand Ballroom of the Plaza Hotel. One of Paul Whiteman's society orchestras was on the bandstand, the maestro himself conducting. Champagne and liquor flowed without any consequences from the Eighteenth Amendment, the New York City Police Commissioner being one of the guests. Len told Alice all about it, and she told me (and her diary) about some details that didn't make it into the papers. We were in White Plains, shopping early for Christmas presents on her day off, and stopped in a coffee shop when I needed a doughnut.

"Of course, one Rhinelander is a bishop," she said. "Geez, they do everything, are everywhere! When Bishop Rhinelander pronounced them man and wife, Adelaide lifted her veil and 'licked her lips like a lizard to make them glisten.' That's what Len said."

Alice was as happy as I've ever seen her, talking away as if it were gossip about movie stars. "The groom is a banker and was a lacrosse star at Penn, Larry 'Tiger' Shackno. His upper lip sweats, and it glistened almost as much as Adelaide's two did." She laughed as if she'd been there. "Len was standing eleventh down in the

row of groomsmen to the side of the groom. After the Shackno's wet kiss—
well, it must have been— Adelaide was worried about her lipstick being smeared.
So when she took her bouquet back from her maid-of-honor, turned her back
to the congregation, and faced the altar to press and roll her lips together. Only
after that did she take her husband's arm—first things first, after all. Then they
went down the steps, walking down the center aisle on a white silk runner that ran
the length of the church. Can you imagine? White silk to walk on?"

"You think they re-use it," I asked, all eyes, "or sell pieces of it because
Rhinelanders walked on it? They could sell it as bedsheets."

She laughed and went on. "The other groomsmen moved toward the center
aisle to take the arm of their bridesmaids. Len knew there was no bridesmaid for
him, which was just cruel. He had to follow the last couple down the aisle alone. He
looked at his father as he passed, but... remember those pulleys? Len said his father's
eyes were lifted again, 'to a convenient level between heaven and earth to avoid
seeing anyone that was merely human.' "

Having recently seen a number of pictures of Philip Rhinelander, I laughed in
recognition. "Len has a way with words."

"He does. He describes ideas so exactly. Ideas come out of me like a big lump
of dough. You know what else Len did? People in the church watched him go by,
smiling with pity, whispering who he was to each other, having heard what the
family had spread about his 'infirmity,' even his 'mental deficiencies'—that's what
the family says about his stuttering. One lady stared so hard that Len picked a lily
from the flowers tied on the end of her pew and, with a crazy smile, handed it to her.
Her mouth fell open, and she was ready to scream, backing away into the woman
behind her as if he was giving her a disease!"

"Len is very intelligent... just not with a lot of life's experiences." That was my
sermon of the day, and I hoped she heard the warning.

"If you'd been treated like he has, you'd be inexperienced, too!" She was
defending him, so my warning was lost. "That bitch sister of his cut him out of the
whole wedding, and he didn't even want to be there! Em, they despise him for being
in their family, and he hates being there!"

I paused, then said, "And?"

"And what?"

Smiling, I asked pointedly, "Is he making other plans?"

Alice tried hard to stay angry but gave way to glee. "Stop being so smart."

"I try all the time, but..."

She stood up and came around to sit beside me in the booth, giving me a kiss
and a hug. "You must be a witch. You know too much."

"I've been where you are now, is all, so I have an advantage."

She turned serious. "Okay, where am I now?"

"On the edge of love's thrilling, dangerous cliff."

"I know the thrilling. What's the danger?"

"You know that, too."

She didn't answer right away. "What if I don't care about all that Rhinelander stuff?"

"That's even more dangerous."

She turned to me. "He's the one for me, Em. He's my man. I'll do anything..." She didn't finish.

"Fine. But while you're doing it, don't go running blind into what you're up against."

"I hope you don't think I love him just because he's rich."

"I never thought that. None of us did."

"Well, he's not in control of any money. He gets an allowance from his father."

"Does his father know about you?"

"We don't know. He hasn't said anything to Len. I suppose The Orchards tells Mr. Rhinelander about Len being away so much, the letters he mails to me, the phone calls."

"So Len hasn't said anything to him."

"No."

"I'm not saying he should, Alice, but secrets are always where the danger lies."

She nodded, then her head fell forward. "There's a bigger problem. I want him to sleep with me so badly that I ache with it. I can't sleep alone anymore."

Ever since I can remember, Alice has cried with no sign of it other than tears, no gasping for breath, no wailing. She can go on talking as normally as before it starts. It started. "I'm crazy with it. We've done everything else but in the front seat of his car. We have nowhere else to go... He wants to, too, but I'm scared I'll lose him, that somehow the desire, the mystery, will be gone. And then it gets into when we'll be able to, and the idea of marriage floats around, which I don't want to mention, because it'd seem like I was blackmailing him into marrying me as the price of getting me into bed!"

"You don't really think he'd believe that?"

"No! But I do!" She crumpled in her seat, her head falling on my shoulder. I put an arm around her, and we sat silently for a time. "So, what do I do, dear, dear big sister?"

I took a moment, then said, "Don't get pregnant."

She didn't react at first, but when she did, she jerked up, backed away from me in the booth and stared at me wide-eyed. "Are you telling me to go ahead?"

"No! Not at all. I'm only saying that if you do, be careful because that would be one disaster of many you want to avoid."

She took that in. "He went out and bought rubbers. I put one on him one night."

"No more, please. I'm very shy." She mock slugged me on my shoulder. I said, "Alice, it's not a sin. More and more people indulge before they get married. The world's changing."

"You think so? I don't know. You read about the famous people, the Hollywood stars, the politicians, the gangsters fucking whoever as much as they want. I know my friend Kitty has been to bed with a couple of guys that she doesn't even see anymore. And Grace…"

"No!"

"I'll let her tell you, not that you'll get the whole truth… But don't you think most people want to be decent, keep it private, share it, just between two people who love each other and

want to be together the rest of their lives?"

"Ideally, of course. But neither sex nor marriage is ideal. What I'm saying is that now, in this situation, you should worry more about pregnancy than principle."

"Would I lose him if we…?"

"You will for a hundred other reasons before that one."

She nodded. "I'll always worry about the hundred. But the one—I might have to let something happen."

For nearly fifteen years since the day of that conversation, I've blamed myself for it—not that I said anything I didn't believe then and now, but that it gave Alice a rationalization that her own ethic didn't include. I've regretted it ever since, and although I've never admitted it until now, on this page, I partially hold myself responsible for what happened next, for them and how long she suffered.

Soon after that conversation, I started dealing with what my doctor and I eventually discovered were Braxton-Hicks contractions, not a threatening complication but one that makes pregnancy unpredictable and rest vital. I didn't see Alice for a couple of weeks but heard from Mum and Daa that she was seeing a lot of Len, and they'd made some plans, as yet undefined—or unrevealed. Then just before Christmas, Alice told them that she and Len had finally arranged to have a big New York City date. They planned to go to dinner and the theater on the night that Len left the clinic for the Christmas holidays.

The family that Alice worked for had gone down to Florida, so she was free to go. She told Mum that if the theater went on too long, she'd stay with an old friend from the Catskills resort where she'd worked who lived down in The Village. Then, as I heard, she'd stayed in for a couple of days with her friend, missed Christmas at home because Len had something special to show her, then there was a three-day blizzard that shut down the trains, so she had to stay in even longer.

My Braxton-Hicks routine had become fairly regular, so I was beyond caring about much else, having to go to bed every time the contractions came. Fortunately, I had them pretty much under control on the night Alice showed up unexpectedly at the Weingold garage a few days before New Year's. A taxi somehow had made it through the white-out wind and snow that was still falling. Alice was blue with cold, had not eaten, was unable to speak and was shaking so badly I thought of calling an ambulance. Bob was up at the main house running a party, but he'd made a fire in our fireplace and stacked a lot of wood beside it. I got her warm and made her soup. The shaking stopped eventually, and I sat with her, waiting. Finally, she said, "The disaster came."

As we sat together in front of the fire, this is the story she told me, and I still remember it pretty well. As always, she spoke of sex with complete candor, but that night it was in a lifeless murmur. Len had told her his parts of it, as long as he was able, and most of it ended up in her diary.

Two days before Christmas, Chidester was sent to Stamford in the Packard to bring Len and his luggage home for the holidays. He'd arranged theater tickets that night to *Blossom Time*, the hit Schubert brothers' operetta. Alice was coming with him, with the idea that she could catch a late-night train back to New Rochelle after the show. As Chidester carried the two suitcases out to the Packard, Len followed him down the stone steps carrying a large Tiffany box.

"You want that in the trunk, sir?"

"No, I'll hold it, a Christmas present for Miss Jones. I'll leave it at her house when we pick her up. And that second bag goes to Gerald, suits for pressing."

"You're giving her a Christmas present?" Chidester said with a daring smile.

"Yes, a clock. Why?"

"Well, you know her father's a colored man?"

"What?" Len was furious. "I don't give a damn if he is. It's not your business. Just drive me there, Chidester."

He opened his own door to get in and slammed it shut behind him. Chidester stood a moment, apparently shaken, then closed the trunk and took his place behind the wheel. Len slid the window shut between them as well as the curtain over it.

Arriving at the Jones house, Chidester scrupulously did his duty of opening Len's door and waiting patiently at the curb. Len went in to deliver the present. He and Alice finally came out, and she greeted Chidester with her usual cheerfulness. He said nothing but tipped his cap as he held the door open for them.

"The Ambassador Theater, Chidester," Len said. "We're having dinner next door."

Within moments of the car starting, Leonard and Alice were lying across the back seat in an embrace, his hands rushing up her legs, one of them quickly around him, kissing urgently, trying to suppress ecstatic groans even though the glass was closed and the curtain drawn. By the time they crossed the bridge into Manhattan, control was fracturing.

"We have to decide, Len."

"I already have."

"What?"

"That we're going to make love to each other or go insane."

"Yes, but what's going to happen with us after?"

"There'll be no 'after.' We'll never stop."

"'Never'? Do you mean that? Len, if I do this, you can leave me behind anytime you want."

"Good Christ, Alice, could you ever believe I'd do that? I love you and I don't plan ever to stop loving you, ever."

"Can I trust you? How long will you mean that?"

"Only until I die."

"Oh, God, Len." Her decision was made. "Listen, I told Mum I'd stay in town with this girlfriend of mine if the show got out late."

"You did? Perfect! We'll go to a hotel."

"Len, we…"

"There's no reason not…"

"I'm afraid."

"Of what?"

"Oh, do that, do that. Oh God. I'm afraid if we start, I'll never be able to stop."

"Why should we ever stop?"

She pulled away to see his face. "Ever? What…?"

"Never. Never stop. Come here."

Ten minutes later, Chidester was surprised when the curtains parted, and the window between the front and back seats was opened.

"Chidester, a change of plan. Miss Jones has decided to stay in town tonight. I remember there's a hotel on Broadway, in the 60s."

"Yes, sir. The Marie Antoinette."

"I want to stop there on the way to the theater to book a room for her. Once you drop us at the theater and deliver my bags home, you're done with us for the evening."

Without hearing a response, Len slid the window closed again. "I'll reserve a room for Mr. and Mrs., what?"

"I don't care. I just want to go to this show and get back to the hotel."

"Here," he said as he pulled out a money clip and gave her a bill. "When I go into the hotel, give this to Chidester. A Christmas present from you. Be sure to do that."

"This is a lot."

"It doesn't matter."

"It doesn't? No, I guess it doesn't."

At the restaurant, their hands were outrageously busy under the table. In the theater, their seats were on the aisle, which proved fortunate. They held hands, first in Alice's lap, then in his. By the time the applause began after the wildly popular song "Three Little Maids," they had lasted through most of the first act. They rose and hurried out to catch a cab. When they crossed the lobby of the Marie Antoinette, they didn't care about the attention they attracted from the hotel staff. As soon as the elevator man let them out on their floor and closed the door behind them, they were racing each other down the hall to their room. Clothes fell to the floor from their door to the bed. Alice crawled naked onto the covers and lay on her back, her legs apart. In an instant, Len was between them, on his knees, slipping on a rubber.

In the bare light coming in through the windows, Alice gasped. "Oh my God! Len, that's... Here! Come here, here!" Their lovemaking was urgent to the point of recklessness. Curiosity, discovery and even subtlety followed with no thought of danger or consequences over the hours, other than "getting the log in its raincoat." Sleep was occasional, and waking from it was another chance for variation. At some point, Len staggered out of bed to the window and threw open the curtains. Instantly blinded by a day for which he was not prepared, he started to close them.

"No, leave them open," he heard Alice say. "I want you to see me in the sun. Come back here." He turned to find her standing naked at the head of the bed, legs apart, leaning back against the wall. Sometime that day, they learned what could be done in a shower with flowing hot water while soaping each other. Finally, not caring whether it was night or day, they found themselves in naked stillness. She sprawled over the armchair that had been their latest platform; he collapsed on the floor next to her. He reached up for her hand, and she guided it to her thigh.

"Len, we haven't eaten since, well, sometime a long time ago."

"I hadn't noticed. I've been very busy."

"I'm afraid to leave the room, afraid it'll all disappear."

"I know. Tomorrow we'll have to. You have to call your parents again."

"I will. You going home for lunch sure does spoil Christmas."

"Rhinelander tradition. If I weren't there, they'd start looking for me. I'll be back for more of you, because obviously I can't get enough."

She bent down to kiss his hand. "I love you so much, Len. I'm so scared of getting this crazy. What if there's nothing more to it than this?"

He sat up on the floor and looked at her a moment, then stood up. "There'll be a good deal more to it than this." He started collecting his clothes from where they lay on the floor. "We really ought to hang these things up." Rummaging through the pockets of his suit, he pulled out an unwrapped Tiffany ring box. "I have something for you."

"Len, I haven't opened the present you left back home."

"Let's say this isn't for Christmas. Let's say it's because I love you."

She opened the box and stared. "My gosh. Len. It's a ring. Does this mean...?"

"It means everything that it can mean right now. There'll be a time for the formal thing. This represents everything of myself that I can give you at the moment."

Alice watched him, deciding whether to ask more or just accept it. "It's such a beautiful ring."

"The woman at Tiffany called it a *bijou d'amour*. Amethysts, lapis lazuli."

"I love it. Whatever 'beejoo damore' means, it means a whole lot more to me because, my dearest man, you gave it to me."

She stood up and put it on, going to the window to see it in the light. He followed and embraced her from behind, holding her breasts in his hands.

"I'm glad, because I love you. And your body shines in the sunlight?"

"Len, what're you doing? We have to eat. I'm starving."

"For me, I presume."

"No! For a big banana split!"

"I have just the thing!"

"Leonard Rhinelander! That's terrible!"

"But not bad, as you may remember."

CHAPTER FIVE

On Christmas day, they left the hotel together. Parting on the street, Alice walked down Broadway to the pay telephone she had used previously. After hearing instructions from the operator, she put coins in the slots at the top of the phone and dialed her home.

"Merry Christmas, Daa... Oh, I know, I wish I were there too, but the party lasted until so late, and Mimi said I could stay over with her. Yes, from the Catskills resort, and I may stay a while, because Leonard says he can get away from his family later today and wants to take me. No, he has to be there for lunch, Rhinelander traditions and all that. So I'll stay over to see him tomorrow, and I'll call."

Len managed to arrive at West 48th Street without seeing any of the family, reaching his room without having to greet anyone besides the servants. He took off his badly wrinkled clothes, bathed and dressed for the occasion in a dark suit, but put on a particularly garish tie that Oakley had given him years ago as a joke. As he was tying it, he looked at himself in the mirror. Surprised by what he saw, he tried to define why. What had changed? Nothing, really, except that for some reason, he appeared to himself as not bad looking, and at a certain angle with an arched neck so that his head tilted down, he was almost—well, not to go too far—attractive. Well...

He could hear the rumble of conversation begin to grow as the family came in and passed through the hall on their way to the drawing room. So many times he'd stayed in his room until the last moment before he had to go down. He put on his suit coat and took a last look at himself in the mirror. Smiling at himself, he thought of it as a rakish grin. It pleased him greatly. He went down the stairs feeling as if he might be dancing, knowing it was all because of Alice. He wanted to tell her about it.

As host to the family, his father, Philip Rhinelander, was near the entrance to the drawing room, speaking with a cousin, the bishop at Adelaide's wedding, Benjamin Rhinelander. And, thank goodness, his favorite relative was there, too.

"Hello, Aunt Lucy." Len kissed her on the cheek. "Merry Christmas."

"Where've you been?" his father demanded. "How's my dear boy?" Aunt Lucy said.

"Upstairs changing. Benny Darlington had a party out on Long Beach, and I stayed over. Hello, Bishop, how are you, sir?" The bishop was in a clerical collar, a dark suit with a blazing scarlet waistcoat over which ran the heavy gold chain of his pectoral cross.

"I'm very well, my boy. What are you up to these days?"

"Thrilling adventures, nothing less."

"How exciting," Lucy said, "tell us all."

"Well, to start, I smuggled the cognac for Father's eggnog, ran it down from Albany. Bishop, d'you think Prohibition is preventing evil?"

"Frankly, I think Prohibition is causing evil."

"You didn't do that, Leonard," Lucy said, "did you?"

"Of course he didn't," his father said.

"I think I'll go get some, excuse me."

Len started across the room toward the punch bowl. He heard Aunt Lucy say, "Philip, he doesn't stutter at all anymore." His father did not respond.

Len shunned P.K. and avoided Adelaide, who had recently returned from her honeymoon on Capri with her Tiger. Paying his respects to the titular head of the family, Uncle Chalmers at the eggnog, Len realized he didn't recognize him. The eldest Rhinelander, a retired investment banker, asked what he was doing, to which Len replied, "Nothing," and laughed. Then he turned to the Schermerhorns, cousins by marriage, who knew exactly who he was but were not particularly eager to talk with him.

Maxwell announced dinner, and everyone went into the dining room. Len was happy he'd been seated mid-table next to his Aunt Lucy. His father sat at one end of the table, Maxwell standing behind him, directing the serving staff with his eyes. Adelaide, as the immediate family's hostess, was at the other end with Tiger on her left, his upper lip already glistening. P.K. was on her right, having once again come without his wife and daughters. Len had overheard that one of his children had croup, allowing them and their mother to be absent from yet another Rhinelander ritual. While Aunt Lucy was talking with a cousin on her other side, Len overheard his sister at her end of the table.

"Oh, we'll go back to go skiing in Gstaad, won't we, Tiger?"

"Perhaps, Darling, but why not," he broke into a bad Italian accent, "*Cortina d'Ampezzo? Italia! Ah, bene, grazie tanto.* Do you know Cortina, P.K.?"

"Loved him, hated her," P.K. responded with rolling eyes. Tiger gave the hoary joke an ingratiating chuckle.

"So, dear Leonard," Lucy said, turning to him, "it's Christmas. If you had your choice of anything, what would you wish for?"

"A choice? What's that? Never had one of those." They smiled, accepting the sad truth of the matter. "I'd travel. A million places I want to see. But I have very little say about anything I do at the moment."

"Well, dear Leonard," she leaned closer, "it won't always be that way."

"Why not?"

"Because when you come into your inheritance, you'll have a freedom of choice about a great many things. You know that."

"'Freedom of choice?' I know nothing of anything like that. My father will never die. You know that. Even if he did, I'm sure he'd leave me nothing more than the measly allowance he gives me now."

Turtle soup was served to both as Lucy spoke confidentially, "No, no, no, not from your father. The Rhinelanders skip generations in their estate planning and spread money around to bind the family. When you're twenty-one, you'll come into a good deal of it. And your father has nothing to say about it. Hasn't anyone told you about this?"

Len was astonished. "No. Never. I thought everything came through Father."

"You should know about this, and you should prepare for it. And most of all, you should be careful. Don't tell anyone."

As she lifted her soup spoon, Lucy was drawn to her other dinner partner. Len sat transfixed, holding his spoon in mid-air just above his soup. Could so much happen at the same time? Was it astrology? Was it luck? He couldn't contain his elation and stood up. Noticing his soup spoon, he abruptly pinged it on his crystal water goblet until the table became quiet, all astounded by who was standing.

"Merry Christmas to the family!" he toasted as he picked up his wine glass. "Yes! It's a very merry Christmas. Let us drink... to the wonderful 'freedom of choice' we all have here..." and for no reason he added, "in America!"

Everyone raised a glass, but there were as many raised eyebrows. Lucy looked pleased and inquisitive at the same time. Adelaide scoffed her contempt a bit loudly, for which she received a withering glance from P.K. A Rhinelander did not criticize another in a public gathering, particularly a family one.

Len smiled happily and took his seat, glancing down the table to see his father's reaction. Uncharacteristically perched as if he was about to spring up to attack, Philip Rhinelander sat staring back at his youngest son as if he had gone mad.

Len tried to smile at him beguilingly. He couldn't wait to tell Alice. Yet his twenty-first birthday was two-and-a-half years away. Who cared?! It would pass in a second in hotels all over the world!

Three days later, the blizzard's wind from the Hudson River still blew the snow and sleet almost horizontally between the buildings on the cross-streets of the city. The lovers idly watched it from their room on the fourth floor of the Marie Antoinette Hotel. They lay on the bed, viewing the chiaroscuro wash against the brown-black background of the row houses opposite. Icicles had formed on their roofs, and those lengths of ice were the only way they chose to measure the time passing.

"How does a butler get dinner served with his eyes?" Alice asked. "Everyone around that table knows exactly what's expected of them, family and servants. God help anyone who messes up."

"Didn't you mess up with that crazy toast to America?"

"No. I startled but didn't mess up."

"Your family is beyond anything I'll ever understand," Alice said. "Don't waste a second on trying to. I'll be leaving all of it as soon…"

"Len, please don't leave me here alone again."

"I won't have to. Since we discovered the hotel has room service, I don't even have to go out, the great hunter and gatherer, to provide my mate with raw meat." He laughed and kissed her.

"You sure are happy. You've never been so happy after you visited home."

"Alice, you've never been to Venice, have you?"

"I've never been anywhere, Len. You know that."

"We'll make love in a gondola, blindfold the gondolier, '*Oh sole mio…*'"

"You're crazy!"

"Totally, about you. Happy New Year!"

Alice smiled. "You're getting ahead of yourself. Three more days."

"And I plan to say it every day of 1922, because now I have you."

"Len?"

"Umm?"

"We have to think about going back."

"We'll never go back from here."

Alice turned in his arms to look over at him. "Where are we, Len? Where are we going from here?"

He kissed her. "As far as two people can go in a lifetime. As long as life lasts."

"Oh, my darling man, you can't mean all that."

"I do, and a lot more that I can't think of the words for yet. I hope you feel the same."

"I feel everything I can feel. I want to make a home with you, wake up with you every day, spend days making love, just like this."

"Wouldn't that be wonderful… A home. A real one. With you."

She kissed him. "We can spend weeks planning that. But I have to get back to New Rochelle."

"Why? Your parents certainly believe you about the blizzard, a good excuse for at least another day, and my family doesn't care where I am."

She couldn't help but laugh. "Len, we've been here almost a week."

"Maybe I should rent by the month, or the…"

He was interrupted by a soft knock on the door.

"Yes?" Len called.

"Room service. Collecting the tray, please, sir."

Still naked, Len got up and went to the tray on the table. "I'll hand it out to you," he called.

Holding the tray in one hand, he unchained the door. The moment he turned the bolt, it was pushed open with such force that Len and the tray were thrown backward across the room. He sprawled on the floor, as china and glasses crashed around him. Alice screamed and tried to cover herself with the bedding.

Two large men stood in the doorway. They barely looked at the two of them but swept their eyes over the rest of the room. "What're you doing? Get out of here," Len yelled, starting to stand up. Alice stopped screaming just as an old man with white hair came between the two men at the door, both of whom came further into the room toward the lovers. Another man came in behind him. All four wore heavy overcoats and hats.

Len was aghast. "Mr. Bowers? Oh, good Christ!"

"Who is it, Len?"

"Cover yourself, Leonard." The old man looked away with distaste, his jowls shaking as he shivered from the cold.

Len stood up and went to Alice on the bed. "He's my father's lawyer." He took the bedspread and draped it around himself.

"Leonard," Bowers said, "this is not a duty I thought I would ever have to perform, and be assured, I despise it. I have here a letter, signed by your father, giving me power of attorney over your care and supervision as a minor. I have no desire to embarrass you or Miss Jones, only to be certain that you're safe, which is all that your father, your legal guardian, wishes."

"Safe from what?"

"This is Mr. Leon Jacobs, an associate in my firm who will supervise this business."

"What business? Is that what this is?"

As if Len hadn't spoken, Bowers went on. "This is Mr. Brown and Mr. Stevens. They are licensed security officers. Mr. Brown will escort Miss Jones to Grand Central Station and help her board her train for New Rochelle."

"I don't need help. I know how to go home."

"And Mr. Stevens will be going with you, Leonard."

"Where?"

"You'll hear about that in the car. I suggest you both get dressed."

"GET OUT!" Len shouted as he threw the bedspread at Bowers and lurched toward one of the men. Holding a blanket around her, Alice leaped out of the bed and started toward the other man. Jacobs intercepted her, holding a hand up to stop her.

"All of you, get..." Len didn't finish. The man he took a swing at stepped back, grabbed Leonard's arm and twisted it so hard that he flipped Leonard around and forced him to his knees. When he continued to fight, the second man grabbed his other arm, and the two of them drove his forehead into the carpet.

"Don't hurt him anymore!" Alice shouted.

Bowers directed a disdainful look at her before turning back to Len. "Leonard, we don't wish to distress either of you any further than we must. Your father urges you to remember the example of William Copeland Rhinelander."

"What?" Len stopped struggling. "What are you saying?"

"Please: Just get dressed."

Len turned his head on the carpet to look up at Alice. "All right," he said and stood as the two men guardedly let him loose. He took the blanket again and wrapped it around him as he compliantly gathered up his clothes from the chair. Following his example, Alice went to the closet for hers, and they both turned to the bathroom. Jacobs preceded them to check the window and take the key out of the lock.

Once the door was closed behind them, they let their clothes fall to embrace each other. "I don't believe this is happening," Alice said, shaking.

"My family is capable of anything. It's as if a switch was thrown."

"How did they know?"

"It doesn't matter now. We have to get dressed."

As they put on their clothes, Alice said, "Can't we fight back? Run?"

He stopped and held her shoulders so that she faced him. "Alice, Father will commit me if he can, then come after you with everything he's got."

"Commit you? What do you mean? He wouldn't do..."

"I know what he'd do." He was severely intense. Alice nodded and picked up her clothes.

Now dressed, they embraced again. Alice was still shaking. "What'll happen now?"

"Alice, what we have is stronger than what they can do to us. It has to be."

"My darling Len, it is." She kissed him.

Someone knocked on the bathroom door. The couple looked at each other, took each other's hand and went back into the hotel room. The four men looked at them, then Leon Jacobs opened the door to the hall. The two security officers held the couple's overcoats for them. Bowers went out first, and Jacobs indicated that Leonard and Alice follow. Nothing was said in the elevator, nor when the six of them crossed the lobby to the hotel's main entrance.

Outside, sleet was packing down hard in the street, on parked cars and lampposts. Three black limousines were lined up at the curb. Mr. Bowers went to the first one, where a chauffeur jumped out to open the back door. Without another word, the old lawyer stepped in and was driven away. Jacobs escorted Alice and Leonard toward their cars. One of the security men took off his overcoat and offered to put it over Alice's shoulders. She shook her head, refusing it. She turned to Len. "I love you."

They embraced and kissed. "I love you so," he said.

"Mr. Rhinelander," Jacobs said, indicating one of the limousines. As Leonard and Alice approached it, they saw a steamer trunk strapped to the back. An edge of sleet had collected on it.

"That's my old school trunk. It seems I'm going away."

"From what I understand," Jacobs replied.

"I won't ask where. But can you tell us how you found us?"

Jacobs hesitated. In the cold light from a streetlamp, Alice thought she saw the barest flicker of sympathy. "You told your father about a party at the Darlingtons."

"He called them?"

"No, I did, on Mr. Bower's order." He glanced away. "Then I interviewed your chauffeur."

Len nodded. "Thank you, Mr. Jacobs."

He embraced Alice, then got into the limousine. Before the door was shut, he said to Jacobs, "As you seem to be the messenger, tell my father I said goodbye, that we're stronger than this, and that he'll fail."

Jacobs nodded.

"I love you, Alice," Len called out as the security officer got into the back seat beside him and shut the door. As the car pulled out into traffic, Jacobs turned to Alice.

"Miss Jones."

Alice walked over to the limousine, got in, and Jacobs shut the door. But she opened it and stepped out, facing Jacobs again. "I don't want your fancy car. I know where Grand Central is."

"Miss Jones, it's still snowing."

She saw the security man jump out of the car and hustle around to join them. "If you force me, wouldn't that be kidnapping?" She turned and walked away down Broadway.

Two hours later, she arrived at our apartment. After she told me what had happened, I stood up to put another log on the fire. By the time I turned around,

Alice was asleep in her chair. I made up the couch for her and led her to it. I don't think she ever woke up that day. I called Mum and Daa and told them she was safe and would be home tomorrow. Bob came back soon after, and I started to explain to him why Alice was there. At one point, I stopped abruptly.

Who was William Copeland Rhinelander?

CHAPTER SIX

I must warn the reader that what happened over the next two-and-a-half years is close to impossible to believe. It certainly was for me even as it happened. More astonishing than Alice's blunt determination and self-control beyond the limits of a young woman's endurance was what we learned of the ruthless extremes to which a prominent family would go to dominate their own.

Until Len's first letter arrived, Alice seemed to wander through her life in a similar state of shock to what she was in the night she told me what had happened at the Marie Antoinette Hotel. Why she didn't get pneumonia that night, I'll never know, but she never missed a day of work when her employers came back from Florida. Other than what she told me—and asked me to tell Mum and Daa nothing except that the Rhinelanders had broken them up—she spoke only when necessary. She let us all know she was waiting, that she was certain a letter would come. I offered her any support I could, but I was dealing with some problems of my own. As the weeks passed, I admit I feared the abominable strategy that Mr. Rhinelander had put into effect had worked.

Six weeks went by, but then:

The Princess Hotel Room
667, Bermuda
February 17, 1922

My dearest Alice,

Did you get my letters from Atlantic City? I wrote at least two
dozen in the time I was there, but they might have been intercepted.
Apparently, that wasn't far enough away from you, so here we are in
Bermuda. Please quickly write me a letter here at the hotel so I can see
if my "pal," which is what he calls me and wants me to call him, rather
than "jailer" or "keeper," will steal it before I get it. If so, I'll figure out
another way, General Delivery or something. I need a letter from you
like I need air to breathe.

Bermuda, at least, is better than Atlantic City. I suppose I should
be grateful Father didn't send me to Devil's Island. Here, in the
morning, I can bicycle down to the beach and swim. I imagine you
here. If you were, I'd never leave.

As it is, I do almost everything alone. I can't run away on an island
with no money, so my keeper lets me go out on my own. Other than

the beach, I spend most of my time reading, a lot of Edith Wharton (her mother was a Rhinelander, but even so, she sees all the nonsense very clearly). I've never read this much in my life.

The bad time is the evening. My pal and I dress for dinner. I have to tie his black tie. He befriends every New York female that comes into the hotel, using my name to ingratiate himself. His instructions clearly include introducing me to anyone "suitable." His judgment about that is ridiculous. I've met about fifteen of them. I talk to each one for about ten minutes before I excuse myself. They all smoke; they all drink like fish. They get tight and loud and truly dumb.

You've told me how distant I can be with other people. It's true. When I'm not with you, I'm a completely different person. With other people, I do become "distant" and very boring. I certainly bore myself.

When the band starts playing for dancing, all the people go out on the floor and do what they do. I don't. I just sit and listen to the atrocious orchestra and get very blue when I hear the songs we used to play on your Victrola. "April Showers" or "Love Will Find a Way" drives me right out of the room and back upstairs to a book.

What's truly terrible is that I don't know how long this will go on. I've tried to find out from my "pal," but he seems to know nothing more about it than I do. He's just doing his job as long as it lasts. He's not a bad guy and doesn't impose. He gives me a little money each day, and it's enough for postage to send these letters. As soon as possible, I'll start saving to send you a gift.

Alice, we can do this. We have to win. Our love has to be stronger than the Rhinelanders or anything my father can do. I think of you all the time and hate not being there with you.

Write me soon. Please write to me.

Len

Over those years, there were hundreds of letters back and forth. Alice shared a few of his with Mum and Daa, more of them with me. Unfortunately, most of them would be entered as evidence at the trial to become part of the public record. I include a bare selection here only to advance the story and to reveal Len's and Alice's super-human resolve to keep love alive.

763 Pelham Road
New Rochelle, N.Y.
March 16, 1922

> *Dearest Len,*
>
> *I wish you had me, the two of us alone, in a room, any room, away from here, very far away. Instead, you're the one who's alone, very far away. Can I stand this, not knowing where you are, where they'll take you next, when in the world you'll ever come back here to me? No, I can't stand this. But I will. I will! Do all rich people break up lovers this way?*
>
> *The way things are now, I love you, you know that. It's hard being home. If it's not Grace with mean questions about my losing you (which I don't answer), it's Mum and Daa wondering how a family can do what they're doing to you. I can't tell them the whole truth about the Marie Antoinette after all the stories I told about staying with friends and blizzards and all. If they ask, I say anything that comes into my head, usually about your family not wanting us to be together, and that sure is the truth. Emily says, trying to be helpful, that secrets are dangerous. She's right, but I need them now.*
>
> *Every little thing like that makes me feel very blue. I have to make a change. I have to get away from everything around here that reminds me of you. I'm just so furious all the time, so sad that they did this to us. The only thing that gives me pleasure is knowing we're stronger than whatever they can do, and that someday—soon?—we'll be together.*
>
> *I better stop. I have to work tomorrow. Dearest, dearest Len.*
>
> *Lovingly yours, Alice*

It's April something,
I don't keep track, and the hotel has bugs.
Havana, Cuba

> Darling Alice,
>
> Don't write any more letters about men you're seeing, or parties, or going to Proctor's. Of course, you have to go out. Just don't tell me about it. I'm being true to what we promised each other. I plan to be true to you until I see you again, and we can go on with whatever we're going to be. I know you're suffering as much as I am and hating it as much as I do. But we have to bear it and survive until this crazy separation is over. I think they're sending me on through the Panama Canal to California, so don't bother to write here.

If I could be interested in anything, Havana seems an interesting place. But I can't. I wake up with no will even to get out of bed. I spend so much time trying to memorize what we did together so I won't forget a moment we had. I think of all that time we had at the Marie Antoinette, when we actually wasted time, just lying around. What I'd give for just one of those times.

My pal takes me to anything that he thinks might help me forget you, but most of the time, they're things that are entertaining to him. Tonight, for instance, we went to a huge nightclub to see a floor show that included two dozen nearly naked Cuban women. One of them came over and threw her feather boa around us both and pressed her naked breasts against my pal's face. He was delighted, as you can imagine. All I could think of was running after you, catching you, and having you on any surface that could hold us. Do you remember? Do you go over and over what we did? Do people write these things in letters? I don't care, I need to. It's about the only thing I enjoy, and I don't need a naked chorus girl to get me started. I need you, oh God, how I need you!

I can't write anymore. I love you.

Your Len

Pinewood Resort,
Pinewood, New York
August 13, 1922

Dearest, dearest Len,

I just got your letter about you leaving San Francisco and going over to Hawaii. How much farther away are they going to send you? China? India? Do you get my letters, all those pages I send, never even knowing if you'll ever read them? And when will you come home? This fall, it has to be. When will they— no, not they—when will <u>your father</u> let you come home? Do you have any idea? If you did come home, you could start school in the fall, or get a job, or go back to The Orchards if he wants, even though I think I did a better job on your stuttering than all those specialists. I just wish your father would pay me what he must pay them.

This resort is the same as the others where I've worked each summer, but at least it's a change from being a maid to being a waitress, and I'd rather be here than in the laundry. The fat, sweaty men get drunk when their wives aren't looking

Those old guys look at me as if I were theirs for the taking. And then the boys on the staff look at me the same way, wonder why I'm so "stand-offish," as one of them said the other day. No, I don't go telling everyone it's because of my Len, but it is, it is, there's no other reason why I'd be keeping to myself the way I do. Simple as that, and that's all that keeps me going.

I work hard up here, but the tips are good. I don't have any time to enjoy being in the mountains—if you can call the Catskills the mountains. It's been awful hot, but like I said, I'd rather be here than home. I love them all, but Emily has no time for anything since Roberta was born. She's beautiful, can't figure who she looks like, has straight brown hair, not as dark-skinned as her Daddy but isn't white either. Our house is shrinking even after Grace left and married "Footsie" Montello, a nice Italian guy who didn't know what hit him. I'm happy for her because she wanted it so much. He seems to love her a lot, and they have a nice little house near to ours in New Rochelle and all. So when I go back at the end of the summer, I'll be alone with Mum and Daa, the old maid of the family, with fewer and fewer chances of finding anyone else but you, not that I ever want to.

I'm sending this to the Clift Hotel in San Francisco like you told me. When you get back from Hawaii, there'll probably be twenty or thirty letters waiting for you. I'm not kidding. I don't have anything else I like to do. Are you still keeping them all? I keep yours. I read them over and over. Nobody else will ever read them, like we promised. Just us, writing things we'd never write if we ever thought anyone would see them, love going back and forth on pieces of paper. How pathetic.

You've got to come back to me, Len. Please. Please.

Your own Alice

The Arizona Ranch School Chandler
(near Mesa), Arizona
Sept. 8, 1922

Dearest, sweet Alice,

After all that expectation of coming home, here's what happened (and it'll explain why I haven't been able to write anything for so long). We came back to San Francisco from the cruise to Alaska (Did you get the stuffed polar bear I sent you?), and two nights later, my pal's appendix burst. I had to get him to the hospital and then look after him. Within a week, a couple of San Francisco lawyers showed up at my hotel with instructions and, thank goodness, money to pay the hotel and hospital, for I had none. I figure that a doctor got the information back to my father, and arrangements—as they always are—were made.

The lawyers said I had to pack right away and that I was "headed East." I was thrilled! There was a big railroad strike, so they'd hired a car and driver to take me. I figured it would take maybe two weeks, but I didn't care. That's when I managed to send you the postcard saying I was coming back. And that's when I learned never to trust a lawyer's tricky words again.

We drove for four days. The driver, who barely spoke, showed me he was carrying a gun for our safety, probably to shoot me if I tried to run away. I had no idea what any danger was, but I didn't care. I was going back to you! But I wasn't. We stayed in motels in the middle of nowhere, ate in greasy spoons. I didn't pay much attention to the direction, so I was horribly surprised when we drove into this ranch. The silent driver dropped my bags in the dust and, without a word, drove away.

At first, I didn't even know which state I was in. This is a "school" with about twenty guys around my age, all from the East, all in some sort of trouble at home, all from very wealthy families who don't want to put up with us, a lot of them like me being "detached from a female acquaintance", which is how it's officially described. It seems that this is the way the rich do it. It used to be a grand European tour (according to Cousin Edith), but that was for girls.

We started "classes" yesterday, which seemed concentrated on making us into cowboys. We're also supposed to read books when we have free time between learning to lasso a pair of horns attached to a wheelbarrow, to muck out horse stalls, to run all over the desert, and then do chin-ups on the pipe running from the windmill to the water tank. I can't do one. All our "city-slicker" clothes we brought are in a storage closet, and we wear something called Levi's, a denim material that takes two months to break in and be wearable. The cowboys who are our "teachers" say to sit in the water trough and then let the pants and shirts dry and shrink on us. I also have boots and a straw hat, neither of which fit. The cowboys say to do the same thing with them.

We ride every day, and I'm still so sore that I eat standing up. The cowboys say we'll get used to it. But apparently, once a week, we ride into Chandler to spend the dollar that the owner, the head of the school, gives us for candy and stuff. We went there for the first time yesterday.

It's about five miles away through nothing but desert and cactus. Chandler is a grocery store and three houses, one of which is a blacksmith, another a vet. But the man who runs the grocery store has a little booth in there that's an official U.S. Post Office, and the dollar will cover postage for my letters to you. I'm getting this written so I can put it in the mail the next time we go. I convinced him to hold your letters to me separately (address yours to General Delivery, Chandler-near-Mesa) instead of putting them in with the mail that comes out to the ranch. Yes, they read all mail and report to the parents before any of us see it— if we ever see it.

But the truly bad news is that this is where I'm going to be for the foreseeable future, and on a ranch, there are no holiday vacations. The twenty of us are not wanted at home, and though we'll celebrate Christmas and Easter, I hear we don't go anywhere unless we're taken in an autobus to Phoenix to see some Indian ceremony or something. That's about two hours away. And during the summer, we go on a cattle drive to Colorado, as this is a working ranch.

I'm very worried about what this will mean to you. I think Father intends to keep me here as long as possible. I can't write him about it anymore. I've done that since Bermuda, always demanding to come home. He's never answered, and I'm sure he never will. I do despise the man with everything in me, which of course is totally useless.

I love you, Alice, somehow more now than I ever did when I actually was with you. I create scenes in my mind of us being together, living together, in a house like those pictures from The Saturday Evening Post that you sent me a while ago, yes, with the car out front in the driveway. I keep reminding myself that all this will change, that he can't keep me here after I'm 21. I know, now a year and nine months away, but then I'll have my freedom and enough money for us to live on, and Mr. and Mrs. Leonard Rhinelander will do whatever we want, live where we want, and not be afraid of anything!

But can you wait for me, Alice? I know, it's a long time. And can any love last on nothing but letters? I wonder what I'd do if you decided to stop writing. I don't really know. I do know that I'd go on loving you, probably as long as I live, no matter what. I can't ask you to wait, but I can beg you to, because I believe our lives are already tied together, for better or worse, and every day that passes now will get us closer to the better.

I love you, Alice, with every beat of my heart, every breath.
Len

Home
Feb 20, 1923

    Len, dear, dear Len,

    I got over the shock of you not coming for Christmas, when I wanted to kill you, me, and the neighbor's dog. I started going around a lot to get over it, like I told you, mainly to get out of the house, more important to dance, but I stayed true to you no matter what, out of habit, I suppose, because none of those boys has anything to like about them, much less love. I'm still going out, but it's to dance and hear the jazz as some kind of distraction, even them pawing me or grabbing me on the dance floor is just that. I've just got to get out of here. I'm worrying Mum and Daa to death, moping around here all the time, her being as sure as I am that there's still hope, Daa, not predicting but always interested in where you are.

    Hope! Ha! It sure is hard to live on that. I can keep doing this, Len. I'm loving you no less. God, sometimes I wish I could do that! But what my life is now is waiting around for you. I work day and night at these big houses, earning what you'd spend on socks. I dream of money, I dream of someone taking care of me, I dream of having that little house in The Saturday Evening Post. It's so hard, Len. It's more than a year until you're 21. What am I supposed to do? Please tell me, what am I supposed to do?

    If you ever do come back, you'll find a dead thing, the way it's going. Don't you dare think I love you any less,

    Your Alice

The Arizona Ranch School Chandler
(near Mesa), Arizona
July 5, 1923

    Dearest darling Alice,

    I totaled it up, and here's what I've accomplished at this place: Twelve chin-ups—more important to me than anything I've learned. I came in 18th but at least finished the annual 5-mile run from the ranch into Chandler at dawn. I can jump off my horse onto a dogie and twist it to the ground, but still not any good about tying up the hooves. I also read Crime and Punishment. Took me a year but I read it. I like Cousin Edith better.

I got to know one of the cowboys, named Buck. A fine man, been wrangling for 30 years. Over my time here, he's become kind of my adopted uncle, or at least what one ought to be. I told him something about me, my family, and even you. And from nothing I thought I'd said, last week he asked me, "What if you give your father something of what he wants?" I said I didn't have anything my father wanted, and I didn't want to give him anything anyway. He spat (tobacco), said "Bull-shit! He wants a son, and you got that to give him." I said, "Why should I, after all he's done?" He looked at me as if I were a mule. "Because he's always going to be a big part of your life, whether you like it or not. Give him some of what he wants, so's you can have some freedom and live your life."

I haven't decided what to do yet, but what Buck said hit me right between the eyes. Everything I do from now on will be to get back to you with the freedom to live our lives together, no matter what I have to do.

I love you, I live to be with you,
Len

c/o Alderson
34 Round House Road
Greenwich, Conn.
December 29, 1923

Dearest Len, darling Len,

Is this the thousandth letter? The ten-thousandth? Are you keeping them? Do you read them over and over like I do? Do you keep them in a locked iron box under your bed like you swore to do? I do. Have you become an old mean "scold" as Mum calls me when I'm in a really bad mood? Mrs. Alderson let me off for Christmas Eve, and I went home hoping for some cheer. The whole family came over, Emily brought little Roberta, who is so sweet and dear. She smiled at me. But everyone else saw how unhappy I was, so of course, Grace went over and put on "Love Will Find a Way." Soon as I heard it, I charged over like some crazy woman and took the record off the Victrola and smashed it on the table. I said, It's a lie, you can't believe the words of a silly song. The little girl started to cry, and so did I, and I spent the rest of the night up in my room.

Merry Christmas, Len. I've written that in the last four letters because I never know which ones you'll get. Did you get my present? It was silly, but I knitted them myself, trying to remember how big your feet were, but I've said that four times, too. Aren't you completely bored with me? I am.

And Happy New Year! Will 1924 be another year of letters between us? Or will your magic 21st let you out of your prison? I've read your letter so many times about what Uncle Buck said and I wonder what he's getting at. Did you ever write your father, giving him what he wanted? God, I hope not. I wouldn't give him a thing after what he's done to you. And to me. But then I started thinking that if he believed you were something of who he wanted, that might be enough for him, and I'd get the rest of you!

I wear the beautiful turquoise Fourth of July ring you sent me on my wedding finger. Did I tell you that? Because you said, "it means so much more than what it is," so I wear it where it means just as much to me. I haven't taken it off since I got it.

Len, I'm going to go out on New Year's Eve with Eddy Holland, a nice boy who has no ideas about me but just likes to dance. He wants to take me to Proctor's, and I want to hear the jazz band they're bringing in from Chicago. I don't know what you'll be doing, of course, but maybe you'll be having some fun. I hope so, dear Len. And I'm sorry I'm going out; I have to, to stay sane, and I hate it at the same time. I always tell Daa where I'm going in case a boy cuts up and I have to call for a ride.

Working at Mrs. Alderson's place is the best job I've ever had. Living here is such a relief from home, where I just mope around. But she goes to France in May. I'll have to go back home, and probably have to go back to a resort in the summer. That idea just about kills me. Anyway, she treats me like a human being, and likes to talk, and I've told her all about you—no names of course —and she gives me lots of advice, that if you're true to me, I have to be true to you, and that time is on our side. But what does that mean? Time is life, and it runs out. And you can waste a lot of it being true to someone who isn't there. Here. Here, Len, when will you be here?

I'm sorry. I'm sorry about so much. I'm sick of being sorry. I want to be Mrs. Leonard Rhinelander, and have a home with you, and love you, and hold you. Oh God, I can't think about that without feeling sick and blue.

This is a lousy letter. I promise I won't write anymore like this.

The next one will be happy. Oh God. What am I saying?

Your loving, happy Alice, you remember her.

The Hanover Trust Bank

40 Wall Street New York, New York

May 1, 1924

Mr. Leonard Kip Rhinelander c/o

The Arizona Ranch School

Chandler (near Mesa), Arizona

By Special Delivery

Dear Mr. Rhinelander,

Under the terms of your grandfather's trust and your two great-uncles' trusts, as well as those of several Rhinelander family bequests, you are to receive certain assets upon reaching your majority, on May 7, 1924.

May I request a meeting with you here at your earliest convenience to discuss the process of directing these assets for your benefit?

Noting your location, I will presume that you may be available soon after your school term ends. To hasten our meeting, a check is enclosed (#7395), for $5,000 [five thousand dollars] drawn as an advance from cash accumulated in these various accounts to cover any and all travel and sundry expenses that you may have until we meet. I have arranged with Valley Bank in Phoenix for you to have check-cashing privileges. Ask for Mr. William Holmes there.

I look forward to our meeting and offer congratulations on your birthday.

Sincerely,

M. Caldwell Fleming Senior

Vice President and Director,

Trust Department

I read this letter after Alice ran up our steps yelling, waving it in her hand. Len had sent it from Arizona. She shoved it in front of me. "READ THIS!" I did, including what had been written by hand on the bottom:

Dear Miss Jones, I've taken a position in my father's firm.

I've retained a real estate agent to find a suitable HOME in New Rochelle so I can commute.

Will you marry me at the earliest? Our secret. Please advise.

CHAPTER SEVEN

The secrecy bothered me from the moment I read it, as I told them both at the first opportune moment. I don't trust a secret when only one person is keeping it, but this one was of necessity going to be shared by the whole Jones family. That included Bob as well as Grace's husband, Footsie Montello, whom we hardly knew. It wasn't that I didn't trust them, but mistakes are made, and each person in on the secret multiplied those chances of it slipping into notice.

Len had been back for two weeks before he and Alice came over to our apartment for dinner. It was Bob's day off, so he was in New York at NYU, working with his NAACP committee. Even so, Alice wanted to come over. I'd heard about Len's return, his surprising her late one night at a club where she'd gone dancing, to which Daa had led him. Since then, Len has been spending most of his time in New York, taking his place at Rhinelander Real Estate, spending nights at his home to reassure his father of his purpose, and establishing a commuting schedule as he looked for a place to live out of the city. To anyone who asked, he explained, "The Orchards gave me a taste of what living in the country is like." This routine allowed him to see Alice every other day and on weekends. They had just managed to spend two nights together at Lake George.

"It was perfect!" Alice was elated. "We slept on a tiny island in a tent."

"What did Mum and Daa think about that?"

"As proper Victorians, I think Daa convinced Mum not to think about it at all, and Mum's so glad Len's back, she doesn't. In fact, she offered him Grace's old room if he needed to stay over."

"Blow me down, that's amazing!"

Len played it as if it were a five-star hotel. "I was shown the room and happened to notice it was just across the hall from Alice's, so I accepted the offer."

Len had brought Roberta a foot-long Indian totem pole he bought at a fish shack on the lake. My daughter had inherited something of my reticence, but at two years old, she already liked getting presents. "I'm not sure how useful this is to you, Roberta, but maybe it'll grow on you." Gurgling her pleasure, she ran to her room to study it. "Emily, I stole another bottle of wine for us from the cellar."

"How fine, Len. Thank you. I still remember the Chateau d'Yquem."

Alice smiled. "I do, too, that wonderful night."

"You'll remember this one too." He showed me the label. It was so old and faded I couldn't read it. "My grandfather bought it at the château in Bordeaux."

"Does it go with pasta?"

"It'd go with hay."

It wasn't easy to bring the conversation down to any level of seriousness, ecstatic as they both were about each other, with exciting diversions about their search for a home, Alice learning to drive his Oldsmobile, and his commuting. But my sister has always had sharp powers of observation.

"What is it, Em?" Alice asked. "What's wrong?"

Len looked at her, surprised, not having seen anything.

"You know me too well, dear sister." We'd finished our pasta. Roberta was asleep in her crib by then, still holding tight to her totem pole. I took a good slug of the remarkable wine, then a deep breath to say the sentence I'd prepared. "Secrecy is always dangerous, usually impossible, and destructively retributive, not necessarily in that order."

"No big book words, please, Em. What do you mean?"

"I mean that one deception, one lie always leads to another, and sooner or later they'll come back and bite you in the ass—poisonously."

Alice sank back in her chair. "We know that."

Len pondered, then sighed. "You're right, Emily, but there's no other way."

"Tell me why, Len. You have your own money. You're not a minor, so they can't control you. Why keep your family in the picture at all? Why can't you marry Alice openly and live openly, happily ever after, forget them, and let them forget you?"

He gazed at Alice. "Wouldn't that be wonderful?" Then he turned to me.

"Emily, I have forty-seven cousins. My family regards each one of its many members as a vital part of the whole. Marriage is considered in terms of financial merger and blood-breeding. Some choose to go their own way and have great success, but nobody turns their back on the golden goose, and everyone marries appropriately. Alice and I know from our recent experience how they regard this relationship, and to what extremes they'll go to prevent it. Secrecy—along with deception—is our only choice." Smiling bitterly, he raised his glass to me.

Impressed as much by how he'd grown up as by the terrible clarity of how he saw his life, I lifted my glass and touched his, taking long enough for Alice to lift hers to make a third. We all drank, and Alice said, "We need you with us on this, Em. As a matter of fact, I don't think I can do it without you."

"I'll be with you 'til the cows come home, you know that. I just know the trouble secrets can cause, and I had to warn you."

"Emily, Alice knows in detail what we're facing. I've made sure of that. The world turns, and families—even the Rhinelanders—have to change or they die out. So one fine day, maybe we'll be able to walk in the sun."

"Bob and I'll be there cheering." We tapped glasses again, even as I suppressed asking if there was time enough in their lives to wait for such a change.

"And we'll be getting married," Alice said, "as soon as... um, possible."

It took longer, no matter what they planned. Len was meticulous in setting up his role as a commuter, carefully getting to RRE each day ten minutes early, staying at his father's house often enough to convince him that the former prodigal was dedicated to his role as a true Rhinelander. His father didn't seem to care what else Len was up to, just as his father had little interest in what Adelaide or P.K. were doing. "As long as I give him something of what he wants," Len repeated like a refrain, "he'll be satisfied, and the rest of my life is mine. As time goes by, I'll make more of it mine until I have it all." He studied zoning laws, RRE maps, mortgages and contracts.

As the summer passed, he gained confidence that commuting by train to New Rochelle was safe. Alice picked him up at the station in the Oldsmobile and drove him to the Jones house. She did love to drive that car. For Alice, living at home had never been as pleasant. First of all, she wasn't working. On the nights when Len slept over, he stayed in Emily's old room out of deference to Mum, who insisted on the proper appearance of things. The arrangement did not prevent nocturnal visits once Daa's snores resounded sufficiently through the walls to guarantee that both parents were asleep. And then they had the weekends, in many of New England's best hotels. Alice told me about most of it and half-jokingly said, "Why do we need to get married? This is so perfect." I spouted the usual justifications, but looking back, coasting along as they were might have been a better option.

As summer turned to fall, they finally found a country cottage they both loved only ten minutes from Pelham Road. Len bought it, hired an architect and interior decorator to work on it, and together with Alice, spent days driving around the countryside looking for antique furniture, old hooked rugs and pictures to hang on the walls. They wanted nothing from New York City. I wasn't surprised when they showed up one evening as Bob and I were cleaning up after dinner. Without a word, she presented her hand with a very large diamond ring on it. And Len, of course, had a bottle of champagne.

Bob looked closely at the ring. "Sorry to say, Alice, it's fake." Len laughed. "I'll sue Tiffany's."

I looked at it, trying to be casual. "I suppose this means you're giving in to married life."

Alice nodded. "October fourteenth, hope you'll be free."

"Of course we'll be free!" I said. "What's the plan?"

Len popped the champagne. "The barest ceremony possible at the town hall, then a grand reception at Pelham Road, which the royal caterer, Mrs. Jones of Yorkshire, has demanded to create..."

"You told them?"

"I formally asked Mr. Jones for his daughter's hand in marriage, to which he replied 'Only if you'll take her arm and spleen as well.'"

Bob loved that. "Sounds like they were happy."

"Ecstatic is more like it." Len was pouring champagne into the glasses I provided.

"We all are!" Alice let out a whoop. "I can't be this happy!" Len gave her a glass. "Then why on earth are you crying?"

"I'm not!" Alice shouted. "Tears come, happy or miserable."

"This is only the beginning," Len answered, and raised his glass. "As our great American philosopher Al Jolson says: 'You ain't seen nothin' yet!'"

On the day of, the Jones' dining room table displayed Mum's three-layered chocolate cake with a bride and groom statuette stuck on top. The whole family was there, all shouting at the same time as the bride and groom came through the door directly from the town hall. Bob was at the piano, banging out the Mendelssohn. At the same time, I tried to rein in Roberta, now almost three, with straight brown hair and blue eyes like her grandmother, who doted on her to the exclusion of all other responsibilities. Our little girl could hardly wait to throw the rice, but Alice distracted her by throwing her the bunch of daisies she'd been carrying. Because everything was out of order anyway, Footsie Montello, Grace's husband, cut a piece of the wedding cake and shoveled it into Len's mouth. From the moment the nearly hysterical couple appeared at the front door, Mum had tried to control everything to create dignity for the event, but quickly gave in to the happy chaos. Sitting down in Daa's chair, exhausted from the months of alternating stress and joy, she allowed a jubilant smile.

Realizing the party was moving faster than anticipated, Daa hurriedly poured the bottle of champagne he'd bought for toasts. They had just the number of historical containers needed, collected over the years. As he poured, Daa recalled each of their origins, his mug being an English crockery marmalade jar dating from their first month off the boat. He'd bought it as a memory of their past English life, a splurge when they could least afford it. He'd drink from nothing else, particularly on their daughter's wedding day.

A move to the table for cake followed, and Mum rose to scold them, "Supper is coming, and you're eating dessert at the wrong time!"

"Dear Mrs. Jones," Len shouted to her over all the comments, "this wedding reception is like no other! Happening just as it happens, it's perfect!"

A cheer of agreement dissolved Mum's objection, and she excused herself to get her glass, the only one of six that had survived that she and Daa had received years ago from a bank for opening their first checking account.

The familiar song came on at top volume from the Victrola, and all turned to see Grace standing proudly by it. "I bought a new record just for today!"

"Oh, Grace," Alice said. "Thank you, dear."

"Well, the bride and groom have to dance to something."

Alice looked across the table at Len, and he came around to take her hand. They stepped to the center of the living room, and as applause began, he took her into his arms. "Love Will Find a Way" filled the room, and the couple made several turns around the floor until Alice whispered something in Leonard's ear. They parted, and Alice went to Daa, asking him to dance, Len to Mum. The two couples stepped forward and, with considerable pomp, took a turn or two.

"Mrs. Jones," Len announced loud enough for everyone to hear, "I think it's time I called you Mum."

"Oh, Len..." she started, but quickly reverted to, "I'll have none of you softening me up with your treacle and flash."

"Len, you may call me..." Daa called over the music, "'Patriarch'!"

The Brooks family left at six to get Roberta bathed, read to and in bed on time. I heard later from Alice that the celebration went on until nine, when Leonard had to leave to catch the late train into New York. The Jones family knew about his leaving, expressing regret and affection when he and Alice went out the door. Being secretly married on the day before he was made a junior partner in Rhinelander Real Estate was an added triumph. Yes, it was their wedding night, but Alice, too, enjoyed the special twist of it. They'd had their honeymoon all summer.

"It's amazing," Len mused as Alice drove the Olds toward the station.

"What?"

"We've never said anything to them about keeping all this quiet. They just seem to know. I feel they'll all keep it to themselves."

"If she says anything, Footsie'll murder her."

"It's so admirable. The Rhinelanders can keep their bad secrets, but your family can keep the good ones."

Alice drove quietly for a time.

She said, "I was wondering again what your family would do if they found out."

"We've made plans for everything, Alice."

"Nightmare plans."

"Let's just hope they never find out until it won't make any difference."

At the station, they kissed longingly before he got out.

"I'll see you Friday. Think about where we can go, 'Mrs. Rhinelander.' Maybe back to Lake George."

As she watched him hurry up the stairs to the platform, Alice told me she had been in some kind of trance, thinking, "Here I am putting my husband on the train to go into New York for work." Then she shook her head, thinking she had a long way to go to catch up with accepting it. I'm not sure she ever had the chance. She always seemed to have doubts that the marriage was plausible, even during the happiest times.

The weeks went by in a haze of making fantasies real. At home, Alice told Mum that she thought she was floating through the days, never touching the ground; she was so happy. "Our house will be painted, papered and ready in two weeks! Then we can move in all the things we've bought. I can't stay this crazed. I have to get back down to earth, try to figure out how this can possibly be my life. I keep waiting for something bad to happen."

"Oh, it's real, luv," Mum said. "There's a document signed, sealed and on record saying it's real. You have every right to float, or jump up and down, or scream if you want to, but please don't." She hugged her daughter at the kitchen sink. "You waited a long time for this. Myself? I waited for it too, and now when I'm alone, I go around the house singing the old bawdy songs I haven't sung since we came across."

"Mum! You don't sing bawdy songs!"

Challenged, Mum stood very straight and with dignity, let fly in her best music hall belt:

> *Let her face be fair, and her breasts be bare,*
> *Let her have a voice that can warble!*
> *Let her belly be soft, and to mount me aloft,*
> *Let her bounding buttocks be marble!*

Alice yelled and hugged her mother. "Does Daa hear you singing those songs?"

"Oh no, he'd be shocked. He's an innocent, you know."

"I thought you were the innocent!"

Mum smiled. "So does he. That's how clever I am. Now go along, don't you have a train to meet, a husband to fetch?"

"I do," Alice said and headed for the door.

"Don't forget your coat. There's already a little November in the air."

"What if someone heard you singing like that, walking by outside?"

"They'd believe they'd died and were hearing an angel sing."

"You have to teach me that song. I want to sing it to Len."

"Don't you dare tell him I sing such filth!"

They hugged each other, both laughing. "I love you, Mum."

Later that night, Alice, in a new silk nightgown, tiptoed down the hall to her room, carrying her bathrobe back from the bathroom. Opening the door, she was seized by Leonard, who wore nothing and closed the door behind her.

"Len, behave yourself," Alice whispered. "This is how husbands behave."

"Not in the bride's family's home!"

"The bride has to control her animal noises, is all."

"Mine? What about your banshee cry?"

"I'll suppress it." Len lay back down on the bed, clearly aroused.

Alice let the bathrobe and her silk nightgown fall to the floor. Then she stepped to the bed and took her place astride. Their only sounds were the rhythm of the bedsprings, and even that caused them to control their urgency and to enjoy more about the slow, long pleasure that silent restriction allowed.

She never wanted it to stop, the lovemaking, the silk nightgowns, making a home, buying things without asking the price, making love whenever they wanted, over and over again. And then collapsing and going to sleep without thinking about having to get up and go to work, but lying in his arms, and listening to him breathe, and waiting for his eyes to open to see her smile, seeing how delighted he was to be there, and then starting another day together.

CHAPTER EIGHT

On November 13, 1924, Len went down the Jones' front steps to get the morning paper. I wasn't there but learned later from each of them all the details of what happened.

A young woman was standing on the sidewalk holding the paper.

"Good morning, Mr. Rhinelander."

"Oh. Good morning. I'm sorry, but I don't remember…"

"I'm Barbara Reynolds. I'm a reporter for the New Rochelle Standard Star. I was over at the county clerk's office the other day and happened to see your name in the marriage records. Congratulations. You and Alice Jones are going to get a lot of attention from the press."

He stared at her and stepped backward. "I doubt that, Miss Reynolds. I'd hope the press had more important news than a simple marriage."

"It's not so simple, Mr. Rhinelander. I put it on the wire services about an hour ago." She had the wide-eyed anticipation of hope for a reaction.

He gave her none. "Put what?"

She handed that morning's *Standard Star* to him, opened to the headline.

Leonard took it, and as he read, she asked, "Is it true?"

He stepped backward again and tried to smile. "Yes. We're very happy." He turned to go back into the house.

"Mr. Rhinelander, does your family know you're married?"

"Not yet," he said as he walked away from the reporter.

"Any chance I could have an interview; let you tell your side…" Len reached the front door and closed it behind him.

Alice was sitting with Mum and Daa at the dining room table. "Back so soon, Mr. Rhinelander? Long time no see." She was beaming. Then she saw his face. "What's wrong?"

Daa stood up, already alarmed; Mum reached out to grasp his arm.

"Everything's about to change," Len said.

He put the newspaper down on the table. They all could read the headline:

RHINELANDER SCION MARRIES DAUGHTER OF COLORED MAN

They sat in shocked silence. Daa sat down. "They didn't even talk to us."

In a fury, Mum blurted, "Why didn't they say you'd married the daughter of a white woman?"

"That's not..." Alice began. Something hit her. She told me later it was like an engulfing wave at the beach had smacked her. The headline "COLORED MAN" seemed huge and public. It hit her so hard that past worries about the Rhinelanders seemed puny.

Len picked up the paper and read it again. "My father will know now. So it begins. Mum, George, my darling Alice, right here at the start, I profoundly apologize for my family."

Daa waved it away. "We've lived with this before in our lives, Len." He went over and sat in his chair. "Besides, no one in New York reads the Standard Star."

"The reporter out there said she'd put it on the wire services."

They were all silent. Restlessly, Daa stood up again. "Len, we can take care of ourselves here in New Rochelle. You'd better tell us what we're in for from your family."

"An endless war." He looked blankly toward the window. "They'll come first with lawyers. But that's only the part we'll be able to see... Oh God! Excuse me!" He went up the stairs two at a time, gagging and slammed the bathroom door shut. They heard him retching and flushing, then he finally came back down the stairs. "Well, I suppose if I had the choice, I'd rather have my bad stomach back rather than the stuttering." He took Alice's hand. "I'll be all right. It was the surprise."

Alice squeezed the hand she held. "Len," she realized she was gasping, "we're worth fighting for. What your father did to us made us stronger."

"All of us," Daa said.

"All of us!" Mum repeated with rage.

Len hugged Alice, then reached an arm out. Mum and Daa quickly took his hand. "They'll start with the law, so I have to find a good lawyer. Not from New York, someone local who won't be afraid to..." Abruptly, he turned and stepped away from them. "We have to see what they'll do first, be ready for anything. Because once they've started, they'll never stop."

Mum followed him. "What else can they do? What can't we see coming?"

Len gazed at her. "Mum, I hope you'll never know."

"I have to call Em."

"Let me start calling lawyers first. George, do you know a good firm?"

"I'll give you a list of the big ones around here..."

Daa told me he stayed home as long as he was useful, calming Mum's fury, giving Len the names of the lawyers he knew in and around New Rochelle, reminding Alice that if she could survive the years of waiting, she could survive the tussle of keeping what she deserved. By the time Grace arrived, waving her copy of the paper, Daa felt he could leave. Before Alice could reach me on the telephone, he slipped out to the garage and drove away in his taxi. Going back to the station offered the familiar calm of waiting for a fare.

In the cab line, the other drivers didn't come over to talk as they usually did, which he appreciated. He didn't believe they were shunning him because of the headline, but rather that they understood something of what he was dealing with and allowed him his privacy. He sat and fretted, trying to think ahead to what was going to happen. The complexities were beyond him, just as he had feared when Len—whom he was very fond of—came into their lives. One thing was certain: The color-blind acceptance that the Jones family had enjoyed over thirty years in the narrow confines of their lives in New Rochelle was over. The ugly, vicious racist regard that was everywhere now would focus on his skin, and it would be the only thing anyone—black or white—would see. Because of it, his family would suffer, and Alice was going to be hurt, badly hurt, no matter how things turned out. And Daa felt completely helpless to do anything to protect her.

The 11:32 pulled in, and his taxi was fourth in line. He doubted he'd have a fare, as few commuters came out from New York in the middle of the day. That was fine with him. He wanted the time to try to figure out something he could do.

Suddenly, about a dozen men leaped off the train even before the conductor could put his step down on the platform. They jostled each other on the platform steps and ran across the parking lot to the cab line. Four reached Daa's cab, yelling.

"No, no, this is mine, buddy. Take me to..."

"You gotta share. We're going to 763 Pelham Road."

"Me, too."

"Just a moment, gentlemen, that's my house. What do you..."

"Yours! Are you the bride's father?"

"Where's my photographer?"

"Is she as, ah, dusky as you are?"

Daa rolled up his window, pulled out of the line and drove away, leaving the men bellowing and scattering to find another cab. He arrived back at the house in time to warn the family what was about to happen.

I was outside painting a chair with Roberta so that I couldn't hear my telephone ringing. Two cabs pulled into the driveway of the Weingold estate. Half a dozen journalists jumped out to photograph and to try to talk to Roberta, playing with her doll in the yard beside the garage. My little girl was fascinated; her mother was not. I carried the paint can and started yelling at the reporters. This did not stop the flashbulbs or the shouted questions.

As I threatened them with paint, Bob ran down the driveway from the main house, followed quickly by Mrs. Weingold, he in his daytime livery, she in a print frock with pearls. She forcefully ordered the journalists to leave the property. Fortunately, the taxis had remained and were able to drive them away. I quickly climbed the steps to the apartment with Roberta. That's when I heard the phone ringing, and Alice told me what had happened. I picked up Roberta and drove over to Pelham Road.

We were there most of the next two days. Roberta was a welcome distraction for Mum; I was a listener and on occasion an adviser, but only if someone asked. The crowd of journalists outside on the sidewalk steadily grew in number, often coming up the steps to ask questions. They kept coming, knocking on the door, some polite, but some so insistent that Daa refused to let any of them in. He was coldly polite to the woman from the *Standard Star*, mainly because he'd driven her father many times, the owner and publisher of our local paper. We were all happy when Sergeant Kelly showed up to tell us that the police department would be patrolling regularly, and if any trouble arose, to call them.

When he wasn't in a corner talking in whispers with Alice, Len was edgy, pacing back and forth, worried about why he was being turned down by every law firm he called, about what was going to happen next. The second morning, he saw an exclusive in The New York Times that he read aloud to us. "You'd better listen to this," he said. "'The following is a statement from Spotswood Bowers, Mr. Philip Rhinelanders' personal attorney: "Mr. Rhinelander states that his son, Leonard Kip Rhinelander, who is more than 21 years of age, was married on October 14, without his knowledge. Mr. Rhinelander has never met the young lady whom his son has married, but understands she is of English parentage. He further states that he has authorized no other statements to be made, and that neither he, his family, nor his attorneys will have any further comment."'"

Mum looked around hopefully. "That sounds final."

"It isn't," Len replied.

Mum and Daa didn't want to leave the house; Alice and Len didn't dare to. Instead, the couple sat together whenever there was a private moment, apparently in deep discussions about what was happening. We gave them as much time alone as the house allowed. The journalists were always out on the sidewalk talking to each other, even at night. Grace and I brought the New York papers as well as groceries in the morning as early as we could. Neither of us spoke to the press after something Grace shouted at them appeared in one of the tabloids: "My father is of West Indian descent. Understand? And Len? Well, there are a lot of girls around here who are just sore they didn't cop off a millionaire like my sister did."

The morning of the second day, I was helping Alice wash the breakfast dishes. She leaned against the sink, letting her head drop. "We need more dish soap."

"I'll pick some up tomorrow."

"Thanks.... When are we going to be able to get out of here again?"

"When there's no more news, they'll leave."

"It's spreading. They're tying us up with all the rest, the KKK, lynchings, and race riots. They're making Len and me into some kind of emblem. Did you even hear the word 'miscegenation' before this? Em, I can't stand what this is doing to Mum and Daa. And to you and Bob. Len and I had talked it all out before we knew anything would happen, so we're ready. But my family..."

"Well, the way I look at it is this. Every family faces a crisis sooner or later. That's when a family gets tested. This is ours. You did nothing wrong, marrying someone you loved. His family disagrees and is probably going to attack us. So the Joneses get to find out how great we are... as we beat the shit out of the Rhinelanders."

Alice almost dropped a plate. I'm not sure I'd ever used the word with her before, very seldom with anyone else. I'm a prude about profanity.

"Oh, Em, wouldn't that be great!"

"You remember what Daa said about their time in the slums? 'Your Mum and I are as tough as goat guts crocheted with a crowbar.' They are, Alice. I'd put them in a ring with any four Rhinelanders."

"I'd put Mum in there alone!" She laughed for the first time in days.

"And don't worry about Bob and me. We're pretty tough, too, and we have Roberta to fight for."

"I doubt if the Weingolds were too happy about those taxis driving up with screaming journalists."

"No, they weren't, but not in the way you think. That evening after serving dinner, Bob told them why it had happened and, in deference to their privacy, offered to resign. I was ready to start packing. The Weingolds wouldn't hear of it, sat Bob down and gave him a talking to about never giving in to bigotry, one, or snobby families, two. They're putting in floodlights around the garage and have hired a security company to patrol the property."

"Do people like that really exist?"

"Let's hope a lot of them do."

Len came in and picked up a dishtowel to dry the silver. "Another law firm just turned me down. I think the word is out from father's lawyers not to touch me."

"Can they do that all the way out here?" I asked.

"Professional courtesy and the Rhinelander name are a potent mix to any law firm in New York State."

"So what else can you do, Len?"

Alice answered. "We can do anything. We're ready for everything, no matter how horrible. What we have to know first is what they're going to do."

"What about getting out of here," I suggested, "going somewhere and hiding out for a while, even some foreign country?"

Len put the towel down and put his arms around Alice. "How many times have we thought about that?" He kissed her on the cheek as she answered me. "Because they'd find us, Em. And every second, we'd always be waiting for them to come. No, the fight's here and now. We just have to wait, wait for them to show us what they'll do."

We finished the dishes, not saying anything more. They seemed so ready, but for what, I couldn't tell. I couldn't imagine what they apparently anticipated. I wanted to ask more, if they knew more, but my reticence shut me up again.

That night turned into a nightmare that no one could have expected. Alice described it to me in detail when we had a chance to talk. The journalists outside had left by midnight, and I left, too. Everyone in the house went to bed, exhausted. Alice held Len and kissed him softly as he slept. She knew she was scared and didn't want to be. She kissed him again. At least they were together. Something hit the outside of the house very hard. She sat up, waking Len, and heard Daa shout, "What was that?"

Then her window shattered, and she heard windows shattering all over the house. Mum started yelling as both Alice and Len began crawling toward the bedroom door. A rock crashed through her second window, sending shards over them. Alice put on her nightgown as Len pulled on a pair of pants. He was bleeding but had no idea where he had been cut. They crawled across the hall and pushed open our parents' door. Daa was on the floor, spooning Mum to protect her from the flying glass and rocks. Her yelling changed from fear to rage. Alice comforted her as Daa and Len ran down the stairs. The living room and dining room windows shattered, and rocks flew in. They ducked as Daa crawled over as quickly as he could to the breakfront that held their good china. Reaching under it, he pulled out a World War I carbine, and lying on his back, checked to see that it was loaded. Then he got to his feet and went to the side of the front window.

Len saw what he was doing and leaped across the room to grab the gun.

They both fell to the floor, and Len yanked the carbine away. "If you shoot and they have guns, they'll have the excuse to blow the house apart. They're only breaking windows."

"They terrified my wife!"

Suddenly, it was quiet.

From upstairs, they heard Mum bellow, "You filthy cowardly bastards!

Come in the day to fight, and we'll show you a thing or two!"

Len went to the front door, forgetting that he was still holding the rifle. He opened the door and stepped outside. In the bright half-moon light, he saw at least a dozen men dressed all in black rushing to get into two cars.

"Gun!"

"He's got a gun!"

Len put it down and held his hands up so they could be seen.

"Nigger lover!"

"Mongrelizer!"

"The KKK is God's righteous arm!"

The cars sped away. Len ran after them, trying to see a license plate.

Alice came to the door and shouted, "No, Len, come back." They all heard sirens in the distance.

Len was bleeding from his forehead, and he'd cut his foot on something. Limping back to the house, he stopped to throw up in the gutter. Then he picked up the carbine as Mum and Daa came out on the front porch.

Alice reached for his face. "Len, you're bleeding."

He handed the carbine to Daa. "Get rid of this, George. You don't want the police to see it here."

"Every colored man in the country keeps a gun, and I've just been reminded that I'm colored."

"No gun, George! Not you. Not tonight." Daa took the gun and headed to the garage. The sirens were at the top of Pelham Road.

"Come inside!" Mum ordered. "They could come back, may the good Lord help us." She herded Len and Alice into the house and slammed the door shut.

CHAPTER NINE

SOCIETY DAZED BY RHINELANDER NUPTIAL

A bombshell was tossed into the aristocratic ranks of blue-blooded New York and Newport society last week. It was revealed that young Leonard Kip Rhinelander had been married on October 14 to Miss Alice Jones, daughter of a West Indian taxi driver. Her older sister had previously married a colored butler. The groom is the youngest son of Philip Rhinelander, a many-times millionaire and many-generational New York society man. The bride and groom had kept a close relationship for three years before they were married. Last summer, Alice spent six weeks in the company of the fashionable at Newport.

***

When Alice gasped, then laughed, we looked up from our papers and coffee in surprise. Besides the excited joy that Roberta displayed when she came over to visit her grandparents, little laughter had been heard in the Jones house over the week since the night of the "sneak attack," as Mum called it.

"They'll write anything," Alice said. "Len, the Daily News says you took me to Newport for six weeks last summer."

He grimaced. "They're making things up now. It'll only get worse."

How could it, I wondered. The couple were prisoners in our parents' home, fearing what else might happen in the night, what else might be said in the papers, what Len's father, Philip Rhinelander, was going to do to them. The paper I was reading was still focused on the KKK's stoning and why: "...the foul mongrelizing mixing of races happening inside." Scaffolding was up all over the house for the glazers repairing the windows. The crowd of journalists on the sidewalk had doubled, now supervised day and night by the New Rochelle Police Department, overseen by Sergeant Kelly, who kept everyone off the lawn and away from the house.

Believing that if she told the truth, it might help their cause, Alice had given a few interviews and allowed some photographs. But the press had twisted almost everything she said into her being a salacious gold-digger. Still determined to appear unaffected by the stoning, she and I went out one day to the grocery store. People there felt free to ask for autographs, give her advice, ask her intimate questions, or insult her at a level of viciousness we didn't know existed. A smiling man in a suit and tie had said quietly in the checkout line, "No matter how white you look, Alice, you're still a black nigger whore." She didn't go out again.

As Alice drank more coffee, I watched Mum nervously twirl her wedding ring around her finger, knowing her fear as well as her courage. She and Daa had both been shaken to their bones by what had happened in the night, and neither had slept well since. Alice stood up and went over to the Christmas tree that we'd all forced ourselves to decorate. This was Roberta's happy habitat, where she seemed to stay busy all day.

Piles of newspapers were stacked on the dining room table, as well as hundreds of letters that had arrived in the mail, threatening more Ku Klux Klan actions, described with violent, hate-filled Christian slurs. Len was pushing at crumbs on his plate from breakfast with a fork, bandages still covering the cuts on his face and arms. He stood up to stretch his legs and idly took one of the rocks out of the bucket in the middle of the dining room table. We'd collected the stones thrown by the nightriders and placed the bucket there as if it were a centerpiece trophy.

"When will they go away?" Mum went over to peep through the drapes. "Let me see, fifteen of the press now, and a dozen of those strange people who come just to gawk. Aren't they cold out there? Bless his heart, Sergeant Kelly is ordering two of them off the lawn and back onto the sidewalk. I wish it would snow."

Len smiled at Alice and took her hand. "I ran into the sergeant once."

"That was a good day."

Mum flipped the drape shut. "How can we get them to leave?"

Len put the rock back in the bucket. "They won't as long as the story sells papers."

Daa was reading one. "The mighty New York Times has just come right out and said I'm a Negro. Is that progress? 'Dusky' has been their word of choice until now."

"It's a white man's paper, luv," Mum said. "They don't know what to call you."

"True, but you notice they have no such struggle with 'white' now, do they?

You don't read about 'the milky President Coolidge,' or the 'pasty-faced Charlie Chaplin.'"

Outside, the low murmur of the crowd fractured into shouts and yelling. Len went to the window, pulled back the drape, then turned back to them, alert and agitated. "They're here. Finally. We'll find out what we have to do."

Alice looked shaken. He took hold of both her hands. "We knew this had to happen, and we're ready." She nodded without relief.

We all went to the window and saw through the glaziers' scaffolding what was going on outside on Pelham Road. The journalists and photographers had surrounded a limousine that had pulled up in front of the Jones house. Sergeant Kelly was talking with the driver as five other policemen held the rest of the crowd back on the sidewalk. An agreement reached, Kelly moved to open the back door of the automobile, ordering journalists out of the way, including Barbara Reynolds, who objected to being herded but then smiled at Kelly and moved to the side. When the limousine door opened, a man stepped out whom Alice and Len knew. He followed the sergeant toward the front door.

"Oh my God! It's that man from... Remember, Len?"

"His name is Leon Jacobs. He's one of my father's lawyers."

"We won't let him in!" Mum declared.

"Of course we will, Mum." Len smiled at her. "We've been waiting too long to hear what he has to say."

His eagerness struck me. He seemed oblivious to any threat. I was missing something.

Two other men got out of the limousine and followed behind Jacobs. All three wore overcoats and fedoras; all three ignored the crowd and the shouted questions of the journalists. They walked up the steps to the front door, and Jacobs used the knocker.

Mum hurried back and sat at the dining room table with me. Alice reached out for Leonard, and he put an arm around her.

"Ready?" Daa said, then opened the door. He confronted Leon Jacobs. "You're surely not welcome, sir, but you'd best come in." He turned and went to sit in his chair.

Jacobs stepped in and closed the door behind him, leaving the two men who had accompanied him to stand on the porch. He looked around the room, taking it in, and took off his hat. "Mr. and Mrs. Jones, Mr. and Mrs. Rhinelander. And Mrs. Brooks, isn't it? Thank you for letting me come in."

Alice looked surprised to hear herself called that by anyone connected to the Rhinelander family. She glanced at Len to see if he, too, noticed it. He gave no sign.

"My name is Leon Jacobs. I'm an attorney, and I represent the Rhinelander family. I'm sure my being here isn't a happy visit for any of you. But I assure you, it's done for your benefit and safety. Since the intrusion by the nightriders last Wednesday night was reported, it's clear that each of you is in considerable danger. Your father is deeply concerned, Leonard."

"No need for his concern, Mr. Jacobs. We're protecting ourselves with the police's help."

"Yes, I see that. And you also tried to hire a private security firm. It's clear that you're as deeply alarmed as we are." The lawyer made no move to sit but stood two steps in from the front door, holding his hat. "We've also become aware that the Ku Klux Klan has ordered a national letter-writing campaign regarding your marriage. There are sixty thousand members just over in New Jersey, almost as many in New York. Your father's received hundreds of vile, unsigned letters already, promising untold violence."

"We have, too," Mum said, smacking her hand on the stack of letters. "They threaten to do terrible things to us."

"That's cowardly and disgraceful," Jacobs said. "I'm sorry to hear that, Mrs. Jones. Our greatest concern is what the KKK might do next." He turned from Mum to face Alice. "They're using your marriage to recruit new members. I'm sure you understand why they'll continue to harass you and your family, Mrs. Rhinelander. Because anything they do to you, no matter how heinous, will attract more attention to their cause in the press."

"You call this harassing?" Daa was angry as he stood and picked up a large rock from the bucket. "It's attempted murder, Mr. Jacobs. They could have killed us."

"Precisely, Mr. Jones. I agree. Such a danger is real."

I disliked Jacobs, distrusted his respectful "misters" and "missuses," but suspected he was right.

Len took a step toward Jacobs. "Why haven't I been able to retain a lawyer? You know why, don't you? I've hired three firms, and each one called back after a day, giving some pathetic excuse why they can't take me on as a client."

"I believe, Leonard, that your father wishes to provide you with all the legal assistance you might need," Jacobs said. "That's why I'm here."

"I don't want your assistance or his." Len was very calm. "I'm sure you understand the obvious conflict of interest."

"What are we to do?" Mum was shaken. "I don't want those KKK people coming here unless we can fight back!"

Daa smiled bitterly. "Luv, I'll bet you a fin this fellow is brim-full of ideas."

"Let's hear them, Mr. Jacobs," Alice demanded, "right now."

Jacobs was ready for the opening and instantly addressed the newlyweds. "Unfortunately, the Klan knows exactly where you two are. You're their target." He paused for their reaction. Alice and Len didn't give one. "As long as you're here, this is where they'll come. Until the danger passes, it'd be best for you both to go into hiding. I can leave people here to look after…"

"You leave any of your people here," Daa gestured toward the front door, "I'll throw them off the property. We'll take care of ourselves, you can be sure."

"Certainly that's your choice, Mr. Jones."

"How do you mean, hide?" Alice scoffed with contempt. "Len and I have our pictures in the newspapers every day."

"I agree, Mrs. Rhinelander. It's a difficult problem." The lawyer nervously shifted his stance. "A famous couple is very hard to conceal. That's why it'd be best for you to go separately at first, because..."

"What?" Leonard smiled. "Well, well, well. Finally, we see the plan. Jacobs, it's clear what 'separately' means. No need to lay the fear on so thick. Tell us what you're after."

"Please hear me out, Leonard." He looked plaintively at Mum, then at Alice. "We have the means to protect you and your family if you'll let us. If you don't, there's nothing we can do, and you'll be on your own."

Daa waved the warning away. "Us and the New Rochelle Police Department."

"Sir." Jacobs had his orders, I thought, but was earnest with his warning. "How long do you think that level of local police commitment can go on, or will go on once the excitement dies down? Not long, I assure you. The Klan, however, has a long-lasting interest here."

Mum groaned. "George, we can't fight them in the dark."

"I'm planning to hire people." Len was trying to reassure her, but it was a losing battle "Around the clock. How did you know I tried to hire a security firm?"

"You wrote them a check. The bank alerted us."

"That's against the law."

"It's a Rhinelander bank."

The full realization of what this meant affected Len instantly. "Is what you're saying that Father's worked his way into my trust accounts?"

"That's beyond my purview." Jacob's discomfort was palpable. "I'm here because of your safety, and I urge you to remember McKinley. Presidents are shot, surrounded by bodyguards. If the location of the target is known..."

"Oh dear God!" Mum reached for Daa. He tried to comfort her, but he, too, looked worried.

"What do you want us to do, Mr. Jacobs?" Alice was bitter and cold. "Now that you've scared the hell out of us?"

"If you could stay with some trusted friends, Mrs. Rhinelander," Jacobs adroitly turned to me, "perhaps your sister, Mrs. Brooks."

"Whoever I stay with will share the danger."

"Not if no one knows where you are. We'll be sure that Leonard is safe until the threat passes. Then you could be together again."

Both Alice and Len watched him, then at the same moment turned to face each other. I watched as he smiled so sadly at whatever they shared; her tears started as she nodded agreement. Then he turned suddenly back to Mr. Jacobs and asked,

"Another William Copeland, Jacobs?"

The lawyer seemed honestly perplexed by the question. "I don't know what that name means."

But I did, from Alice's tale of her disaster at the Marie Antoinette Hotel. I'd never been able to find anything about a Rhinelander of that name. All I remembered was that it had stopped Len fighting that night and warning Alice of extreme though undefined family dangers.

"You won't succeed, Mr. Jacobs." Alice was like a stone. "Remember, you people separated us for more than two years, and we still got married."

"I can well understand why separation is your concern, Mrs. Rhinelander. But your safety—and that of your parents—is mine."

"What's your plan, Jacobs?" Len was contemptuous of the noble statement. "What're you really up to?"

Abruptly, Mum sobbed, and Daa sat her down in a chair at the dining table.

Alice went over to take her hand.

"Don't mistake an old woman's tears, Mr. Jacobs." Mum was as angry as she was scared. "We're as strong and tough as any of those cowards who come in the night. But if we can't see them coming..." She could not go on.

Len stepped forward. "What do you want us to do, Jacobs?"

"I suggest Mr. Rhinelander leave with me now. Your father's valet packed a suitcase of your clothes. It's in the car."

Len and Alice turned and looked at each other, amazed. "You predicted that, too!" Alice's tears fell with no effect on her astonishment. "You knew they'd pack a bag."

Realizing they'd foreseen it all, I was staggered.

Len nodded. "Father, anticipating little resistance to his orders, thinks far ahead. But he'll be surprised by what he's getting. All right, Jacobs, any last horrors for us?"

Jacobs hesitated, and I thought he looked sympathetic for a moment. "No. When we leave, the press outside will take note of it and report it widely. Then, when there's an opportunity, maybe late tonight, Mrs. Rhinelander will go to her sister's house. Later, the press will be told, maybe even shown, that she's gone. Once the two of you are gone, attention here will dissolve. The KKK won't have their target, and neither will the press. It won't be long before the two of you can join each other in a safe place."

I had to say something to Len and Alice. "Why are you two making this so easy for him?"

They were startled and looked at each other. Len then said to me, "Because it was going to happen, Emily. Accepting it, getting it started makes it easier on all of us."

"Will the KKK come," Mum asked, "to burn a cross on the lawn?"

"Never." Daa seemed reassured by the plan. "Sergeant Kelly wouldn't allow it."

Jacobs nodded. "Besides that, they'd have much less reason to, if Mr. and Mrs. Rhinelander are gone."

Len laughed, which startled us all. "Justifying our separation with the white sheets of the KKK is masterful, Jacobs." Then he became intensely serious, turning to us. "Alice knows that my family's capable of anything. We don't know exactly what'll happen. But it won't be what either Mr. Jacobs or my father is expecting." He looked around the room. "No matter how ready you try to be, it's hard to leave... All right. Alice and I know we have to do this. But don't ever believe it's what it appears to be. And no matter what, my dear, dear Alice, I love you with every breath I take. I'll call you every day. Without you, I'm dead, but with you loving me, we'll find our way back to each other, just as we've planned."

They embraced. Then Len turned to Jacobs and nodded. "Let's go."

Jacobs went to open the front door. "We're both coming," he said to the two men waiting on the porch.

The crowd outside began shouting as soon as the door opened. Flashbulbs popped. Len started to go, squeezing Alice's hand. She struggled to hold it but finally let it go. Jacobs led him out, and Daa hurried to shut the front door. He turned to Alice, seeing her tears.

She walked over to me. "Em, have I lost him?"

"No!" Daa interrupted. "It's a new battle, just beginning. You never give up until it's done!"

The yelling outside swelled. Alice said, "But in a battle, aren't you supposed to see the enemy coming? I can't see a thing except half of me walking out the door." She took my hand, and we went back to the window.

Outside, the two bodyguards preceded Jacobs and Len. Sergeant Kelly had anticipated the exit, and his men moved quickly so the bodyguards had little to do but open the back door of the limousine. The flashbulbs were blinding, even in the daytime. The local reporter, Barbara Reynolds, yelled loud enough for Alice to hear, "Hi, Mr. Rhinelander, where ya going?" Smiling, he shrugged and stepped into the backseat next to Jacobs. Slowly, the limousine drove away through the crowd.

CHAPTER TEN

I called Bob at the Weingolds' right away. They were in Florida until May. Bob called them to ask permission for Alice to stay with us. They had read about the KKK night riders, and their response was immediate: She was welcome, and Mr. Weingold would increase the security patrol around the estate. Bob then waited until I called again when all the press people outside had left for the night. It was one in the morning. He came over in the Model T with a sleeping Roberta to pick us up. Alice was packed, and we drove back to our garage apartment.

We barely talked as I put Roberta down and made up the couch for Alice. She put her clothes away in a coat closet and a set of empty drawers in the kitchen. When we were both in our bedclothes, I found her standing by the couch.

She handed me a letter. "I'm too tired to talk, but I wanted you to have this right away. Len did, too. We hesitated until now because it's another secret, and we knew you don't like those. But this'll explain a lot that we both want you to know."

"We'll talk tomorrow. Get some sleep."

"Sleep. What's that?"

Even so, she was out within minutes. Bob was asleep in our room, so I took the letter into the kitchen and read it through twice. It didn't make sleep any easier.

A Havana Hotel,
can't spell the Name
April 11, 1922

Dear, dear Alice,

In the letters you sent to Bermuda, you asked me three times who William Copeland is, the Rhinelander that my father's lawyer mentioned at the Marie Antoinette. I suppose I never wanted to tell you about him, hoping his name wouldn't come up again. What's happening now makes it clear that it must. Although I'd rather tell you how much I miss you and love you, I know that you have a right to know what you're getting into. So in this letter, I'll tell you. Here goes.

William Copeland Rhinelander was my uncle, my father's older brother. He was disinherited, wiped out of the family history, and erased by society. Ever since, he's been deemed nonexistent by the Rhinelander family. They even managed to remove any official documentation—birth certificate, passport, everything. Why, you well may ask. Because he ran away with an Irish maid who'd worked in his home and then married her.

He was forbidden access to his house, legally disowned in order to sever his connection to any Rhinelander holdings, and accused of stealing enough to send him to jail. Legally, all that was easier to do back then, more difficult now—but not impossible. It was nearly fifty years ago, in 1876, and forgotten by the public long ago. What's important to remember, at least it is to me, is that the effort to destroy William Copeland was led by his own father and brother, my grandfather and my father. Father knows from that experience how to do these things, which is what his lawyer was reminding me about at the Marie Antoinette. It's easy for me to imagine that Father could recruit my brother P.K. to help him deal with me, "carrying on the destructive family tradition," ha-ha-ha.

The only one who ever talked to me about this was Aunt Lucy. But she felt family-bound to tell my father that I knew. He was mad as hell with her and forbade me from ever mentioning the name. So here I am doing it. Don't ever let anyone see this letter. From what I can figure out, this uncle, William Copeland, was a rebellious force who couldn't adjust to the Rhinelander world. Any control that the family tried to use on him, he battled it as if it were a prison, which, of course, to him, it was.

After they married, he and the Irish maid traveled as long as any money he had lasted. Sadly, there were two children. After a few years, it all started to fall apart. His gambling, drinking, and finally drugs took most of his time, and when things became difficult financially, he abandoned his family. He tried to sue for more family money, and during one meeting, he shot his father's attorney. Those were the days! The family then applied all their legal pressure and had him declared insane. He got out of the country, talked his way out of both jail and asylum, lived on the few small trusts the family didn't bother to break, and died in "genteel poverty" in Canada. He was, after all, a Rhinelander.

In the meantime, Grandfather and my father turned the blame on William Copeland's Irish wife for his downfall and went about breaking her. After years of struggle, where any employment she managed to find was ended by Rhinelander influence, the Irish girl went hopelessly mad. She was allowed to rot to death over many years in a state institution. The Rhinelander lawyers arranged the adoption of their two children.

I just read this over and almost tore it up. I'm worried it'll scare the hell out of you. It scares me! But I'd be such a fraud if I didn't tell you. This is what they might do if you and I were ever to marry, which I so hope is going to happen. But whether it scares you or not, you have to know what we'll be facing.

I wouldn't blame you for writing me back, saying it's not worth the chance and go your own way. But don't. Please.

I love you.

The answers that the letter provided were profound, but the questions it raised were terrifying. Could an elite, powerful human family do such things to itself? I'd read about the Borgias and the Roman emperors who did a lot worse, but they were safely back in easily condemned history. The Rhinelanders were alive and too close for comfort. And my dear, romantic, stubborn sister had taken them on. I was astonished by her and, yes, from that moment on, my fear for her became dread. But at the same time, my perception of her changed from someone blindly idealistic to a person who'd long ago accepted a fundamental challenge. This undertaking ignited my alarm, but also my deep admiration.

The next morning, Alice was up before Roberta woke Bob and me. She had coffee made for us, and we went through our morning routines without family matters being discussed. We explained to her how the apartment worked and figured out how we each could have a sense of privacy in spite of Alice's need to stay in and avoid being seen.

Finally, when Bob went up to the main house, and Roberta was happy building a palace with Lincoln Logs, Alice and I sat at the kitchen table to finish the coffee.

"You read it."

"Yes, twice."

"And?"

"I didn't get much sleep."

"I can't imagine why. Sorry, dear sister."

"It made a lot clear, but as the night went on, it really became troublesome."

"I'm all ears."

"First and foremost, Len's trying to protect you from his family. He hopes that giving himself up to them will keep them from coming after you. You two seem to have thought long and hard about what you'd do if this happened, so it wasn't any surprise to you when Mr. Jacobs showed up. In fact, it was almost a relief."

"For Len. Not for me. Yes, we'd planned on Len probably having to leave, but I hated it, and I'm scared to death what his father will do to him."

"I figure that he went with Mr. Jacobs to avoid the kind of destructive fight that William Copeland had. But what's he think he'll have to do to come back?"

"He doesn't know. The main reason he left was so he'd know what was going on rather than guessing from a distance. He wants to be his own spy. They'd stopped him from getting his own lawyer, and from what Mr. Jacobs said, they're now able to control his money."

"Do you have any? I can loan you..."

"He left me some, but we'll have to give up our house."

She said it bravely, but I could see how much it hurt. "Alice, what's his plan?"

"To let them do whatever they feel has to be done—even to help them do it— to get it all over with as soon as possible. If they want to take away his money? Fine. If they want us to get a divorce? Fine. We were fine without money or marriage. In fact, getting married was our big mistake, nothing but a record that a reporter could find... Em, once his father has done whatever he needs to do to punish Len enough, maybe me too, then we can find our way back to each other and live our lives. It's the only chance we have. Running, fighting them? They'd locate us, they'd defeat us, they'd destroy us."

She was too far ahead of me. I was too muddled to object. "How long will all that take?"

She smiled a little. "I don't know, but Len will be there in the middle of it to hurry it along. And he has an advantage. Money and the family name are crucial— that's Len's word—to the Rhinelanders. Neither one means anything to him because we're more important. He and I agreed that we could do another two-and-a-half years apart if we have to."

I don't cry, and I didn't then, but the wave of dread and pride I felt for her went over me and left me speechless. I just sat staring out the window at a tangle of branches in the leafless willow tree in the yard. Were they crazy to think such an amorphous plan would work? Was I crazy for doubting the strength of character each of them was now willing, and perhaps too eager to put to the test?

"Em?"

"Sorry. It's hard to talk. Let's just leave it for the moment with my saying that no matter what happens, I'm with you to the bitter or happy end."

"Fine," she said and reached across the table to take my hand. "I won't need much more than that, but that I'll need a lot."

She stayed with us for three weeks, during which we saw what she was going to be facing. For the first five days, Len called each night at eight, and they spoke as long as they wished. Jacobs and the two security men charged with guarding them, plus the chauffeur, moved from one rural motel, hotel, or to get a haircut to change how he looked. He wore sunglasses, even inside, as well as a baseball cap with its brim pulled down to cover his face.

Alice told Len that the crowd of journalists and gawkers dwindled to a bare handful within days of their leaving. Daa had invited the reporter from the Journal-Star into the house to show that Mrs. Rhinelander wasn't there either. Alice told me that she thought everything was going well.

But then, without warning, the phone calls stopped. Alice was a caged animal until a letter arrived at Pelham Road five days later, which Daa rushed over to deliver to her. She read it standing at the window in the living room, then she crumpled and fell on her couch, holding out the letter to me. "Read it out loud."

There was no greeting.

> *I have no idea if I'll be able to get this off to you. Everything's changed. I'm now a prisoner, Jacobs having all kinds of court papers giving him authority over my 'care.' I'm not sure what their plan is, but a lot of lawyers are involved, and Jacobs keeps talking about 'the case.' He's also trying to turn me against you, presenting a copy of your birth certificate yesterday, which has you down as 'mulatto,' asking if I knew that. When I laughed at him and said I didn't care if you had zebra stripes, he said—sadly, I thought—'Leonard, try to understand what can be done to you, to your wife and her family.' I asked for details, but he walked away. I don't know what's going to happen, but Jacobs seems to be preparing for a legal battle. Once I know what it is, I'll be able to negotiate. I hope you'll have better luck finding a lawyer than I did. I'll write when I can. Phone calls are now forbidden. Oh yes: I tried to make a run for it a couple of days ago, but one of the security men used to play football for Penn, and he tackled me after a hundred yards.*
>
> *Never forget how much I love you, Alice.*

None of us could speak. Roberta came out of her room and stopped when she saw Alice's tears falling freely. Looking at Alice from just in front of the couch, my little girl said, "Aunty Ally, please be all right now."

Alice opened her arms and hugged the child. "Okay, 'Berta, I'll do what you tell me." She wiped her eyes with the back of a hand and asked, "Now where's

Cora?"

"Asleep in her cradle. You want to see her?"

"Cora's my favorite doll."

"Mine, too!" Roberta said and ran to her room.

Alice looked up at me. "As Len said, everything's changed. Again."

"I doubt if you were ready for this."

Daa came over and took her hand. "None of us were. I think we have to find a lawyer."

"Not yet." Alice shook her head. "We have no money for a lawyer. If the Rhinelanders hear we're getting lawyers, they'll get more and get meaner. It'll make it that much harder for Len to negotiate anything. We don't know what they're going to do."

"It'll be wicked, for sure." Daa kissed her hand.

Roberta returned, carrying Cora. "She has a cold but wanted to see Aunt Ally very much."

Alice picked the doll up. "You know something, Cora? I had the happiest four-week marriage that there ever was..."

While Alice stayed with us, it was crowded, which she acknowledged every day and apologized for it. She covered her moods by reading to and playing with Roberta, babysitting while Bob and I went out, listening to the radio and reading science fiction about which I knew nothing. We cooked together a lot until all three of us realized that the pies were ending up around our waists.

Then we cooked healthy meals that no one wanted to eat. So, we went out, Alice in a heavy disguise of hats, Bob's enveloping overcoats and dark glasses, but we all ended up being worried about discovery halfway through the meal or that Len might call. We left without finishing, Roberta complaining loudly about no dessert.

Heavy snow finally came and at last drove the last journalists hanging on in front of Daa and Mum's house. Alice packed up what she'd brought, and late one night in January, I watched her go down our steps to the garage. We all needed the relief, but watching her go was deeply disturbing. I felt like I was watching her walking down a bottomless canyon. I couldn't know what she would be facing, whether it would be Len's disappearance from her life, or the world wounding her again. I also couldn't have known how quickly it would begin. The details were sickening, and her survival was miraculous. I was soon to learn just who this sister of mine had become.

The night she left, Bob steered his Model T down an icy Pelham Road, just past the Jones' house, and parked. Alice looked up and down the street. She and Bob nodded to each other and got out, quickly walking up the recently plowed garage driveway and around to the back door. Daa was waiting inside to open it, and Mum hugged her daughter as soon as she came into the kitchen. "It's so good to have you home."

"Did he call? Any letters?"

"Not yet, darlin' child."

Daa took her coat. "Bob, thanks a million for bringing her over."

"She's welcome back whenever she needs to come."

"I'm so grateful for those weeks, Bob, and all you and Em explained to me. If he calls, tell him I'm here, will you?"

"Of course. Goodnight, all, have to get back."

After Bob left, the three of them sat down at the kitchen table and stacked all their hands on top of each other, an old family tradition. "Popcorn!" Daa made it with cheese and was proud of it.

Alice looked from one to the other. "It's so good to be home."

"Even at home, it's hard to survive without popcorn."

Alice put a hand on Daa's cheek. "I wouldn't mind having some sleepy tea. I really want to rest tonight."

"I'll put the kettle on." Mum stood up and started. "What did Emily explain to you?"

"A lot, about what's happening in the country, what Len and I mean to people, what we really are in the papers to people, which hasn't much to do with who we really are. And she warned me that a lot of people I thought I knew aren't going to be the way they used to be."

"Oh yes, indeed." Mum lit the gas under the kettle. "Lots of people are different toward us, too."

"Can we talk about all that tomorrow?" Alice stood up. "I'm dead tired and just want to lie down. Mum, will you bring the tea up?"

"Of course, luv. I put a clean towel on your bed, but I didn't have time to change the sheets."

"I put clean ones on the morning Len and I left. Dear God, how long's it been since then?" She left the kitchen, not wanting to hear an answer and went upstairs to her room. Turning a light on, she looked around, remembering more than she wanted to. Going to her chest of drawers to find a nightgown, she listened as the Tiffany clock's three bells struck the quarter hour. She put her hand on the clock and said, "Please bring better times."

She undressed and put on her nightgown, too tired for a bath. She did want the tea, and she lay down on the bed to wait for Mum. Taking a deep breath to relax, she felt something under her. With one hand, she tried to feel what it was, but then got up and pulled the covers back.

She dropped them and recoiled. Spread out on the bed was a rope tied in a lynching noose. A full-page picture of Alice from the *Daily News* was in the loop. Uncontrolled, she staggered back against a wall and sank to the floor, still staring. A scream started, but she couldn't get breath. She tried to think of what Em had said, then heard her mother coming up the stairs.

"I've got your tea, luv."

Alice lurched toward the bed and, on her knees, spread the covers over the noose. She lay down by the time her mother came in.

"Here we are now, you drink this and have a good night's sleep. Tomorrow you'll feel..." As Alice sat up and took the cup, her hands were shaking. "Oh, luv, what's the matter?"

"Just tired, Mum. So, so tired. I'll be fine. We'll all be fine. We can't let them scare us!" She suddenly stood up, put her cup on the chest of drawers next to the clock and looked in her closet, then under the bed.

"What is it, luv?"

"Has anybody been in the house, plumbers, cleaners, since I left?"

"Nobody cleans my house but me. No, no plumbers, no one. Oh, don't worry, luv."

"Have you both been away for any time?"

"Well, your Daa and I snuck out one night and went to a movie."

Alice nodded. "Thanks, Mum. I love you so much. Good night." She hugged her mother.

She'd tell Sergeant Kelly in the morning. He'd keep it to himself if he could. And she'd sleep with that thing right in the room with her and get the locks on the house changed tomorrow.

When she called me in the morning to tell me about it, I instantly asked her back to the Weingolds' garage. She refused. "They will not bring me down! This is where I live. Let them come."

Something had changed in my sister. It was more than the iron resolve I heard in her voice. If anyone wanted to analyze this story, I think that was when Alice realized—maybe not consciously—that she was no longer going to be a victim. In that moment, she chose to be a warrior.

CHAPTER ELEVEN

For two months, Alice had no word of Len. The winter was hard, so not much distraction was available except for the movies. We saw every movie within twenty miles of New Rochelle, sinking into the black-and-white distraction with hypnotic concentration. We kept a running vote of our favorites. We sisters seldom wavered from Rudolph Valentino; Mum chose Charlie Chaplin every time ("He's British!" she explained.) We accused Daa and Bob of having a secret lust for Theda Bara that they refused to reveal with a vote, virtuously choosing "America's Sweetheart," Mary Pickford, instead.

It's safe to say that I went over to Pelham Road just about every day when Roberta was in nursery school, as it was hard for me to stay at the Weingolds' garage when so much anxiety was flooding my family's life. Grace was over there too, but not as often, as her husband and his Italian family demanded a lot of attendance. That's why I was there the morning that Barbara Reynolds of the *Standard Star* arrived at the door. She informed us that a legal complaint against Alice had been filed at the Supreme Court of New York in White Plains the previous day, and asked if anyone had a comment.

We were all speechless, not even able to come up with any of the thousand questions we thought of later. Daa said with perfect courtesy, "Miss Reynolds, I'm sure you understand our hope for privacy at this time. When we have something to say, I promise you'll be the first to know."

"I'm at your service, Mr. Jones," she said with a sympathetic smile, "but I have to warn you that this will bring the crowds back outside."

It took four hours. More than a dozen journalists gathered. Sergeant Kelly was there again with his fellow officers to control them. In spite of the dread of it happening all over again, the four of us fell back into a bunker mentality. We prepared for a resumption of battle conditions so that when we heard yelling start outside, we were ready for whatever was coming.

The large limousine parked in front of the house again, and Leon Jacobs and his two bodyguards got out. The sergeant cleared a path through the bellowing journalists, and Jacobs approached the front door and knocked. Alice, Mum and I went to three chairs at the dining room table and sat like judges.

Daa saw we were settled, nodded, and opened the door. He said not a word, but went over to his chair and joined us, staring silently at the lawyer.

Jacobs came in and took off his hat, realizing our silent strategy. He turned to close the door, reached into his pocket for an envelope, then said to us, "I have a letter from Leonard."

So much for strategy. Alice was on her feet, reaching out for it. Mum uttered a cry, and Daa asked, "Why are you the deliverer? You might have put it in the mail!"

"Leonard has agreed to certain arrangements, as you will hear." He opened the envelope and started to read. "'Dearest Alice…'"

Alice immediately objected. "Wait a minute! If it's to me, I don't want you reading it to me."

"Mrs. Rhinelander, this is what Leonard agreed to. I must read it to you all, or you won't be able to hear it. He wanted your family to hear it as witnesses." Jacobs stood, trying not to allow the slightest emotion. He had not taken off his overcoat, an unnecessary burden on the warmest day of a March false spring. Outside, the restless crowd, more vehicles, shouts, and orders being given were clearly heard.

Alice stood, then shifted her feet to stand firmly as if against a wind. "Then read it."

Jacobs continued in a monotone. "'Dearest Alice, First and last, I love you. Second, I'm so desperately sorry that because of *my* family, yours is dragged into this horrible situation. Most important: Get the best lawyers to advise you. I don't care about the outcome. My lawyers will prove in court that I'm a fool and an idiot, and Alice, remember: I'll help them do it. You prove that you're white, 'whatever that is' as your good father said once, and we'll laugh them all out of court. It will be over.'" Jacobs said, "That's underlined. Twice." Then he continued reading: "'All of this, including this letter, is part of the arrangement I've made with my father's lawyers. After whatever legalities are settled, we'll pick up where we left off, again after a long absence, a sad waste of time with which we're very familiar. We can do this, Alice, as you said. Until then, as part of the deal, I've agreed not to contact you anymore in any way until the case is settled. But as I said, first and last, forever, I love you. Len.'"

Jacobs looked up at Alice. She stepped forward. "May I have it, please?"

"I'm sorry, Mrs. Rhinelander. The original may be germane to the case. A copy will be sent to your attorney. I was only required by your husband to read it to you."

Alice couldn't believe it. "That's ridiculous!"

"What attorney?" Daa stepped up beside his daughter. "What 'legalities' is he talking about?"

Jacobs glanced at him, then pulled a document out of his inside pocket. "This is a copy of the Summons and Complaint that was filed yesterday morning with the Westchester Supreme Court in White Plains." None of us moved to take it from him, so he laid it on the top of the piano. "Somehow, the press has been alerted. We had nothing to do with that and regret it. You have twenty days to choose an attorney and respond if you plan to contest the suit. If, however, you choose to accept the terms of annulment described herein, an appropriate arrangement will be made."

"An annulment?" I said it reflexively, surprising myself. "Are you talking about a divorce?"

"No, not a divorce." Jacobs spoke too carefully, I thought. "A divorce ends a marriage but admits its existence. An annulment declares a marriage null and void. It's retroactive, meaning that an annulled marriage is invalid from its beginning, almost as if it had never taken place."

"'Never taken place?' " Alice exploded. "What kind of legal magic is that, to make our marriage vanish?"

"It's a legal device." Jacobs looked away hopelessly.

"Tell us about the 'appropriate arrangement' you mentioned," Daa commanded.

"An arrangement." Alice was intensely alert. "You mean money?"

Jacobs nodded carefully. "A figure commensurate with what you have had to bear."

She almost leaped at him. "How much, Mr. Jacobs? A million? Two?"

Jacobs watched her but did not answer.

Alice went on, rage taking over. "So my accepting money will mean that our marriage never existed? Does it?" Jacobs gave no response. She stepped toward him. He held his ground. "Listen, our marriage is genuine and end... What's the word? Enduring! That document you brought is a ridiculous, horrible lie! So I refuse your bribe! And the press ought to know about it."

She walked past the lawyer to the front door.

"Don't do that, Mrs. Rhinelander. You'll invite the whole world into this."

"It's been here since the first headline, Mr. Jacobs, and the whole world should know exactly what kind of animals the Rhinelanders are!"

She went outside. There was no opposing her. She charged past the two bodyguards who were standing on the porch and strode down the steps toward the crowd on the street. Yelling started, and flashbulbs went off as Sergeant Kelly shouted orders to his men. Alice saw Barbara Reynolds and went toward her. Jacobs went out the front door, followed by Mum, Daa and me. We all stood together on the front porch as the two bodyguards with Jacobs looked at him, wondering what to do.

Alice raised her arms for quiet. "I have something to tell you. You can put it on your wire service," she said to Reynolds, then yelled to be heard by the rest of the crowd. "Please, be quiet so you can hear me. I've just been served with papers suing me for an 'annulment.' I never heard that word before today. My family and I are wrecked by this, frightened almost to death by what's already happened." She fought off the emotion in her throat. "The Rhinelanders just offered me a bribe to accept this thing, this annulment." The crowd reacted with questions. "Please! Listen! I will never accept it. I'll fight it until my last breath of life, for any life without my husband is not worth living. I'll never give up! I love him dearly, and I know he loves me as much. And all the Rhinelander millions cannot take him away from me!"

The resulting roar of questions staggered Alice. She was close enough to Barbara Reynolds to hear her shout, "Good for you, Mrs. Rhinelander!" Alice ignored them all and turned back to see Jacobs and the bodyguards coming toward her on their way to their car.

As he passed, Jacobs stopped to say, "Never underestimate millions in America, Mrs. Rhinelander. And please: watch out for the Klan. We can't help you anymore. I honestly regret to say, we'll see you in court."

The uproar continued as Alice went back up the steps and grabbed my hand. Mum and Daa led us inside. When the front door was shut behind her, Alice's legs gave way, and she sank to the floor. Daa and I tried to hold her as Mum knelt on the floor beside her.

"No! No!" Alice said, more to herself than anyone else, pulling on my hand to stand again. "I can't be weak, not for a second. Yes, it's a war, and they're trying to destroy us. How am I going to fight them?"

I said, "We have to find a lawyer."

"Yes! Like Len said. Right now!"

Daa said, "Stay in the house. The sergeant'll look after you. I'm going to see Judge Swinburne, and I'll drive right over that lot out there if they don't get out of the way."

"Daa, he's a judge!" I said. "He can't be a lawyer for us."

"He'll know who can! We'll get the best there is, Alice. Then we'll figure out some way to pay for him."

We all stood there, suspended in the impossibility, until Mum bellowed:

"Go!"

CHAPTER TWELVE

Alice and I sat on a varnished wooden bench across a hallway from Daa and Judge Samuel Swinburne, seated on another. She whispered to me, "I'm thinking of all I don't know. I hate being behind a problem, waiting to react, and being on the defensive. Len and I had to do that for so long. But now, I want to attack, want to get ahead of it."

"Maybe today we'll get ahead of it."

"Yeah, maybe." She smiled grimly. "You remember when I worked in the laundry at the Yacht Club. I didn't wait there to get hit. I hit that bitch first!"

After reflexively smacking her hand on the bench's arm, we glanced over to see if she'd been noticed.

The two men noticed but didn't hear what we'd said, dealing with their own thoughts.

"You all right, luv?" Daa said, his deep voice and Yorkshire accent echoing on the marble walls. His eyes were sunken from lack of sleep. We nodded.

"No matter how bad all this is for me," Alice whispered to me, "to him it's worse, like punching him while he's 'dancing on my straight razor,' as he calls it. All this vicious attention to his careful life at a time when he has a right to relax and enjoy himself. That idea is pretty much shattered now." She shook her head at that enormity and looked down at the floor.

"Please don't blame yourself for something that's going on all over the country. You didn't go out and volunteer to be a lightning rod." She took my hand and held it.

The judge sneezed. Over the years, Daa had spoken about Judge Swinburne not only as a steady client for his taxi business but as a good man. He was a "city court judge," but also practiced law on the side. Daa wasn't sure how that worked, but the judge had assured them that it was legal. He'd promised to make whatever time was needed to handle the complaint against Alice.

We liked the judge, mainly because he was so easy-going when he explained the law to us. Then, when we agreed to meet with the newspaper people, the judge was with us so that when reporters tried to trap Alice with questions, he took over. Most importantly, he'd "answered" the Rhinelander complaint, filed it with the court, then sent a copy to the whole slew of Rhinelander attorneys. Since then, we'd had five meetings with him, Alice from the first wanting me to be along as "my silent advisor." Judge Swinburne admitted right off that he could never handle such a complex trial, but promised he'd find someone who could. We were waiting to meet this new lawyer who'd lead the fight against the charges made. "Fraud," they called it.

None of us knew exactly how it applied to Alice. Ironically, Barbara Reynolds had explained it succinctly one day during an interview, saying Alice was accused of lying to Len about being white. She'd yelled, "I never lied to Len!" Alice was certain that he knew that. But we didn't know if Len knew what his lawyers were saying on his behalf. Probably not. Could he ever demand to know or tell them to do anything? Never in a million years. We all knew who was telling his lawyers what to do. His father's lawyers were putting such charges as fraud down in legal papers. And as Len said in his letter, he was doing whatever they told him to do, just to get it over with, to get to the other side of the legal procedures and then come back to her. But could that ever happen? None of us would dare to speculate.

Judge Swinburne leaned forward to speak to Alice. "Alice, when Mr. Davis asks you his questions, it's mostly to see what kind of client you'll be, whether or not he can depend on you, as you'll depend on him. So be very honest, no matter how difficult a question might be. The man tried and convicted thirty first-degree murderers when he was the district attorney. He'll know what's the truth and what isn't."

"I have nothing I need to lie about, Judge," Alice said.

"Thatta girl," the judge said, pleased with her answer. "And remember, you get to choose to retain him or not. He's a good lawyer, but don't feel he's your only choice. We'll find somebody else if we have to."

We all sat back on the benches to wait. The office building where we sat was just across the street from the Westchester County Supreme Court in White Plains, where the trial would take place. We could see it out of the window at the end of the hall, white pillars and wide stone steps leading up to the doors going into the dark inside, where the courtroom was. Alice had said, "I have no idea of what'll happen in there, except what I've seen in the moving pictures. And they always had happy endings."

"Would you please come in?" a nicely dressed woman said as she held the door for them.

The two men let Alice and me precede them. We followed the woman through a busy office of five secretaries' desks and corresponding side offices to a door with black letters painted on it that spelled out "Lee Parsons Davis." The woman opened the door and nodded us in.

We saw a huge desk, piled high with what must have been legal papers. In the middle of them was a stack of newspaper clippings. Behind the desk, a man stood up, paused a bare second to look at Alice and came around.

"Hello, Mrs. Rhinelander. I'm Lee Davis."

His voice came up from deep in his throat. It sounded kind, but I had a sense it could bellow down a building. His eyes concentrated on Alice as if she were under his microscope. Tall, fit, probably in his fifties, he was a handsome man, but stern, severe looking. Wearing a dark gray three-piece suit with a gold chain running across his vest, he offered to shake her hand.

She took it. "I'm Alice Jones."

"'Alice Jones Rhinelander.' At this point, I'd keep that part of the name."

"You're right, I should."

He smiled, which was a relief, then passed by to welcome me, Daa and the judge. Three chairs had already been placed for us behind one directly across from his desk.

"Mrs. Rhinelander, would you sit across from me? Mrs. Brooks, gentlemen, just behind." We did what we were told. "I'm always pleased to see you, Judge Swinburne, so that you can tell me from a judge's lofty perspective all the secrets of the bar of justice."

"And I know them all," the judge said. The two men had a nice chuckle together. "But Lee, I'm here today to introduce my client, Mrs. Alice Jones Rhinelander, to you, as she is a fine young woman in great need of your services. I've known the Jones family for thirty years." He leaned forward in his chair and spoke intently. "George here has driven me all over the county in his taxi, and we've become friends, good friends. He brought Alice to see me because she needed an attorney. What she truly needs is a trial lawyer, because hers is going to be one hell of a trial, as you've no doubt read in the papers. She needs a litigator, and I'm not one of that ilk, that's for sure. Someone who's won thirty first-degree murder convictions might be just the ticket."

The whole time that the judge had gone on, Alice had watched Davis. He concentrated on every word that the judge had said, to which he responded, "Your modesty is admirable, Judge. But I'm confused. In all these documents and news clippings you've sent, I didn't see that murder was involved." He then looked at Alice and allowed a brief smile.

Daa cleared his throat. "It isn't yet, but I'm bloody close to it." Alice saw that Davis was watching her.

"Mrs. Rhinelander, my first question must be to you. What do you wish to accomplish with your defense, beyond winning the case?"

Alice hesitated. "'Beyond winning'? I don't know what... I'm just trying to defend myself against the Rhinelanders."

"I understand. But if you're successful, do you imagine further benefits?"

"You mean, what else am I hoping for?"

"Yes. As I understand it, you were originally offered a simple annulment to end your marriage to Leonard Rhinelander. I have no doubt you would have been offered a great deal of money to accept it. Yet you turned it down. Now this family wants to force an annulment in court by accusing you of fraud. Again, I'm sure you could still settle for the money at this point, probably a lot more. I'm curious why you've accepted the perhaps painful course of going to trial?"

"Their offer of money is a bribe." Alice was trying not to be angry. "It'd be like them paying me off, like a whore. And this court thing is accusing me of lying. I don't lie, Mr. Davis." He tilted his head to look at her from another angle. "Since you ask, the main thing I want from this is to save my marriage. I also want to protect my family from the Rhinelanders. They're horrible and cruel."

"I see." Davis paused without taking his eyes off her. "Mrs. Rhinelander, I must tell you that if you retain me, my only interest will be to win this case, to prevent the annulment and preserve your rights as Leonard Rhinelander's wife. I cannot suggest how you'll realize your ambitions about your marriage, or that I'll have any interest in them."

She stared hard at him. "Will you win it?"

He looked away. "Predicting jury decisions is similar to forecasting earthquakes," Davis said. "What I can offer you is this: I don't make a habit of taking on cases I'll lose."

Alice paused to take that in. "Do you want to take this one on?"

"I do. I believe it's a unique case of great legal interest."

"Why is that? A simple annulment?"

"Hardly simple."

"What do you mean?"

"Aside from preventing the Rhinelanders from stealing your rights, I see this case as having a profound influence on women's rights in a marriage, and if I'm not mistaken, a new clarity about race in our country."

Alice cringed, and Davis saw it. She turned around to look at Daa. Sitting rigid in his chair, his eyes were closed against what Davis had implied. She turned back to the attorney.

"Mr. Davis, we aren't used to a lot of attention. What's happened to our family already has been very hard, what they say in the papers every day, what people say to us when we go out. Isn't there a way of doing this without a lot of... noise?"

"Yes. Accept their financial offer and the annulment, and the matter will be settled."

No one said anything. Alice watched Davis as he watched her.

"Mr. Davis." Daa stood up and stood awkwardly. "This is for my dear daughter to decide, but I'd not have her suffer this another second. But I've learned since coming over to this country that if you hide from a fight that's needed, a part of you begins to die." He reached forward and put a hand on Alice's shoulder. "I'm not willing to let the Rhinelanders start that process."

Alice put her hand on top of his. "Neither am I. So, is this when I'm supposed to decide to—what do you call it—'retain' you?"

"The moment will serve, if you're ready."

Alice looked around at her father again, then at Judge Swinburne. He'd brought her here; she knew what he thought. Still standing behind her, Daa made a bare gesture with his hands that she read as, "Who else?"

She turned back to Davis. "Sir, if you'll win the case, I'll figure out those other hopes I have. We'll take what comes. You're retained, Mr. Davis."

"I'm very pleased, Mrs. Rhinelander. Judge Swinburne, I'm honored to join you on the defense."

"Before we go any further," Daa was gripping his cap in his hands, "I must tell you, sir, what I said to Judge Swinburne ten minutes after I barged into his office. He told me not to worry about fees, so I said nothing more. But a Yorkshireman worries about grass growing. I own our home in New Rochelle and some nearby rental properties. I have $36,578 saved to get my wife and me through the rest of our lives. And my taxi, I keep it together with baling wire and chewing gum. I offer it all for Alice, but even with that, I don't see how we can afford you."

"Once again," Davis said, "the Honorable Judge Swinburne proves himself to be elegantly sagacious. You have no worry about legal fees, Mr. Jones. Your daughter is married to Mr. Leonard Rhinelander, and when we defeat his suit of annulment, she will still be Mrs. Rhinelander." He turned to Alice. "As long as you are married to Leonard, he is legally responsible for his wife's reasonable expenses. We will immediately make a motion to the court that until the trial is over, you will be provided with alimony to cover your living expenses, as well as all funds needed to cover your legal fees. I'm certain that the Rhinelander lawyers have informed your husband of this."

Daa stood, amazed. "That's very good news!" He sat down again. Alice leaned forward. "How much is it going to cost?"

"Depending on the extent of their prosecution, it could be substantial."

Alice nodded. "Mr. Davis, I'm not interested in getting a lot of money, only getting my husband back. But it'll give me some pleasure knowing it'll cost the Rhinelanders something for all they're doing to us."

"Noted, Mrs. Rhinelander. The pleasure will be mine." He reached across his desk and picked up a heavy book, opening it to a page he'd marked. "I want to explain 'dower rights' so we're all aware of why the Rhinelanders are fighting so hard for an annulment rather than a divorce."

"What kind of rights?" Alice asked.

"Dower rights, established back in colonial times. They were to protect a woman if her husband tired of her, walked away and left her destitute. In effect, the law says that the moment a woman marries a man, she is forever entitled upon his death—even if she has been divorced or abandoned—to one-third interest in his land. Not his money, or gold, or jewels, or any other possession—but his real estate. The law was made when land was the primary asset that a couple had. Today, assets are usually more diverse. But in the case of the Rhinelanders, who presently own a good deal of Manhattan Island, dower rights will serve you very well."

"So a divorce wouldn't solve their problem," Alice said slowly, "because that dower right would still be mine."

"Exactly."

"Even with them accusing me of lying about being colored?"

"That's not germane. The statutes in New York State no longer define or consider anybody's color or race. He married you. The dower rights are yours."

"Unless it gets annulled, meaning our marriage never was, so that I wouldn't have that dower right, or I guess any other."

Davis gave her that slight smile again. "You are a quick study, Mrs. Rhinelander."

The praise moved her. "Thank you, sir."

"Which third of their Manhattan property do you want, Alice?" Judge Swinburne added, laughing. "I'll get a map."

Davis got up and went over to the judge to give him the law book. "Sam, that idea will never be mentioned again until the court settles this case. Future negotiations aren't part of our agenda, and I don't want to even hint at avarice. Agreed?"

The judge said, "Oh sure, Lee, just having fun."

Davis went back to his chair behind the desk, but he didn't sit. He reached out for the stack of newspaper clippings. I thought that he had more of them than we'd collected on the dining room table at home.

"I want to address something else." Davis was dead serious, more so than he'd been since we walked in. "Sam, I see in these newspaper articles that you gave interviews to The New York Times, as well as a number of other papers."

"Just trying to clarify all of what those press boys didn't understand."

"Judge, the press is not looking for clarification. They are looking for sensation, particularly with a case like this one." He picked out an article. "You state that your client's main purpose in the case is to prove that she is white."

"Well, isn't it?"

Davis disregarded the reply and went on to another article. "You also said that you'd prove that her father, George Jones, is not a colored man, and that you'd neither affirm nor deny that Mrs. Rhinelander herself is a Negro but leave it up to the Rhinelander lawyers to prove their charge that she is."

"I said all those things." Judge Swinburne looked sheepish, knowing he was in trouble. "The complaint is accusing her of fraud, that she deceived Leonard by claiming to be white. Therefore, they have to prove that she isn't. It's about fraud. It isn't about race."

Davis glared at him for a moment. "Judge, with the great respect you know I have for you, I must strongly disagree. All over the country, the Ku Klux Klan is now a national political force in spite of its idiotic and violent traditions. The Jones family has already been their victims. Here in Westchester County, where our jurors —inevitably white—reside, everything about this case will be infused with race, *particularly* this case. We must all accept that right now. I must ask that no further statements be made by anyone to the press about our strategy."

To me, his voice, though not loud, came from way down and could go through a wall.

"The show is yours to run, Lee." Judge Swinburne owned up to the error. "I'll refuse any further contact with the press."

"Thank you. I'm most grateful, Sam. Truly. We have months to wait before we get to court. I don't want the press to have formed their own verdict before the jury does. And I certainly don't want to stimulate any further KKK attention."

I realized, and I think Alice did, how completely Lee Parsons Davis had just taken over the direction and control of her case. But it seemed that he'd put a big sign on it that said: *Race.* To us, that wasn't it. The whole mess had to do with Len's father wanting control over his son and what kind of woman he was allowed to love. And now that we understood about that dower right, it was clear it had a lot to do with money. Her dower rights wouldn't matter to her until Len was dead, but she'd learned from him that the Rhinelander family always thought about money way ahead, and they had a lot of lawyers to think along with them.

Mr. Davis turned to Daa. "Mr. Jones, you and your wife are naturalized American citizens, are you not originally from Great Britain?"

"We are, sir."

"Both you and your wife? Were you not originally from the West Indies?"

"My father was. I was born to an English mother in Yorkshire."

"Are all your papers in order and in a safe place?"

Daa coughed, one thing we recognized as a sign of nerves. His legal status was a part of his life about which he'd never allowed himself to be certain. Seldom did he show it, covering worry with concentration on his purpose of being worthy of his citizenship.

"All that's in the garage where no one could ever…"

"Garages burn down," Davis interrupted. "I'd be happier if all your papers were in a safe-deposit box."

"Yes, sir. Of course."

"I think we must be clear that this trial may be particularly difficult for you, Mr. Jones. You've already been identified in the press as a 'colored man' and as a foreigner. With Sacco and Vanzetti waiting on death row, and the Ku Klux Klan spreading, particularly here in the Northeast, you potentially could be targeted by either the anti-immigrationists or the bigots, both dangerous and carelessly stupid."

"I'm familiar with both groups, and I'll be prepared for whatever might come."

"You and your family will never be alone. Judge Swinburne and I will see to that."

To me, Davis seemed smarter than God, could stand up to anyone, and had a strategy already working in his head to win the case. I hoped Alice felt the same way. She watched the lawyer as he searched the pile of clippings, handing one to her. It was a newspaper picture of her.

"Mrs. Rhinelander," Davis said, "you'll note that in that picture, your skin has been tinted darker by the newspaper, from white to colored. Please don't provide them with any more opportunities to photograph or to write about you."

"All right. Can I ask a question now?"

"You may, if I may after."

"Mr. Davis, are the Rhinelander lawyers going to try to turn me into being colored? It's not a big worry of mine." She turned to look at Daa. "My father has his dark West Indian skin. My sister's married to a Negro. I've worked with black people all my life, as a laundress, waitress, and in-house maid. It's just that, until all this came up, I've been like my mother: white, not hiding anything, not ashamed of anything, looked on as such at school, at church, same with my friends and family. Is it better for the case that I go ahead and change?"

Davis was not surprised by the question. "You are who and what you are, Mrs. Rhinelander. That does not change." It wasn't the answer to her question, but he asked his question before she had a chance to respond. "My only question to you is, do you still want me to take this case?"

"Yes, sir."

"Good," he said, and went behind his desk. He sat down and picked up a pencil to take notes on the yellow pad before him. "Let's start at the beginning. When did you first meet Leonard Rhinelander?"

I heard her throat close. She almost couldn't breathe. Finally, she explained, "Those memories haven't been allowed for a long time. They just hit me like a truck."

"I understand. No hurry."

"September 21, 1921."

"And Mrs. Rhinelander, I need you to tell me about every detail you can remember, even if you don't think it's important."

"Even what I was thinking? A lot of times it was different than what was going on."

"I'd be most grateful for that."

Alice looked out of a window. Dark clouds were gathering for a predicted storm. "That was a nice day..."

CHAPTER THIRTEEN

Waiting for a trial to begin is a special hell that Dante didn't cover, probably because there aren't words for it. The mental battle, I think, for all of us, was between each of our distorted degrees of doubt and hope, and doubt was always an easier sell. Ever wary of what we read in the papers, we clung to whatever one or the other of us heard from Lee Davis, both in our private interviews with him, or from any information that came from his office.

He interviewed each member of the family separately, weeks apart and didn't ask us to keep the conversations to ourselves. In fact, he urged us to compare notes with each other. If anything was remembered or clarified, he wanted to be informed. In my meeting, he showed no modesty in his questions about racial or sexual questions, leading gently to personal specifics with an ease that few white men could muster in the presence of a black woman.

"Your sister, Mrs. Montello, mentioned that each of the sisters had various...

How should I say? Birthmarks? Mis-colorings? Small areas of skin coloring that contrast with the rest."

I laughed. "Do they teach a course in law school on graceful definitions of awkward subjects?"

"At the moment, I wish they had."

"You don't need it. You did fine. Grace does enjoy the drama of revelation. Yes, we all have some blemishes, and before you can ask, I'll say that they haven't meant much, never seemed like a brand of race. I suppose if any of them were ordinarily visible, on our faces or something, it might be different, but they're all covered by clothing."

"As Mrs. Montello so graphically informed me."

"About all of us?"

"She did so with some enthusiasm."

"Oh dear. Am I blushing?"

"I'm a bad judge of blushing."

"Good! But in answer to your next question, no, we never thought that they were any indication about our race, only that we were our father's daughters."

"But your father has very dark skin."

"He was always a West Indian to us, and probably because of our mother's insistence, any clarification edged toward Spain. For years, we imagined he was descended from matadors. Race is a state of mind, I think. As a matter of fact, just recently I've begun to accept that I'm black, or 'octoroon'—according to that perverse racist math established by slave traders and owners. Of course, none of those classifications has any basis in genetic science. So is your next question about genetics?"

"Mrs. Brooks, I'm so glad that I don't have to cross-examine you."

"Me, too. But why?"

"You know what my questions should be before I ask them. What if I made a mistake?"

Yes, after my interview, I liked him and trusted him even more.

And no, I don't know exactly when I decided I was black. It happened without my realizing it, although I suppose what was happening around us every day, the hate in the papers, the unsigned obscene letters only cowards can write that Klansmen, their wives and even their children sent to my family, and of course, my dear daughter who was lovely and most definitely her colored father's child—all those things changed the gene pool for me. When I accepted the change, I felt good about it, because by then I wanted in on that fight, for Daa, for Roberta, for Alice, and for all of us. I made no big proclamation about it. By now, the reader must know I don't do things like that. I just started living it while dealing with the pressures that the public's attention forced on us, each of us reacting in different ways.

For instance, on a hot August day, Daa, without a word, went out on the steps of the house with the bucket of KKK nightrider rocks that we'd collected six months ago. Bellowing disjointedly, he threw the stones at the journalists behind the rope set up by the police. The rope kept people off the Jones property and separated the press from the two-dozen members of the general public, a changeable and expanding mass each day. In anticipation of the trial and because of the steady newspaper exposure, Pelham Road had become a New Rochelle attraction.

The press ducked as Sergeant Kelly made a careful but steady progress toward Daa, shouting to his old friend to stop throwing the rocks. Flashbulbs went off as Mum and I came out and grabbed the bucket's handle and frantically tried to pull it away from him. He held on and threw another missile. Other police officers moved the press out of range into the street.

An automobile blew its horn as it moved down Pelham Road. Mum and I pulled Daa by the bucket handle back toward the front door and shoved him inside with the bucket. Then she turned, her face in a rage. Plodding straight down the path toward the press, she saw Barbara Reynolds, who pushed herself forward and called, "Good morning, Mrs. Jones!"

Her colleagues, knowing her local contact might result in news they might share, quieted down to record any response. Sergeant Kelly protectively moved behind Mum as she eyed Barbara. "You're the young woman who writes for the Standard Star?" Her voice wobbled with emotion.

"Yes, I sure am."

"We've been very pleased with how you've been writing about us," Mum said, attempting control, but then gave in to bellow, "unlike so many of THESE OTHER LIARS!"

Objection and derision were expressed by the other journalists, above which Barbara said, "How are you all doing, Mrs. Jones? Any chance I could get an interview?"

A policeman standing by the car that had pulled up was calling urgently to the sergeant. Exasperated, Kelly hurried over. The howling of the press enraged Mum, who shouted, "Stop all this caterwauling!" Then she pleaded to Barbara, "Luv, can't you make this bunch of hooligans go away?"

Through hoots of contempt, Barbara smiled sympathetically. "I'm afraid we sharks have to be fed."

Mum therefore chose to address them directly: "Why should I tell you anything? You write terrible things about us in your papers, saying month after month that my Alice deceived Len. That's the lie you tell!" The press was silenced enough to write down the diatribe. "He loves her! That's the story you should be telling!"

Sergeant Kelly, having escorted Lee Davis from his car, cleared the way for him. "Coming through! Let him through!"

The press responded with flashbulbs and shouted questions, many to Barbara Reynolds.

"He's Lee Davis," she informed them loudly, "lead counsel for the defense, former D.A., thirty first-degree..."

Davis gently took Mum's arm. "Come inside with me, Mrs. Jones." He escorted her up the front steps. Alice opened the door for them and closed it quickly behind them. Inside, Davis saw Daa sitting slumped in his chair, looking at the floor. Mum hurried to his side. Alice and I stood together, trying not to distract.

Daa's rage had settled into despair. "They're stealing our lives, lying about us. How can they do that?"

"Sharks!" Mum barked. "That's what she called them. SHARKS! When will they leave us alone?"

"They won't!" Mr. Davis shot back. "As long as you keep giving them what they crave." His anger shocked them. Mum sat back on the arm of Daa's chair. "Throwing rocks? Giving them quotes, photographs?" Davis was severely annoyed. "It does damage to your daughter's case. From this moment, no matter the circumstance, no member of the Jones family will say or do anything involving the press without my permission. Is that clear?"

Abruptly, Mum caved in on the arm of the chair. "I'm so sorry, Mr. Davis, so sorry."

"Agreed." Daa put his arms around her. "It's getting the better of me.

They've been out there every day."

"I realize how hard this is on you." The harsh tone that Mr. Davis used did not change. "No one should have to go through this, particularly the innocent. But in a hot summer, sap and emotion flow. Last week in our nation's capital, 50,000 members of the Ku Klux Klan were allowed to parade down Pennsylvania Avenue in their ludicrous, white-sheeted regalia. Men, women, and children from around the country were cheered by the crowds watching. Fifty thousand! We do not wish to gain their attention in Westchester County!"

Daa nodded. "I agree about that."

Mr. Davis glanced at Alice. "May I take my suit coat off?"

"Oh, yes, of course." Mum got up and gave the suit coat to Daa, who stood and laid it across his chair.

Mr. Davis gazed piercingly at our parents. "Mrs. Jones, since meeting you and Mr. Jones, I've become convinced that one of the strongest parts of our defense will be you two—your humor, your style, and particularly your strength of character. I'm hoping to use those qualities when we get to court. But be assured, they'll be tested between now and then, severely tested, as all of us will be. I'm confident that, realizing how vital you are to your daughter's case, you'll not only survive these dreadful times, but triumph over them."

They looked at each other and took each other's hand. "Thank you, Mr. Davis." Daa was clearly contrite.

Mum was not quite there. "You can be sure, only when it's over will we spit in their eyes!"

"That will serve."

"It's hard waiting, sir." Daa sighed deeply. "Any idea when the trial will start?"

"When I know, you'll know. The Rhinelanders are being extremely thorough in their preparations. Now I must speak with my client, if you'll excuse us."

"I'd like Em to stay."

Davis debated it for a moment, then nodded.

Without a word, Mum and Daa went into the kitchen, letting the swinging door close behind them. Davis turned to Alice. I backed up into a chair where I'd offer no distraction.

"I did try to stop them from going out there, Mr. Davis. My father has a temper, but this is more than that. It's causing him damage."

"It's poisonous, I know."

"It sure is. You want to sit at the dining room table? I've had just about every grown-up conversation there since I was born."

They both took chairs facing each other. "How are you holding up, Mrs. Rhinelander?" He glanced at me to include me out of courtesy, but I let Alice answer.

"All right, I suppose. The crowd doesn't bother me as much as it used to. Sometimes they don't come, and there's only one policeman. It's just that... Mr. Davis, I haven't seen or heard from my husband in... now it's half a year. We were married for one month before he left. Where's my marriage?"

"I regret to say that it's in limbo, where sadly it'll remain as long as your husband's lawyers and their investigators continue their discovery. They're being very conscientious."

"Investigators?"

"They have twelve. We have four."

"Good Lord. What're they trying to discover?"

"Everything about every step you've taken since you were born, as well as anything they can find about your parents and grandparents."

"Good luck to them. *We* don't even know much about the grandparents.

But what do I do to keep Len and me alive? Couldn't I at least write him a letter?"

"Do you know where he is?"

"No." Leaning forward intently, she put her elbows on the table. "I was thinking if I wrote something, you could put it in with all the stuff you send back and forth to his lawyers and maybe they..." She stopped. "They'd never let him see it, would they?"

"I doubt it greatly. The statement about not communicating with you that Len made in his last letter—the one that Attorney Jacobs read to you—I think was a vital part of his negotiation with the Rhinelander attorneys... to what purpose, we cannot know."

She nodded. "It's just that he and I both believe that if we don't have something going on between us, we'll start dying. Or at least love will. I'm worried about that."

"I certainly sympathize, Mrs. Rhinelander. If you write a letter, I'd also have to read it, because I assure you, his lawyers will."

"Oh Lord, what would I write for all of you lawyers?" She smiled, hoping to amuse, but gave up.

Mr. Davis looked toward the windows as the crowd outside made itself heard. "I notice the police are out in force."

"Here, night and day, taking no chances of having more nooses turn up. They never did find out how that thing got in here.... Listen, Mr. Davis, what you said to my parents just now was wonderful, and I thank you for it. But they're scared all the time. Can't they be left out of the trial?"

"At this point, I can't leave anything out. I mean that quite literally, Mrs. Rhinelander. I came over today because I've reached a point where I urgently felt it necessary for you to know how brutal this trial may be... and to give you the chance to get out of it."

"'Brutal.' Aren't you supposed to protect me from that?"

"Mrs. Rhinelander, I'm supposed to win your case. How I do that and how our opposition chooses to contest us allows a very broad range of behavior, from courteous to vicious. Yes, I can protect you from their excesses. But whatever truths they might discover and present, you and your family must be prepared for them. I cannot refute the truth."

"What 'truth' are you talking about?"

"The legal case for annulment is about fraud, but the trial will focus on your social class, your race, your powers of seduction, and your sexual proclivities, all in explicit detail."

"I know 'explicit.' What's 'proclivities'?"

"Your natural way of doing something, your personal inclinations that others, particularly regarding sex, may view as sordid or even perverted."

Alice looked over at me as if she'd been kicked in the stomach. "Sounds like it could get pretty dirty."

"It most certainly could."

Alice turned back to face him. "What's happening here, Mr. Davis?" He waited for her to continue without responding. She sat back in her chair and glared at him. "I fell in love with a rich man and him with me. We did sexual things. That's a natural part of it, isn't it? An important, aching part of it. Is that so—what'd you call it? 'Sordid?' 'Perverted?'"

"I don't think it is, but I'm only your lawyer, not your judge. It's the jury that may form those opinions, particularly about interracial sex. And that's my concern. It's possible that if they consider you guilty of purposeful miscegenation, mixing races, they could also decide you're guilty of fraud."

"'Mixing races' never occurred to Len and me. The sex was between two people, that's all." Alice stopped, sensing that something was about to change. "What're you saying?"

"I'll select the jury as carefully as I can," he said, "but there isn't a single soul in the Westchester County jury pool who'll come into that courtroom without a preconceived notion about race. The whole country is consumed with it."

She stared at him. "You mean I'll already be colored to them. That's fine with me. It'll be fine with Len. So what?"

He nodded. "The question of miscegenation is still there. You two have run into an acute issue in American society: the menace to white racial purity. This case may very well define the future, in the courts as well as in the culture, of what the mixing of the races will mean. Your marriage represents a profound challenge to a bigoted society, one that's been deeply established since America's very beginning, which any number of constitutional amendments cannot erase."

"I don't know much about American society, or until now, not much about it being bigoted. All I know about, or care about, is Len and me being married and what's happening to us."

"Mrs. Rhinelander, your marriage infuriates, I'd say, the majority of the white population. They're outraged that the purity of their race is threatened. Twelve men of that majority will judge you."

"Wait. Let me try to understand this. The Rhinelander suit is charging me with lying to Len that I was white before I married him. That's the so-called fraud. But the jury will have to decide on that only because we got married?"

"That is a distinct possibility."

"What if Len and I never married? Lived in sin, but didn't make it legal?"

"I doubt if we would have ever met."

"Do you think I lied about being white?"

"I don't believe you ever lied."

"I didn't! Ever!"

"But my opinion doesn't matter in the court. I'm deeply concerned about that jury. They've seen pictures of your father and will see him sitting in the courtroom beside Mrs. Brooks and her proudly colored husband." He looked over at me. "I so hope I can depend on that."

"We plan to be there every day. Or I do. Bob may have to work."

"That will serve." He turned back to Alice. "The jury will hear the Rhinelander lawyers present evidence to prove you have inherited some modicum of black blood. To most white people, even in New York, the one-drop rule of the Jim Crow South prevails; that is, having a single drop of black blood makes you a Negro."

"Fine!" Alice said, furious. "But at the time, Len didn't care if I was white or green or had polka-dots! At the time, I thought of myself as white, if I even thought about it at all. If I'm all of a sudden something else now, well, that's all right with me. I'm learning very fast about that. But I never lied to Len or anyone else."

He nodded. "I believe that."

Alice looked at me. I trusted this straightforward lawyer. I thought Alice wanted to as well. I said, "I believe Mr. Davis."

Alice nodded once. She turned back to him. "Can you convince the jury of that?"

He sat up straight and let his voice go very low. "I want to force them to decide something else. You'll be happy to know that the Rhinelanders have spent a small fortune gathering their proof of your racial makeup, that you have mixed blood in your veins from your father, his father, the West Indian sailor, etc. But before it's even presented, I wish to admit to the court on your behalf that, yes, you have some drops of mixed blood, and in effect, 'So what?' Therefore, all the Rhinelanders' expensive evidence about your blood will be moot, irrelevant."

"That'll be fine with me, but what does it do for our case?"

He folded his hands on the table. "Then all that's left for us to prove is, to whatever degree you're black, that Leonard Rhinelander must have known it. He knew your background, knew your father and brother-in-law, and knew you under the most intimate circumstances. He saw everything about you that there was to see."

Right that second, I wondered if he was talking about our skin coloring, the blemishes. I looked at Alice to see if she was thinking the same thing. Apparently, she wasn't.

"And therefore," Mr. Davis continued, "he must have known all that can be known of your so-called racial makeup. If Leonard *knew* that you had mixed blood in your veins, it makes no difference if you told him you were white or not. He knew you weren't! If he knew that, there is no fraud. And without fraud, there'll be no annulment and the Rhinelanders will fail to take away your rights."

Alice stared at him, then stood up and took a few steps over to one of the windows where she could take my hand. "Len saw everything, but I can tell you he was never thinking about race." Parting the drapes slightly, she looked out at the crowd. "You know, Mr. Davis, I've worked in a lot of rich people's homes where their spoiled kids didn't care about what they said to servants, where some husbands didn't care what I thought about them handling me." She turned back to him. "When they got mad, I got called 'high-yeller' and 'dusky bitch' and 'colored slut' and 'nigger' trying to pass as white. I was fired for spanking a kid for saying it once. I fought against some of the husbands for saying it, got fired for that, too. Of course, they'd hired me because I was white enough for their standards of servants' skin, but all of a sudden, in their eyes, I'd turned black. A miracle!"

Mr. Davis nodded. "That pathetic irony is another reason I can believe you

never lied to Leonard Rhinelander about it." He paused. I thought I could hear his mind working. If he believed it, why'd he want to say anything different in court? I suddenly thought he had a plan that he wasn't going to explain.

Before I could ask, he said to Alice, "I'm sure you realize that you're involved in a different fight now, a considerably bigger one. You perhaps stand for something far greater in the world than yourself or in this case."

"I don't want any of that," Alice said. "I'm not the one to be standing for anything more than saving my marriage." She watched him for a response.

When none came, she returned to the table and sat down. "How much about these prock—prosliv-..."

"Proclivities."

"How much about them is going to be discussed in front of everybody?"

"In order to prove how completely your husband knew you, I'll cross-examine him about every physical detail. Also, the Rhinelander lawyers will use the letters between the two of you describing your sexual activity. Many letters, as you remember, are... explicit."

For a moment, Alice could hardly take a breath. "Yes. I remember. How many will they read out loud?"

"I'm very sorry to say that his lawyers have entered into evidence all the ones you sent him. I will have to do the same with those he sent to you. That's not to say they'll all be used."

"Just the really dirty ones. Have you read them?"

"They're the reason I came over today to warn you."

She choked, deeply. Both Mr. Davis and I stood to help her. She waved us away. "I'm just embarrassed. I'll get over it." She took a deep breath. "We swore we'd never show them to anyone. I guess this is what the law does to promises."

"The letters will be used. I'll try to use them to your benefit."

"Can't you stop that? They're so private."

"I regret that they were discovered. But they were, and we must attack them and use them if we can."

"Mr. Davis, how much of Len and me will be left for us?" She shook her head.

"Look, I'm not too shy, but it'll be so awful for my parents, and even worse on Len. What if I tell you not to use them, not to make anything of the ones they use?"

"You can ask me to do that," Mr. Davis said without offense. "I'll surely consider your wishes, but I won't promise you anything. If I go on with this case, I'll do what has to be done to defeat the Rhinelander lawyers, who I assure you will not be kind about those letters, no matter what we do."

She looked at him in despair. "Why did he even let them have my letters?" Mr. Davis was sympathetic. "If we're correct in assuming he's trying to protect you, I'd suggest that Leonard is in complex negotiations with his father's lawyers on a daily basis. The letters were probably an element in some trade-off."

Alice closed her eyes. "All right. I'm going on with this. But please, don't you ever dare leave me in it alone."

"I never leave, except when I'm told by a client to go."

"I'll never tell you that."

"I do trust that... Mrs. Rhinelander, I think we're done."

"Thank goodness. I don't have anything more to say anyway. Too much to think about."

"You're certainly permitted that."

Mr. Davis stood and retrieved his coat from Daa's chair. "Long before the trial begins, I'll make a list for you and your family of every question that I think will be asked, in hopes of preventing surprises. But be assured—and warn them—even after such a list, there'll be surprises, hard ones."

"We'll be ready for anything." Alice looked over at me for confirmation. I nodded in agreement. "I'm just worried about Len. I want there to be something left of us."

At the front door, Mr. Davis shook my hand. "Goodbye, Mrs. Brooks. I know how much it means to your sister to have you at her side."

"Thank you, sir. It'd be hard for me to be anywhere else."

Then he turned to Alice. "I don't expect you to always agree with me, Mrs. Rhinelander. But I do need your respect for whatever I must do."

"My God, you've had that since the second I met you. I can't always agree with you because of what I think you're going to have to do to Len. And probably to me."

"I accept that. And may I say, you impress me greatly."

"You don't have to say any nice stuff. I'm sure not very impressed with myself."

"You should be. You didn't take their money and decided to fight. You've been astonishingly adroit in dealing with the extremes of altered circumstances. And you're willing to consider a new world rather than straight away rejecting it. These are admirable qualities."

"You mean my new black world? How could I reject it, even if I had the choice? The money? I like money, same as anyone else. I loved the presents he gave me, I loved going around with him in the car, I loved making us a home—for that one month." Tears came but did not affect her.

"But I don't like money like the Rhinelanders do, destroying their own family when they think they have to, like that uncle, now like Len. My taking the Rhinelander money would have destroyed me, and that's just what they want to do. But they're not going to do it, Mr. Davis, not so long as I have a pulse. You're stuck with a trial."

"You're reassuring your counsel," Davis said, allowing his bare smile. "Thank you." He reached for the latch and opened the door.

"You know," Alice said, "Len and I... it was so... simple."

"It seems so." Davis nodded his goodbye and went down the steps. The crowd welcomed him with a great din. Alice closed the door behind him. Then, as the full force of memory hit her, she said, "Em, it was so simple."

I had nothing to say to that. I just folded her in my arms.

CHAPTER FOURTEEN

On a cloudy, unseasonably cold afternoon in early November 1925, the trial began. By then, we'd been told how to dress (church clothes), how to act in court (no matter what we heard or thought, we must not reveal the slightest emotion), how to act outside the court (any of the public's expression—whether a single person or a crowd, whether it was sympathetic or offensive—was to be ignored), and how to regard the press (they: jackals; we: sphinxes).

In our slow water torture of occasional information, we also had learned something of the legal cast of characters, that Judge Joseph Morschauser would preside (Mr. Davis liked him as a "fair judge"), and that the Rhinelanders had retained as lead counsel a popular local judge of their own, Hubert Mills, who'd served at one time on the New York State Superior Court. He was both courtly and waspish, with a fervent proclivity for fundamental religious invective. (Mr. Davis was delighted as he regarded Mills as "a postulating fool, needing to be loved by all.")

Alice had been shown the courtroom and told me she'd felt lost in it. "Full of echoes," she said. "The jury box seemed like it was right on top of where I'll sit, and on the other side, the press table—which Mr. Davis said would be jam-packed—was placed so there was no place for anyone to hide from them. Our table faced the judge and the witness stand, and…" she hesitated, "and Len's lawyers—and Len! —will be at a table across from ours, not twenty feet from me. Mr. Davis has said over and over again that I sure as hell can't speak to him, and I can't even look at him until he's in the witness box or stand or whatever it is. How am I supposed to do that?"

That question was never answered, even though we talked about it incessantly right up to the day of the trial. We did agree that we had to get together every night, either at our apartment or at home with Mum and Daa, to talk about whatever had happened during the trial that day, since we couldn't say anything to each other in court. Bob and I would be sitting behind a railing with Mum, Daa and Grace in the first row of spectators' seats. Alice, Mr. Davis and Judge Swinburne would be just in front of us at the defense table. The presiding judge and the press would have an unrestricted view of us. Any communication would be noted and publicized with unlimited speculation. We were all going to sit there, motionless, expressionless, like mannequins in a store window, no matter what was said or what happened. I asked Mr. Davis once if we were allowed to think. "Not out loud," he said.

That first day, Alice had stood with Lee Davis inside the ground-floor entrance of his office building, waiting to be summoned. Above and beyond her own anxiety about appearing in court for the first time, she was worried about Len's absence. That morning, the call to order had been delayed because he hadn't arrived. His own lawyer, Judge Mills, apparently didn't know where he was. Was he sick? Was he refusing to come? The presiding judge, Judge Morschauser impatiently kept granting extensions from his chambers, the final one being until two in the afternoon, the plaintiff present or not. It was already past that. If they didn't start by three, Davis said the trial would be put off until the next day. We all dreaded another night of waiting.

The clamor from hundreds of people across the street had been going on since they had massed that morning outside the courthouse. Most of the crowd had arrived too late to secure a place inside the courtroom. Alice pictured the courtroom that she'd only seen empty, now crowded with strangers, soon to be watching her every move, every look, every breath.

"No privacy in there, I guess."

"In court?" Davis smiled grimly. "No. Think of it as a fishbowl." He looked at his pocket watch and put it back in his vest pocket. "Won't be long now."

He seemed so calm, but he watched the door as if he wanted to attack it. Maybe he was thinking of the courtroom, too. Then the thought hit Alice again that in a matter of minutes, Len—presuming he was all right—would be sitting across the aisle from her, not twenty feet away. How the hell was she not going to speak to him, not even look at him, not going to leap up and rush over and tell him how much she loved him? She'd do none of those things. She'd sit there at the defense table with "a confident (phony) look on your face," what Mr. Davis had suggested, a look she'd tried to discover in the mirror over her bathroom sink at home. She hadn't found it and hoped some blank mask would appear that would do the trick.

What if Len looked at her, and because she was obeying her lawyer, she missed seeing it? But what if she did see it? What could she do about it? And what would happen if the press saw it and made whatever they could out of it, or if the lawyers saw it, or the judge? So much trouble for just a look. And this would be in the first minute. How could she stand it over the hours or days or even weeks that the trial could last, according to Mr. Davis?

And what would it be like for Len, these crowds, him sitting so close to her, after a year, a solid year since he went off with Mr. Jacobs, a year since his last letter, read aloud by his lawyer. All she remembered of that was "Get the best lawyer," and "first and last and forever, I love you." Well, she sure did have the best lawyer, and she'd murmured the other phrase until it was frayed almost to meaninglessness by repeating it so often to herself.

Judge Swinburne's double knock sounded outside on the door, and Davis opened it. The crowd noise tided in; coming through the door, it was like a force against Alice's body.

"The plaintiff still isn't here yet," Judge Swinburne said, "but Morschauser wants to get started."

"Ready, Alice?" Davis picked up his two briefcases. He'd asked her permission to use her first name, as he needed to be less formal in court.

"Been ready a long time."

"Walk straight across and right up the steps to the door. Don't hear or see anything else. We'll be just behind you."

"Mum and Daa are already in there?"

"They're sitting right behind you in the first spectators' row." Judge Swinburne was excited. "With your sisters and Mr. Brooks."

"They all right?"

"Displaying courage and pride, a fine, strong American family!"

"Not to some." Alice hoped she could do as well. As she stepped out of the doorway, everyone across the street started yelling. She walked quickly into the street and saw Sergeant Kelly holding back the traffic for her. He gave her a quick wink and smile of encouragement as she passed. He'd winked like that when Len hit his car. She wondered what the sergeant was doing in White Plains, feeling gratitude that he was there. She headed up the wide steps toward the courthouse door.

The crowds on each side were shouting at her; she couldn't hear what, and she didn't look to see their faces. Policemen were holding them behind barriers, and suddenly she was nearly blinded by dozens of flashbulbs exploding, seemingly all at once. Once at the building's entrance, two sheriff's deputies held the door open for her and her attorneys. Moving quickly down the hallway, they passed through another crowd milling around outside the courtroom door. The deputies cleared the way through people staring at Alice as she passed.

"JESUS' JUDGMENT WILL DAMN YOU TO HELL!" a male voice shouted, and a deputy went into the crowd.

Mr. Davis was right behind her. "Keep going into the courtroom, Alice, and right down the aisle to our table on the right."

She knew where it was. She'd had dreams about that table, screaming mean ones. The shouted curse didn't bother her, not after all the Christian hate and threats she and the family had received in the mail over the last year. But the first sight of the courtroom staggered her, every seat filled, people lined up against the walls in double rows, deputies standing on guard throughout, all watching her walk down the center aisle. She saw the elderly man, who must be Len's lawyer, Judge

Mills, sitting at the plaintiff's table, apparently paying no attention to her arrival. He was older than she'd thought, balding, with rimless glasses propped on a pug nose almost too short to hold them. When he suddenly looked up to see her, Alice saw that he pursed his lips to smile and raised his eyebrows in anticipation. Of what? She thought that it was probably her autopsy.

At a long table up against the wall on that side of the courtroom's well were some two-dozen journalists watching her, some already making notes. On the opposite side of the well was the jury box, too near the defense table for Alice's liking. It was filled with a dozen respectable-looking men, all in suits and dark ties, which is all Alice allowed herself to see before she took her place at the defense table in a chair between Mr. Davis and Judge Swinburne.

As soon as they sat down, she heard the big doors of the courtroom bang shut at the back. The spectators started talking, and Alice was startled by how loud they could be. Through the noise, she heard Daa's deep voice. "We're all right here, luv." Mum added, "We love you." I was there too, content that she knew it.

Alice looked over at Davis, who was laying out the contents of his briefcases in neat piles on the table. She wasn't even supposed to look around at her parents! Then she glanced at the press table and understood why. They were all watching her, probably hoping for any sign of grief or agony. Recognizing Barbara Reynolds among them, wearing what looked like a bright new yellow dress with Oriental decoration for the occasion, Alice sat back and worked on finding the "confident face" that Mr. Davis wanted, wondering if just looking blank would do.

"All rise!" a deputy called out as a nice-looking man in his early sixties came out behind the judge's stand in a black robe and took his place. "The court of the Honorable Joseph Morschauser is now in session."

"Please be seated," the judge said pleasantly, like a preacher in church. He looked out over the courtroom, first at the jury, then at the spectators who had gone silent, then at the press. He didn't look at Alice or any of the lawyers, but said right off, "Judge Mills, we've waited for your client to appear for many hours."

"Your Honor, I beg the court's pardon." Judge Mills stood at the other table. "My client is, indeed on his way. The reason..."

The doors at the back opened again, and Davis put a hand on Alice's as a warning. She didn't turn to look, and neither did any of us. The disturbance at the back grew into a loud chatter from the spectators. Alice knew Len was near, and as chairs across the well scraped back, she knew he was about to sit in one. Daring to look, all she saw was Jacobs, a man whom she hated. Behind him, only a shock of slicked-down hair. She closed her eyes and let her head sink but then snapped it back to a neutral position.

"Judge Morschauser, we apologize for the delay," she heard Judge Mills say. "We offer no excuse, only the well-known explanation that time to big-city lawyers is different than it is to those of us who humbly labor in the vineyards of country law."

The spectators expressed their enjoyment of the sentiment, and I saw Jacobs glance at Mills as if he'd like to kill him. Judge Morschauser cracked his gavel on his desk. "The spectators will be aware," he said in a surprisingly commanding voice, "that they are here at the court's pleasure. I will not hesitate to withdraw that privilege if spectators misuse it. The deputies will have you out of here in two minutes."

He stared out at the spectators as they became as quiet as a congregation. Then he turned toward the jury. "Gentlemen of the jury, good day. Be assured, I will do everything in my power to prevent any further waste of your valuable time." He then looked directly at Judge Mills, who smiled and gave a little bow of contrition.

Morschauser then took up papers, studied them for a moment, and turned to the jury again. "Gentlemen, under New York State law, your consideration as jurors is different in this case from more dramatic proceedings that involve a crime. Rather than deciding guilt or innocence, in a trial such as this one, you are charged only with resolving specific issues germane to this single procedure. These issues are defined by the court—that is, by me—and submitted to you, the jury, for your consideration. The verdict, which only the court will decide, will be based on your decisions about these issues, as well as the law. Copies of the issues will now be provided to you in order that you may refer to them as the trial continues. Bailiff, please distribute."

As the bailiff passed a single sheet of paper to each jury member, Davis moved a legal yellow pad in front of Alice and wrote, "Be ready for what's coming."

She took the pencil out of his hand and wrote, "Did he look at me?"

Taking the pencil back, Davis wrote, "Of course not."

"Gentlemen of the jury," Morschauser continued, "the first issue to be decided by you: At the time of the marriage of the parties, was the defendant colored or of colored blood?"

Alice felt a jolt of heat go through her and tried not to move a muscle. She felt her face go rigid, as if every muscle had tensed. "At the time of the marriage of the parties." Was Len remembering that day? For the first time since, she remembered her hesitance, worried that marriage—the ritual, the papers—were going to change things. What if they'd stopped right there, never married? Would they be here now?

"The second issue: Did the defendant, before the marriage, by silence conceal from the plaintiff the fact that she was of colored blood?

"The third issue: Did the defendant, before the marriage, represent to the plaintiff that she was *not* of colored blood?"

Alice closed her eyes but didn't let her head sink. What was Len thinking? Was he screaming inside like she was?

"The fourth issue: Did the defendant practice said concealment, or make said representation with the intent to induce the plaintiff to marry her?

"The fifth issue: Was the plaintiff by said concealment, or by said representation, or by both, induced to marry the defendant?"

Alice opened her eyes. She must have turned her head because she was looking right at the jury. They were listening to every word the judge said. All wore suits, ties and starched white shirts. She knew those shirts; she'd ironed so many of them. Could these men ever believe that she didn't lie to Leonard Rhinelander, only loved him?

"And finally, the sixth issue: If the plaintiff had known that the defendant was of colored blood, would he have married her?"

YES! YES! YES! Alice shrieked inside her head but only closed her eyes again to keep herself from looking over at Len. She heard papers being sorted and moved about on the table before her. She didn't look at anything until she heard Judge Morschauser speak.

"Judge Mills, your opening statement."

A murmur of anticipation swelled from the spectators, then deflated with a bare look from Morschauser. Alice figured that everyone would be looking at Judge Mills as he walked over to the jury box, so she glanced at Len. Clearly visible as Jacobs was leaning forward over the table, recording the trial on a yellow pad, Len wore a dark gray suit and had his hair parted severely in the middle, brushed flat against his head. His glasses looked slightly crooked on his face. He was slumped back in his chair, staring up at the ceiling, his lips tight across his mouth. Alice felt a sudden urge to call to him and turned away to suppress it. She understood why she shouldn't look at him again but knew she would.

"Thank you, Your Honor," Mills said. "And may I say once again how pleased I am to practice law here in your court."

As fast as lightning, Alice was furious. Later, she wrote in her diary, "What a kissy-kissy thing to say!"

"Gentlemen of the jury, good day," Judge Mills said. "We are about to partake of a journey together. It leads us toward a common understanding of both the facts and the law. It is a fascinating journey that, in spite of the sordid nature of the present case, I have little doubt will stimulate and challenge your intelligence and wisdom—by the way, for which you were chosen." He wiggled his head and snickered, presuming his compliment was appreciated. Then he went back to the plaintiff's table and put on a skullcap to cover his thinning hair. "It's very drafty in these old courtrooms. Please forgive this necessary attire for an old fighter in the trenches of the law."

Alice couldn't resist taking the legal pad and writing, "What hat will you wear?"

Davis read it and wrote "!" She turned to Judge Swinburne to see if he might laugh, but he was busy recording everything that was said.

"To begin with, the law," Mills said. "In the state of New York, any misrepresentation or concealment of a material fact—such that if known to the other party, it would have prevented a marriage—is sufficient ground for an action of annulment. The law also states that each party to a marriage has a duty to reveal all facts material to said marriage. The law in this case would be violated by a lie by the defendant of being entirely of white blood. That'd be fraud. Therefore, in this trial, the plaintiff, Leonard Rhinelander, has the evidentiary burden of answering this question: Is the defendant, Alice Jones, colored? Then, did she misrepresent herself to Leonard Rhinelander as being white with no colored blood? In other words, did this boy marry Alice Jones in the full faith and belief that she was white, pure white?"

He paused dramatically, then pointedly turned and looked at Alice. Many of the jurymen followed his example. Alice did not dare to breathe. She met his look with what she hoped was a dead face. "In answering these questions," Mills continued as he turned back to the jury, "we'll prove that the plaintiff, Leonard Rhinelander, is of pure white stock, in contrast to the substantial strain of black blood that has come to Alice Jones through her father and his father before him. From investigations in England, we have learned that Mr. Jones was indeed known there as a colored man. Here in Westchester County, his children are known by some as mulattoes. I will leave no doubt in your minds that Alice Jones is of substantial colored blood. Here and now, I challenge any statement to the contrary."

Alice was ready for all that and was delighted that Judge Mills had sunk into it with such eagerness. Mr. Davis would make him look like a fool. At the same time, she wondered how much it had affected Len. Was he concerned that she was now colored?

"Please remember throughout the trial," Mills continued, "that when Leonard Rhinelander met this woman, he was a boy of 18, left motherless by a tragic accident five years before, and whose beloved brother subsequently died in the war 'over there' only three years later. We'll show you that Leonard suffered throughout his youth from a serious physical infirmity that tongue-tied him. The reason for this is a lifelong mental backwardness, which finally caused him to be admitted to an institution for his care. This is the helpless boy whom Alice Jones, almost four years older than he, ensnared with her licentious charms. We have letters from her that will clearly illustrate how she bewitched Leonard, as I say, a mere boy, upon whom no woman had ever smiled before, a tongue-tied, diffident innocent who was fair game for an experienced, clever gold-digger."

"Objection, Your Honor." Davis was on his feet so fast it startled Alice, struck as she already was with mention of the letters. "My distinguished colleague sullies himself by using such petty insults for fact."

"Sustained," Judge Morschauser said without thinking about it, "but without the editorial comment."

"Thank you, Your Honor," Mills said. "We will also show you that before they were married, the boy Leonard and this sophisticated, experienced woman stayed together in a New York hotel, The Marie Antoinette, for many days and nights! A responsible parent separated them, and the boy was sent away, far away. No matter! Alice Jones used hundreds of letters over the two years of separation that followed to hold him in her web of passion. One example, this from May 1923: 'I dreamt of being kissed by you all over while showered with ten-dollar bills.' That lewd, greedy expression is typical of what the boy was fed on. He became utterly infatuated, and in this condition, he did not know black from white, or anything else."

Alice looked at Mr. Davis. He seemed to be listening intently. Why didn't he object to that? A shaft of apprehension stabbed through her, hating that they had her letters. She thought of the night Mr. Davis had told her that, how she wanted to give up the case. Her expectation that her letters would be read in court caused her more sleepless nights than almost anything else.

"Being so innocently trusting, Leonard Rhinelander was ready to accept Alice Jones' inferior social position," Judge Mills continued. "But after he learned the truth about her race, Leonard would not inflict upon his ancient and proud lineage the undying disgrace of an alliance with colored blood. As to color, he drew the line! We will therefore prove that she has black blood in her veins and that she hid that shame from him in order to marry a very rich and very innocent boy!" He was nearly shouting, then abruptly he leaned forward heavily and placed his hands on the rail of the jury box. Speaking with intense passion, he said, "I do not make these revelations —the sordid character of this defendant and the pathetic weakness of my client— recklessly. I try this case, gentlemen, only so that God's truth shall be revealed, let it cut where it may!"

He swept his eyes over the jury, then bowed his head to them. Pushing himself off the rail, he turned and, with an air of exhausted triumph, made his way back to his seat.

"Because of the delay in starting today," Judge Morschauser said, "it is my suggestion that the defense make its opening statement tomorrow morning, if counsels agree."

"Agreed, Your Honor." Davis was too quick to agree. Alice turned to him angrily.

"Yes, indeed," Mills added.

She couldn't understand why Mr. Davis wouldn't immediately crush all the lies Judge Mills had just told. Then the thought hit: What if they weren't lies? What if, over the year that Len had been away from her, he'd changed his mind, or had it changed for him, had sunk back into being a Rhinelander and was seeing her as colored to get rid of her?

"Gentlemen of the jury," Judge Morschauser said, "it is incumbent upon you not to begin forming any opinion, as you have heard barely one side of the case. Do not discuss it with anyone, and do not allow yourselves to be influenced by anything you read in the press. Journalists have the great luxury of deciding a case for their readers at the end of each day. You do not. Adjourned until ten tomorrow."

"All rise, the court of the Honorable..."

The protests from the press almost drowned out the bailiff, but Alice wasn't listening. As she stood, she was aware that the lawyers around Len were swiftly gathering their papers and preparing to take him out of the courtroom. She didn't look directly at them, but she, too, started to go.

"Let them leave first with their bodyguards." Mr. Davis put a restraining hand on her arm. "Let them get all the attention."

They did, and we all watched as bodyguards came down the center aisle of the spectators to meet Len, who stared at the floor as Jacobs urged him out. For a second, he hesitated, then looked up at the ceiling and followed the bodyguards, many of the spectators gawking as he passed. The photographers and most of the other journalists followed, asking questions and taking pictures. He did not look at Alice.

She sat down in her chair, feeling a kind of doubt that she hadn't felt before. By chance, she looked across the courtroom and saw Barbara Reynolds from the New Rochelle paper watching her. Surprised to be caught observing, the journalist smiled at Alice, more in understanding than in friendship. Then she turned to her pad and began writing again.

Alice looked back just as Len and his lawyers exited the courtroom.

"Let the mantle of fame fall on him." Davis was filling his briefcases. "It distracts and destroys."

"I don't want him destroyed. I told you that, Mr. Davis."

"Yes. And perhaps your husband doesn't want you destroyed either. But as you've just heard, Alice, they've started to do just that."

"Why didn't you answer all those lies that Judge Mills said about me?"

"Because Judge Morschauser obviously wanted to go home, and because, having the evening allows more time for me to consider how best to skewer Mills' opening statement."

Mollified, Alice turned around to see us, her family in the seats behind her. None of us said a word, waiting for permission from Mr. Davis to move. She smiled at us, then turned to Davis. "How much worse will it get?"

"Much worse."

She looked around the courtroom. Deputies had led the jury out, and the last spectators were straggling out. A few journalists were still writing at their table, and two deputies waited to escort her and her family out to their cars.

"They won't destroy me, Mr. Davis." Alice stood up. He turned to face her. "No matter what those twelve men decide, no matter how much the Rhinelanders spend, no matter how black they make me, Len loves me. And I love him. It's this trial that'll distract and destroy. It's all posing, speeches, and nasty fights, isn't it? How can anything get decided?"

"Alice, it's a miracle of reasoning, a labyrinth of contradiction."

She turned away from the explanation. "I just wish he'd look at me."

She wanted Mr. Davis to say that maybe Len would. But Mr. Davis said, "He won't, Alice. He can't. He's been forbidden, as you have, for the same reasons. I'm sure it's painful." He went back to filling his briefcases.

CHAPTER FIFTEEN

From that first day, Alice and I met each night. Sometimes we were too tired to say a word, sometimes too upset to trust what we might say. But all in all, I had a pretty complete sense of what my sister went through. Her diaries subsequently made it clear that what she was thinking about some particular thing was pretty much what I was thinking. During both the boring and the explosive days, when the court's attention was taken up with either legal detail or dramatic revelation, Alice's attention was so often focused—without hardly a glance—on her "accuser," sitting at the prosecutor's table just across the courtroom's well.

None of us slept very well the first night, a combination of adrenaline and fear. We spent too much time talking after the dinner Mum gave us, all of us scared that those twelve men in the jury box were sitting at home, believing what Judge Mills had said. Alice was afraid that Len might have changed, yet angry with herself that she was distrusting him only because of what his own lawyer had lied about. She went up to her room "to do the diary," and I went home to try to sleep. It hadn't worked out too well.

"Mr. Davis, your opening statement," Judge Morschauser said, and the Jones family as one focused through fatigue on "our" attorney as he stood. We watched him take several steps toward the jury box. All attention on him, I saw Alice look quickly over at Len. I did, too. He'd missed brushing a section of his hair that stuck up behind his ear. It was my first look at him in over a year. He looked terrible, had lost a lot of weight, was sickly pale, with eyes sunk back in his head. He looked like he hadn't slept either. Alice told me later that how he looked made her feel better, misery liking company and all. But what was he thinking? "Oh, God, to know that!" she'd said the previous night.

"Gentlemen of the jury," Davis said, his deep voice ringing easily throughout the courtroom. "First, I wish to address a legal technicality. Alice Jones Rhinelander, the defendant, on advice of her counsel at the time, in all innocence, made a previous denial about her blood. In the interest of focusing on what is truly important in this trial, we hereby withdraw that confusion and readily admit that she has some unknown amount of mixed blood in her veins." A loud reaction came from just about everyone, particularly from the press table. Judge Morschauser used his gavel to bring a quick silence back to the courtroom.

"Your Honor," Judge Mills rose to say, "I wish to state that I regard such an admission on the part of the defense to be honorable and appropriate." Alice wondered what he was so happy about, a big part of his argument and investigations being useless.

Mr. Davis ignored him as he turned to Judge Morschauser. "Your Honor, I further request that you instruct the jury to disregard Judge Mills' gratuitous and truly bizarre portrayal of his own client's questionably diagnosed mental deficiencies. They have nothing to do with the question before this court, that of fraud."

Morschauser took little time to say, "The statements will stand, being subject to your further examination of them. Continue, please, with your opening statement."

Mr. Davis didn't seem bothered by the judge's ruling, maybe because the jury had heard his message. He walked back to the jury. "Gentlemen, I feel a tremendous responsibility in the face of what was presented to you by opposing counsel. It comes coupled with the anger I felt during Judge Mills' opening statement. I cannot conceive of a more effective confusion of the questions in this case than was presented to you. Therefore, let me define the issues in a nutshell. Until just now, the first issue was: Has Mrs. Alice Rhinelander any colored blood in her veins? Because this is now an admitted fact, it's no longer a question you need to consider. The second issue is now the only relevant issue, and it is simply this: Did Alice represent in any way to Leonard Rhinelander before their marriage, that she was white, pure white? And even if she actually said it—which we utterly deny—did Leonard Rhinelander believe when he married Alice Jones that she was pure white? Knowing her as intimately as he did when making his decision to marry her, could he possibly have believed it?"

Tired as she was, Alice moved forward in her chair and sat up straight. She thought she understood where he was going, and it was exactly right. Was Len thinking the same? And was he excited for her, or worried that his own case would be hurt?

"Because, gentlemen," Davis continued, "that is the essential point: Leonard should *not* have believed she was pure white, *could* not have believed it, unless of course he was blind." He came back to the table to retrieve a sheet of paper. "In Judge Mills' opening statement, he explained the New York law to you by saying this: '...any misrepresentation or concealment of material fact—such that *if known* to the other party, it would have prevented a marriage—is sufficient ground for an action of annulment.' 'If known,' gentlemen. The fact is, in this question of fraud, it makes no difference what Alice Jones may have said or not said—if Leonard already had known the truth! If she had said to him a thousand times that she was green, he knew that she was not. The question for you, therefore, becomes this: At what point in their relationship, before or after their marriage, did Leonard Rhinelander know, had to know, must have known that Alice Jones had mixed blood in her veins."

He turned and looked directly at Leonard. Alice saw most of the jury look that way, too. She looked over to see him completely engaged, sitting very straight in his chair, but his head was hanging over strangely.

"Now, Judge Mills has argued that perhaps Leonard had indeed gone blind, blinded by his own moral weakness to the evils of sexual temptation. But gentlemen," he said, turning back to them, "even if morally blind, it's impossible to believe he did not see clear and obvious evidence to suppose, to suspect, to deduce, to conclude, *to know* that Alice Jones was not a pure white girl."

Davis turned to look straight at her. Startled, Alice sat up straighter. They were judging her right then, she knew that. "I cannot help but believe," Davis continued, "that the truly vicious, uselessly cruel opening statement made by Leonard Rhinelander's counsel on his behalf against this girl wasn't inspired by any righteous truth, but rather by the Rhinelander millions. I therefore do not believe this young man, Leonard Rhinelander, had anything to do with it. But his father, Philip Rhinelander, did. His explicit intention in this trial is to crush under the weight of privilege and social influence an innocent member of a concededly humble family. Leonard Rhinelander is taking this legal action—how willingly we may question— in order to save what the grand Rhinelanders consider to be their ancient and 'honorable' name. But gentlemen, they are not going to do it if it is within my power to prevent them. In this instance, the word 'honorable' turns to ash in my mouth."

Alice didn't move. She wanted to yell and cheer. She had no idea that Mr. Davis would, or even could, say these things in court. She kept expecting Judge Mills to object. How could she have believed anything that Mills had said yesterday? How could she have doubted Len? She snuck a look at him. He was watching Mr. Davis with great intensity.

"Here is Judge Mills' case," Davis continued, then gestured toward Leonard. "This poor blighted son, this dear young man, descended from his long blue-blooded line, is—may I use the current expression? —bughouse! This sad fellow who used to stammer and was so brain-tied, they're saying he couldn't even understand that quote from Alice's letter that the Judge read—so thrillingly, didn't you think?" He paused to see a number of jurors smile "Judge Mills' achingly righteous conclusion? That this girl must have ravaged that helpless boy into marriage. That is their case! It is astonishing! I've prosecuted much in the world of crime, but this is the first time I've heard of a girl being charged with raping a man into marrying her."

"Objection!" Judge Mills jumped up to say.

"Sustained," Judge Morschauser said. "Rape is not charged, Mr. Davis."

"Your Honor, I agree. The word is not actually there, is it? But so much else is. Gentlemen, it was not enough that this son of immense wealth comes into the girl's very humble home and takes her as his wife. But because his papa becomes cross about it afterwards, judging from atop his social plinth that such a wife for his dear son is unworthy, he will now try to have her dragged through the slime to get rid of her, to throw her away like so much of their luxurious trash. But, gentlemen, this is not something with which Rhinelanders wish to dirty their hands. Here in this courtroom, you must understand that dirty work is what the Rhinelanders want you to do!"

A number of the jurors quickly glanced at each other and shifted in their chairs.

"To that end, look to what lengths the Rhinelanders went to discover Alice's father, George Jones's racial heritage. What did they find after such vast expense, wasted time and effort? Exactly what he has always acknowledged ever since he arrived here to fulfill his dream of America. His mother was white; she told her son that his father, who had died, was from the West Indies. The Rhinelanders could have learned that by simply asking him. Why didn't they do that?" Davis turned toward the plaintiff's table, holding his hands up in inquiry. The Rhinelander lawyers ignored the question, and just for a split second, Alice thought she saw Len barely smile. It jolted her, and she felt like she lifted right up out of her chair.

"Now, gentlemen, may I ask you to use your eyes? I'm going to ask Alice's two sisters to stand." That was a surprise! The jury looked over as Grace and I stood. "Emily, the elder, is next to her husband of five years, a respected colored butler, Mr. Robert Brooks. Grace, the younger, married an Italian American who is unable to attend this trial as he's employed in the construction business. You may be seated, ladies. Thank you. Those three sisters' father, Mr. George Jones, an English West Indian, sits beside his wife, their mother, a woman who comes from the purest kind of ancient Anglo-Saxon stock. Gentlemen of the jury, Leonard Rhinelander, for years before he married Alice Jones, *knew them all*, and well!

"Incidentally, this is the same Leonard Rhinelander whom Judge Mills would have you believe was in an 'institution.' No doubt the good judge was hoping to suggest an asylum, the young man being 'brain-tied' or whatever, mentally backward. *Gentlemen, he stuttered!* He had a chronically nervous stomach. He was sent not to an asylum but to a very expensive private clinic to address those specific problems. When ‧he met Alice, Leonard was not insane or brain-tied. Instead, he was close to cured, and he fell in love!"

Alice felt intense heat go through her and became aware that people were looking at her; surely the jury and the press were. Was Len? "He fell in love!" Had he looked at her? The spectators released a vocal appreciation that Judge Morschauser ended with a single rap of the gavel.

Mr. Davis waited for complete silence. "We will prove that it was Leonard who wanted to keep the marriage secret because *he feared his own father*. Remember that even after the marriage, even when the press proclaimed to the world that Alice was colored, and after the KKK attacked them, Leonard stayed with her. He was not shocked. He was oblivious to the universal accusation that she was colored. He was happy! He did not care. He was not fooled. So then the basic question that must be answered is: Exactly when and why did Mr. Leonard Rhinelander realize that Alice was so suddenly colored, and exactly when was she colored enough so that he'd be motivated to bring this sad case for an annulment to this court? I suggest, therefore, that there was no fraud in the marriage, but rather the lies in this legal action that has been forced by a father upon a young love-besotted lothario."

"Objection," Mills said. "A suggestion of pure conjecture."

"Sustained."

Mr. Davis ignored the objection and went on. "Gentlemen, I will try not to throw filth in this trial, but I am forced to say now that if such a course is continued by the other side, we will meet kind with kind. I came here originally to try this case on the issues I have outlined to you. Unfortunately, Judge Mills has taken the lid off the garbage can." Davis turned to face the plaintiff's table. "If it is to be that kind of fight, let the fight go on. But be sure that we will not shrink from any onslaught."

After a moment, Davis returned to his chair at the defense table. What surprised all of us was the spectators' utterly silent reaction. Alice didn't move, aware again that she was being watched. Yet her gratitude and admiration were so deep that she let herself feel a little safer.

In order to break the silence, Len's lawyers moved quickly with a lot of business and a quick calling of a first witness, someone from the Secretary of State of New York to present a document about the census taken in 1920, where it was recorded that Daa was black, another with my birth certificate that classified me as black and Alice's that stated she was mulatto. We knew from Mr. Davis' list of questions that all this was coming, that all of it had already been admitted as evidence.

Each submission was objected to by Mr. Davis, who took "an exception" each time when the judge overruled him. But Judge Mills still went on, making it clear to the jury that everyone in the Jones family except Mum was officially designated as some degree of black. We realized that even after Mr. Davis had admitted that Alice had black blood in her veins, Judge Mills wasn't going to hold back any of the details. Alice didn't understand a lot of the skirmishes that followed as Mr. Davis objected to them. Instead, as she wrote in her diary, she thought back over his opening statement, "He was happy, he did not care, he was not fooled," or "Leonard was not insane or brain-tied... He fell in love!"

"Yes! Yes! Yes!"

For several days, officials appeared as plaintiff's witnesses to present such documents, and each time Mr. Davis rose to object that the evidence of colored blood was moot, in that the point had already been admitted. Nevertheless, another piece of evidence about the Jones family's blackness was presented, angering the family by the endless repetition of what they had never opposed—anger we did not indicate in any way. We hoped it was boring everyone else. Alice gave up looking over at Leonard. As far as she knew, he had never looked over at her, slumping in his chair and staring at the ceiling, as he'd probably been ordered to do.

He had said in the last letter that he could have no contact with her. Mr. Davis explained why his lawyers had certainly instructed him not to look at her. But surely they had shown him all this black evidence. Had he accepted any of it? Had he begun to think of her as colored, and did it matter to him? Alice couldn't let that thought get loose in her head.

Abruptly, one morning, a familiar face appeared. The memory of her wedding day seeped through Alice as Judge Mills began his questioning of the county clerk who had filled in and signed their wedding license. Alice remembered that the woman had been an imperious personality in her own domain. She was a nervous wreck in the witness box.

"But you did question both the bride and groom," Judge Mills asked, "and you recorded their answers?"

"Yes, yes, I did, I surely did."

"And in both cases, each is identified on the marriage license as white?"

"Well, yes, of course. But..."

"Just yes or no, please. And the bride said absolutely nothing to oppose that?"

"No, but..."

"And you," Judge Mills quickly continued, "with two of your colleagues, witnessed their signatures on this document that states that they were both white?"

"We did, all of us, I remember that."

"Thank you, ma'am. Your witness, Mr. Davis."

Mr. Davis took his time and stared at the woman. "I must confess I'm curious about those 'buts,'" he finally said as he stood and approached her.

She pushed back in her chair as if to get away from him.

"What? 'But?'"

"Concerning the racial identity of the couple," Davis explained. "I believe Judge Mills said something to the effect of, 'each is identified as white,' and you said, 'Yes, but,' before he, with astonishing alacrity, interrupted you. What were you going to say?"

"I, I, don't..."

"You did say that you recorded the answers on the document."

"I always do. People scribble..."

"Could it be that you did not ask about their racial identity aloud, but filled in the answer yourself, based on your own hurried observation?"

"I, I, it wasn't necessary," the county clerk said. "They seemed, well, white. I never ask that question."

"You never ask that question?"

"No. It'd be embarrassing."

"Embarrassing? Only if the answer was anything but white." Davis turned to the jury. "What is important here is that Alice Jones did not identify herself as white on her marriage license, but was so defined by a busy, but clearly observant, civil servant. I submit that all the so-called 'official documents'—birth certificates, immigration papers, licenses to which we have been inflicted over the last long days —are tainted with doubt by similar hurried bureaucratic judgments and 'embarrassments,' whether they say black or white or torturously something in between."

"Objection!" Mills said. "Utter conjecture."

"Sustained," Judge Morschauser said.

"No further questions, Your Honor," Davis said and returned to his chair. As the judge excused the county clerk, who fled the witness box, I watched the jury and wondered if they might accept the "conjecture" that all the official documents about the shades of black in our family were pretty muddy.

"In light of the hour," Judge Morschauser said, "we'll recess for lunch. Court adjourned until 1:30."

Alice turned around to greet her family as we stood with the other spectators. We smiled bravely at her, then turned to watch as the bodyguards came for Leonard. He again followed them through the gawking crowd, looking at no one. Alice saw a number of the female spectators actually sigh; one signaled a puckered kiss. Disgusted, Alice asked Judge Swinburne, "Are they allowed to do that?"

"I imagine as long as Judge Morschauser doesn't see it," Swinburne said as he packed up his notes.

"Let's go, Sam," Davis said. "Alice, are you and your family being looked after when you go to lunch?"

"They assigned Sergeant Kelly to escort us."

"Good. Be back early, please, and don't run into the plaintiff."

"You've said that, Mr. Davis, a couple of times."

"Have I? Forgive me." He went out the center aisle, followed by Judge Swinburne. Most of the crowd had left, so Alice joined us, and we made our way out of the courthouse. Sergeant Kelly was waiting for us on the front steps, at that moment speaking with Barbara Reynolds. When they saw the Jones family, the journalist hurried away, and the sergeant came up to greet us. We all turned to watch as Leonard was ushered into a parked limousine with curtains over the windows. Several photographers took pictures.

"Where does he have lunch?" Alice asked.

"I hear they go back to their hotel over in Bronxville," Sergeant Kelly said. "Hello, George, bearing up?" He led us down to the sidewalk toward the coffee shop we'd used previously for our breaks. Other policemen discouraged any of the curious crowd still there from approaching.

"I'm surviving, shall we say. Elizabeth grinds her teeth through it all."

"I'm chewing glass."

The sergeant laughed. "Don't let the rich get in close to you. They're dirty fighters."

Mum took his arm. "Sergeant Kelly, you're so right! I'm glad you're here."

"These White Plains bulls couldn't get along without the New Rochelle contingent. But I'm telling you, with all the attention this trial is getting, I won't be surprised if the Royal Canadian Mounted Police shows up."

At the entrance to the coffee shop, Daa held the door for Mum, and Grace and I followed. Bob asked Alice, "You doing all right?"

"I'm getting through it. Can't tell you what it means to have you all behind me. Hope this isn't causing you trouble with the Weingolds."

"They insisted I be here."

"I never had an employer like that."

"I don't think many do. Sure do think Davis is fine."

"No worry about Mr. Davis. It's Len. What's he thinking about?"

"I think it's pretty safe to say, you."

"You think so?"

"He sure seems bored by everything else. Something else, though."

"What?"

"He moves heavy. When he walks up the aisle, he's, I don't know, as if he's weighted down. Something's not right."

"We're all weighted down."

We went in, followed by Sergeant Kelly. The patrons, many being spectators at the trial, grew silent and stared. Daa led the family to the large booth we'd been using. Before he got there, the owner came around from behind the counter and stood in his way. Alarmed, Alice looked around the restaurant. She saw Barbara Reynolds sitting at the counter.

"Excuse me, but I'm sorry," the owner said. "We can't serve you in here."

"Why on God's green earth not?" Daa's temper was instant. "We've been in here every day for…"

"We've been visited, told things." The owner was not enjoying being heard.

"We don't want trouble, and that's what we'd get."

Daa stepped toward him. "What things did they tell you?"

"What if you get trouble from us?" Grace stood right in his face. "My husband will…"

"What about me?" Mum interrupted, loud enough for all to hear. "They're my family!"

The owner shrugged. "Sorry."

Mum was going to say something else, but Alice pulled on her arm. "Mum, let's go. We're black, haven't you heard? Let's go."

As the family headed back to the door, the owner called, "That's just the way it is now."

Sergeant Kelly turned at the door and said to the entire restaurant, "Never knew White Plains had sunk so low, right down into Mississippi." As he came outside, we could see the sergeant's face had turned a deep red. We gathered in a tight clutch on the sidewalk

"I can't believe it!" Mum was hopping mad. "Aren't we human?"

I was no less angry. "To them, the answer to that takes one word."

"'That's just the way it is now,'" Alice quoted. "It's our new Jones family world, Mum, compliments of the Rhinelanders."

"Come with me." Sergeant Kelly started walking. "I know a place."

Alice and I noticed Daa, his face constricted in a fury we'd never seen. Alice took his hand. "Daa? Are you all right?"

"Just an old, cold hand on the heart, darlin' child. Haven't felt it for a long, long time. I thought that White Plains was just twenty minutes from New Rochelle. I fear for us; we're on the dark side of the moon."

We all had been well aware of the shift in our lives, but the public expression of it was painful. We didn't discuss it over the relatively silent meal we had at the Irish bar where the sergeant had led us. Alice was surprisingly calm. At one point, she offered, "It doesn't matter anymore what color I think I am, or the court thinks I am. The rest of the world has made its decision—and it's based on a trial about an annulment. It's crazy."

The family went back to the courtroom, each deep in thought. Our attention was finally diverted when the next witness, Dr. L. Pierce Clark, was called. A distinguished man in stylish rectangular glasses with a carefully cut head of hair, he took the stand with assurance, dressed elegantly for the occasion.

"Leonard Rhinelander was in your care at The Orchards for about eleven months," Judge Mills said. "Please describe his physical and mental state during his time there, Dr. Clark."

Mr. Davis was on his feet immediately. "Your Honor, I must object. An opinion of plaintiff's mental and physical state at some amorphous period in 1921 has no bearing on this case of fraud, presumably perpetrated by marriage in 1924."

"Overruled," Morschauser said. "History applies. Judge Mills, continue."

"Thank you, Your Honor. Dr. Clark?"

"During his time with us," Clark said, "Leonard's primary difficulty was with speech, a chronic stuttering disorder; a lesser concern was a stomach syndrome."

"The cause?"

"As to the stomach, an excessive release of acids caused by stress. We found that the stuttering was based on a deep sense of social inferiority."

Having heard so much about Dr. Clark from Len, Alice was amazed to see what the man looked like. I thought that he was probably a good doctor but was trying to rise above and escape whatever was going on in the courtroom.

"Now, Dr. Clark, in your medical practice beyond the speech therapies at the clinic," Judge Mills said, "you specialize in nervous and mental disorders, do you not?"

"I do."

"Isn't stammering often accompanied by a chronic mental weakness?"

"Always."

Mills acted surprised. "Did you say 'always?'"

"Always," Dr. Clark repeated.

"Thank you, Dr. Clark," Mills said with delight. "Your witness."

"Dr. Clark, as you know," Mr. Davis said as he pulled a large file from one of his briefcases, "Leonard's treatment files at The Orchards have been introduced into evidence. I'd like you to corroborate some of the information contained therein for the jury."

"With pleasure."

"Thank you. Could we clarify the difference between stuttering and stammering that what Leonard Rhinelander did was stutter and not stammer?"

"That is correct."

"And that the mental weakness that Judge Mills so cleverly mentioned is connected to stammering, as he led you to reply, not stuttering, which was Mr. Rhinelander's struggle?"

"That is also correct."

"Then it's safe to say that stuttering does not suggest the slightest mental incapacity?"

The doctor shifted nervously, not wishing to offend. "Very seldom."
"Good. This report describes Leonard on the day he arrived at The Orchards with his father. Quote: 'He talks only when directly addressed.

Typically, his main problem with stuttering takes place when getting started. Once a sentence begins, he seems able to go on unless a 'w' presents itself. However, there is present in him a profound sense of fear.'"

"'Fear,' Dr. Clark, when he arrived with his father?"

"I must presume so," Dr. Clark said, looking uncomfortable. "But those reports were written some time ago."

"Ah, but as Judge Morschauser so wisely observed, 'History applies.'" Mr. Davis smiled up at the judge, who ignored him. "Now the files further reveal that Leonard, quote, 'had a general physical condition below par,' unquote. And that you confronted this condition by, and I quote, 'administering three daily doses of Hormotone.' Doctor, what in the world is Hormotone?"

"A physiologic cell stimulant used to treat neurasthenia."

"And neurasthenia is?"

"An often chronic mental and physical fatigue and depression."

"But you prescribed this, Doctor, for Leonard's weight problems, not for any mental lack?"

"For the most part."

"And you prescribed it, even though the Council of the American Medical Association in a study of Hormotone done only two years before, declared it, quote: '...inadmissible as a drug because its composition is secret, its therapeutic claims are unwarranted, and the routine administration of polyglandular mixtures is irrational,' unquote. Is it some kind of snake oil, Doctor?"

Dr. Clark revealed his discomfort by looking toward the door of the courtroom, as if to flee. "Hormotone is a highly respected drug commonly used for such cases as I've described."

"Highly respected, is it? Apparently not by the American Medical Association." Mr. Davis turned a page. "Now, in September of 1921, Leonard bought himself a car. Your file says, quote, 'He is greatly pleased with it and shows a general feeling of being decidedly more confident.' I point out to the Court that this is exactly the time he met Alice Jones. Thus, the file subsequently reveals, quote, 'Leonard is becoming a changed man. He has recently made the acquaintance of a young girl. He calls on her, waits for phone calls, talks normally over the telephone.' Dr. Clark, would it be safe to say that Leonard's meeting Alice Jones was at least as beneficial to his stuttering and physical health as Hormotone?"

The spectators laughed, and Alice was surprised to see that Judge Morschauser tolerated it. Dr. Clark said, "I do not offer an opinion."

"Then could you agree that Leonard Rhinelander, by the time he left your care at The Orchards, was physically and mentally sound, 'a changed man,' as it says here, from the condition of fear when he arrived with his father?"

"I believe that Leonard was much improved by having stayed at The Orchards," the doctor said, then looked at Leonard. "He was a pleasure to have with us."

"Last question, Dr. Clark." Mr. Davis closed the file he held and put it back on the table. "In those eleven months, did Leonard Rhinelander's father, Philip Rhinelander, ever visit, or through The Orchards' switchboard ever telephone his son?"

"No, not to my knowledge." I thought the doctor had answered with a slight edge of annoyance. "He was taken home for occasional weekends and on holidays."

"Occasional weekends over eleven months? Leonard was 18. He'd traumatically lost his mother and tragically a brother in the war. Did such a circumstance of gross parental neglect by his father make any impression on you, Doctor, specializing as you do in mental disorders?"

"I was aware of some of the difficulties Leonard had at home."

"'Some?' One does wonder about the others. No further questions."

Again, the courtroom went quiet.

That evening at home, Alice told me that she'd begun to believe that silence was a more meaningful spectator reaction than any kind of noise they made. After the rest of the family had gone to bed, she said how she was torn by the idea that if Philip Rhinelander could treat Len like that in the past, what had he done to Len over this last year? She asked me if I knew about what Bob had said about Len's walking heavy, something not being right. I didn't, but said I'd find out.

She looked at me suddenly and said, "I'm going to piss on Philip Rhinelander's grave, Em. He can't imagine what's coming at him... But now I have to learn how to stop my mind from worrying. Any ideas how to do that?"

"Ethel Waters singing. Rudolph Valentino kissing. Al Capone naked."

I got her to laugh. "Howzzabout Al Capone singing, Ethel Waters kissing and…"

In chorus: "Rudolph Valentino naked!"

CHAPTER SIXTEEN

Judge Mills stood majestically. "If it pleases the court," he said, "I now call the plaintiff, Leonard Kip Rhinelander."

We heard the rush of curious comments swirl around the courtroom. Based on what the newspapers wrote, we figured the spectators' questions were along the lines of whether he was a spoiled racist loony. Or was he a super-rich, depraved sex maniac? As we watched Leonard stand up and go to the witness stand, I recognized the slow, heavy movement that Bob had mentioned. Was he sick? In pain? Bob had told me that he thought Len might be on some kind of drug for something.

The spectators muttered their excitement. They were there for entertainment. All that Alice and Len were going through was, to them, amusement. I saw that Alice held a white handkerchief. Mr. Davis had allowed it because in recent days her tendency to shed tears arbitrarily had become noticeable. Whether they came from tension or exhaustion, Alice didn't know, but the tears were a maddening source of copy for the press.

"Do you swear to tell the truth, the whole truth, and nothing but the truth, so help you God?" the bailiff droned.

Leonard, with one hand raised, the other on the Bible, said, "I do." He took his seat and crossed his legs. They were too long for the space, and he shifted around to find a comfortable position. Folding his hands in his lap, he then grasped a knee. He did not look at Alice, but she was free to watch him. "The ache of missing and loving him stabbed at me like an ice pick," she wrote later in her diary. "Then the fear that I'd lost him made that pain numb."

"Now, Leonard," Judge Mills began, "you realize, of course, that you are one of two people who know the entire truth of this sad story. We so look forward to hearing from the other person when she takes her turn on the witness stand." He said that as a challenge. "But for the moment, we need to know of your involvement from the first time you met the woman, Alice Jones. Had you ever had any experience with a female, any sexual experience, before meeting her?"

"Your Honor," Mr. Davis rose to say, "I must object. I cannot see how the plaintiff's sexual history is germane to the racial question of fraud before us."

"Your Honor," Mills testily responded, "I'm certain that my learned colleague is aware that fraud is a complex undertaking often involving subtle strategies. In this case, we aim to prove that sex in all its ungodly lascivious corruption was one strategy so used."

"Overruled. Continue, Judge Mills."

"Leonard, tell the jury how you met Alice Jones." We all heard the patronizing tone in Mills' voice, as if Len were about ten years old.

"I, I had a new car," he began. "I drove it to New Rochelle and had an accident. I bumped into a police car. Alice saw it happen and helped me with the policeman. She knew him because of her father."

"She was walking on the street and saw the accident?"

"Yes, and..."

"And after she helped you with the policeman," Mills said, "she stayed there to talk with you?"

"Yes. She noticed I had... difficulty... At the time, I stuttered."

"And you picked her up, a woman on the street, alone. Did she hesitate at all?"

"I didn't pick her up," Leonard answered. "I was grateful. I offered her a ride home."

"Is that where you went?"

"No."

"No? Why not?"

"The accident happened about ten yards from her home."

"Did she tell you that?"

"No. We..."

Mills turned to the jury. "Deception began instantly." His lips pursed, he nodded to them as if they all agreed with him, then turned back to Len. "She didn't tell you because she wanted to go with you in that car. And she had her way, didn't she?"

"We went for a drive."

"Did she like that new red, very expensive Oldsmobile convertible?"

"We both did."

Judge Mills went back to his table and shifted some papers. I thought he was annoyed but wasn't sure why. He continued his questioning in the same condescending tone as if Leonard were a child or an idiot. "Where did you go, Leonard? How long was that first meeting?"

"We just drove, and we walked on the beach, a long walk, then went back to her house and I met her family, or some of them."

"And that's when you realized her deception, why she originally didn't want you to drive her home?"

"I thought that was pretty funny."

"Precisely," Mills said and strode over to the jury again. "And she saw how easy it was to deceive a defective boy and so began her entrapment."

Mr. Davis rose with a long-suffering effort. "Your Honor, not only is Judge

Mills leading his witness, but he is erroneously describing my client's intentions for her."

"Sustained."

"Very well," Judge Mills said. "We will let Alice Jones reveal her web-weaving ways in her own words—as I will see she does—when she testifies before this court." He returned to the plaintiff's table. "Gentlemen of the jury, from that first night on, Leonard and Alice Jones carried on a correspondence amounting to hundreds and hundreds of letters." Jacobs quickly supplied him with one. "We have placed into evidence nearly a hundred of those sent by this woman to young Leonard. Here is a sample of what she wrote in December 1921, barely six weeks after meeting: 'Just think of me, being here at home, all alone, thinking of you, dear heart. I only wish my Len was coming down this evening. How I would caress you, dear. Because I know how you love for me to caress you.'" With his free hand, Mills reached to heaven, declaiming, "Get thee behind me, Satan! Lead us not into temptation!"

"Objection!" Mr. Davis didn't rise but was as loud. "This is not a revival tent but a court of law."

"Sustained."

"All right, then," Judge Mills continued, "we will read the letters to the jury one by one at a later time. But to continue revealing what we are dealing with here: Leonard, there was a time, was there not, that you went to the Marie Antoinette Hotel in New York with the defendant?"

No matter how well Mr. Davis had prepared her, I knew Alice had dreaded the questioning about the hotel. It came so suddenly.

"Yes, we went there," Len said, looking up into a corner of the courtroom.

"Can you tell me what the date of that was?"

"December 23."

"In 1921, only three months after you'd met?"

"Yes."

"Now, up to that time, had you had any sexual intercourse with Alice Jones?"

Alice did not breathe and kept an expression she had begun to use, her "dead face."

"No."

"Had you made any attempt to have any at that time?" Leonard hesitated. "I, um, I'd expressed the desire."

"I must object again, Your Honor." Mr. Davis rose again. "Mr. Rhinelander's success or failure in sexual matters obviously has nothing to do with a fraud case about Alice Jones being white or not."

"Overruled again, Mr. Davis," Judge Morschauser said with an edge of irritation.

Judge Mills nodded happily. "Well, Leonard, how did the two of you end up in that hotel room alone?"

Len looked so tortured that Alice had to use her handkerchief in front of her face.

"I, I'd invited her to the theater. We went in my car. Alice told me that, because it would be a late night, she planned to stay overnight with a friend. I suggested a hotel and that I... accompany her."

"And her reaction?"

"She refused."

"But she did let you stay with her that night, did she not?" Mills was abruptly impatient. "How did that happen?"

"We had time in the car to persuade each other."

"May we presume you were not driving?"

"Our chauffeur was."

I saw Davis write on his legal pad. I learned later he'd written: "What chauffeur?" and pushed it in front of Alice. She took his pencil and wrote "Chidester."

"And then the two of you stayed in the hotel for nearly a week, from December 23rd to the 28th, is that correct?"

"Yes."

"And may we presume that sexual intercourse between you took place repeatedly?"

"Yes." Len barely whispered.

Judge Morschauser interrupted. "Mr. Rhinelander, may I ask that you speak up for the benefit of our court recorder?"

"Yes, sir, I'm sorry. I said yes."

"That period of time included Christmas." Judge Mills was now strutting back and forth between the jury and the witness box. "How did each of you explain your absence to your respective parents?"

"I went home for Christmas dinner. Seeing me there, my father wasn't really concerned where else I'd go."

"That proved to be an error, did it not? It turned out your father was deeply concerned, wasn't he? And Alice Jones's parents?"

"She spoke to her mother by telephone."

"And to your understanding, what did she tell her mother?"

"I believe she said she was staying with a friend in Greenwich Village."

"You mean she lied? To her own mother?"

"I didn't mean that at all. She didn't want her mother to worry."

"Or perhaps something else." Judge Mills leaned very close to Leonard. "Perhaps she was reporting her progress to her mother of ensnaring a rich white husband by sleeping with him!"

"Objection!" Mr. Davis was angry. "It's outrageous to force a witness, particularly one's own client, to such far-fetched speculation."

"Sustained."

Judge Mills was becoming increasingly annoyed. "Your Honor, I would wish to read those letters the defendant wrote to this boy to give the jury a view, as well as the flavor, of her lustful provocation."

"I object to Judge Mills' prejudicial description."

"Your objection is sustained, Mr. Davis." I thought Judge Morschauser's tone of voice was a warning to Judge Mills to be careful.

Mr. Davis continued, "And as the plaintiff has seen fit to enter more than a hundred of these missives into evidence—and because we might wish to plan the remaining years of our lives—could my honorable colleague give an idea of how many letters he might choose to read out loud to us?"

"I believe the jury will benefit greatly from hearing at least sixty of them, perhaps a few more."

"Sixty! To what purpose of proving fraud could they possibly pertain? They are love letters!"

"They pertain to the character of the defendant. I believe that the letters will be germane to the jury's clear understanding of her proclivities."

Alice turned to give me a quick look at the familiarity of the word.

"Your Honor, I take an exception to every letter to be read as having nothing whatsoever to do with this case."

Judge Morschauser took an irritated breath. "As you know, an exception to each piece of evidence will need to be stated as each letter is read, Mr. Davis. Judge Mills, you may proceed."

Judge Mills went over to take the first letter from Leon Jacobs. He returned to the witness box and handed it to Len. Alice took a sudden breath, fearing what it said. Mr. Davis gave her a look, leaned over and whispered, "You've read them all. No display, please." How could she not "display" with Len sitting right there?

"Mr. Rhinelander, I show you a letter dated May 25, 1922, and an envelope postmarked the next day. It is addressed to you at the Clift Hotel in San Francisco. Is that letter in the defendant's handwriting?"

"It is." Len could barely sit comfortably, shifting his long legs around in the witness box. His face was haggard with discomfort.

"And did you receive it at the hotel through the mail?"

"I did."

Mills gave the letter and envelope to the court clerk, saying, "I offer it in evidence."

Mr. Davis rose. "And I object as advertised, for old love letters have nothing whatsoever to do with fraud."

"The advertised objection is overruled," Morschauser said.

"I take an exception." Mr. Davis would do so for each letter that was read. When Alice asked him what that meant, he explained that exceptions were the basis of appeals.

The clerk stamped both objects, saying, "The letter and envelope are received in evidence and marked respectively: Plaintiff's exhibit number 59, and 59A."

Judge Mills cleared his throat. "Gentlemen, I will read them as written. The structure is often tortured." Alice looked around and saw that everyone in the courtroom was watching Mills read. Maybe she could...

He began.

> *My dearest man,*
>
> *Well, to start, I am very interested, dear Len, for you to write and let me know if you have laid out your future life, compared to your past one. I'd like you to tell me about it as if I was lying in your arms, because you always knew that I love to be in your loving arms and hold your warm lips to mine. I knew many times, Len, dear, how I have made you feel very happy, and in time to come, I'm going to have the same chance again…*

Len looked at her! I didn't see it, but Alice told me later that it was a painful look, and then Len shook his head slightly. She noticed that his face was damp with sweat. He brushed a finger over his lips, signaling his silence, and returned his gaze to the ceiling. But he had taken the chance and looked at her, and what the look meant seemed to be such great regret for what was going on. "Oh God, Len, thank you," she told me she mouthed, but he didn't see it.

> *… and it's heaven when a couple loves each other like the both of us do. The other night, while I was lying on my bed, I wrote another poem, something that is true in my mind. This is your poem, just for you. I hope you'll like it.*

Judge Mills looked up to heaven and said, "The Devil's doggerel, may it be forgiven."

"Objection, your Honor," Mr. Davis sighed for emphasis, "... whether for my colleague's attempt at literary criticism or for his inclination toward prayer, the court may decide."

"Sustained."

As Judge Mills went back for another letter, I noticed the intense quiet in the courtroom again and realized no one was looking at Judge Mills but at Alice. Some of the people at the press table were smiling with surprise at the poem. I hoped it would be in The New York Times' summation on the front page. Her reaction was to make her face go dead with no expression. Len was in the witness box, still looking at the ceiling, but for a second, he had the barest smile.

"Mr. Rhinelander, I show you a letter dated..."

An hour and a half later, after listening to Judge Mills read seventeen of Alice's love letters to Leonard Rhinelander, even the most passion-craving romantic in the courtroom had to be close to stupor. The press table was busy, knowing that the occasional sex described would sell papers, but even they wanted relief from listening to Judge Mills drone. Len was being careful, I thought, and Alice couldn't just stare at him, waiting for the next glance. She'd have to wait until tomorrow. His one look and a tiny smile, after so long—for it was an honest-to-goodness contact—was thrilling! But why was he sweating so much? The courtroom wasn't that hot.

Judge Morschauser finally spoke with a certain relief, "I believe that the hour is right to adjourn for the day. Gentlemen of the jury, again I remind you of my order not to even glance at any newspaper. The attention paid to this case by the press has reached a fevered pitch, and often, quite a fantastical one, not to be shared by you. 10 AM."

"All rise," the bailiff called. "The court of the Honorable..."

***

That night, we again went back to Pelham Road for dinner. Bob went home to relieve the sitter we'd arranged for 'Berta, and Grace went home to feed her husband, she begging off attending the rest of the trial because he was becoming impatient with her being away so much.

After the meal, Alice's joy with Len's quick look gave way to the absurdity of the brief moment in contrast to the months of separation. We all gave in to a dull lassitude, together with our own thoughts or lack of them. Daa paced slowly back and forth across the living room with his marmalade jar of tea. Alice sat in his armchair with her mug, staring. I presumed she was trying to think of nothing but bet she was failing.

At the dining room table, Mum was reading through a stack of newspapers. "The New York Times is still putting our day in court on the front page. But not one paper is like any other," she said. "If you read all these papers, you'd think twenty different trials were going on."

Daa scoffed. "Notice the twenty different skin shades of George Jones, orangutan."

"Some of them like us. They call you 'dignified,' George, right here."

"Ah! A step up to a dignified chimpanzee." He turned away from her in his pacing. "They don't like us, luv. They're looking down their noses at our monkey cage."

Mum persevered. "No, they do. And Alice, some are standing up for you. Here's one that says, no matter your race, you had the same rights as any other woman who was trying to win her man."

"You mean even though I'm black, I still have rights as a woman? Not to sound bitter or anything. Sorry. Mum, if you can find something you think is good in the papers, it's all yours. I've stopped reading them because none of them get it right. They seem so certain about everything they want to say, and they torture the truth to death! It doesn't seem to matter much in court either, with Judge Mills wanting to tell the story his way, Len being 'an imbecile' in one paper, and in another, me being 'a one-drop gold-digger that the Rhinelanders have every right to ruin.'"

I couldn't resist: "Sounds like you've been reading a whole lot of papers." It took a moment, but Alice laughed out loud. "Stop being so smart."

"I try all the time, but…"

Our old back and forth gave Mum and Daa an excuse to hug us goodnight and go to bed. I planned to stay over so Alice and I could talk some more.

When we were alone, she took a piece of paper out of her pocket. "You know, Em, yesterday I asked Bob about the one-drop rule, that if I was black because of one drop of black blood, what about a colored man who had one drop of white blood in him? Bob just laughed. 'Alice, don't ever expect white courts to make sense about anything black and white.' I wrote down what he said for my diary as soon as I could." She looked at her notes. "'Ever since the Civil War, no legal categories or definitions about color exist in the law books anymore. But attitudes, superiorities, prejudices are carved real down deep in people's souls. So the courts have to make up color rules as they go along, depending on whatever the collective minds of each community want at the time, whether village, state, or the whole nation. Now today, black or whatever in all hell you are, if you're not white, you're… different. In any white man's court, they don't know what to do with you. To any white community, that's dangerous.' Em, your man Bob is really smart."

"Bob knows what he's talking about. I don't think your jury has any idea what they're going to do yet. I watched them during all those letters being read, trying to get a fix on what kind of men they are. They're listening hard, Alice, but this is all new to them. As Bob says, maybe it's scary dangerous to them."

"You mean me?"

"There's a whole circus of ideas going around in the center ring of that trial, and you're up there on the high wire in the spotlight." I stole the metaphor from a story I'd read in *The Atlantic Monthly.*

"It's sure a circus, all right." She stood up and went to look out the front window. "The police car's there, glad to say. I just wonder, after the trial's over, when will the police *not* be there?"

"When the trial's over, people will start thinking about something else."

She shrugged. "I usually stop myself from thinking about any future that far ahead. It always leads to wondering if Len and I will be together in it. And that's painful. If I let the future go forward, I start thinking that Len giving up my letters might mean that he's decided that he's finished with me, that he's helping the lawyers to break the marriage, that he's not going to be in my future, that the trial will end, and the marriage—annulled or not—will be over. And I'll be left with nothing else to do but go back to making rich people's beds and cleaning their bathrooms."

"Darling Alice, dear sister, that's crazy fear talking."

She looked around the living room. "If that happened, this is where I'll live the rest of my life. Nobody else is going to marry me, not after what everyone in the world knows about me now, what I've done with Len from my letters being read out loud in court! Good God, how horrible is that?"

"Alice, you're creating the worst and doing damage to yourself."

"Maybe I need to! To cut out all the wonderful, joyous body-aching needs that he and I discovered together and—oh God, satisfied! Now they're all filthy, sinful. You and I remembered Mr. Davis' word today— 'proclivities.'" She shook her head. I stood up, and she let me hold her. She said, "Hard way to learn vocabulary."

We scoffed, and she hugged me. "I really don't want to think about our lovemaking being read out in court anymore. That's a kind of torture that love letters should never cause."

"Agreed. I wish I had a magic wand to put you to sleep. Or a baseball bat." She chuckled. "I love you, big sister. What would I do without you?"

"The same as you're doing: taking whatever they can throw at you, with courage and a lot of guts. And Mr. Davis hasn't even begun your defense yet. Alice, those Rhinelander bastards don't stand a chance!"

She laughed, and we went into the kitchen to gorge on pecan ice cream. Did I believe what I said? No one will ever know.

CHAPTER SEVENTEEN

The next day, a Thursday, was spent in court listening to the rest of Alice's selected letters to Len. It was interminable to the family and to those at the defense table. It was intensely humiliating for Alice. Her love and physical passions for Len were orated with a steady tinge of disgust by Judge Mills. Len, trapped in the jury box, sat gazing skyward as usual, but again with a shine of sweat on his face that was slowly soaking his high starched collar.

> *I have to go now, darling boy, and take a shower, get ready for work tomorrow. Remember the showers we took together in the Marie Antoinette, what you did with that bar of soap, moving it all over me with one hand and doing all those things with the other? Oh, Len, just thinking about all that, well, I have to get in there and take my shower right now. It better be a cold one! When you read this, I hope you have to take a shower, too!*

Other than considerable impatience with having to object and take an exception to each letter, Mr. Davis seemed to feel that the endlessness of the Mills monotone was probably driving the jury close to delirium as well. At one point, Davis touched Alice's hand and indicated with a nod that one juror was fighting manfully against dozing off.

> *…Do you remember that last day at the Marie Antoinette, when we had to get out in five seconds? Len, it felt so terrible to come home alone. Wasn't that a sad day? I haven't been happy since you haven't been my bed pal. Will you ever be my bed pal again? I so hope that you will. We did have good times! Len, we'll be happy again soon. I'll have you forever by my side, and no one can ever part us. If they do, I would never want to live on this Earth anymore.*

One of the last letters was one Alice particularly dreaded, not that it involved a lot of sex, but rather a big hint of a marriage proposal. Judge Mills took his sweet time with this one, pointedly emphasizing her demands.

> *… Do you think for a minute that if I had not loved you, that I would have lived with you at the Marie Antoinette like a married woman, doing things that only married couples should do? I could not help it. I loved you. I do hope you'll reward me for making you so happy. I pray and hope every night that you'll be my husband.*

After that letter, everyone in the courtroom was looking at her, including Judge Morschauser, including Jacobs, Mills and the jury, and Len for a second, with a quick smile before he sank back into the witness chair again. The smile didn't help. The letter had made her sound like she was demanding marriage for sex, and that wasn't it. She had just wanted to marry him.

At the end of the day, Judge Mills indicated to a very relieved Judge Morschauser that after concluding the sixty-third letter, he was done. Within seconds, Morschauser dismissed the jury and ended the day's long discourse. Jacobs and the bodyguards hustled Len away without the slightest sign to Alice. I stood behind her on the other side of the rail as the rest of the family went out to the car. I had Bob's car, as he had to work that day.

"I think Leonard liked hearing the letters you wrote him." Davis was waiting for the courtroom to clear.

"Why do you say that?" Alice said.

"As time went on, he seemed more relaxed in the box. Occasionally, I saw a bare smile, which I think was intended for the jury... and you." He checked to see if I agreed. I did and nodded.

Alice was clearly affected. "I saw him smile. I'm not sure what it means."

Mr. Davis was loading his briefcase. "I sense that poor Judge Mills is struggling with his client as a hostile witness... How are you, Alice?"

"I began thinking as the letters were read out loud that everyone in the courtroom—and when the papers come out, everyone in the world—is going to know me as well as Len did. It's horrible."

"That's called fame. It's a dreadful part of this. I truly regret that you have to go through it."

"Mr. Davis, what part of this isn't dreadful?"

"Winning."

She looked at him, incredulous. "You truly believe that there'll be something left of us to win?" She stood up and went to the center aisle, where I joined her.

Walking up the aisle, she said to me, "Em, don't misunderstand this, but tonight, I'm just going off on my own. I have Len's car, and I need some time to get ready for whatever's coming. To do that, I can't have anyone to lean on, even you."

"You know where I'll be."

"I do. I'll see you in court tomorrow morning."

I stopped and let her go on ahead of me.

It was a long night. She didn't go back to Pelham Road. Mum and Daa thought she was with us. When we arrived in the courtroom the next morning, she wasn't there. Mr. Davis asked us where she was and was disturbed that she'd been away all night. Then just before the bailiff rose to call the court into session, she hurried down the center aisle and took her place at the defendant's table, looking at no one. All I could tell was that she was wearing the same clothes as when she left me.

Len was called back to the stand, and Judge Mills continued his questioning.

"Now, Leonard, you came back from the ranch school in Arizona in May of 1924. What motivated your return?"

The courtroom was stuffy with radiator heat. The spectators were restless, taking off their layers of clothes worn on a particularly wintry day. Len still wore a three-piece suit, still with his hair plastered down, parted in the middle. That day, we all noticed his sweating. Aside from wilting his shirt collar, it was matting his hair. Even so, he displayed an edge of cold indifference in his testimony. We wondered if he'd been angered or numbed by the letters as much as we had. He didn't look at Judge Mills when he answered the questions but gazed up at various corners of the courtroom. Maybe something had happened between the two of them overnight.

"I left Arizona after I'd turned twenty-one."

"And you'd inherited some money," Judge Mills said, again talking to Len as a child.

"Yes."

"Where did you live when you returned?"

"At my father's house in New York. And the Joneses were kind enough to let me stay overnight on occasion."

"And on any of those occasions, did Mrs. Jones, Alice's mother, discuss the marriage of Emily, her oldest daughter?"

I was ready for this and, as instructed, became a sphinx. Bob took my hand; that almost ruined it.

Len said, "Mrs. Jones mentioned she'd done everything to prevent Emily from marrying Bob Brooks."

"Why would she do that, do you suppose?"

"I suppose because he was a Negro."

"Indeed? And what happened, Leonard, when Emily disobeyed them and married him anyway?"

"From what I understand, the Brooks were not allowed to come into the Jones home for about a year." Len crossed his legs and pulled up a knee to allow it. Alice could see how distressed he was. He was sweating, using his handkerchief to wipe his face.

"Did Mrs. Jones offer a reason for this?" Mills said.

"She hadn't wanted her daughter to go through what she and Mr. Jones had experienced as a mixed-race couple. She often said the Jones family was English, which they were, that is, not considered to be colored, so that…" Leonard pulled back, regretting what he'd said.

"Beg your pardon, what?" the judge said. "What's that last phrase you said?"

"Not considered to be colored." Clearly, he was angry with himself as much as Judge Mills.

"Ah, meaning Mrs. Jones stated that her family was not colored. And did Alice Jones share such opinions with you?"

"Yes, but it wasn't to deny anything. She was explaining a fine point, about the difference between African and Spanish, not that the difference meant much to her. Her father is one-half West Indian, Caribbean, or whatever he is. So she's one-fourth. She said about that, '…if you like doing math. But genes aren't so neat.'"

"One-fourth black!" Judge Mills said, "What was your reaction to this?"

"It seemed the obvious truth."

"What obvious truth do you mean?"

"That Alice honestly believed she fit into whatever category is considered white more than any other. She'd believed that all her life."

The answer seemed to perplex Judge Mills, and when Alice glanced at Mr. Davis, it seemed to please him very much.

Judge Mills said, "And was anything else said to you at any time by Alice Jones in regard to her being of Spanish extraction?"

"She wrote me once that someone asked her, 'What are you, anyway?' She told him, 'I'm of Spanish extraction.'"

"And you, poor innocent boy, you believed that, didn't you?"

"Of course I did," Len said, glaring at Judge Mills. "I've been to Havana, Judge Mills. I saw many Spanish people of pure Caucasian blood. They had very dark complexions!" He was noticeably irritated, which caused Judge Mills to take a step back, then return to his table.

Davis wrote on the yellow pad, "Why is he sweating?"

Alice wrote, "Don't know."

Returning to the witness box, Judge Mills asked with a smile, "Then Leonard, tell me this: When did you begin to believe that Alice Jones did indeed have black blood in her?"

All Leonard's anger dissolved, and he slumped down in his chair. "I suppose when I saw her birth certificate."

"And when did you see that document?"

"The day I left her," he said sadly, "after the news came out."

I saw Mr. Davis lean forward and write forcefully on his yellow pad, but he did not show it to Alice.

"Leonard Rhinelander," Judge Mills turned and projected to the courtroom, "if you had known that Alice Jones was of colored blood before you had married her, would you have done so?"

Len struggled in the witness box, shifting forward and back as if trying to find a way to escape the courtroom. He said something that no one could hear. Before Judge Morschauser could say anything, Judge Mills ordered, "Speak up clearly, Leonard! Would you have married...?"

"ABSOLUTELY NOT. NO! Clear enough?"

As Judge Mills literally recoiled, Alice did not react. She sat calmly as if listening to a story. I knew that she'd been wounded over the days of testimony, but the shock of Len's blast of a denial had no apparent effect. I think she realized before I did that he'd said it in such a strange way, almost shouting at Judge Mills, for a purpose. Len was sweating heavily, and it seemed clear that he was saying what he was supposed to say. Then it became even clearer to me: The court stenographer would record the "required" words, but Len's telling them in such a way might let the jury understand that he didn't mean what he was saying. I knew better than to hope, but I did.

Mills was again taken aback by his client's vehemence. Even so, the judge remained icily calm as he asked, "When you married her, did you believe her many insinuations that she was white?"

"I don't remember her insinuating it. She simply believed she was white. And I always believed her."

"You 'always believed her.'" Judge Mills allowed the phrase to hang in the air, then shook his head as he walked away from his client. "Your witness."

Before Mr. Davis stood up, he wrote on his pad: "Coached! Had to say 'absolutely not.'"

Alice understood. She said, "Thank you."

"Mr. Rhinelander," Davis started briskly, "from the first day of your relationship with Alice, you knew that she worked as a maid, a laundress, a waitress, didn't you?"

"Yes. She told me."

"And on the first night that you met her, you met her family, saw their humble home?"

"Yes."

"Being a product of wealth and privilege as you are, Mr. Rhinelander, do you believe your pursuit of a maidservant from such a family, from such a humble home, pursuing her with the intention of having her fall for your lures, and having intercourse with you, do you consider such actions those of a gentleman, yes or no?"

"I..." He swallowed and wiped his face.

"Yes or no, Mr. Rhinelander?"

"Yes or no is not the whole truth, sir. I'm under oath."

"Oh, I see," Davis said appreciatively as he turned to the jury. "The young man has a very sophisticated and intelligent grasp of the law, doesn't he?" He returned to face Len. "Well, how soon after you met Alice did you fall in love with her, Mr. Rhinelander?"

Len was watching him attentively. "Very soon."

"Is it fair to say that you pursued her?" Davis said.

"Yes, it is." It seemed that Len was suddenly eager to answer Mr. Davis's questions.

"And when you pursued her, did you do so with the idea of marrying her?"

"I... Not at first."

"Then did you pursue her to make love to her with no intention of marriage?"

"At the beginning, I saw her because I liked her. Very much."

"Mr. Rhinelander, what do you call it when a man writes to a girl, saying he loves her, for the purpose of accomplishing an intimate relationship, simply wanting to satisfy his carnal desires? Is that not deception?"

"No, sir, it's, it's... courtship."

The spectators started to laugh, but Davis went right on, forcefully enough to silence them. "Which is worse, Mr. Rhinelander: to lead a girl on to love you, for her to believe you're going to marry her, and then to take flagrant advantage of her? Or for a colored girl to say, 'I'm white and have no colored blood'? Which is the worse deception, Mr. Rhinelander?"

Len collapsed back in his chair and looked at the floor. He finally said with clear regret, "The latter." Again, Alice did not react. I had to believe that he'd been instructed how to answer such questions. I looked at the jury. Were they thinking it too, or was I hoping too hard?

"Well, of course!" Davis said. "You'd say that, wouldn't you, being the blue-blooded gentleman, being the Rhinelander that you are. Some would surely disagree. Now you say that before the Marie Antoinette, you had not had intercourse with Alice. What had you done with her?"

Len looked surprised, then shut his eyes to answer, "I was fairly intimate with her."

"Sexually intimate?"

"Yes."

"And during this time, was sex your major interest in the relationship?"

"No. It was never like that."

"Oh? Then tell the jury what else there was going on between you."

His eyes still shut, he said, "We learned to trust each other. She was the most honest person I've ever known. We learned about the differences between our lives and tried to overcome them."

Davis watched a moment. "Leonard," he said. At the use of his first name, he opened his eyes. "I hate to ask you these questions," Davis said. "But you understand that the manner in which your counsel has presented your case sadly makes it necessary for me to do so... to defend my client, your wife, Alice."

"Yes, sir. I most certainly do."

Davis nodded and said, "When you said, 'fairly intimate,' what did you mean?"

Len took a deep breath. "I... touched her. With my hand."

"Where? Between her legs?"

"Yes... and other places."

"And were you 'fairly intimate' during the drive to the Marie Antoinette when you 'persuaded' each other to let you stay with her in the hotel?"

"I suppose so."

"And certainly at that point, you hoped to have sexual intercourse with her?"

"I suppose so, yes."

"Mr. Rhinelander, do you 'suppose' you were in love with her? Do you suppose that you intended to marry her at that point?"

"Yes, I loved her very much. As to marriage, I don't know exactly. I only know I'd never have asked her to marry me at that point because I didn't know, legally, financially, what I could do, or even if I could marry her at my age."

"If that is so, then at that point, Mr. Rhinelander, weren't you mainly focused on sexual intercourse and persuading Alice Jones to engage in it with you?"

"I suppose."

"Mr. Rhinelander, what is the color of your wife's body?"

"Color?" He looked at Davis aghast.

"You were in the hotel room for almost a week. Surely you saw it."

"Her body is," Len said, angry again, "like the rest of her."

"Would you say darker than what is generally called white?"

"No, I never thought so," Leonard said. "And what do you mean by white?

You mean, pure white? I've never seen an albino if that's what you mean. Her color is what anyone would consider white, and certainly lighter than the bodies of women that I've seen in Havana."

"Thank you. That's very helpful. Now then, look out at Mr. Jones. Does his complexion resemble Alice's?"

"No."

"I see." He turned to his client and, in an easy tone, said, "Alice, would you please push up your sleeves and hold out your arms?" Slowly, she pushed the sleeves of her sweater above her elbows. "Now, Mr. Rhinelander, please tell the jury if your wife's arms are the same hue as the rest of her body?"

Alice and Len were suddenly forced to look at each other. She wanted to indicate something but was staggered by what she was asked to do.

"They're..." He choked, then managed, "...the same." He wiped the sweat from his face.

"And you base that observation on knowing her intimately, seeing her at night and in daylight during your time at the hotel?"

"Yes. And being married to her."

"And are there any areas on her body that are discolored?"

"Discolored? What do...?"

"A spot, a patch, a blemish..."

"None that I ever noticed."

"You're not color blind, are you, Mr. Rhinelander?"

"My eyesight is fine."

"Good. And in preparation for your stay at the hotel, did you bring those rubber affairs?"

A collective gasp came from all parts of the courtroom. Stunned, Alice looked at Judge Swinburne, but he was busy taking notes. I thought she wanted Mr. Davis to stop.

Len had to swallow several times as if his mouth had dried. "I... good Christ... yes."

"You know what I mean, don't you?"

"Of course."

"'Of course?' Oh. Interesting. Where did you learn about condoms?"

"I learned about them in boarding school."

"Of course. In boarding school. Mr. Rhinelander, when were you sent off to boarding school?"

"It was, I was twelve, that would be in..."

"How soon after your mother was killed so tragically were you sent away to boarding school by your very busy father?"

"Within two weeks."

"I see. And while you were at boarding school, what other knowledge, other than about condoms, did you learn about sexual matters?"

"Very little."

"Yet you seemed to be quite expert with Alice when you persuaded her to do these things?"

"We weren't experts. No one persuaded. What we did was simply human instinct."

Davis paused to look appraisingly at Leonard, then said, "And you went about following these instincts naturally with her?"

"Yes."

"Nothing unnatural about it at all? Nothing indecent beyond the natural intercourse between you?"

"No, nothing."

Abruptly, Davis went back to his table and picked up a paper that he had left there. "Your Honor, I introduce into evidence a letter Mr. Rhinelander wrote to Alice. Just one, I promise you." He handed the letter to the court clerk, who marked it. Davis then gave copies to Judge Morschauser, to Mills, and finally to Leonard. "This is one of twenty-three letters we entered as evidence. Copies are for convenience of the court."

The court clerk stated: "Item marked Defendant's Exhibit N-1."

"Now, Mr. Rhinelander, please read the letter to yourself, to refresh your memory about it."

As Len read, Davis returned to the defense table. The spectators and the press found it hard to contain their speculation about the letter. Alice knew what it said and dreaded it. Judge Morschauser gaveled for quiet. Len indicated he was finished reading by letting the hand that held the letter hang over the edge of the witness box. Then, for a split second, he looked at Alice, dismayed, then down at his feet. Mr. Davis and many others saw it. Comments followed that Judge Morschauser silenced.

From his seat, Davis said, "Mr. Rhinelander, after reading that letter you wrote to Alice, do you really want to continue this trial?"

"Your Honor, I object!" Mills said, shooting up out of his chair.

"Sustained," Morschauser said quickly, hoping to quell further debate, but to no avail.

"Your Honor," Mills continued in a fury, "for counsel to suggest ending this trial to my client while he is testifying is the most outrageous behavior on the part of a defense I've seen in all my years!"

"It's within his rights, Judge Mills," Morschauser said.

Mills would not be placated. He held up his copy of the letter. "This kind of filth is beyond jurisprudence!"

Davis said, "Oh, now, Judge Mills, after choosing to read aloud 63 very steamy letters, surely you jest."

Morschauser put up a hand to end the discourse. "Perhaps we'll adjourn. An adjournment all right with you, Mr. Davis, here in the middle of your cross-examination?"

"It will serve."

"Judge Mills, will you so move?" Morschauser said and gaveled for quiet.

"I most certainly will. Your Honor, I request an adjournment. An unspeakable circumstance has arisen in this case about which I hadn't the slightest intimation."

"We'll take the weekend," Judge Morschauser said. "Gentlemen of the jury, please heed my warnings about the press and any discussion of the case with anyone. Bailiff, give them their weekend instructions." He used his gavel. "Ten Monday morning."

"The court of the Honorable..."

Even before Morschauser was gone, Mills stormed out of the center aisle of the courtroom, angrily signaling Jacobs to get Len out of the witness box. Everyone waited to watch them go. They passed by the defense table, and Davis took no notice of them. The spectators and press then released a roar.

Alice was shaking, and I reached my arm over the rail to hold her shoulder.

"Alice, are you all right?" Davis said as he stood.

"What are you doing?" she said, being careful not to be heard by anyone else. "You kept changing the subject, confusing him, going from one horrible, embarrassing thing to another."

"I was aware of the hour. I wanted to give the jury a weekend filled with numerous points of contemplation." Davis glanced at Judge Swinburne for appreciation.

"Mr. Davis, that letter's going to kill him."

"He wrote it, Alice. Both he and Judge Mills have known that the letter was submitted to the court. The judge's shock is pure performance. After he read your sixty letters, I must show the jury that you weren't a predator and that Leonard wasn't the innocent they now think he was."

"And what do you mean about blemishes?" she said, incensed.

"That question was on the list I gave you before..."

"I want you to stop. I order you to stop. I can do that. I can dismiss you."

Davis paused and looked around, then turned to Alice, his back blocking any view of her from the press table. "Yes, you can," he said quietly. "But if you do that, you'll have to find a new lawyer. It's a bad place in the stream to change horses just now, to risk Philip Rhinelander having his triumph here, robbing you of your rights and leaving Leonard to his fate. Think it over, Alice. Judge Swinburne and I will be in my office over the weekend working. I'll plan to be here Monday morning unless I hear from you." He then leaned toward her so that he could speak close to her ear. "Alice, I must do this. They're painting you as the prototype of the black seducing whore. Without our strong resistance, the jury may choose to believe it."

He gestured with his head at the jury box. She turned, and they both saw the deputies escorting the twelve men out. Several gazed at her with grim interest but turned away when they saw she was watching them.

<h1 style="text-align:center">CHAPTER EIGHTEEN</h1>

I suggested that Alice could use a Saturday night out of town, away from Westchester County, away from the trial, and surely away from home with the police controlling the crowds outside. The Weingolds were in Europe, so Bob was free. And Roberta loved being looked after by her grandparents because they spoiled her in any way they could.

Alice resisted us at first. "Em, somebody'll recognize me. Depending on who it is, I'll be on the receiving end of insults—or that jumpy gawking that people do when they get close to someone in the papers."

"Alice," I said. "Sheryl's. The Jazz Kings. Good booze. You want to go."

She hesitated, then, "Yeah, a lot!"

Bob laughed. "I'll call a friend from my committee who runs the place to save us a table. And how'd you like to see what the NAACP is all about?"

"Just so long as Judge Mills doesn't show up."

"Fat chance of that!"

The crowd outside the house thinned out over the weekend, both the press and the public. Bob conspired with Sergeant Kelly; Alice and I created a disguise. Putting her hair up under a tight-fitting cloche and wearing a pair of my dark glasses made an effective cover. She dressed down in slacks and an overcoat, the collar of which, along with a muffler, could conceal most of her face if need be. When we went out to Bob's car, I yelled to the press people that we were only going over to my apartment for dinner. When we drove away, a New Rochelle police car pulled out and blocked Pelham Road in case anyone tried to follow us.

Alice remembered Sheryl's from a night she and Len had gone to a half a dozen Harlem clubs, one after the other, drinking champagne and dancing to the jazz. The nightclub brought musicians directly up from New Orleans and had been Len's favorite. I offered that maybe it would be better to go to a new place that had no memories weighing it down. But the music won out, and we were excited, agreeing from the start that we would not talk about the trial, no matter what.

Even so, on the drive into Manhattan, Alice said all of a sudden from the backseat, "I never dream of Len. Ever. Instead, it's Judge Mills, Jacobs, and Rhinelanders I've never even met. Worst of all, they're not nightmares, so they don't wake me up. We all have tea on cliffs!"

"Oh boy," Bob said. "I'm not surprised you leave Len out of that."

"Oh, no. Len sits there in my consciousness, as he does in the witness box, crammed in and bent over, saying nothing... Bob, you mentioned this before.

What's wrong with him that's causing all the sweating?"

"I'm no doctor, so I don't know. But it could be some drug he's taking for whatever reason."

"I wonder," I said, "if Mr. Davis could ask about it in court."

We were all quiet for a time until Alice asked, "What's he thinking? Is he tired of me and wanting the marriage over with? Or is he still hoping, hoping like me, that somehow we'll find a way to be together again?"

"I believe we're edging close to tonight's forbidden subject," Bob said. "Anything else on your mind, Alice?"

We were going over the bridge into Manhattan. "Okay, sure. How's this? Am I black? If so, fine! I'll be black. Did marrying Leonard Rhinelander make me black? And if I hadn't married him, would I still be white? What's driving me even more insane is that I haven't changed at all, but that everybody else gets to change me."

"Sounds like a perfect time to introduce you to the NAACP!" Bob laughed. He drove us way downtown on unfamiliar streets, and soon I was lost. "You sure you know where you're going?" Alice said.

"You have to have faith, Alice. Here we are. I'll let you two off at the front and park. Whoops, there's a place."

"Where are we?" she asked. "What are we seeing?"

Bob held the doors for us as we got out and then locked the car. "This is a big meeting hall called Cooper Union. We're going to a speech arranged by the NAACP —National Association for the Advancement of Colored People—an organization that does just what the title says. And we're late."

As they hurried along the sidewalk, Alice said, "This doesn't sound like you, Bob. You're always so careful about... Well, all this."

He glanced at her, smiling at the implication. "I'm a Negro living in white America, working in a white family's house. All of us know our roles. I know exactly what my place is and how lucky I am to have employers like the Weingolds. But when Roberta came, it changed things."

Alice was hurrying to keep up with us. "How do you mean?"

I took her hand to pull her along. "Roberta made us consider her future more than ours; we have to find ways to deal with what we know is out there and what she'll have to face. This is a good group to start with. You'll see."

As we entered the lobby of the great hall, we heard a large crowd's laughter give way to shouts and applause. Once inside the auditorium, we looked for seats but ended up standing against the wall with many others. The place was packed tight with colored people of all ages. A good-looking man—balding with a careful mustache and goatee—stood at a lectern on the stage in the middle of his speech, holding up a piece of newspaper. A sign on the lectern identified him as "Dr. W.E.B. DuBois."

"...And here's something else we found in our continuing search for what's honest and true about race in America." He had a great voice that easily filled the auditorium. "A friend sent us an editorial printed just last week in the Newport News, Virginia, *Daily Press*."

I watched Alice. She was surprised by the loud response of the audience as it shouted for the news. We noticed everyone in the audience was holding the same magazine, using it as a fan, or to wave it when they yelled agreement to something Dubois said.

"You won't be able to believe the problem the white people, the ofays down there in Newport News, are trying to solve! Listen to what it says: 'The Anglo-Saxon race has no moral right to amalgamate'—To amalgamate! How do you like that euphemism?'—to amalgamate with any of the colored races, for in so doing, the Anglo-Saxon race would destroy itself. We would prefer that every white child in America be sterilized...'" A huge roar went up. He held up the newspaper. "Oh yes: '... sterilized' is what this Virginia paper suggests, '... every white child in America be sterilized, and the Anglo-Saxon race be left to perish, in its purity!'" The audience was on its feet, laughing and yelling, waving the magazine—we could see it was titled "CRISIS"—held up and moving like a choppy ocean over them.

"Don't you love that phrase, 'in its purity?'" Dubois was enjoying himself. "How noble that is! Can't you see all those Anglo-Saxon ofays of Virginia 'in their purity' leaning off their verandas—along with the two million mulattoes *of the white South's own creation*!" The cheers resounded off the wall behind them. Bob and I joined in.

"Let's respond, shall we? Dear *Daily Press* of Newport News, Virginia, your rodomontade does make us laugh out loud. Please tell us this: Who will be the first brave Anglo-Saxon to volunteer his little white boy to be sterilized? Which white man will proudly step forward, holding his little boy's hand, ready to make the sacrifice as Abraham was prepared at God's command to sacrifice Isaac? What white man in Newport News is ready to make the sacrifice? Of course! We're sure that, in his purity, it'll be your white editorial writer!" During the laughter, Dubois became deadly serious. "And answer us this Newport News *Daily Press*: In all of human history, who has ever compelled a white person 'to amalgamate'—or in simpler language, 'to couple with'—who has ever forced any white man to join with someone he doesn't want to join with? And then tell us, and tell yourselves, of the millions of black folks upon whom the white man has so violently and viciously forced himself!"

As the crowd's cheers filled the hall, Alice spoke into my ear, "I wonder if our marriage will fit into that history." We heard Dr. Dubois mention the law.

"... and daily, the Negro is coming more and more to look upon law and justice, not as protecting safeguards on which most white citizens can depend, but as sources of humiliation and oppression that every black citizen must fear. In America, laws are made— and enforced— by white men who have little interest in, and knowledge of, black people. Laws are executed by white men who have absolutely no motive for treating black people with courtesy or respect. I leave you with this: I've said it a hundred times. If white America does not eradicate such ignorant behavior, then that ignorance will destroy these United States! Onward, my friends, to find solutions! Ever onward. Goodnight."

When the cheering subsided, we moved along with the crowd. Outside, Bob and I said nothing, waiting for Alice to respond. When we reached the Model T, Alice said, "Who is that man?"

"Dr. DuBois?" Bob said. "He helped found the organization, edits the *CRISIS* magazine you saw everywhere, and wrote one of the great books about being black in America."

"What's he a doctor of?"

"Philosophy. He's the first black man to get a Ph.D. from Harvard."

We got in the car, and Bob turned it around and headed north. "What'd you think?" he asked Alice.

She didn't answer right away. "I don't even know if I'm black or white or what. He's talking about changing the world, and I'm just trying to save a marriage. But my God, so much truth! Black or white, I've got so much to learn!"

"That's fine," I said. "We just wanted you to see what the future can be."

Alice sat back. "I hope it's a good one for Roberta. But I can't imagine all that future. I have to force myself to think even one day ahead."

"Well, that includes tonight," Bob said, "so let's think about scotch and jazz."

Inside Sheryl's, the jazz was loud, the air was thick, and the place was packed with colored people having a good time, drinking and dancing. Alice and I followed the wing-tipped, tight-suited, conked, and brilliantined maître-d to a small table near the back wall that Bob had requested from his friend. Alice kept a hand to her face, pretending to wave off the tobacco smoke. She and I sat down, and after parking the car, Bob joined us. He ordered a bottle of scotch, and when it arrived, we were assured it was the real McCoy. For a time, we drank and listened, the music and whiskey being so fine that it edged out the rest of the world's cares, or at least Bob and I thought so. He was about to ask Alice if she wanted to get out on the floor and dance when she reached across the table to take hold of both our hands.

She didn't say anything, but then she looked at us with an expression of pure purpose.

"I've decided some things. You two have to know about them," Alice said.

Bob and I looked at each other, and I said, "You know we'll help anyway we can."

"The other night, when I went off by myself," she said, and went quiet for a moment, looking at the band. "I drove over to the beach where Len and I had walked and talked on our first day. It was 'our place.' By then, I'd decided that the most dramatic and meaningful thing I could do, even the bravest thing, something that would shock the papers and turn everyone against the Rhinelanders, was for me to walk into the water and drown myself. I sat there in Len's car for a long time, went through the memories, then—not making the decision, that was done, but imagining what'd happen afterward—the scenes, the results, the surprise, the grief and regret that I thought everyone would feel. Me being such a symbol, as everyone says, how my suicide would maybe change the whole understanding about race. I was really thinking big! After I'd had a wonderful time with that, I carried my shoes down to the water and let my overcoat fall in the sand. Then I walked in, got up to my knees... Goddamn, it was cold!" She started laughing. "There was no way in hell I was going to die in that cold water."

We weren't quite ready to laugh. Bob gave her his other hand. "You can't depend on people seeing the drama the same way you do."

"Alice, don't you *ever* do that." I was angry.

"Don't worry. The main problem I had was that I could never do something that big without talking to you first, Em."

Bob sat back and took a drink. "I hope you put your coat back on."

"I did, went back to the car, turned the heater on, and for whatever reason, started thinking about one of those crazy guys who knows absolutely for sure that he's Napoleon. No doubts at all because he's been Napoleon all his life. Of course, he isn't, and all of a sudden, the rest of the world knows that. So everyone tells him he has to be someone else. So tell me this: What's the guy supposed to do, knowing for sure who he is? Go along with what others tell him, right? Pretend he isn't Napoleon, right? Be whoever everyone says he is and wants him to be. Or should he forget whoever the world wants him to be, and go right on getting ready for Waterloo?" She laughed at herself, taking her hands from theirs and having some more to drink.

"Stay Napoleon," I said with conviction. "Let the world go to hell."

"Sure," Bob said, "but there's nothing wrong with doing both, staying Napoleon but being Rudolph Valentino."

Alice looked at him. "That isn't allowed, Bob. Against the rules."

"Oh hell, Alice, you're being forced to break so many rules, you get to make a few of your own. You know who you are. That's the basic truth here. All of a sudden, a lot of people insist you're something else, but for their needs, not yours. You get to be whoever you want."

"I don't think I can do that anymore," Alice said, and took another drink.

"I don't either," I said.

"I'm off-balance," Alice said. "I'm falling through a mirror, backward, upside down, and I have to see all the way back to when I was born. Hard to go back that far, hard to change my spots as I go along." She looked at her sister. "And speaking of spots, Em... our 'blemishes.' Remember when I was about ten? You told me, 'Sister, they aren't going away, even with Dixie Cream Skin Bleach.'" We laughed, but then Alice asked, "Did you tell Mr. Davis about them?"

Surprised, I reached across the table and took Alice's hand again. "I told him something when he first interviewed me. Didn't you?"

"Beg the ladies' pardon," Bob said, "but weren't we going to avoid this subject?"

"We were, dear," I said, "until it became of interest to us, and it just did."

"Oouwee," Bob said, "I know my place. I'll just step up to the bar and listen to that soprano sax."

When Bob had left, Alice said, "What'd you tell Mr. Davis?"

"I hardly remember; it didn't seem important in the middle of everything else he was asking. He told me what Grace had said about our 'discoloring.' Mr. Davis kind of slipped that in, apologizing very politely, but confirming it with me. We'd been talking about how Mum's genes might have mixed with Daa's genes, and vice versa. I said that's what genes did, and described the thing on my back, down on my ankles, then yours."

"I wish he'd told me."

"I saw it on the question list he gave us, so I thought he had." Alice nodded. "Does that mean he thinks of us as colored?"

"I really don't think he cares," I replied. "It's all about winning the case with him, and if such information might be useful. And honestly, Alice, I don't care. If people are coming after me, it's because of my marrying Bob. My 'blemishes' won't make much difference in that tangle."

"I don't think Len ever even noticed. And if he did, it didn't matter."

"Well, you use enough powder on them sometimes to fog out Boston!" She smiled as she reached over to slug me. "Anyway," I said, "your blemishes aren't as dark as mine..." then I whispered, "...except maybe your nipples!"

"You shut your mouth, you terrible girl... I just wonder why Mr. Davis never asked me about it," Alice said. "I wonder why he asked Grace."

"She probably said you had Scotch plaid on your butt."

Alice let loose with a laugh that Bob heard over at the bar, so he wandered back to the table. Content to see us enjoying ourselves, he sipped his drink and listened to the soprano sax doing things that could hardly be believed.

"Lord, how wonderful to laugh," Alice said. "Thought I'd forgotten how."

"You said you decided that you want us to know some things," I said.

She sipped at her drink and said, "I sat in the car that night and started to figure some things out, make some decisions. I don't know what makes lawyers tick, but I came to realize, finally, that Mr. Davis is some driven automatic force, that he'll do whatever it's going to take to win this case, almost like he can't help himself. Well, fine. I think beating the Rhinelanders in this trial will hurt them, wound them, I don't know exactly how, but a lot more than just their pride and bad publicity, something deeper. I want to do that. I want to damage them badly. I'm going to stop interfering with Mr. Davis's methods and go along wherever he takes me, whatever hurt it might cause Len and me. I want you to know that and why."

"I heard you came close to firing him yesterday," I said.

"What I have to do in the trial was still blurred. Now, it's clear. And as a matter of fact, what I heard and saw downtown tonight makes it clearer. I want that man's book."

I nodded in agreement. "We have it at home. Alice, this'll be over. You'll come out the other side of it because of how strong you are, which I never knew until all this started. You stay who you are and count your lucky stars you have Mr. Davis."

She nodded. "Bless you two for getting me out of the house, taking me down to that meeting, and bringing me here with you. Sometimes I forget there's the rest of the world."

"You'll be fine," Bob said. "No one's going through the kind of changes you're being forced to make. I sure wish we could do more than sit behind you in that courtroom."

"Listen, knowing you and the family are there is like being backed up by an army."

"I'm worried about ol' Len. Seems trapped up there, has no way to fight back."

I agreed. "Len's sure hurting."

Alice looked out into the dark. "That letter of his that's going to be read? I think it'll tear him apart."

"He knows what it says, doesn't he?" Bob said. "He'll be ready for it."

A commotion at the club's entrance announced the arrival of a group of young, formally dressed white couples. They came in loudly, greeting the proprietor, some hugging the musicians whom they seemed to know, some going to the bar and ordering champagne.

We watched them. I saw Alice's sadness. "Once, that was Len and me."

Bob turned to her. "It's already different, isn't it?"

"What do you mean, now that I'm black?" She looked back at the arrivals. "Who the hell do those 'ofays' think they are, coming in here slumming with the colored folk?" She drank, then gazed at us. "What if I just took the Rhinelander money and ended the trial. Could that be us again?"

Bob shook his head. "I'd say it's too late. You've come too far."

"Don't you dare stop this trial!" I spoke with some heat. "You're going to win it."

She stared at me, then said, "And after my lawyer, with my blessing, cuts Len to bits, then what?"

It was another question I couldn't answer. She was asking a lot of those.

The three of us gave up, took a drink and listened to the perfect music.

CHAPTER NINETEEN

Everyone in the courtroom looked better after the weekend, even the jury. I thought Alice looked worse. Anxiety didn't take days off. What was going to happen that day had prevented sleep.

"Mr. Davis, do you intend to read, or have read, the letter you gave to Mr. Rhinelander on Friday?" Judge Morschauser queried after the court was called into session.

"I will read it, Your Honor," Davis said.

The press and public reacted. We'd all seen the headlines of the newspapers that young boys had been hawking outside the courthouse to the crowd who could not get in.

"SECRET LETTER TO BE READ."

"LOVE LETTER OR FILTH?"

"SEDUCTION BY MAIL?"

Alice told me she'd tortured herself over the rest of the weekend with the idea that Len could stop the trial, just as she could. He could order his attorneys to withdraw the suit. Mr. Davis had told her Len could but suggested it certainly would break whatever agreement he had with his father. Then she told me that she was bone-deep angry at the trial going on, at her life being fed out to the world. But not for another second did she consider ending the court case herself.

Two quick cracks of the gavel returned the courtroom to silence. "I'm going to ask every woman to leave the courtroom," Judge Morschauser said. "I'm familiar with the contents of this letter, and if I were a woman, I would not wish to hear it. There will be a brief recess to allow all females to exit, including the defendant and the female members of her family."

He gaveled the recess and watched as the bailiff and other officers herded us out. I didn't see it, but Alice turned for a glance at Leonard and was startled to see he was watching her leave. In the crowded aisle, she held up her hands, her face questioning. He responded with a quick gesture with his hand as if holding a needle for injection and pushing it into his arm. He watched to see if she understood, just as Jacobs saw him. The lawyer turned to see Alice before she turned away and followed the rest of us. Outside, she told me about it as I was fuming about the absurdity of us being excluded. What did Judge Morschauser think would happen? That we tender flowers would have a mass faint?

Alice and I went back to Sergeant Kelly's Irish bar to wait. She was very distraught and wanted to tell Mr. Davis about Len's gesture. I agreed, and she wondered if he could ask Judge Morschauser somehow if Len was ill and how he was being treated. His sweating continued; his ambling walk often gave way to trouble balancing. If he was being given drugs, it was another control that his lawyers and family could exert over him.

The distraction helped us get through waiting to hear what had happened in court during our chaste protection from it. We were informed of every detail of what happened later from the newspapers:

During our female evacuation, a male journalist had approached the bench, gesturing toward the few women at the press table, including Barbara Reynolds. Judge Morschauser nodded, assenting to their remaining. He then gaveled for order. "Mr. Davis, please continue your cross-examination."

"Mr. Rhinelander," Davis said, approaching Leonard in the witness box, "last Friday, you told the jury that your relations with Alice Jones were always natural, did you not?"

"Yes," he said, gripping the arms of his chair.

Davis held the letter up before the jury. "This letter, previously entered, is dated June 6, 1922, written by Leonard Rhinelander from San Francisco.

> *It makes me feel so happy, darling, when I hear from you, especially when you write about how I used to touch you, not letting yourself resist me crawling all over you and lying on your stomach. Do you ever think about how I asked you to make me passionate with your lips and tongue, then how I used to put my head between your legs and where I used to touch you with my lips and tongue? You loved to have me do that, didn't you? And you shouted, 'Oh, Len, Oh! Len!'*

"How's that? You asked me to write a letter to interest you, so I've tried my best. Have I made you imagine that I'm right next to you in bed? And what I would do again and again if I could?"

In the shocked all-male silence that followed, Davis walked back to the defense table and put his copy of the letter down. "Mr. Rhinelander," he said finally, "when you performed the act that you described in this letter, did you have any idea that it was an abnormal thing to do?"

"No, I didn't."

"Have you any suspicion about it now?"

"No."

"You would tell this jury that you think it's a perfectly natural thing to do?"

"As far as I know. We made love as we discovered it together."

"You mean that each of you had the same idea at exactly the same moment for you to put your head between her legs? Or did one of you have the idea first, and if so, was it you?"

"Objection!" Judge Mills said. "Leading my witness."

"Sustained."

"Mr. Rhinelander, when you made love to Alice, is it possible that you had some original ideas about it, as she did?"

"Objection," Judge Mills said again. "The plaintiff cannot speculate on the defendant's ideas. Let my distinguished colleague ask that of the defendant when she testifies."

"Sustained."

"All right," Davis said. "Mr. Rhinelander, during your courtship of Alice Jones before you were married to her, when you made love to her, did you ever do anything of your own choosing, your own instinctual creation?"

"I'm sure I did."

"And these actions you say that you chose to do on your own, with no instructions from your partner, were perfectly natural ones?"

"Yes."

"So natural that you could write about it in letters to someone you loved?"

"I did love her!" Leonard said. "I had no other way to express that, except in those letters. Good Christ, they weren't intended for public proclamation!"

Davis paused to allow Leonard to calm down and untangle himself in the witness box. "Did Alice express her love for you in such vivid terms in her letters?"

"I can't remember exactly."

"I did not read anything similar in the hundred or so letters she wrote to you that Judge Mills has so meticulously entered and read ad nauseam as evidence. Would you agree, Mr. Rhinelander, that the writings in this letter of yours to her are a high grade of sophisticated smut?"

"It might appear so to others."

"Indeed, it might. Yet you were willing to marry the girl who allowed you to do these things to her in the Marie Antoinette Hotel, but you are unwilling to stay married to that same girl, not because of anything you observed, but because you've been told she had a few drops of colored blood? What kind of reasoning is that?"

"Oh God, you..." Leonard stopped himself and looked directly at Judge Mills sitting at the plaintiff's table. "As to color, I drew the line." Then he seemed to collapse in his chair, his head bowed down.

Davis followed Leonard's look, took a few steps toward Mills and pondered. Then he turned back and said, "On which side of this line was your love for Alice Jones? On which side was your sex with her, waiting more than two years of cruel separation for her? On which side was your marrying her and living and planning a home with her, even after the press of the world informed you that she had a few drops of black blood from her heritage?"

"As to color, I drew the line," Leonard repeated, looking at the floor.

"Yes, you said that, Mr. Rhinelander. And as I'm sure we all remember, Judge Mills used that exact phrase in his opening to the jury. It must be an oft-repeated phrase, bantered about between the two of you. But I'm very curious about that line you drew, and when you drew it. It couldn't have been a very straight line, this line of color, considering you knew her father, spent time with her brother-in-law, knew Alice herself intimately, all of that for years before you married her. When did you start drawing this astoundingly circuitous line?"

Len again looked at Judge Mills, then struggled to say, "It's a figure of speech."

Davis, too, looked back at Mills, then seemed to study the jury. He turned abruptly to Judge Morschauser. "Your Honor, I'm done with the witness for the moment. I request a recess until tomorrow in order to confer with my client, as she has been absent from this recent, most telling testimony."

When someone came into the Irish bar and told us the court was finished for the day, we hurried back to find most of the crowd gone and Daa waiting at the top of the courthouse steps. He came down to greet us. "Mr. Davis and Judge Swinburne said that things have changed, and they have homework to do. They'll call us tonight to explain."

That made for a silent dinner, each one of us developing a theory of what had "changed." Daa told us of what had happened after we "girls" had been ushered out of the courtroom, and I heard nothing that indicated any great "change." I called Bob to tell him I was staying over, and then we waited. At eleven, Mum and Daa went up to bed. I waited with Alice for another twenty minutes and said, "We should get to sleep too."

I was three steps up the stairs, and the phone rang. Alice picked it up and said, "Hello," and listened. I heard Mum and Daa start down the stairs, and we all went back down to the living room. Alice said, "Thank you, sir," and hung up. "They're coming over."

"Now?" Daa looked alarmed by what that meant.

"Oh, oh, I'll make coffee." Mum started for the kitchen. "Will they want something to eat?"

"Mum, don't do anything. It won't be social."

Just before midnight, we watched from behind the living room drapes as a car pulled up behind one of the New Rochelle police cars. Two officers got out to check on what this arrival might mean, whether more trouble with either the press or the KKK. When Lee Davis and Sam Swinburne got out, they didn't need to identify themselves. The lawyers were escorted up the walkway. Davis knocked, and Daa opened the door. "Thanks for calling a warning."

"Sorry we had to wake you."

"We're ready for you." Daa ushered them in.

Inside, Alice, Mum and I stood motionless in bathrobes by the dining room table. As the lawyers took off their hats, mufflers and coats, Mr. Davis seemed preoccupied. "I regret we couldn't meet when the recess was called. Sam and I had a great deal of work to do, which we've come to tell you about. Please, may we all sit at the table?"

"Is something wrong?" Alice asked.

"No more than usual," he said. "We came tonight because we have to re-focus our strategy and develop an ultimate defense."

Daa offered one. "I have a baseball bat."

"I'll keep that in mind." Davis looked straight at Alice when everyone was seated. "To summarize, we've concluded that no matter what we do, our jury of white men can still easily believe that you were passing as white in order to marry Leonard Rhinelander, a very wealthy boy. At the same time, we believe that your husband's deep love for you is becoming his attorneys' biggest dilemma in winning this case."

Alice nodded. "It's my biggest dilemma, too."

"I'm sure. We know, and they know, that millions of Rhinelander dollars are potentially at stake through your dower rights. For reasons we may only hope, Leonard is allowing himself to be the family puppet. What I don't think his lawyers or his father anticipated is that Leonard would try to cut his puppet strings in court."

Mum was delighted. "That makes good sense to me." She turned to Mr. Davis. "To this day, we know that dear boy loves our Alice."

"Do we?" Alice surprised us with that. Her lawyers overlooked it.

Davis continued. "I've spent a lot of time cross-examining Leonard, getting him to a point of admitting that he knew you had mixed blood, or that it didn't matter to him. But I've come to believe that he has a misguided conflict of purpose. After Judge Swinburne and I went over our notes this evening, it's clear to both of us that Leonard is saying what he must say, but fighting his own counsel to protect you, Alice."

"'Protect?'" Mum interrupted again. Mr. Davis listened tolerantly. "What that nasty little man is saying is more like slow torture."

The lawyer nodded kindly. "I say, 'misguided,' because I fear Leonard is under the impression that if he can only get through the trial, doing whatever he has agreed to do and say, that you and he will be able to return to your married life as it was before, win or lose in court."

"Mr. Davis, win or lose, I don't care either!" Alice jabbed the table with her forefinger for emphasis. I'd never seen her do that. "I want it over so we can see what'll happen."

Davis nodded. "We believe he must give answers that he's been coached to say. He seems under enormous pressure to say these things out of concern for what his father will do to him—and to you. Therefore, I've become convinced that he'll never admit in court that he knew you had colored blood before he married you. The jury knows none of this. I can ask Leonard 'til the cows come home how he could possibly not know. But he has implied not knowing by saying that when he found out you were a mulatto, everything changed for him. He 'drew the line.' Our white jury, seeing you as a white woman every day, could easily believe that. I'm sorry to say, I already believe they do. We therefore have to prove beyond doubt to our all-white male jury that he did know, or should have known that you were of mixed blood."

"Alice," Sam Swinburne added, "as long as Leonard doesn't admit knowing you had colored blood before the marriage, the jury may very well make the easier choice to believe him."

"How could they?" Alice was trying hard to control her temper. "How could they doubt he knew everything there was to know, after what they've heard, what we've admitted, after what Len himself has said? My God, that jury knows everything!"

"No, they don't." Mr. Davis was intense and calm at the same time. "They don't know what being colored is, or more to the point, what having some fraction of mixed blood might look like—unless it's clearly visible. And in your case, it's not. But they do know what a white woman looks like. Every one of those white members of the jury has a white wife. When they look over and see you at the defense table, even though we've admitted you have colored blood, even though Leonard's lawyers have done everything they can to make you black, the jurors see a white woman—as you are, as you've been 'seen' all your life."

"I can't change that!"

"No, you can't. But from what they've heard so far, you may be a seeming white woman who might have lied. We, and those jurors, live in today's racist nation. We therefore must prove beyond doubt to that very white jury that the very white Leonard Rhinelander had to know that you had mixed blood before he married you, even if he denies it in court."

I think the whole Jones family could have shouted in unison, "HOW?"

Daa only grumbled, "Are you coming round to telling us it's hopeless?"

"Mr. Jones, you know me better than that."

"I was hoping I did, sir."

Alice revealed a certain bitterness for the first time. "Mr. Davis always has something up his sleeve."

"Mr. Davis." Mum took on her regal air. "I can't imagine that you and dear Sam came over here at midnight to tell us this. What are you going to do?"

"Mrs. Jones, your perception is noted and appreciated. Alice, we had to get to this point in the trial before we could see clearly what we had to do. Here's our plan: I'll finish cross-examining Leonard—hard, in hopes of getting an admission that he knew you had mixed blood before marriage. If any doubt remains, then I'll call a few witnesses to try to make the case. But then..." He folded his hands on the table. "Alice, if you consent to our strategy here tonight, you'll prove to the jury beyond any doubt that Leonard Rhinelander must have known you were to some degree colored. And you'll do it without ever having to say a single word in court."

We all stared at Davis in confusion and disbelief, then we glanced at each other for some kind of reassurance. Alice reached for my hand. "You'd better tell us what we're in for." But Judge Swinburne raised his hand to speak, and Mr. Davis nodded. "Alice, I've known your family for a long time, as you know, and regard your parents with the greatest respect. I've grown to respect you as much during this trial. What Lee and I are about to suggest, we do only because of that respect. Our greatest hope is that you'll trust us in this."

"Just tell me what it is."

Judge Swinburne looked at Mr. Davis, who did not hesitate, "We must let the jury see the decisive evidence, Alice, all of which Leonard saw before he married you. I want to present to the jury the visual proof of parts of your skin coloring, as described to me by your sisters, which the jury as yet haven't seen, those parts of your body that your clothing always covers, those parts with which Leonard was obviously familiar before he married you. Those parts that, better than any witness or any other evidence, clearly indicate a genetic mix of blood."

No one said a word. Davis watched Alice, who was still holding my hand as if it were a lifeline. She struggled to speak. "The trial's over. You're both unretained, relieved, and fired! Whatever the word is!" Her voice rose with her fury as she let go of me and gathered her bathrobe around her. "Tell the court anything you want. If you have to have me undress in front of those twelve men to win this case, if all this time and effort only brings you to needing me naked, what in hell does the court matter? Is this how the law works? If I take off my clothes like a stripper, is that what I have to do to get justice?"

"How do you two dare suggest such a thing?" Daa rose from the table. "Trust you, you say? My God, Sam! No, gentlemen, no! I want you both right out of the house!"

Swinburne tried to answer. "George, wait to hear how it'd be done. She won't be totally…"

"It won't be done, Sam!" Daa leaned across the table. "Didn't you hear me?"

"We did, Mr. Jones!" Without moving, Davis met our father's rage with fierce intensity. "And I will *not* leave until you hear me out! I know full well what I'm suggesting, how grotesque and hateful it is. But whether I'm Alice's attorney any more or not, she'll benefit by understanding what I have to say."

"No!" Alice pushed back her chair and stood. "I've heard you and heard you for a year, everything you've said, what everyone has said, and what do I have left? A little self-respect—that you'd have me peel off with my underclothes! Do you think about what the newspapers would do with this? What my family and I would have to live with?"

"Alice! Daa!" I didn't shout, but I was loud enough to stop the argument. "Let the man speak! He deserves that. Remember what he's done for us."

My dear father and the daughter he would die to protect stared at each other for a moment. Then Alice turned back for her chair and sat to face Mr. Davis. Daa remained standing.

Having been given a cue, Mr. Davis took a moment to time a response. "As you remember, I've tried a good many criminal cases, often involving murder. Not once did a trial go as we expected. Not once did we ever have all the evidence that would eventually convict. We'd discover what was needed only during the trial."

"You need my 'blemishes', that my sisters told you about in confidence during their interviews with you—that you never said anything to me about, until right now."

"Oh, good God!" Daa was disgusted.

"Yes, I need them. Those indications on your skin are the most powerful verification we have that Leonard knew before your marriage that you have mixed blood. And the jury hasn't seen them. Once seen, you will win the case. It will prove that Leonard must have, or should have, realized you were of mixed blood."

"I didn't 'realize' it!" Alice blurted. "It was never a conscious fact to me! And I had those blemishes all my life! Why would Len know what they were?"

Davis became deadly calm and again, forcefully intense. He let Alice's emotion pass, then spoke with profound empathy. "Alice, you've been accepted from the beginning of your life—in your home and out of it—as being white. To you and to anyone who asked, your father was Spanish, West Indian or whatever, loved and respected as such. Leonard had no such upbringing. He knew enough upon seeing your father to realize you were not pure white, particularly when he saw you…”

“Naked,” Alice interjected without bitterness, “like you want me to be in front of those twelve men.”

“You won’t be totally exposed, only those parts of your body—your lower back, your arms, the back of your legs…”

“And my breasts?” she challenged. “You know about those?”

“Yes.” Mr. Davis responded without apology.

Alice stared at him, then shook her head in amazement. “Why would I do this?” She grabbed at her upper arm, then a breast. “Do I let you take away any idea of my being a human being for the sake of showing pieces of my skin?”

“If you want success in this case.”

“*Your* success, Mr. Davis! Not mine. In that courtroom, I’m black, and you’re part of it, and the law is not on my side.”

“That’s not true, Alice.” Surprisingly, Judge Swinburne interrupted. “It’s also unfair. If the law ever gets on anyone’s side, it’s the end of America. No, it’s what we’re able to make of the law, move it forward or move it backward, the struggle that goes on in every trial in every courthouse in the land. We’re part of that. We’re not making you black. You haven’t changed, Alice. You’re stronger and finer than ever. But maybe someone in the courthouse has changed, from the presiding judge to the old man in the back row. That’s what the law does. It often fails to change anything and sometimes makes things worse. That’s because human beings created it, struggle with it, break it, … but sometimes we make it shine.”

Alice’s tears began to fall. “What should I do, Judge?”

Judge Swinburne checked with Mr. Davis before continuing. “For your sake, for your family’s sake, you’ve got to think beyond this trial. What we suggest is one minute of gross embarrassment against the rest of your life. If the Rhinelanders win this annulment, you’ll have nothing to defend yourself against them—and win or lose, don’t think they’ll walk away after the trial. They have enormous power. You’ll have no financial standing, no reputation, and a future facing an unforgiving public.”

“I’ll have Len.” I heard the doubt in her voice.

So did Mr. Davis. “Are you sure? Alice, as we know, his father is capable of anything. I so hope that Leonard’s return to you is possible. But if it is to be, he will need you to be his wife. I would add that it will be useful to you, no matter what happens, that he is your husband.”

Alice stared back at him, then turned to me. I barely nodded. She looked down.

"What else?"

Mr. Davis indicated that Judge Swinburne speak again. "For what the Rhinelanders have caused you, you're entitled to more than a ruined life. Don't think we don't know what we're asking. Don't think we don't hate to ask it."

As Mum looked at Daa, hoping for solace, Alice remained seated. Then she put her hands flat on the table, turning to her parents. "Mum, Daa, I have to go to bed. I'm too angry and too tired to decide anything. Em, please come up with me."

She looked back at Sam Swinburne, then at Lee Davis. "If you two still want to go on with this, that's up to you. But don't ever expect me to be grateful. I'm going to lose everything I was trying to save, and probably a lot more." She stood and went to the stairs. Turning back, she looked from one attorney to the other. "If I do this, what will Len think of me? I hate this trial! I hate whatever the law's supposed to be, and at the moment I hate myself."

As she disappeared up the stairs, Mr. Davis stood up. "Goodnight, Mr. and Mrs. Jones. And Mrs. Brooks, thank you for being here." Swinburne followed him to the door as they put on their coats. "I hope somehow you can believe our intense regret but respect our determination."

Mum was near tears herself but wouldn't give in to them. "We do, Mr. Davis."

Daa took her arm. "Maybe I will if I can see beyond what it's doing to my daughter."

Mr. Davis stood very still. "Mr. Jones, I've no doubt whatsoever that she'll survive this. She's as strong as anyone I've ever defended or prosecuted. She's remarkable, sir. No matter what she decides to do, you may be very proud of her, as I am to represent her."

"I'm very proud of her, sir, you can be sure of that."

Mr. Davis nodded. "Mrs. Jones, in a day or two, will you please bring a long coat for Alice in a valise to court? Just in case she decides. Goodnight."

When I reached her room, Alice was watching from the window as Mr. Davis and Judge Swinburne spoke to the policemen and drove away. She turned to me and said, "Close the door." I did. She went on. "We have to talk. I'm not tired at all. I'm angry, white-hot angry because I'm trapped."

I sat on her bed. "How?"

"I can't talk to Mr. Davis about this. But I know he's right, and I hate it."

"Alice, I'll stay as long as you want. Take it slow, and tell me what you mean."

She became icily calm, slowly pacing around her room in the small circle that the space allowed. "Say I have the choice now, to lose the case or win it. Okay. And say my only purpose is for Len and me to end up together. Okay. So, if I don't do what Mr. Davis says, that white jury won't believe that Len knew I was black before we got married because he implied he changed his mind after he found out I was. Whether Len cared or not doesn't even matter! So it's fraud, and we lose the case. Agreed?"

"For the sake of the argument, agreed. But if you lose, it'll be over, the Rhinelanders won't be threatened by your dower rights or any other. You and Len can..." Alice was shaking her head, so I stopped.

"Len's father, that 'pillar-of-society-Mr.-Philip-Rhinelander,' as they call him, has proven what he can do. He's proved it twice! Em, he's a killer, and he's been shamed, publicly shamed. In his strict, unreal world, shame means gashes have been cut in reputation that leave deep scars. He knows as long as Len and I are alive, we'll fight to be together, maybe even marry again, and what if we have a child?" She stopped pacing and looked at me. "That possibility will drive his father to destroy him, to addict him, to commit him, and then Philip Rhinelander will come after my family and me."

That included me, and she wanted me to know it. I nodded that I got it and that I agreed with her analysis of Mr. Rhinelander. I said, "But you have another choice: win the case."

"Yeah," she said, and sat on the floor, leaning back against my legs. "I show myself to the jury, causing a sensation that goes all over the world. Len, who's spent the last two years fighting his family to protect me from them, watches me having to shame myself to a point of disgrace that his father could only dream of—and all because of Len! He couldn't stand that. He wouldn't ever be able to..."

She didn't finish and didn't need to. I slid down to the floor next to her and put my arms around her. She accepted the gesture, but her rigidity remained. I said, "Mr. Davis said at the beginning that juries can't be predicted."

"He's pretty sure of this one now."

"Seems to be. So maybe you should think of what other benefits might come from the choices you have."

"'Benefits'? Good Lord. What benefits?"

"If you lose the case, you lose your power—to defend yourself and your family, to get what you deserve, to harass and do damage to the Rhinelanders. If you win the case and remain Mrs. Leonard Rhinelander, you'd keep all that... even if you lose Len, which, if hope is anything..."

"It isn't."

Slowly, I felt the tightness ebb out of her, and we held on to each other.

"You really have to stop being so smart."

"This isn't being smart. These are cries of love for my sister, who's facing the impossible choice."

She kissed me. "Thanks, Em. More than you know."

We sat on the floor holding each other, leaning up against the bed. "If I lose him, what'll I have?"

"Memories. A lot of good ones."

"Hard to remember. They're getting lost in the cesspool."

"So make notes."

She kissed me and stood up. "Get some sleep, Em. I want to do the diary."

CHAPTER TWENTY

The next day, the trial was delayed because the courthouse's heating system broke down in the night. When Mr. Davis woke the Joneses at eight to inform us, Alice had not slept at all. The unexpected reprieve sent her happily back to bed. I took the opportunity to have a brief conversation with Mr. Davis about the pantomime of injection that Leonard had displayed to Alice the previous day.

"Was she sure that Mr. Jacobs saw the exchange?" he asked.

"Alice believed he had. She was worried that Len would be punished somehow."

"Thank you, Mrs. Brooks. That's very interesting. Tell Alice I'll see what I can do in court."

The repair and reheating of the courtroom took until the afternoon. The crowd outside the courthouse waited in a gray cold. The press drew straws to see who would remain to alert their colleagues waiting in several coffee shops and bars, previously selected. The delay was hard on everyone, particularly the participants, although Alice relished the time. It even allowed her the luxury of a bath.

Arriving at her seat at the defendant's table refreshed, she nevertheless was no more comfortable with what her lawyers had presented the previous night. She barely greeted either of them as she sat down. She did not look over at Len, but I did. Something was wrong. His body seemed to have caved in on itself; his eyes were sunken and rimmed with gray. As usual, he was sweating profusely, using his handkerchief to wipe his face.

When Judge Morschauser finally gaveled the court into session, Mr. Davis wasted no time in rising. "Your Honor, might prosecuting counsel and I approach the bench?"

"Please." Judge Morschauser moved his chair so that he could more easily communicate over the dais. Mr. Davis started what turned out to be a spirited session of whispers among the three of them, shielded by their hands from the courtroom. Finally, some sort of agreement was reached, and the two lead attorneys returned to their respective tables.

Judge Morschauser gaveled to silence the conjecture running through the courtroom. "A concern has been expressed about the physical health of the claimant. Judge Mills wishes to make a statement for the record, to which Mr. Davis wishes to respond."

Judge Mills stood at his place, directing his comments to the jury. "Gentlemen, my client Mr. Rhinelander, has from his earliest years had any number of infirmities, as you have heard. One that has not reached public attention is a long-standing effect on his digestive system when stress has its way with him. On the insistence of the distinguished counsel for the defense, I now must place in the public record another sad struggle which my client faces and for which he has received the best medical attention available. I hope this allows an unnecessary and certainly embarrassing circumstance to be appropriately put aside." He sat down with a disdainful glance at Mr. Davis.

"Mr. Davis?" Judge Morschauser didn't look up from what he was writing.

Mr. Davis paused long enough to cause the judge to watch him. "Your Honor, my learned colleague goes on so mellifluously and yet manages to leave so much out. Succinctly: vomiting, for which 'the best medical attention' has prescribed a diet of white rice, Pepto-Bismol, and oh yes, laudanum. It is a tincture of opium. I've gained knowledge of it in previous criminal matters. I can tell the court it's a notoriously addictive drug, that if used over a period of time, can lead first to euphoria, then slowly to a pronounced languor, a breakdown of synaptic processes in the brain, and finally death. The good news is that in spite of these obvious life- and mind-fracturing dangers, it is regarded as a superior analgesic to Hormotone." He sat down. As the press and audience responded with gasps and some laughter, I glanced over at Judge Mills, who looked like he was chewing a nail but chose to say no more.

"Mr. Davis," Judge Morschauser said impatiently, "without indulging in further levity while considering the serious matter before us, please continue your cross-examination of the plaintiff."

"Your Honor, with great respect, my apologies," Mr. Davis said as he approached Len in the witness box. "Mr. Rhinelander, other than the Jones family, could you please tell us what experience you've had with colored people?"

In spite of his elegant evisceration of Judge Mills, I thought Mr. Davis was edgy, perhaps aggravated by the morning's delay, by the time lost, and probably by Alice's reaction last night. He'd said he was going to be hard on Leonard, to try to get him to admit that he had known about Alice's mixed blood.

"None," Leonard answered.

"None? You don't know any? Servants? When you traveled? Getting your shoes shined?"

Leonard thought a moment. "No, I literally don't know any other than Bob Brooks, who became a good friend. Our servants are British or Irish. When we travel, we're usually in sections of a ship or a private railcar where there are none."

"First class."

"Yes."

"But you do know what a colored person is?"

"Yes."

"Then, if you had no exposure to colored people at your level of society, when did you first discover what a colored person is?"

"When I was a child, I'd see them..."

"Where exactly?"

"On the street. As I got older, I heard about jazz and went to clubs."

"And as you grew up, did you become aware of any prejudice toward them?"

"It's everywhere."

"Your family? In school?"

"From them and school, yes, jokes mainly, insulting jokes about colored people's inferiority. Cruel jokes. But my family and the boys at school made jokes about me, too, about *my* inferiority. But I never knew a Negro."

"So, before you met Alice Jones, you had no prejudicial feelings about Negroes, one way or the other?"

Until then, I believed that Leonard answered Davis' questions about race with a certain interest. With the last question, he suddenly looked alarmed as he seemed to realize where the questions were leading. He sat up very straight in his chair and wiped his face. "We had certain standards..."

"Standards? Are those different than prejudices?"

Judge Mills was on his feet. "Your Honor, I object to the badgering nature of the defense's questioning."

"Badgering?" Davis offered mock surprise. "I thought my line of questioning revealed a quiet reserve, a genuine curiosity about how those of a certain social status can so completely insulate themselves with their luxuries from seeing, hearing about, or even discussing perhaps the most corrosive dilemma in American culture today."

"We know exactly what you're getting at." Mills had no sense of humor. "To that, I object!"

"But Your Honor, shouldn't I be allowed to get there before it is objected to?"

"Overruled, for the moment," Judge Morschauser directed patiently. "Mr. Davis, you may go where you are going."

"Mr. Rhinelander, you went to a prestigious private boarding school. Did you study the Civil War there?"

"Yes."

"So you do know about slavery, the Emancipation Proclamation?"

"And the three resulting constitutional amendments."

"How impressive. And do you keep up with current events in the newspapers, the goings on of the Ku Klux Klan, the NAACP, the race riots and lynchings that take place from time to time?"

"I've avoided newspapers for over a year. Before that, I read them, but not everything. I know what the Ku Klux Klan is from a movie I saw once. I've heard of lynchings, about race riots, but I've not heard about the NA... whatever it is."

"So is it fair to say, Mr. Rhinelander, that before you met Alice Jones, you had little knowledge of, or experience with colored people?"

"Yes."

"And even after getting to know Mr. Brooks and Alice's father, you had no particular intolerance against colored people?"

"No. And I didn't regard her father as colored."

"But you did notice that he was darker than, well, a Rhinelander might be."

"Yes."

"And yet after three years of knowing Alice and her family and marrying her, only weeks later, you brought this case to court, accusing Alice Jones of fraud. Why? For allowing herself to be thought of as white by you when she was actually black, because—as you and Judge Mills have repeatedly said—as to color, I drew the line.' Mr. Rhinelander, when exactly did you, on your own, draw that line? When did your sudden 'standard' about colored people rear its ugly head?"

"Objection," Judge Mills had been coiled for some time, and sprang up. "This is badgering, pure and simple."

Judge Morschauser thought a moment. "I sustain the objection, with the idea that Mr. Davis may go ahead at his point from a less hyperbolic angle."

"Thank you, Your Honor," Davis said. "There are indeed many points and many angles. Mr. Rhinelander, you spent a good deal of time in Alice's father's company, did you not?"

"Yes."

"When you first met him, were you surprised by the color of his skin?"

"No. Alice had told me about it. I was more intrigued by his English accent. I believed he was an Englishman with a West Indian father."

"You did not, as you've said, consider him a colored person?"

"No. I still don't."

"Mr. Rhinelander, when you met George Jones and saw the color of his skin, did you not question his daughter, Alice Jones' race?"

"No, not at all. Before I met him, she'd told me about his background, that Mr. Jones's mother was English and his father was a sailor from the West Indies. The color of his skin made perfect sense to me."

"But if he was so dark, didn't it occur to you that his daughter, Alice Jones, must have inherited a modicum of his racial makeup?"

"It never was an issue. I'd met her mother, too, and her racial makeup was just as clear to me."

"Mr. Rhinelander, you must have known that having a white parent means little in deciding race in our society, but having a colored one always means a great deal. Were you aware of the so-called one-drop rule?"

"No, not until all this business began."

"You mean, after you married Alice?"

"No. As a matter of fact, not until after this case started."

"But could you possibly believe that a person with one colored parent could ever be considered completely white?"

"I'd never thought about such a thing. And when I did, it didn't make sense. If one drop of black blood made someone black, why didn't one drop of white blood make someone white?" He shook his head. "As I said, it was never an issue between Alice and me."

"If it was never an issue, why are we here today, Mr. Rhinelander? It must have become enough of an issue at some point for you to sue Alice Jones Rhinelander for an annulment of your marriage based on the fraud of her implying by not correcting your idea that she was white. When did the 'issue' float into your mind?"

"I was informed of certain things."

"Ah. Then, may we hear what things, and who informed you of them, and exactly when this happened?"

"As I said before, her birth certificate. Mr. Jacobs showed me a copy the night I left the Jones house."

"And what did the birth certificate say that convinced you in an instant that your wife was colored?"

"Where it said 'race,' 'mulatto' had been entered."

"And with that one word, presented to you by one of your father's attorneys on a document more than two decades old, all that you had believed over the previous three years about Alice being white was erased, and in that instant she became 'mulatto?'"

"It wasn't as simple as that."

"I agree, Mr. Rhinelander. After all, your marriage license, barely one month old at the time, stated she was white. So, isn't it possible that you had many suspicions, many racial doubts about Alice from the beginning that you had simply suppressed, and that seeing that word on an official document allowed you to accept what you'd had in the back of your mind all along?"

"Objection! Outrageous conjecture."

"Conjecture, yes. Outrageous, no!"

"Sustained." Judge Morschauser glared at both attorneys. "I believe the long day has made us all a bit testy. Perhaps a night of rest will return us to a calm consideration of the facts in this case. Ten, tomorrow morning."

He banged his gavel and retired to his chambers as the bailiff intoned. Len sat exhausted in the witness box. Just as Leon Jacobs started up to get him, Len rose suddenly and headed straight toward Alice. Losing his balance, he lurched sideways. Alarmed, she stood in anticipation, but Jacobs intercepted him and forcefully steered him toward his own table. Alice heard him say, "I have to talk to her."

Mills ordered, loudly enough to be heard, "Get him out! Remove him!"

Jacobs immediately guided Len up the aisle toward the back of the courtroom. Two bodyguards quickly met them. Len suddenly stopped and shook them all off. He stood up straight, adjusted his tie and coat, and without looking back, walked out.

Alice watched, frustrated, angry, and finally depressed. I was standing just behind her. "He was coming over here, said he had to talk to me."

Mr. Davis was not sympathetic. "The press would have gone wild."

"What was he going to say?" She allowed the conjecture for a moment, then shook her head furiously. "God! Why can't we talk!"

Both her lawyers were surprised by her anger. Judge Swinburne stood to talk with her. "For obvious and painful reasons, Alice, neither of you has that choice."

She glared at him. "Why do you want to go on trying to win this thing?"

Davis spoke very calmly. "To preserve your marriage, and to protect your rights as a woman to have a financial future."

"What marriage?" she shot back. "And what do you mean by 'financial future?' I know what you mean. If I do what you suggested last night, I'll show my body to a bunch of men and get a lot of money. What does that make me, Mr. Davis?" She shook her head in frustration and walked away to join the family, waiting in the center aisle.

In the car going home, Alice said to Mum, Daa and me, "Don't take this badly, but I don't want to have to talk anymore tonight. I have to eat and not think and go to bed. Okay?"

CHAPTER TWENTY-ONE

"No further witnesses at this time, Your Honor," Judge Mills said the next morning, "but I wish to reserve the right to redirect examination of witnesses."

Judge Mills seemed particularly perky as the court began. I had no idea why, maybe because he was finished with the prosecution, and thought he'd done such a swell job. Alice had said she felt particularly rotten. She'd lain in bed all night, sat upright repeatedly before collapsing again, thinking over and over of what Mr. Davis wanted her to do. That morning, she told Mum to bring the bag with her long coat in it. When I arrived, my sister said she wanted me with her if the worst happened. And as chance would have it, we all had arrived on the courthouse steps at the same moment that Len did. Still, we had to pretend that we didn't see him. He looked like he hadn't slept either, and he shuffled when he walked.

"Mr. Davis, your defense."

"I call Mrs. Barbara Reynolds."

We all watched the reporter rise from the press table, enjoying her colleagues' surprise. Reaching the witness box, she stood primly as she was sworn, in a new dress, I thought.

"Mrs. Reynolds, you are a reporter for the New Rochelle *Standard Star*, I believe." Mr. Davis seemed to take on a fast, efficient manner in his questioning of his own witness.

"Yes, sir."

"And were you the first reporter to meet Mr. Rhinelander after news of his marriage to Alice Jones appeared in the press?"

"Yes, sir. I broke the story in the paper that morning, and I wanted to follow up."

"What did you ask him, and what did he answer?"

"I checked my notes this morning," she said. "I asked, 'Is it true?' I was showing him the headline, 'Rhinelander Scion Marries Daughter of Colored Man.' And he replied: 'What? Well, yes. We're very happy.'"

"Mrs. Reynolds, forgive me, I missed that. Would you repeat the answer?" Barbara got what he was doing right away. She repeated, "'Is it true? The headline said, 'Rhinelander Scion Marries Daughter of Colored Man.' 'What? Well, yes. We're very happy.'"

"'We're very happy'?" Davis repeated. "Yes, sir, 'Very happy.'"

Davis paused, said, "How fleeting it was. Thank you, Mrs. Reynolds. Your witness."

Judge Mills, seething quietly, rose. "Mrs. Reynolds, when you had this exchange with Mr. Rhinelander, did anyone else hear it?"

"No, it was pretty early, and..."

Interrupting, Judge Mills said, "And when I recall Mr. Rhinelander, and he refutes what you said, it would be your version against his, would it not?"

"Yes, sir, but I have my notes."

"A journalist's notes are not sacred scripture, Mrs. Reynolds. You surely had a professional interest in creating such a good quote for your readers, did you not?"

"I don't create quotes, sir!" Barbara said angrily.

"No more questions." said Judge Mills.

"You're excused, Mrs. Reynolds." Judge Morschauser liked Mrs. Reynolds and smiled at her. "Your next witness, Mr. Davis."

Still fuming at Judge Mills, Barbara rose and went back to the press table. Davis spoke with calm gravity. "Please call Mr. Ross Chidester. Your Honor, he was not on the witness list because our investigator just located him late last night and arranged for him to be here today."

Turbulence broke out at the plaintiff's table. Len, startled, turned to watch Chidester come down from the rear door. For a moment, Len's glance met Alice's. They both quickly turned away.

Chidester went to the witness box and was sworn, looking uncomfortable in the suit he wore. It was clear from his frightened eyes and nervous frown that he was not happy to be there.

"Please state your name and address," Davis said. "I'm Ross D. Chidester, 614 Oak Street, in Valhalla."

"Where you drive a truck for a local bakery?"

"Yes."

"But in 1921 and '22, you worked as a chauffeur for the plaintiff's father, Philip Rhinelander, did you not?"

"Yes."

"And indeed, you are the one who drove Leonard and Alice to the Marie Antoinette Hotel on December 23, 1921."

"Yes."

"Mr. Chidester, please tell the court about that day, particularly about the Christmas present that Leonard had with him when you picked him up."

"I picked him up at The Orchards, brought his bags out and put them in the trunk. He was carrying a Tiffany box, and I asked if he wants it in the trunk as well. He says, no, it's a present for his lady friend, and he'd leave it at her house when we pick her up on our way to the city."

"Did this surprise you?"

"Nearly knocked me over. Him and me were pretty friendly for a time. I drove him a lot, talked about investments and jazz clubs, so I felt like I ought to warn him, 'Don't you know her father is a colored man?' I'd seen her father from the car before. Someone like Mr. Rhinelander might keep someone like her as a mistress, but giving her presents from Tiffany's seemed, well…"

"Did Mr. Rhinelander answer your question?"

"He sure did. He said, 'I don't give a damn if he is.' I had a notion to grab him and kick the living…"

"Mr. Chidester, just to be clear, what that meant to you was, 'I don't give a damn if he is a colored man,' correct?"

"That's exactly what he was saying."

"Now, later that evening, did Alice Jones give you a Christmas present out of gratitude for your kindness to her?"

"I didn't want to take it," he said, looking increasingly uncomfortable. "Who was she to be giving me something? But I had some presents to buy, and five dollars helped."

"Ah, of course. The spirit of Christmas. Your witness." As he came back to his seat, Mr. Davis looked at Alice to see her reaction. She nodded her appreciation. He'd managed to get evidence from Chidester and make him look stupid at the same time. Mr. Davis didn't look as sanguine.

Judge Mills attacked him right away. "Mr. Chidester, the conversation you describe happened nearly four years ago. Are you certain you remember it correctly? Leonard is here to corroborate, and you are under oath."

"I remember the words, sir. They changed everything between him and me. Probably the reason I left their employ."

"I believe you were fired. Is that true?"

"Nothing to do with this."

"No. It seems you drink. And since then, you've had seventeen different jobs, from which you've been fired for the same reason. We've been looking for you, too, you see, and heard a great deal about your problem. After so much drinking over the years, can you still recall those exact words?"

"I never drank on the job! And I remember the words!"

"Nothing further, Your Honor."

"You're excused, Mr. Chidester." Judge Morschauser looked toward the defendant's table. "Mr. Davis?"

As Chidester left the courtroom, Mr. Davis said, "Your Honor, as much has transpired, I must consult with my client. I would request a recess, but perhaps in the interest of time, Judge Mills might wish to do any redirect now."

"The court has no objection. Judge Mills?"

"Absolutely," the judge stated. "Call Mr. Rhinelander back."

On a legal pad, Davis wrote something in large letters and slid the pad in front of Alice. I learned later that it said, "Still too much doubt. We must do it now, if at all. I will respect your decision."

I knew she'd so hoped that the witnesses Mr. Davis had called or his cross-examination of Len would be proof enough for the jury of Len's acceptance of her being black. But Judge Mills had damaged their testimony, and no telling what he'd get Len to say now. We watched him shuffle awkwardly back to the witness box. Alice picked up the pencil and wrote several words and sat back, gripping her chair's arms as if bracing for a crash. "DO IT!"

"Leonard," Judge Mills said, "I want to go back to that letter you wrote to Alice Jones, the one that Mr. Davis insisted on reading to us. It described that thing that the two of you did together. You've said you went into this relationship with no sexual experience. I want to clarify the basic understanding that we have about that occasion. Here's a simple question for you. Who instructed whom about that particular activity?"

"I've said before, it happened naturally."

"But the first time you did it," Judge Mills said with an edge of impatience, "you knew nothing of such matters. I doubt if it was natural for you to put your head down there. Who suggested that idea?"

"We suggested things to each other. I suppose Alice asked me to try that."

"Of course she did. And did she describe the details, all the details of what you were to touch? Come, come, Leonard, I'll be asking her these same questions when she's on the stand. You might as well tell us."

"It was just things people say to each other. People ask for things they like done."

"And you did what she asked, as usual?"

"I tried to."

"Even though it was a disgusting, sordid thing to ask?"

"It was never disgusting to me."

"I don't care what you thought of it. Did she tell you what to do?"

"She asked me to do things, just as I asked her to do things."

"And you did them, without question?"

"As she did for me."

The two of them faced each other, both obviously incensed, until Judge Mills turned away and said, "Your witness." I noticed that his hands were tensed at his sides as if he wanted to strangle Leonard. Was he so angry that he'd forgotten to question Len about Barbara Reynolds and Chidester? Could their testimony stand and be meaningful to the jury? Of course not. Stupid hope.

Davis remained seated to ask, "Mr. Rhinelander, have you previously testified that before you married Alice Jones, you did not see any personal, physical evidence that she was colored?" He spoke in a monotone, seemingly bored.

"I didn't see any, yes."

"You also stated that your eyesight is good aside from slight myopia for which you wear those glasses, but not color blind, correct?"

"Correct."

Standing abruptly and with sudden intensity, Davis spoke directly to Judge Morschauser. "Your Honor, I'm going to ask that the courtroom be cleared. Under the rule of procedure called 'real evidence,' I'm going to ask Mr. Rhinelander to identify for the jury certain physical evidence—parts of his wife's skin—not what can be seen here in court, but what Leonard Rhinelander surely had seen and saw repeatedly over the years *before* they were married."

Judge Mills shot up out of his chair. "Now, wait just one moment! I object!"

"Grounds?" Judge Morschauser seemed suddenly alert to the possibilities of the procedure.

"Well, obviously because while he is cross-examining the plaintiff who was called as *my* witness, he cannot introduce the defendant into the proceedings."

"Your Honor," Davis spoke as if Judge Mills were acting like a petulant child. "I am not bringing Alice forward to testify. As Judge Mills has so ably observed, I am cross-examining the plaintiff. But in so doing, I intend to present Alice Jones Rhinelander's skin as physical evidence, to allow Mr. Rhinelander and the jury to see it first-hand, in order to counter the testimony that the plaintiff has just stated about what he saw or didn't see."

The reaction of both public and press threatened to burst out, but anticipating it, Judge Morschauser hit his gavel twice and said over any remaining disturbance, "I assure you all, spectators and journalists alike, that if there is the slightest audible reaction to these proceedings from this point on, I will shut this courtroom down to every one of you. The business of this court is too important to suffer the distraction of any unnecessary comment." He looked over the entire courtroom before turning back to Mr. Davis. "A complex request, Mr. Davis."

"It's an appalling one!" Judge Mills vituperated. "My God, Davis, you'd turn the woman's skin into an object?"

"I believe our culture has done that for us, Judge, and what the plaintiff saw of her skin is now what this case is about."

"Your Honor, we do not need to see Alice Jones's skin. It has been admitted by counsel that she has black blood."

"But Mr. Rhinelander never had a chance to test, see or judge her blood." Mr. Davis was speaking as if to a child again, growing calmer with every word. "He could not tell if she was white or black—except by what he saw."

Judge Mills yelled, "He saw her father!"

"And her mother," Davis smiled.

"You're denying that her admitted black blood defines her race?"

Still smiling, Mr. Davis cocked his head to one side. I had a sense that Judge Mills had unwittingly given him a perfect setup. "Judge Mills, race is defined a hundred ways, a thousand ways, depending on what state you're in, what part of town you live in, which church you belong to, what country club you join. In this case, Mr. Rhinelander, whom I'm cross-examining, denies having *seen* any sign of 'black blood,' to which you so delicately refer, before he was married. He has said clearly and repeatedly, 'As to color, I drew the line.' I think the jury must see the visual evidence of how vaguely, and perhaps blindly, he drew that line. The jury must see what he saw to be able to judge whether he drew his line in error, to judge if he denied to himself what any other man would see and assess. The jury must see the 'real evidence' around which he drew that zig-zag line of his."

"Your Honor," Judge Mills said, "You cannot force this jury of twelve gentlemen to gaze on the naked body of this woman! It would be shameful."

Judge Morschauser considered that for about two seconds. "The law does not flinch at shame, Judge Mills. But I won't allow her naked, Mr. Davis."

"Of course not, Your Honor. She will be covered and will expose only those areas in question. I intend for the jury to see only parts of her upper body and lower limbs."

"The defendant is willing?" Morschauser spoke as much to Alice as to Mr. Davis. Alice managed to nod.

"She is eager, Your Honor, that justice finally be applied to this conundrum."

Judge Mills turned and seemed to stomp his way back to his chair. "This is a Godless, indecent proceeding!"

"I will not clear the court." Judge Morschauser looked around for an alternative and settled on one. "I suggest the jury room. They have facilities there where Mrs. Rhinelander can change. We three and the jury, oh, and the court stenographer. No one else."

"Mr. Rhinelander has to be there," Mr. Davis suggested, "and Alice requests her sister be with her."

"Of course." Judge Morschauser hit his gavel. "For the record, here's the court's reasoning for this decision. The purpose is to resolve whether or not Mr. Rhinelander could have known that Alice Jones was of colored blood by certain physical indications the defense is presenting under the rule of procedure called 'real evidence.' The court does not know what her body is going to reveal, but using it as evidence may show the jury whether Mr. Rhinelander had clear grounds to believe she was white—or to perceive that she was colored."

"Your Honor, I take strong exception." Judge Mills was livid. "Should there be the need for an appeal, I will base it on this specious ruling."

"Noted, Judge Mills. Bailiff, remove the jury."

Mr. Davis returned to his table to confer with Alice. He signaled to me, and I stood, taking the small travel bag from Daa. I pardoned myself out to the aisle and approached the defense table.

"Your courage is formidable, Alice."

She turned to Mr. Davis, saw me standing just behind him with the bag. "This isn't courage, Mr. Davis. I'm doing this dead." She turned to look at Len, still sitting in the witness box, all but forgotten in the latest agitation. He sat collapsed again, bent over in his chair.

Furious, Judge Mills was seated next to Jacobs. He whispered loud enough for us to hear, "I'll cross-examine her with razor blades!"

Mr. Davis immediately turned to him and said quietly, "Judge, that's an egregious threat, and with it, you're asking for a mistrial."

The judge ignored him but was silenced.

Alice and I didn't look over at the plaintiff's table, but I did happen to see that Barbara Reynolds had been seated close enough at the press table to hear the exchange. She looked appalled by it.

"Gentlemen, Mrs. Rhinelander, Mrs. Jones," Judge Morschauser instructed as he stood, "please follow the deputies to the jury room. Bailiff, any disturbance beyond whispered conversation is not to be tolerated in my absence."

Alice rose, and she and I walked out of the courtroom. Going out one door, across a hall and into the jury room, Alice whispered, "Remember that Mata Hari movie about her being a spy led out to the firing squad?"

The jury room was small, barely large enough to hold the single long table and the twelve chairs around it, now filled with the jury. None of them looked at us as we entered. No windows. The three chandeliers that hung over the table were very bright.

A deputy stood at a door at one end of the room. "Toilet," he explained. Alice and I approached it as the men following us came into the jury room and found places to stand against the wall. One of the jurors rose to allow the court stenographer a place to work.

Alice quickly went into the washroom. I followed and closed the door. "I don't want to see Len," she said as she started to undress.

"He's there," I said. "Pick out someone, watch the stenographer, maybe."

"How horrible that it's come to this, for me, for him."

I helped as best I could and carefully hung her clothes on a hook on the back of the door.

"I'm keeping these on," Alice whispered, stripped to her panties. "Of course. Here's the coat."

It was an old coat, but almost a full-length one, so that it completely covered her. "Should I wear my shoes?" she said.

"Go barefoot," I said angrily, "like it's a slave market!"

"Something is urging me to go back in there stark naked and spit on the table."

Alice took off her shoes and went to the door. I opened it, and we returned to the jury room. Alice stood very straight and took two steps to one side to be sure all could see her.

From where he stood across the room, Mr. Davis instructed her. "Alice, please let down your coat and then turn."

I saw Len looking at her, mouth open as if he couldn't breathe, eyes wide in utter horror. Alice shrugged the coat off her shoulders and let it fall so that she was naked above her waist. As she was examined, she slowly turned. The men watching her seemed not to breathe. The only sound was the scratching made by the court stenographer's pencil as she recorded her shorthand.

"Thank you, Alice. Put your coat back up and then please lift it above your knees and turn."

Alice reached down for the coat's bottom edge and held it up as she was examined, then rotated again. "Thank you again, Alice. That will serve." She let the coat fall over her legs and immediately went back into the washroom. I followed. As soon as the door was shut, we heard everyone in the jury room rise to return to the courtroom. Alice sat on the closed toilet, doubled over and gasping.

I knelt on the floor to comfort her. "I've never been so proud of you. Your skin was a weapon."

"They took it all, Em. There's nothing left of me now. I didn't even cry."

"Call it courage, being very strong, very brave."

Alice stood up and helped me up from the floor. She took her chemise from the hook, but before she put it on, she caught her reflection in the mirror over the sink. "Was I black enough for them?" she said. "What makes me black enough for them? Here, inside of the arms? That patch on my back? My nipples? Oh, for sure.

Back of the legs?" She turned to me. "He saw all of me! Did you watch Leonard?" She started to dress.

"He watched, but then when you…"

"He turned to the wall!" She said it as a cry. "He seemed devastated."

Silently, Alice finished dressing. "I'm not going back in there 'til I'm ready."

"Not one second sooner."

When we returned to the courtroom, Len was back in the witness stand, wet with sweat, balled up almost in a fetal position, clearly in a state of shock. Judge Morschauser did not have to silence the spectators as they were immediately quiet, watching us. Judge Mills was whispering furiously to Leon Jacobs. Judge Morschauser settled back in his chair. "Mr. Davis, please continue your cross."

Alice and I didn't know if we should move or not, so we stood in the doorway. Mr. Davis approached the witness box. "Mr. Rhinelander, did you see the physical evidence as presented to the jury?"

Len answered, "Yes."

"Mr. Rhinelander, does your wife's body today have the same varied coloring as it did when you saw her in the Marie Antoinette Hotel, with all her clothing removed?"

"Yes," Leonard said.

"No further questions," Davis said and sat down.

The sudden end of cross-examination had its effect on the spectators who were anticipating more detail.

Morschauser gaveled for silence. "Judge Mills?"

Mills stood and, with obvious ire, directed his response directly to Lee Davis, who ignored it. "Under these sordid circumstances, no further questions. Leonard Rhinelander was my last witness, and we look forward to cross-examining the defense."

"You're excused, Mr. Rhinelander." As Leonard slowly unwound himself and stepped down from the witness box, we started back to our seats. Morschauser idly ordered, "Continue with your defense, Mr. Davis."

Davis said from his chair, "Your Honor, the defense rests."

After an unbelieving moment, pandemonium ensued. The crowd exploded. Judge Mills was on his feet, apoplectic with figuring out something to do. The press was calling back and forth to each other, several slipping out to telephones. Morschauser's gavel began banging in a constant rhythm but without its usual effect. Barbara Reynolds watched open-mouthed, looking in all directions. Len, still devastated, stood in the center of the well and stared at Alice as she was about to sit down. Confused, she stood there when she saw him looking at her. The deputy who had escorted us rushed to his duty position. Standing at the end of my row, I still held her coat, not knowing what to do. I saw Len turn to Leon Jacobs, who was being yelled at by Judge Mills. I was close enough to hear.

"What just happened?" Len had to shout.

Speaking above the clamor and whatever Judge Mills was yelling, Jacobs seemed happy to explain. "If Davis doesn't call your wife, Judge Mills can't cross-examine her."

Len stood bolt upright and turned to Alice. He then laughed loudly with delight. That brought an amazed moment of quiet to the courtroom without Judge Morschauser's need to gavel for it. Len and Alice faced each other, she confounded by his laughter. Then the discord broke loose again.

Jacobs took a firm hold of Len's arm and returned him to his seat at the plaintiff's table, still laughing. Judge Mills yelled something at him. Alice gazed over the courtroom, the jury, the spectators, her family, the press, many of whom were watching her intently as everyone else seemed to be yelling. Then she saw Mr. Davis gesturing for her to sit down.

She went to her chair. I'd made my way back to mine. She turned around and said to me through the confusion, "Did he forget what I just did? How can he be laughing?"

I told her what Jacobs had just said. Her mouth dropped open. She turned toward Len at the plaintiff's table, put her hands on the table for support and rose. She stood there, waiting for him to see her, until Mr. Davis gripped her arm and sat her down. He never looked.

CHAPTER TWENTY-TWO

In her column on the front page of the next morning's *Standard Star*, Barbara Reynolds wrote:

> *… Regarding the couple, are they heroes that we cannot see, fighting battles that we cannot know? Regarding the trial, is it a seminal redefinition of race in America, or a portrait of a woman fighting bravely to be herself up against a family of grotesque and destructive power? Or is it just a love story shattered by law and property protection? The trial hints that it's all these things, but the chances are that we'll never know.*
>
> *When Leonard Rhinelander found reason to laugh at such a shattering moment for his case, it confirmed my suspicion that no matter how much detail the trial manages to reveal (or not), the reality of the lovers' relationship is so much more complex than any of us will ever get right. I knew then that whatever the verdict will be, whatever the law concludes, it will be such a small part of what has actually happened to these two young people who, against incredible odds, dared to fall in love.*
>
> *That's not a big revelation on my part, only a realization that the conceit of the press and the presumption of the law of getting the 'whole truth and nothing but' about a love story told in a courtroom is, in fact, laughable.*

I read it to Alice over breakfast. As I did so, she stopped eating to listen. I finished and waited for a response.

"She comes as close as the press will ever get."

I nodded. "She's been consistently good to us. You can feel good about this."

It was Thanksgiving Day. Mum and Daa had gone to church. We were still in our pajamas. The whole family had agreed to skip any celebration. The long weekend that Judge Morschauser had granted us for the holiday was time to lick our wounds. We all needed to be ready for the two closing arguments that Judge Mills and Mr. Davis agreed to present to the jury on Monday.

"The only thing I feel thankful for is how upset Judge Mills was about not being able to have at me in the witness box. And then you telling me why Len laughed. That had nearly killed me."

"It'll be over soon. Hang onto that."

"Maybe the drugs he's taking let him forget what I'd just done in the jury room."

"Maybe. But he was laughing in triumph, I thought."

"But...we've lost."

"Lost what?"

"Our main battle was to come through all this and be able to love each other again. That can't happen now. The Rhinelanders have won even if I win in court."

"Alice, why do you jump to that conclusion? You and Len survived two years of forced separation, with everything they could throw at you since."

"Did you see the look on his face when he saw what I had to do in the jury room, in his mind, because of him? He'll never be able to forgive himself, no matter what I say..." then furiously, "even if I could talk to him, which they'll never let me do! They'll still be in control of him!" Then bereft, she said quietly, "His laughing was a last letting go. He'll give up now, and I don't blame him."

She stood up and went to the stairs. "Go home, Em. I'll be okay. I'm going to catch up on my diary and sleep. See you in court on Monday... God, what a thing to have to look forward to."

Three nights of good sleep and three days with Roberta and Bob made me feel almost human again. We avoided reading the papers so that when I returned to court, I was unsure if anything unusual had happened. I wished it had because going back into that same courtroom with the same cast of characters gave me a sense of what psychological torture could be like.

Mum, Daa and I took our seats behind the defense table. Poor Grace had influenza. Alice turned to us with a grim smile. She caught my eye and gestured toward Len. He was staring at the ceiling again, but slumped in his chair, slack-jawed, his hair stringy with sweat. I looked back at Alice. She mouthed, "He's gone."

After several preliminary motions and general "housecleaning," as Judge Morschauser termed it, the courtroom became silent in expectation of counsels' final summations to the jury. Mr. Davis rose. We all wished he could have had the last word, but unfortunately, Judge Mills had that privilege.

"Gentlemen," Davis began, "my closing remarks must first consider why this case was ever brought before you. Is it really about fraud, a girl lying about her racial mix? Or is it about destroying the girl, to be rid of her, so she will not be a further taint, a further financial threat, a further legal irritation to a fearsomely powerful, socially entrenched, and fantastically rich family?

"We must remember why this trial is for an annulment and not a divorce. A divorce only severs a marriage; an annulment treats a marriage as if it never happened. Could it be that the mighty Rhinelanders, who own vast packages of property in the most exclusive areas of New York City, as well as any number of lucrative slum properties, so feared Alice's dower rights, rights that gave her a claim to inherit a one-third interest in all her husband's real estate interests? In a divorce, she would still have rights to make claims on that property. After an annulment, she would have no rights at all. She would have nothing. So could this trial really be about real estate rather than a marriage?"

"And without doubt, we must ask if this trial is about race. Certainly your deliberations cannot ignore the context of this nation's historical, current, and perhaps perpetual prejudice and bigotry. You, gentlemen, were chosen for this jury in part because of my profound belief that each of you was certain to rise above such intolerance. The law, on which this nation is based and where its struggle to evolve ensues, depends on my being right about you."

He turned and walked over to stand for a moment looking at Leonard, then turned back to the jury. "I must confess to you that I have great compassion for Mr. Rhinelander. What did he do that caused his powerful family to deny him marrying the woman he loved, that caused his own father to force this trial? Allow me to tell you exactly what Leonard did. He willingly married far below his social class, and he knowingly married far outside his racial heritage. Gentlemen, those measures are crimes to the Rhinelanders. They are most certainly not in this New York court of law."

"Rather, the so-called misdemeanor that you must decide upon is 'fraud,' that Alice Jones claimed to be, or allowed herself to be thought of, as white in order to entice Leonard Rhinelander to marry her. Having heard what you've heard in this court, and seen what you've seen in the jury room, is it possible to believe anything else but that Leonard Rhinelander had to know she was not pure white when he married her, and more important, that he did not care? There is no fraud here. The only 'crime' that Alice Jones committed was falling deeply and truthfully in love with Leonard Rhinelander. And for that, she has lost the possibility of any future happiness with the man that she loves. Can anyone believe these two will ever be able to restore the shards of their shattered relationship after what they have been forced to experience here?"

I saw Alice turn toward Len. I did, too. His head slowly sank forward onto his chest. He looked sick and devastated.

"Gentlemen, you will surely influence the future with your decision on how we in America will understand, tolerate, and finally how we accept and overcome our racial differences. For the good of all, do not let the Rhinelanders throw Alice Jones away as if she were another piece of their luxurious garbage. She has little left after all this, beyond an extraordinary, loving and faithful family. And therefore, gentlemen, let the world in which she must now live at least know the truth of this vile outrage: that the Rhinelanders in their lofty privilege have charged Alice Jones with fraud for nothing more than her presumption to fall in love with one of them.

"Gentlemen, I thank you for your service to this court."

To me, the ensuing silence was a quiet wave of approval from all those who heard what he'd said. Mr. Davis sat down, and Alice turned to him with a look of desolation. She quoted him. "The shards of their shattered relationship."

As the gavel rapped, she turned to me for some kind of support. I felt utterly helpless.

"Judge Mills, your closing statement."

With yet another bowing flourish, Judge Mills approached the jury. I thought his enthusiasm indicated relief that he no longer had to deal with his own client in the witness box. Everyone was startled when he started at an intense pitch, with his finger jabbing in the direction of each subject in his invective.

"Gentlemen of the jury! You might as well bury *that* young man six feet deep in the soil of the old churchyard where his early American ancestors sleep, as to consign him to be legally chained to that woman!

"Why, gentlemen, stop and think. There isn't a father among you who would rather see his son in a casket than see him wedded to a mulatto woman. That is a basic truth, shared by all. Our determination about the purity of race doesn't belong just to white people alone. Decent blacks have the same feeling. Almighty God created the races, white, black, yellow and red, and He placed them on separate continents. But for the simplistic meddling with this arrangement by idealistic fools, there would never be a chance for such sad, pathetic marriages as this one. The very fact that God so separated the races on His Earth shows that He did not intend for the races to mix!

"On the other hand, once freed from this false marriage, what can this woman anticipate? She will gain a husband of her own race, and life will have happiness for her again, as it has for her older sister who did not assume such vaulting ambition, but married a fine colored man."

I thought of standing up and walking out as a demonstration of contempt, but I couldn't be sure how it would be interpreted. I did want to yell at him. But instead of any of that, I sat still.

"I urge you to remember Alice Jones' many letters. You heard them. They show clearly how that boy, under that woman's sophisticated manipulation of his innocent, totally unknown desires, was reduced by temptation and lust to the utter depths of degradation. Remember that vile act of concupiscence described in young Leonard's letter to her. It was done for her pleasure! You, gentlemen, know this. It was not a white man's act. That was an act of the black and tan!" He gestured toward Alice with a sweep of his hand. "And poor Leonard became her sexual slave!"

I thought the jury would follow his direction but was surprised to see that few did. Could it be that they saw through Judge Mills' flim-flam? No. I urged myself to stop hoping.

"In spite of this, I was appalled, as no doubt you were, by her being forced by her counsel to a degree of indecent exposure unheard of in American jurisprudence. You will remember that I opposed it. It was utterly unnecessary for you to see her body. For the proof of her blackness is not only what can be seen, but what is obvious and admitted from her inherited blood. Yes, she looks white, in spite of it. But she did nothing to clarify that mix to Leonard. In fact, she said a great deal to deceive him. And that is fraud, gentlemen, plain and simple fraud, the basic charge of this case."

Judge Mills leaned heavily on the jury box railing, bending in so that he could talk with more passion and less volume. "And now the responsibility for human justice, and for Leonard Rhinelander's freedom, passes from my shoulders to yours, gentlemen. Your verdict shall answer finally and certainly, for all of America, the ancient question asked in Jeremiah, 'Can the Ethiopian change his skin?' For the good of this great American nation, for the truth in this case, your answer to that ancient question must be: 'No! No, it cannot be done!' I must hope that you have no hesitation in giving this young man a chance to redeem himself and his family name, which, by his sad mental weaknesses and his folly, he has besmirched under the bedevilment of the defendant. I beg of you, free this boy from this horrid, unnatural, absurd, and terrible union!"

He had released himself during the last sentence to his previous level of bombast, and those jurors closest to him pulled back. Even so, Mills did a little bow as if expecting applause, I thought, and with a martyred look of self-sacrifice, struggled back to his chair.

Judge Morschauser gaveled for attention and read from a prepared statement. "Gentlemen of the jury, as you remember, there are six issues that you must settle. Please refer to your lists of those issues as you deliberate. In considering the case as presented, I wish to make clear several points in my instructions to you. The first point is this: The fact that defense counsel chose not to call the defendant does not give advantage automatically to the plaintiff's case.

"On the other hand, you may deduce a conclusion from any witness not being called. The second point is, if you should find that the defendant knowingly lied about her color, or in any way purposely concealed her race, the marriage can be annulled. On the other hand, given the visual clues he had, if the plaintiff did not realize by standards of ordinary intelligence that she was of colored blood and not an untainted white woman, fraud cannot be claimed.

"Lastly, gentlemen of the jury, and this is vital: If you allow yourselves to be influenced by any racial prejudice during your deliberation, you do both parties and the law a deep injustice. An honest, courageous and unemotional determination upon the evidence is required of you by your oath as jurors.

"Bailiff, show the jury out."

Both Alice and Len sat motionless, both looking shattered. Suddenly, he began to choke, then gag, controlling a need to throw up. For a moment, the attention of the court focused on him. It passed as he slumped back in his chair, gasping.

Judge Morschauser waited for the crisis to pass and then declared a recess for jury deliberation. Jacobs stood and got Len on his feet. They walked up the center aisle, where the bodyguards met them. Usually, Alice waited until Len was out, but that day she rose and moved quickly to follow him, leaving Davis and Swinburne to lurch after her. I followed as soon as I could.

On the steps outside the courthouse, we stopped to watch as a chauffeur opened the back door of the familiar limousine, and Len got in. Alice stepped forward to call out, but Judge Swinburne put a hand on her arm. The crowd and press were all staring, so again, she said nothing. As she watched the limousine drive away, she said, "I have the ridiculous feeling that I won't ever see him again. I know that's crazy. The trial is still going on... And what would I say to him?" She looked at me. "'I love you,' at least?"

CHAPTER TWENTY-THREE

The jury took two days to decide. Those two sleepless nights and two days waiting in Mr. Davis' office had all of us climbing the walls. Grace had been with us, still miserable from her battle with influenza. Bob had appointed himself the snack-runner, trying to distract us with chocolate temptations and coffee.

During those two days, following Judge Mills' "grotesque" summation—that was the word that Mr. Davis used to describe it—Alice had only one real conversation with her lawyer about the verdict. He told her to try not to react, whether good or bad, but he believed it was going to be good. Alice told me that Mr. Davis had expected her to be as hopeful as he was and knew he was disappointed that she was not. Instead, she'd worried about where Len was, what they were doing to him, and what would happen when the verdict was announced. "Will he come over to me? And what if he does?"

"Cross that euphoria when you come to it, but don't believe it now." This was the advice I gave that I was sure was not taken.

Within hours of those questions, Judge Swinburne rushed over from the courthouse and called from the hall downstairs before he even got to the office, "Jury's ready!"

Alice looked at me. "No matter what, I just want to hold him."

I took her hand, and we all walked downstairs and over to the courthouse. The crowd waiting there for Alice and Len to do their walk-by was larger than ever. A huge number of police were in evidence as well. The photographers were setting off flashbulbs like a blanket of heat lightning. It was a warm day for late November.

"The steam heat in the courtroom'll be on full blast," Alice said.

"You won't be in there long."

"Nothing matters, Em. Sure as hell not the verdict."

"Yes, it does, and you know it."

The whole family was being carried along into the courtroom by everyone else's excitement. We were like wraiths, drifting along on legal gusts, Mum and Daa using determination to endure. Inside the courtroom, the spectators and press reacted to Alice's presence with their usual buzz. What we noticed instantly was that Len was not in his chair. His lawyers were there, Judge Morschauser was already in his place, and the jury—all looking fresh in pressed shirts when led in by the bailiff —sat down with no indication of what they had decided. Alice looked at Mr. Davis, alarmed, but didn't have a chance to ask about Len.

Once seated, the jury foreman handed an envelope to the court clerk. The clerk then gave it to Judge Morschauser, who opened the envelope. "I will warn the public against expressing any audible reaction to the answers that this fine jury has worked so diligently to address." Then he read the jury's conclusions into the record.

In answer to the issues we were given to decide:

One: At the time of marriage, was the defendant of colored blood? "Yes."

Two: Did the defendant, before marriage, conceal from the plaintiff by silence or other means the fact that she was of colored blood? "No."

Three: Did the defendant, before the marriage, represent to the plaintiff that she was white and not of colored blood? "No."

Four: Did the defendant practice any such concealment to induce the plaintiff to marry her? "No."

Five: By said concealment, or by said representation, or by both, was the plaintiff induced to marry the defendant? "No."

Six: If the plaintiff had known that the defendant was of colored blood, would he have married her? "Yes.'"

Judge Morschauser fiercely gazed around the courtroom to contain the palpable response. He then said, "Therefore, it is the decision of the court that in the matter of Rhinelander versus Rhinelander, an annulment is denied."

The requisite explosion of reactions ripped through the crowded courtroom. Most of those at the press table rushed to the exit to get to a telephone. Passing by Mum and Daa quietly embracing, I hurried to the defense table. Alice's only reaction was to ask Davis, "Why isn't Len here?"

"The plaintiff isn't required to be present for the verdict," Davis said. "He's probably avoiding the press. Alice, we won!"

She looked up into his proud and happy face as if he'd just spoken in Chinese. We heard the gavel pounding and turned away from Mr. Davis. Alice and I briefly hugged each other before being urged back to our seats by Judge Swinburne.

Judge Mills made a motion that the decision be set aside, and that there be a new trial on the grounds that the current one had been unfairly conducted, that the judge's instructions to the jury prejudiced Leonard Rhinelander's case. Judge Morschauser quickly rebuffed him, thanked the jury and excused them. He then ordered the police to escort Alice and her party out of the courthouse. Without any further comment, he hit his gavel, ending Rhinelander v. Rhinelander.

"Today, we'll go out first!" Judge Swinburne said triumphantly. He and Mr. Davis went over and shook hands with Judge Mills and Leon Jacobs. Mills was all hearty congratulations as if the trial had been a pleasant game of croquet. Between handshakes, I glimpsed Jacobs looking over at us. I never knew for sure, but I sensed that he was happy with the outcome. The Jones family swarmed around Alice with cries of relief and joy. When Davis and Swinburne were ready, we followed the police up the center aisle and out of the still-exulting courtroom. I glimpsed Barbara Reynolds at the press table, weeping with a happy smile.

Outside, the huge horde still included banks of photographers. Even controlled by the extra police on duty, the crowd pressed forward as Davis and Swinburne, followed by Alice and the family, made our way out of the courthouse and down the steps to the street. Yes, we were jubilant. Alice tried to smile at those yelling questions or congratulations. Sergeant Kelly gave a wink and a smile. He and other police opened the way for the party to cross the street. Davis led us into his building, and the police prevented anyone from following.

The Joneses followed Davis into his office, and all of us took a deep breath, shook hands, thanked Davis, hugged Alice and in general, burst with our triumph. As the others exulted, Alice and I moved to a corner. Davis followed.

"I wanted this for you, Alice."

"For me and for yourself, too. I'm trying hard to be grateful, Mr. Davis, but you'd've had me do anything."

"Only what it took to win your case." Alice nodded. "You won it. I lost it."

"Perhaps not."

"You know better, Mr. Davis. I heard what you said. Remember? About 'the shards of their shattered relationship.' How's he going to let himself love someone he made show herself to the world? He wasn't even there for the verdict."

"As I said, I presume his family wished to avoid any more press, which, as a matter of fact, I think you'd be wise to take advantage of, right now. It'll be helpful in the future."

She looked at him, unbelieving. "What future? It's over."

"Alice, winning this trial was only a first step in gaining what is rightfully and legally yours. You're still Mrs. Leonard Rhinelander. I suggest that his father will fight you every step of the way to prevent any benefit that you surely deserve. It'll help you if the public knows something of your story. You should use the press to your advantage immediately."

She stared at him. "I don't want to fight them anymore."

"I fear you'll have little choice."

"Alice," Daa interrupted, coming over from the other side of the room where the family had gathered, "Judge Swinburne is saying you ought to meet with the press. It's surely your turn."

"Alice, it'll be helpful to have a few reporters up here now," Judge Swinburne said.

"'Helpful?' Since when?" Alice said.

"Since you won," Mr. Davis said. "The press grovels at the feet of winners."

Alice hesitated. She whispered to me urgently, "I want to be forgotten." I knew that was hopeless, so I said, "Maybe Len will see what you say."

"Okay," she said to the others. "Oh, and be sure to ask Barbara Reynolds from New Rochelle to come up."

It took Judge Swinburne ten minutes to select the members of the press to be invited for an interview. During that time, Alice sat quietly in the office. Each excited member of the family described how happy he or she had been with the verdict, and what it would mean. Alice listened to their obvious joy but had no sense of sharing it. Seven journalists finally crowded into the room, three holding cameras. The rest of us hovered behind them as Alice moved over to sit circumspectly in a wooden chair that Mr. Davis placed in front of shelves filled with law books. "Please ask questions one at a time," he said.

"So now, Alice." The first reporter was young and presumptuous. "With the trial done, what do you think of the Rhinelander family?"

"I'd like not to think about them at all." Appreciative laughter followed; Alice did not join in. "I don't know what's happened during all this to the Rhinelanders, but I know that my family is stronger, greater, and finer than any other, including that one."

"Did the trial change what you thought about yourself?"

She glared at the questioner. "You mean something else, don't you, whether I think I'm colored or white now?"

"Yes, I suppose I do."

"I'm surely different from what I was. I know what you think, what everyone else thinks, but I haven't changed my spots at all. I've certainly changed my mind about a lot."

Barbara Reynolds asked, "Mrs. Rhinelander, what about Leonard?"

"An easy question. Thank you. I love Len very much. I always will."

"Will the two of you get together again?"

Alice wasn't ready for that. "I, I'm sure you'll be the first to know."

"Thanks. I hope so." The journalist seemed honestly concerned. "What will you do with your life now?"

Alice stared at her. "What life? Is there one?"

An awkward pause followed, and Mr. Davis quickly suggested, "Before more questions, could you get your pictures? With the parents?"

Another reporter asked, "Mr. Davis, what do you anticipate legally?"

"I'm done. Mrs. Rhinelander is Judge Swinburne's client now." He deferred to his colleague.

"I anticipate the Rhinelanders will appeal, and I will immediately petition the court for Mrs. Rhinelander's continued support."

Mum and Daa joined Alice to pose. Mum adjusted her hat. "We'll give a big smile for this lot, luv, then I'll spit in their eye."

The three of them looked directly into the cameras, and Alice did what her mother suggested and reached for Daa's hand. With empty smiles, many pictures were taken.

A reporter asked a question to anyone who might answer. "Is there going to be a divorce?"

Judge Swinburne did not allow speculation. "No comment."

EPILOGUE

I'm done. Telling the story hasn't been easy, but now that it's been written, the last word has to be Alice's.

> <u>*July 17, 1933*</u>
> 1. *NAACP vote drive*
> 2. *Him*
> 3. *Birthday, dates*
> 4. *Apologies*
> 5. *Laughter explained (again!)*
> 6. *His life, drugs*
> 7. *Goodbye*

Today I worked with my voter-registration team at the corner of Third Avenue and 125th Street. The NAACP summer campaign in Harlem is something I really like being a part of, and Nellie, Ben and I are a great team. Aside from getting a lot of new people to vote, for each voter we signed up, the organization gives us a nickel. The total is split up between us at the end of the day. That corner is always crowded, and today our team was very successful.

After the commission was paid by our supervisor, we folded up the card table and chairs, Nellie put them in her car and we went our separate ways. I noticed a man leaning up against the storefront, and I passed by him without taking notice. But then I hesitated and turned.

It was Len, almost unrecognizable. His body was thick, his face all puffed out, and he had a little bushy mustache, thinning hair, odd-looking round glasses, and a suit that pulled at the buttons. "Len?"

"Happy birthday." He had a deep rasp in his throat when he spoke.

"Oh, God, Len. Thanks. I don't keep track anymore."

"I keep track of yours, not mine. It's your thirty-fourth. I just wanted to see you again, say hello. Don't worry. They don't follow me all the time. I made sure no one did today."

"That's a relief." I didn't know what to say. "Len, I'm not sure how to act. I've imagined running into you again, so often, not so much lately. How long's it been since we've seen each other?"

"I certainly don't keep track of that." He laughed, and in that brief moment, he seemed to be the Len I tried to remember. It didn't last. He seemed to fold in on himself and stared off into the traffic.

"It must be, well, ..." I didn't keep track either. "It was in November. So it'll be —good glory—eight years since the trial."

He coughed, deeply. "Yes." Then he looked at me. "I'm so sorry, Alice."

"Let's not do that. I'd have to start apologizing, too."

"What in the world for? You did nothing wrong."

"I did a lot, Len, during and after the trial. I'll never get over what I did in that jury room. Never. And now that you're here, I want you to know I've hated myself for suing you in the divorce for 'abandonment,' of all ridiculous things, when your father pretty much kidnapped you. Then me, suing your father for 'alienation of affection.' We won all that, but nobody ever succeeded in alienating me. It's just that the lawyers..."

"I did abandon you. They shipped me to Nevada to get the divorce, then to California for drug rehab. That took years. And 'alienating of affection?' Christ, it was certainly alienated by all the drugs. And Father went after you. If you hadn't sued him, he'd have never given you a settlement... And he should have given you much more."

"I know, but I was so sick of suing. And what I'm getting is fine. I was doing what the lawyers told me to do." We both smiled for no reason. "You want to walk, Len? We used to talk pretty well when we walked together."

"You remember the beach? That first day," Len said. "I think of it all the time."

We turned and walked along 125th Street.

"Me too, all the time... How are you, Len? Are you all right?"

"You mean, my new look? I eat too much, the only pleasure left, and on my allowance, I can't afford a tailor to disguise it. I eat, and I listen to jazz. Both pursuits only take one." He laughed at himself but then stopped talking, apparently having nothing more to say. Then, "How are you, Alice? I found out you were working for the NAACP. I asked for Mrs. Rhinelander when I called them. Stupid."

"Not stupid. That's who I am, Len, and I'm still proud to be. Your father's lawyers made me give the name up, swear never to use it, but I do. To myself."

"How petty that was."

"But I'm fine, Len... You know, nobody really remembers the trial."

"I know. We were a juicy distraction." He smiled. "Isn't it pathetic? Our wrecked marriage, my imposed addictions, and your brave, amazing shock of revelation in the jury room made no difference beyond the entertainment."

"I know. Right after, I got some letters, oh well, a lot of hate mail, filthy racist stuff. But a few thanked me for not hiding whatever I was, for shaming the bigots and saying: 'This is me! So what?' But one thing was different, Len: the Rhinelanders lost the case, and the other legal things since."

He gazed at her and nodded. "Yes, you made a slight crack in the family foundation. I hadn't thought that until now. Maybe I'll be able to believe that makes it all worthwhile."

"Do you really think what I did in front of the jury was brave?"

"Incredibly brave."

"Thank you. I can't tell you how—what's the word?—gratified that makes me feel. I remember how you laughed in court afterward. I know it was because of Judge Mills, but I've always wondered what you really thought."

"I was so damned happy that idiot couldn't cross-examine you. But at that moment, I was only half-there, just enough to be totally wrecked by causing you to have to take off... "

"You didn't cause it, Len. My lawyer did, and with time and forgetting, he was right... although I hated him for it then."

We walked around a large family coming the other way.

"Is this what you do, Alice? Work for the NAACP?"

"Yes, whenever I'm needed, mostly weekends and holidays, when the crowds come out. I'm not much of a joiner, but I so believe in all they're doing. Keeps me busy during this awful business depression. I commute down from New Rochelle, still living at home, glad to be there to help Mum out."

"Are your parents well?"

"Daa died two years ago. Mum never changes."

"I'm so sorry. I loved George; he was such a fine man. Please give your mother my love. On second thought, maybe not." He began to cough again. "Sorry. I'm trying to cut back on the medicines I still have to take and have no resistance to any little disease flying around."

I asked, "We heard about the drugs, Len. When did they start doing that?"

"Before the trial. They didn't want any accidents in the witness box. The stress caused a problem. You must remember my volcanic upset stomach." He guffawed, so I smiled. But he was still hurting about it. "They started with drugs, trying to control throwing up, then they started adding things so that by the end of the trial, I could barely think, and when I could, I was so appalled and angry with ... I don't want to start thinking about that."

"No, I don't either."

"During that last week, as I said, I was half-there, and that half was so crazed with what you had to do. And then they gave me more. After the trial, I barely knew where I was. I was addicted, and then, sometime during rehab, my father established a legal guardianship, with control over everything... You know all that." He stopped to look at her. "You do understand that's the reason I disappeared, why you didn't hear..."

"Yes, I know. I've never blamed you." We continued to walk. "I'm so glad you came today, Len. What are you doing? Where do you live?"

"With my father, who won't die. I'm called an 'auditor' at the family firm. They give me little to do, and as the idiot Rhinelander, I give them a lot to laugh at. How's that for horrible?"

"Len, can't you leave?"

He shook his head slowly. "They still worry about you. My sister Adelaide never stops carping at Father to stop your payments. And if I run away, he's let me know they'll come after me and commit me, then go to court to break your settlement, harassing you any way they can."

That disgusted me. "They're still hanging on to it."

"They'll never let loose of it. Father will always pay you as a matter of honor but be careful of Adelaide. Honor is not in her vocabulary."

"I'll do what the lawyers tell me to do."

We walked until Len stopped again and turned to face me. "It may be a pathetic self-justification, but even though I've done nothing else in my life, since I've withdrawn from most of the drugs, I've done what they wanted, in hopes of keeping them from coming after you."

I couldn't talk. Pedestrians passed by us. "I hate that you've had to do that... I'm so deeply grateful to you. But Len, I've come to think that once it all started, it was more than your father. We had so much more going against us."

He nodded. "You mean the salacious press, the whole racist country?" He smiled. "Yes, I suppose it was hopeless. But Alice... my dear Alice, I've always thought that what we had, during that glorious summer and fall, was—well, yes, very brief—but the very best that life and love can offer."

"It was to me, too... Len, I still think of myself as your wife, no matter what I'm called."

"Is that true? I'm so... so glad! I'd try to think like that, but... well, it's too late. You remember once I said, 'Without you, I'm dead.' Well, I died..."

He laughed and turned away to cough again, deeply, taking time, trying to be done. "Thank you, Alice. Thank you for... No, I'd better not do that, either. I'd be here for days if I started thanking you." He finished coughing. "I think I'd better go. It's time. It'll just get more painful."

I started to object but then agreed. "I'm so very glad you came, Len."

"Yes, I am too. It's wonderful to be with you." He looked like he might kiss me but then didn't. "Goodbye, Alice."

He turned away, then, reaching behind him, he held out his hand without looking back. As people went by, I took it, held it until he withdrew it and started to walk away. The sidewalk crowds closed around him. I wasn't waiting for him to turn around, to wave, or to change his mind and come back. I had loved him so much. He turned a corner, and I couldn't see him any longer.

I stood there a minute. I suppose I should have cried, but I haven't done that since the trial. I had loved him, and do, if you can love a memory.

Then I walked over to the 125th Street station to catch the next train to New Rochelle.

EDITOR'S AFTERWORD

Less than three years later, on February 20, 1936, Leonard, aged 33, died of pneumonia at his father's home. He left an estate of $10,301. All of it went to his father in a will his father had prepared.

On May 20, 1939, Leonard's brother, Philip Kip ("P.K.") Rhinelander, aged 42, died of a presumed heart attack, mysteriously living alone in a $1-a-week rooming house in Hell's Kitchen, across town from his and his wife's Park Avenue apartment. At the time, she was in Palm Beach with her two daughters, preparing for the eldest's upcoming wedding at St. Thomas Episcopal Church. Public speculation as to the strange circumstances of his death was suppressed.

Not quite a year later, on March 10, 1940, Philip Rhinelander, aged 74, died alone in his home on 48th Street in New York City. He left his entire personal estate to be divided between his daughter Adelaide and her two nieces, P.K.'s children. Adelaide instructed her father's executors to stop paying Alice Jones her settlement of $3,600 per quarter. Alice sued the estate and won the continuation of the payments until her death.

In 1961, Rhinelander Real Estate, having controlled vast pieces of Manhattan real estate for fourteen generations, land accumulated by the Rhinelanders since the Revolutionary War, sold off the majority of its holdings to a group of investors controlled by Harry Helmsley.

On March 24, 1970, Adelaide Rhinelander, who had dispensed with her married name soon after her divorce, died in her mansion on Fifth Avenue. A recluse, she was alone except for an around-the-clock staff who ministered to her constant, often demented demands. The mansion was sold immediately to pay for many debts that she had refused to acknowledge. The building was razed to make way for a high-end condominium.

On January 30, 1980, the author of this book, Emily Jones Brooks, aged 83, the widow of Robert Brooks, died surrounded by her family in the Brooks' Harlem brownstone, where so many political and cultural events had taken place over the previous decades. A leading philanthropist and board member of a broad range of organizations, she willed her home to a foundation that promotes reading in Harlem's school system. Her daughter, Roberta Brooks Bennett, heads its Board of Trustees.

On September 13, 1989, Alice Jones died, aged 89, having outlived every Rhinelander she had experienced. Her estate of $27,841 and the house in which she had lived throughout her life on Pelham Road in New Rochelle were left to her sister Grace and to her niece, Roberta Brooks Bennett, whose lawyer son, Robert Brooks Bennett, a partner in his late father's law firm, administered it. Alice never remarried and was buried in a plot next to her parents in New Rochelle. She had previously ordered and paid for her gravestone. It reads:

ALICE JONES RHINELANDER

1899-1989

ACKNOWLEDGEMENTS

This book was written over many years and significantly re-written over many more. In the early versions, the editor Walter Bode was a wise presence, and my agent, Erica Spellman-Silverman was a tireless champion.

My method of research is spontaneous and lacks the organization of scholarly work. I read until I must write. Among many books I used as reference, the process for this book was enriched particularly by the scholarly work of *"Property Rites: The Rhinelander Trial, Passing and the Protection of Whiteness"* by Elizabeth M. Smith-Pryor (2009), and *"According to Our Hearts: Rhinelander v. Rhinelander and the Law of the Multiracial Family"* by Angela Onwuachi-Willig (2013).

Two other books of straight history that were particularly helpful about the 1920s were *"Only Yesterday,"* by Frederick Lewis Allen (1931), and *"New World Coming,"* by Nathan Miller (2003). I came into this project with considerable knowledge of the period, having written a previous novel about it, *"Born With The Century."*

Journalism—which is a major dynamic in this book—was astonishing in its revelations of the period (many wildly and cruelly exaggerated). I dug into the <u>New York Times,</u> the <u>New York Daily News</u>, the <u>Daily Mirror</u> (Hearst's organ), and the <u>New York Evening Graphic</u>, the sensationalist tabloid and originator of the "composograph," altered photos for the benefit of scandal—Alice Jones' darkened face for one. Outside of New York, I managed to find some material from the <u>White Plains Daily Reporter</u> about the trial.

By far the most important part of my research was the trial's transcript. It is massive and is carefully housed by the constantly helpful people at the Library of the New York State Bar Association in Manhattan. I'm greatly beholden to Barbara Robinson, former President of the Bar Association, for arranging access to their astonishing library.

Every writer must have trusted readers before the manuscript is sent out into the publishing world. I had mine over the years, but am indebted to three who read this latest version and firmly offered (read "demanded") that I fix things: Inge Heckel, Jared Zelman, and Kaye Sprinkel Grace. I am deeply in their debt. And besides reading, Dave Williams has been a friend and advisor throughout this strange new publishing process.

And beyond debt is my in-house editor, Susan Kinsolving, a poet and novelist in her own right, who gave me more time than she had to give, sacrificing her own work, and dragging me through whatever creative morass in which I found myself. I'm a word guy, but still haven't found sufficient ones for my gratitude. I'll keep trying.

A NOTE TO THE READER

Thank you for taking the time to read *Black and White and Read All Over*. This book has been many years in the making, and I am deeply grateful that you chose to spend time with this story.

If the book moved you, I hope you might consider sharing your thoughts with other readers. Word of mouth and reader recommendations play an important role in helping stories like this find their way to new audiences.

COMING SOON: The Antebellum Series

As the Fairfield brothers and a woman of singular resilience navigate the tectonic shifts of mid-nineteenth-century America, the stakes grow ever higher. From the Mexican War (1846—48) to the Fugitive Slave Act (1850) to the violence of "Bleeding Kansas," the struggle of a nation on the brink of inevitable and violent change intensifies.

The first two books in *The Antebellum Series* will be published later in 2026.

Thank you again for reading.

—William Kinsolving

Also by William Kinsolving

Born With the Century
Bred to Win
The Diplomat's Daughter
Mister Christian
Raven

ABOUT THE AUTHOR

After graduating from Stanford, William Kinsolving began his professional life onstage—first at the Oregon Shakespeare Festival, playing Richard II—then studying at The London Academy of Music and Dramatic Art. Returning to New York, he acted under-, off-, and on Broadway and performed or directed at Stratford (CT), Harvard, Dartmouth, Café La Mama, and the Berkeley Repertory Theatre, where he received the *San Francisco Chronicle's* Best Actor of the Year award.

He wrote his first play backstage, earning a Ford Foundation Playwriting Grant and a production by the Stratford Ontario Shakespeare Festival. That success led to decades of work as a screenwriter and script doctor for every major film studio in Los Angeles, London, and Rome—ultimately contributing to more than fifty films.

Kinsolving later turned to fiction, publishing five novels, including a *New York Times* bestseller and multiple Literary Guild Main Selections. When traditional publishing contracted, he returned to playwriting, with new work presented in theatres across the country. His musical *That Week with the Bachs* premiered in 2023 at San Francisco's Grace Cathedral.

Compelled by the tectonic shifts in America today, Kinsolving returned to another time in American history when its social and cultural foundations were rumbling: The Nineteen-Twenties, and a love story that led to a trial that perforated the facades of privilege, sex, race, and wealth: *Black and White and Read All Over*.